THE
Heart
OF THE
Midwife

4 Historical Stories

THE
Heart
OF THE
Midwife

Darlene Franklin, Patty Smith Hall
Cynthia Hickey, Marilyn Turk

BARBOUR BOOKS
An Imprint of Barbour Publishing, Inc.

Print ISBN 978-1-64352-665-2

eBook Editions:
Adobe Digital Edition (.epub) 978-1-64352-667-6
Kindle and MobiPocket Edition (.prc) 978-1-64352-666-9

All scripture quotations are taken from the King James Version of the Bible.

Cover Photograph © Jill Battaglia / Trevillion Images

Published by Barbour Books, an imprint of Barbour Publishing, Inc., 1810 Barbour Drive, Uhrichsville, OH 44683, www.barbourbooks.com

Our mission is to inspire the world with the life-changing message of the Bible.

Member of the
Evangelical Christian
Publishers Association

Printed in Canada.

Love Charm

by Cynthia Hickey

Dedication

Moreover it is required in stewards,
that a man be found faithful.

1 CORINTHIANS 4:2

Chapter 1

Boston, Massachusetts
1868

"You have no idea what you're getting yourself into." Phoebe Hudson's mother planted her fists on her well-dressed hips and glared. "You'll do more than deliver babies for the hill folk. You'll be doctor as well. The poverty, the ignorance and superstition. . .I can't take it." She put the back of her hand to her forehead and fell onto a chaise lounge.

"Mother, please don't be so dramatic. I'm going to teach them better ways and help them in the process. It's a noble calling." Phoebe straightened the bow at her throat and glanced at the bassinet next to the window. When her younger sister died in childbirth, Phoebe had vowed to do what she could to prevent the same tragedy from happening to other mothers. The women of Possum Bottom, Missouri, wouldn't have access to the finest doctors like her mother had. They needed someone willing to help. That someone was newly graduated Phoebe.

After putting a book on herbal remedies in her satchel on top of her midwifery book, she leaned down and kissed her mother's cheek. "I'll write often. Papa is waiting for me downstairs. Won't you see me off?"

"I cannot." She turned her face away.

Tears pricked Phoebe's eyes as she darted down the stairs to where her father waited. "I will miss you, my little girl." He held out his hand to help her into the carriage.

"No more than I will miss you, Papa." Despite her excitement at embarking on a great adventure, sadness filled her heart at the thought of leaving behind all that was familiar.

They rode to the train station in silence. When they stood beside the track, her father handed her a drawstring bag as porters loaded her trunks. "Food for the journey. Don't talk to strangers on the way to St. Louis. If the person assigned to pick you up is not there, stay at a hotel and have them bill me. I won't have my little girl roaming a strange city alone."

"I'm full grown now, Papa, but thank you." She took the bag, kissed his cheek as the train whistle blew, then skipped up the steps to the passenger car. Minutes later she located her seat and waved out the window as the train pulled away from the station. She waved until her father was little more than a speck in the distance. Blinking away tears, she settled in for the long ride and pulled one of the books from her satchel.

"What are you reading?" The woman sitting across from her set down her knitting.

"A book on herbal remedies." Phoebe smiled. "I'm a newly certified midwife."

The woman looked around, then settled her attention back on Phoebe. "Where is your husband?"

"I'm not married."

The woman gasped, one hand clutching the ruffles at her throat. "An unmarried midwife? That's scandalous. Why. . .you'll. . .see. . ."

"I'm quite aware of what I'll see, ma'am." Phoebe fought to keep her voice calm rather than loudly defend herself. The prejudices had begun before she even left the state of Massachusetts. She'd been warned by her instructors and would take the criticism with decorum. "I delivered babies during my training."

The woman gaped like a fish. "What part of this country will allow a young woman to behave in this way?"

"A small settlement in the Ozark Mountains." Phoebe raised her book in hopes the woman would let the matter drop.

"Where will you live?"

Phoebe sighed. "A house is part of my payment."

"Chaperone?"

"Not necessary." She slapped her book closed and stared out the window. Maybe if she laid her head back and pretended to sleep, the woman would leave her alone.

"Your mother must be mortified." The woman returned to her knitting.

Phoebe bit her bottom lip to keep from grinning. Poor Mother. She'd wanted nothing more than for Phoebe to wed well and give her grandchildren. Now, at the age of nineteen, a spinster to some people, her daughter would be living alone among strangers. Phoebe almost clapped her hands in excitement. Instead, she closed her eyes and prayed she'd be a blessing to the people of Possum Bottom.

"Are you sleeping?" The voice of the woman across from her drew her out of the peaceful state she'd settled into.

"I'm praying."

The woman laughed. "You'll need it."

Sighing, Phoebe got to her feet. "I feel myself in need of a

9

stroll. Please excuse me."

The woman pulled her skirts aside as if she'd be tainted by the mere brush of Phoebe's gown. "While I know you will not listen, I strongly advise you not to leave this car."

Childishly, Phoebe marched toward the door and flung it open. The wind whipped it from her hand, and she stumbled onto the platform.

"Whoa." Strong arms encircled her waist. "You wouldn't want to topple over the edge."

Phoebe stared into the hazel eyes of a man in a brown wool suit. "Thank you, sir." She straightened and gripped the railing.

"Luke Morris, at your service."

"Phoebe Hudson, who, it appears, owes you her life."

"Are you by any chance headed to Possum Bottom as the new midwife?" His eyes widened.

"How do you know that?"

He thrust out his hand. "I'm the man sent to greet you. I had business to attend to in regard to my position as teacher, and since I was scheduled to arrive back on the same day as you, I volunteered." He grinned. "I count myself a very lucky man."

Her cheeks flushed. She hadn't thought of the possibility of meeting a handsome man on her adventure.

Luke prayed he'd convincingly hidden his surprise that the new midwife was barely old enough to know about birthing babies. She'd definitely have her work cut out for her. Not many would welcome the presence of one so young after the death of Old May. She'd delivered more babies than he could remember.

Until the hiring of Miss Hudson, the community had been

making due with a healer woman named Enid. "I hope you'll be happy with us."

Eyes the color of a summer sky widened. "Why wouldn't I be? I think the question here is, will your people be happy with me?"

"In time." He placed his back against the railing. "Hill folk are stubborn, loyal, superstitious, brave, and very set in their ways. It takes them awhile to warm up to strangers."

"But I'm coming to help."

"They'll realize that in time." He glanced up to see a stern-faced woman glaring through the window in the door. "Who is that?"

"She has the seat across from me." Miss Hudson wiggled her fingers in a wave and laughed. "She's been very scandalized by me."

He didn't have the heart to tell her she'd meet a lot more people who shared the woman's sentiment. "I'd best let you return to the first-class car. I'm in this one. I look forward to our arrival in St. Louis."

Her lips spread into a smile that made his heart skip a beat. "I do too. Good day, Mr. Morris." She held out her hand.

"Miss Hudson." He raised her gloved hand to his lips, then made sure she got safely into her car before entering his.

Three days later, he stood on the train platform and stared as porters piled trunks in front of Miss Hudson. "This is all yours?"

She nodded. "Things I will need in order to keep homesickness at bay."

He doubted the small cabin she'd be living in would hold the contents of one trunk, much less three. "I'll rent a wagon."

"Already taken care of, thank you. My father made arrangements. Please watch my things." She hiked her skirt to her ankles, stepped off the platform, and marched across the street to the livery.

Independent little thing. Good. She'd need to be in Possum Bottom.

A burly man followed her back across the street, hefted a trunk onto his shoulders, and returned to the livery. Luke did the same, leaving the last one for the driver. Soon all the trunks sat in the back of a wagon and Miss Hudson perched on the seat next to the stranger.

Luke retrieved his mule, Ole Blue, made sure the shotgun he never left home without was in place, and led the way toward home. With school starting the following week, he still had a lot of work to do. Add to the long list introducing Miss Hudson to those she'd serve, convincing them she would do just fine, and he feared he'd not be ready for the start of school.

"How many students attend school, Mr. Morris?"

Luke glanced over his shoulder, then slowed the mule to walk alongside the wagon. "Twenty, if they all show up. Sometimes the students are needed at home for one thing or another."

"What can I expect when we arrive?"

"I'll take you straight to your cabin. In the morning, I'll have you attend church with me. That's the best way to meet everyone at once. Most of the community are strict church attendees. You'll see those who are expecting, and I'll introduce you. I'll come for you a little before nine."

Worry flickered in her eyes, and her hands trembled in her lap. She took a deep breath, squared her shoulders, and stared straight ahead.

Bravo. She'd need that backbone. He prayed she truly was

trained to help the people he'd grown to love. "Don't worry. It took them awhile to warm up to me."

She nodded. "It will be fine. I truly believe I'm called to do this."

He thought about warning her of the ongoing feud between the Simpsons and the Pettys but decided against it. It would be better if she arrived with no preconceived notions of the people she'd serve. Miss Hudson would have to be unbiased, since she'd be helping both families. If one thought she showed favoritism to the other, things would escalate to a whole new level.

"How much farther?"

"Over that rise and into the hollow. A couple of hours. We'll be home before nightfall."

"Good. I'd like to see my home in the daylight."

Luke choked back a laugh. It would be better if she saw it under the cover of darkness.

Right as the sun kissed the top of Iron Mountain, they pulled up to the one-room cabin. He watched the new midwife as she took it in without speaking. Then she motioned for him to help her down. When he did, she marched to the cabin, pushed open the door, and stopped before entering.

"It will need some work."

"That's putting it mildly." He chuckled. "Where do you want your trunks?"

She tapped her chin with her forefinger. "Against that wall. I'll be putting a board and pillows on top of them to provide a bench for seating at the table. I suppose, in such a cramped place, they'll also be needed for storage."

"You surprise me, Miss Hudson."

"How so?"

"I almost expected you to run screaming into the night. The wind howls through the cracks in the walls, the roof leaks, and it's a chilly walk most nights to the outhouse."

She lifted her chin. "I'm not afraid of hard work. I'm sure I can make this place quite lovely indeed." She stepped inside and waited for her trunks. Once they were placed where she requested, she said, "Good night," and closed the door after them, effectively dismissing both him and the driver.

Chapter 2

Phoebe worked late into the night trying to turn the cabin into a semblance of home. She didn't have time or material to plaster the cracks in the walls or check out the leaky roof. Those would wait until tomorrow. She woke gritty-eyed despite the blankets she'd piled on the sagging straw mattress to provide softness, and stood slowly. With both hands on her lower back, she arched and sighed as her spine readjusted.

She washed with water from the basin and fixed her hair, very grateful her wall mirror hadn't been damaged during travel. With a tug of her shirtwaist, she took two steps to her left, prepared a cup of coffee, and nibbled on some stale cookies, also from her travels.

When she'd finished, she took a stroll around the small cleared plot of land she'd call home for as long as God meant for her to be the community's midwife. The outhouse sat well away from the cabin, the path overgrown with grass and weeds. The mountain rose steeply behind it, full of trees and brush. A red-tailed squirrel darted past her and up a tree where it sat and chattered in outrage. A small barn and corral had been erected under a large oak tree.

Phoebe laughed at the squirrel and noted where she could plant flowers and a small garden. Having read many books on gardening, she looked forward to medicinal herbs for her practice and fresh produce to eat. How hard could it be? She'd helped the family chef as a child and felt confident she remembered enough.

Life would be good in Possum Bottom. She felt it in her heart.

The rumble of wagon wheels in front of her cabin had her rushing to greet Mr. Morris. He grinned at her and jumped from the driver's seat. "Good morning. Sleep well?" He untied a small brown mule from the back of the wagon.

"Not at all." She smiled. "But I'll adjust. Let me grab my Bible and I'll be ready." Physically at least. Inside, her stomach did flips in anticipation of meeting her patients. When she returned outside, Mr. Morris was leading the mule to the barn. "What's that?"

"Your ride. Her name is Daisy Mae. She's part of your compensation. There's feed and straw in the barn, but you'd best hope some of your patients pay with feed or you'll run out before a month is past." He ducked into the barn, returning moments later. "The church isn't far, but you'll have to travel miles to see some of the families."

She nodded, her mind overwhelmed already. "I'll manage," squeezed from her lips with a small squeak. Would she? Her adventure was quickly becoming altogether foreign.

Mr. Morris put both hands on her waist and hefted her onto the driver's seat as if she weighed little more than a child. "I'm sure you will, Miss Hudson. I think you have a spine of steel."

"Please call me Phoebe. I have a feeling we'll be seeing a lot of each other."

"Then you must call me Luke." He trotted to the driver's side, climbed up, and clucked his tongue to the mule. "I insist you contact me with any need you find. I'll do my best to see it met."

"I'll be fine." The words were beginning to taste bitter in her mouth. "I'd like to visit each of the women I'll be assisting. Where would I find a list?"

"The healer woman, Enid Olson, would know. She's been doing the delivering since the other midwife passed on from influenza."

"Will she resent my coming?"

He laughed. "She might, but she also complains every time she's called away from her birds. She'll most likely follow you around for a while and give advice." They pulled into a clearing in front of a charming whitewashed church, complete with steeple. "Here's the Church of Possum Bottom."

She grinned at the simple name, delight leaping in her heart. She knew sometimes her job would call her away, but she'd attend as often as she could. Otherwise, she'd sense her mother's disapproval from states away.

A large crowd watched as Luke helped her from the wagon, no one speaking, all eyes scanning Phoebe from head to toe. She felt woefully overdressed although the white shirtwaist, navy jacket, and brown skirt made up her simplest of outfits. The other women wore wool or calico.

One woman who seemed as old as Methuselah stepped forward. "That's Enid," Luke whispered. "Step one toward being accepted here."

Phoebe's smile trembled as she thrust out her hand. "I am so pleased to meet you, Miss Enid."

"Just Enid." She stared at Phoebe's hand. "Am I to kiss it?"

"You shake it," Luke said, laughing.

"Oh." She vigorously pumped Phoebe's hand. "I'll be over

tomorrow to show you what all needs doin'." She turned and waved her arm at the crowd. "Here's the folks. Y'all be nice now. I'm too old to deal with your foolishness." The crowd parted as she marched through them and into the church.

"What I want to know is what side of the church you plan on sittin'?" A man with a white beard that fell to midchest scowled. "You a Simpson or a Petty?"

Phoebe's eyes widened and she glanced at Luke. "I'm a Hudson."

Luke shook his head. "Settle down, Homer. She isn't taking sides. I sit in the very back wherever there's an opening."

"I'll be sitting with Luke." Phoebe hiked her chin. Of all things, to enter into a family feud was the last thing she'd have thought of. She took a deep breath and linked her arm with Luke's. "Shall we?"

Luke paused with Phoebe inside the door, being the last to enter, as always. He glanced at the Simpson side and the Petty side. Neither had room for two.

"We'll stand," Phoebe said, stepping in front of the closed half of the double doors.

"Sometimes Pastor Wilson gets long-winded."

Her chin hitched higher. "Then my feet will hurt by the end, but I'll survive without having made enemies on my very first day."

Luke was starting to like this woman. She might dress fancy and fix her hair up stylish, but she showed the same strength as the hill folk. Much of his concern regarding her age slipped away.

After a sermon on the damaging effects of holding a grudge, which was clearly aimed at the two feuding families, Pastor Wilson strolled down the aisle. He smiled and held out his hand to

Phoebe. "I do believe you're in my spot." He smiled as she shook his hand. He leaned closer. "I commend you on keeping the peace in a difficult situation."

He turned to Luke, who said, "Good afternoon, Pastor. May I introduce our new midwife, Miss Phoebe Hudson."

The pastor frowned. "A single young woman in such a profession?"

"I've heard all the prejudices, sir. This is what God has called me to do, and this is what I'll do. Excuse me." With a swish of her skirt, she stepped outside.

"Pastor, you'll find that Miss Hudson is every bit as stubborn as these other women." Luke clapped the man on the shoulder. "She'll do just fine. How's the missus?"

"This pregnancy is wearing on her. She isn't as young as she used to be."

"None of us are. I'll bring Phoebe by before taking her home." He raised a brow, waiting for the pastor's response.

"That will be fine. I don't want Sarah delivering with only the superstitions of Enid." He turned to the congregation that had lined up to greet him, leaving Luke free to join Phoebe outside.

He found her next to the wagon. "Before we leave, I've offered to have you visit the pastor's wife. Mrs. Wilson is pregnant with her fifth child and not feeling well."

"Are you sure?" she mumbled.

"That we're going there or that she's ill?"

"That her husband will allow me to visit her."

"I've gotten permission."

"I don't have my bag, but I'll take a look and come back tomorrow."

"That'll do just fine." He crooked his arm. She slipped hers in his, and he led her to the modest cabin behind the church. He knocked and entered when welcomed.

Mrs. Wilson sat in a leather chair, her legs propped up on a stool. "Have you seen my young'uns?"

"No, ma'am, but I'm assuming they'll be coming home with the pastor. This is Phoebe Hudson, the new midwife. Your husband asked that she come by." *Please don't reject her.* He held his breath, waiting.

"You're feeling poorly, Mrs. Wilson?" Phoebe knelt beside her. "I wasn't expecting my first patient today and left my bag at home, but I can do a cursory examination."

Mrs. Wilson nodded. "It's my feet mostly, and my back."

"When are you expecting?" Phoebe stood. "Luke, fetch me some stiff paper or a tube of some kind, please."

"The former midwife said late this month."

"Oh, not long then."

Luke searched the cabin and only found old newspapers. "Will this work?"

"It will have to do." Phoebe rolled the papers into a tube. "I'm going to listen to the baby now. Just relax and breathe normally."

Luke stepped back, content to watch Phoebe work and come to her aid if needed. Having once contemplated being a doctor, he still owned several medical journals. They'd be of more use to Phoebe now.

He watched as she put one end of the rolled paper to Mrs. Wilson's stomach and pressed her ear to the other end. She held her breath and seemed to be counting silently. After a few seconds, she straightened and smiled. "Baby's heart rate seems to be just fine. As for your feet, they're very swollen. I suggest you drink more fluids and use less salt on your food."

"Salt?" The pastor's wife folded her hands over her stomach. "A rare commodity around here."

"I'm sure it is, but I see a container on the shelf. For your sake and your baby's, please limit your intake. Otherwise, you seem to be progressing very nicely. I look forward to assisting you in the delivery."

"Can't come soon enough for me. I'm praying for a girl."

Pastor Wilson and four boys barged into the house. "How's my sweetheart?"

"She's doing just fine, sir." Phoebe met his gaze. "Please send for me if she needs me." Her smile looked forced as she left the house.

"What did you do, John?" Mrs. Wilson frowned.

"I suggested she shouldn't be a midwife due to her age and marriage status." He fished a couple of coins from his pocket. "Please give her this as payment for her visit." He dropped the coins in Luke's hand. "It's best that I, as a married man and pastor, not interact too often with an unmarried woman."

"I'm sure the payment will be greatly appreciated."

"We had to give up a lot of silly ideas when we came here," Mrs. Wilson reminded her husband. "Would you rather Enid deliver this child as she waved some sort of charm over me?"

"No. That's why I let Miss Hudson come." He glanced at Luke for help.

He laughed. An angry or crying woman wasn't easy for any man to deal with. "Miss Hudson is certified from a highly respected college. You'll be safe in her hands."

"If things go badly," Phoebe said from the doorway, "we'll get you down the mountain and to the hospital."

"I won't go." Mrs. Wilson's face darkened.

"I'll do my best to make sure that doesn't happen, but you must do your part. No stress and no salt." She looked at the pastor.

"Sarah loves her salt. What kind of idea is that?"

"Either you trust the midwife or you don't," Luke said, handing Phoebe the pastor's payment. "You can't pick and choose her suggestions based on what you like."

The look of gratitude on Phoebe's face as he stood beside her made him want to take up for her over and over again.

Chapter 3

A banging on the door the next morning had Phoebe jumping out of bed as if she'd been shot. Grabbing a blanket to wrap around herself and cover her nightgown, she lifted the board that held her door closed.

A young boy, barefoot and wearing worn britches, held his doubled-up fist in midair. " 'Bout time, miss. You the midwife?"

"I am." Phoebe smiled.

"Well, get dressed. I've need of ya. Name's Danny McGee."

"I'll be right out." Phoebe dashed to where she'd hung her dress yesterday, quickly donned it, tied her hair back with a ribbon rather than take the time to put it up, and then grabbed her medical satchel on her way out the door.

Danny already had Daisy Mae waiting out front. "It'll be faster if we ride. I'm plumb tuckered out from running."

Using the top step, Phoebe climbed onto the mule and helped Danny climb on behind her. "How bad are the pains?"

"Don't know. She can't talk. Turn left past your outhouse and head up the mountain."

Phoebe had so many questions she wanted to ask, but it

wouldn't be proper to voice them to a young boy. She'd have to make haste and evaluate things when they arrived at the home of the expectant mother.

It couldn't be far if Danny had run the entire way. She did her best to make note of landmarks in order to find her way home. A rock bridge, more rocks that looked like the shell of a turtle, and a creek on their right.

"Right up there." Danny pointed to a cave.

"You live in a cave?" Phoebe slid from the mule.

"No." He frowned. "But this is where Lulu is." He grabbed a bush and started to climb.

Phoebe followed, worry trickling through her. Delivering a baby in such circumstances would be a true test of her skills and not very sanitary.

"She's right there." Danny pointed toward the corner.

Phoebe stared down at a mixed-breed dog on a tattered blanket. "You want me to deliver puppies?"

"You're a midwife, ain't ya?"

"Well, yes, but. . ."

"She's having a hard time."

Phoebe could see the dog laboring. Taking a deep breath, she pulled her apron from her bag, then her stethoscope. "How long, Danny?"

"All night."

"Fetch some water. Lulu is most likely thirsty." Using the stethoscope, she detected several heartbeats as the dog's stomach roiled. The humor of the situation overcame her and she laughed, patting the dog's head. "You're my first delivery, girl. I hope I do you proud. Perhaps you can put in a good word with the other mothers."

By the time Danny returned with water in a wooden bowl, two puppies had been born. After that, the other three came quickly.

With tears in his eyes and a smile on his grubby face, Danny looked up at her. "Which one do you want?"

"I beg your pardon?"

"For your fee. You get first pick."

Oh, heavens. "Why don't you surprise me when they're old enough to leave their mother?"

He started placing the puppies in a burlap sack. "We need to get them home by the fire so a bear don't get 'em."

"Oh. Of course." She suspected poor Lulu would be left to follow the best she could.

With Danny clutching the bag of puppies, they rode farther up the mountain and stopped in front of a cabin slightly larger than Phoebe's. Five children played in the dirt.

"Teacher's here!" Danny slid from Daisy Mae and raced for the house. "We got pups," he told the others as he ran past them.

Phoebe smiled at his exuberance, also happy to see Luke's mule tethered in a patch of grass. She smoothed her hair and skirt, then followed Danny into the house.

"Thank the good Lord above," a man said, taking Phoebe's hand and pumping it. "The missus is ready for ya."

Phoebe shot a wide-eyed glance at Luke. "I've just delivered five puppies." What a ridiculous thing to say.

"Looks like your day isn't over." He grinned. "What can we do?"

"Right. Danny, my bag. Luke, hot water. Mr. McGee, I'll need clean cloths, then your wife and I will handle the rest. It's best the men stay outside." She hurried to the bed where a woman lay in the throes of labor. "Is there something we can spread under you to protect your bedding?" Phoebe took her case from Danny and tied her apron around her waist, then poured disinfectant over her hands.

"Just take the blanket off. We can replace the hay," Mrs. McGee said. Her face wrinkled in pain. "With this one bein' my seventh, it won't take long."

"No, ma'am, it most likely won't. Would you like something for the pain?"

"Already put a knife under the bed. That'll do." She groaned.

Phoebe propped pillows behind the woman's back. "It's easier if you aren't lying down."

Mrs. McGee narrowed her eyes. "You got strange notions. Ah!"

A couple of hours later, Mrs. McGee was the proud mama of a healthy little boy. "Your son is beautiful." Phoebe wrapped the baby in a clean square of flannel. As she went to hand him to his mother, Mrs. McGee groaned and bore down again. Twins?

Phoebe quickly placed the baby in a handmade cradle and helped deliver a baby girl. "Well done."

Mrs. McGee grinned. "Send that no-account husband of mine inside so I can hit him upside the head. How am I supposed to care for these little ones and the others?"

From the look on the new mother's face, she didn't mean the words she said. "I'll go deliver the good news." Phoebe removed her soiled apron and stepped outside.

⌒

Mr. McGee jumped to his feet when Phoebe opened the door. "She's okay?"

"Your wife did wonderfully. You have a son and a daughter."

"Two?" He sagged against the porch post and shook his head.

"I reckon I need to plant that other field to feed 'em."

Luke clapped the man on the shoulder. "You'll do just fine. Go see the missus."

Mr. McGee rushed inside, followed by his children. Shouts of joy came from the open door.

"How are you feeling?" Luke smiled at Phoebe.

"Very well. Mrs. McGee is a strong woman. I doubt she even needed me after having all these children." She sat on the top step and glanced over her shoulder. "So many people in such a small house."

"That's the way it is up here." He sat beside her. "So, you also delivered puppies?"

She laughed and told him of a frantic Danny arriving at her cabin earlier. "I hope word doesn't get around that I deliver animals. I'm afraid I've had no training in that area. But I am getting a puppy." Her eyes twinkled. "As my fee from Danny."

"Can't be so different, people and animals."

"I reckon it is." She arched a brow. "What brings you here today?"

"School starts next Monday. I'm making my rounds, doing a head count. I'll have a larger group of students this year, with children growing older."

"That's good news. Education is important." She stood. "I'll fetch my things and head home. Hopefully I'll remember the way."

"I'll ride with you."

Phoebe went back into the house and returned a few minutes later with her bag and a very excited Danny. "Don't leave yet, Miss Hudson." He raced around the house.

Squeals and clucks rose above the happy sounds of children.

Soon, Danny returned with a small piglet and a chicken. "Pa says this is your payment. Two for two babies."

Phoebe's mouth dropped. "Luke?"

"I'll help you with them. Danny, may I borrow that burlap sack for the piglet?"

"Sure. I'll get another one for the chicken. She's a good laying hen." He ducked back into the house and returned with two wriggling, noisy sacks.

After tying them on Ole Blue, Luke led Phoebe down the mountain. "I suggest you try to sell the pig so you don't have to feed it. I know someone who might be interested. Then you could buy a rooster and another hen or two and have fresh eggs."

She nodded mutely.

He cut her a sharp glance. "Folks up here don't have a lot of money. They pay with produce or labor mostly." He sincerely hoped she had funds to cover her expenses.

"I'm quite aware."

"Then what's nagging at you?"

"The state of the house. Luke, it was filthy and unsafe. There was a knife under the bed!"

"To cut the pain of childbirth." Seeing her genuine distress, he ducked his head to hide a grin.

"Superstition. My job here is bigger than I thought. I need to teach these women about cleanliness. Two newborn babies in a crowded house with a dirt floor, dishes piled in the sink, and tattered clothing. I understand poverty, but that's no excuse not to be clean."

"Tread lightly, Phoebe. These are proud people."

"Surely with you being an educated man, you try to show them ways to improve."

"I do by starting with my students and rules in the school. I request that they wash their hands before lunch and hope the habit will carry home." He pulled in front of her as the trail narrowed. "I appreciate your desire to improve the quality of life here, but the people of Possum Bottom don't believe anything is wrong with their lives. They live as their parents did and their parents before them."

"I still intend to try."

Luke sighed, praying she wouldn't create a chasm between herself and the people he'd grown to love. Word would get around that she'd safely delivered twins. Others would request her services. If she offended one of them, they'd turn their backs on her.

They stopped at Homer Simpson's and traded the pig for a few coins, a rooster, and a hen before continuing to Phoebe's cabin. Although the hour was late, he'd have to see to her chicken coop before heading home. He wasn't sure why he felt it was his place to make sure Phoebe had everything she needed, or why he felt he needed to make sure she understood these people before making a grave mistake. Maybe it was her pretty face or strong backbone. Either way, here he was.

"I'll make something to eat," she said, sliding from her mule. "I've not had anything all day, and I'm famished. It'll be something simple due to the late hour."

Luke hadn't eaten but a couple of stale biscuits. "I'll work on the coop, and I thank you."

He made a couple of hasty repairs to the coop at the back of the barn, then washed his hands at the pump. His stomach growled loud enough to scare away any wild critters around. He stepped through the open doorway to the sight of Phoebe asleep at the table, her head resting on folded arms. What he thought might be stew simmered on the stove.

Smiling, he rummaged around until he found a tin of crackers, then spooned the stew into wooden bowls. He set one on the table in front of Phoebe, then took a seat across from her. "Time to eat," he said softly.

"What?" She jumped to her feet and rushed to the stove.

"I've already served it up."

"Oh." She blinked a few times, then noticed the bowls on the table. "I hadn't realized how tired I was."

"It's fine. The chickens are set. It might take a few days for them to get familiar with their new home and give you eggs."

"I don't know how to take care of chickens." She raised frightened eyes to his. "It seems I don't know a whole lot about hill life."

He reached over and put his hand over hers. "You do know how to deliver babies, and that is a very good thing. The rest will come."

Chapter 4

Phoebe stood at the chicken coop with no idea what to toss in for them to eat. Daisy Mae grazed in the corral, but she doubted the same could be said for the chickens.

"I heard you delivered twins for the McGees." Enid stepped next to her.

"I did. You're late. What do I feed these?"

"Chicken feed. You can get some at the mercantile. Mrs. McGee said you poured some foul-smelling stuff on your hands."

"Disinfectant." Phoebe faced her. "More effective than plain water in cleaning my hands before delivery."

"I don't think there's anything wrong with water the good Lord made." Enid crossed her arms. "You can't be bringing highfalutin city ways here. She also said you offered something for pain. Women are meant to bear the pain of childbirth due to Eden's sin. Looks like I got a lot to teach you."

Phoebe started to inform the older woman that she'd learned from the finest teachers in Boston, but remembered what Luke had told her about proud people and kept her mouth closed. "Come in for coffee, and you can tell me all you know."

"We ain't got time for that. You need to be out visitin' mothers."

"That is on my list today."

"List? Heavens, girl, you don't need a list." Enid shook her head. "Grab that mule and let's go. We'll talk on the way."

Phoebe hurried into the house and grabbed her bag. She shoved paper and a pencil into her pocket. If she was going to be making the rounds on a regular basis, she'd need a map.

"We've got six women expecting in various trimesters. The preacher's wife is due the soonest, but she don't like me, so she's all yours." Enid climbed onto the back of a donkey. "We'll stop at the mercantile before heading up the mountain."

The woman's bossiness would get old very quickly. Phoebe followed her on Daisy Mae to the mercantile, a rock and wood building on what might constitute Main Street for Possum Bottom. The building was the only one on the dirt-paved road. Curtains blew from an upstairs window. Ole Blue, more of a light gray than blue in her opinion, grazed nearby.

"If the Gordons ain't got what you need, you don't need it." Enid dismounted.

Phoebe followed her into the store, her gaze immediately searching for Luke. He stood at the counter, a stack of chalk tablets in front of him.

He turned to greet her with a smile. "The last of my supplies. How are you two ladies?"

"I need chicken feed, and Enid is taking me around to meet my patients."

"Maybe I'll run into you again. I'm still making my own rounds."

A flush heated her cheeks at his warm gaze.

"Hurry up. We ain't got all day." Enid frowned.

"Maybe you will." Phoebe turned to the counter. "I need other supplies, Enid." She browsed the tinned foods and placed an order for what she needed, along with coffee, flour, sugar, and lard with a promise to retrieve them later in the day.

"I'll have them delivered for you. Come in and pay your tab when you can." The portly man grinned, making the large mustache over his mouth quiver.

"Thank you, Mr. Gordon." Phoebe flashed a smile and followed the muttering Enid outside. "Have I offended you?"

"You lollygag too much."

"You told me you were coming. I waited most of the morning for you. I was just about to ask Luke to introduce me to the expectant mothers, since you were late."

"I got busy."

Phoebe stared at the other woman over the back of her mule. "Do you resent my coming?"

Enid hung her head. "No, I want you here. I'm too old. I just don't want to be pushed aside like a worn-out shoe."

"Let's learn from each other." Phoebe's heart went out to her. "I can teach you some modern methods, and you can help me learn the personalities of these people. If I'm ill, they may need you."

Enid's face brightened. "Yes, I can do that." She climbed onto her donkey. "Let me tell you about the Simpsons and Pettys as we ride. You'll be meeting both today."

She'd been curious since church. "Please point out landmarks as we go so I can draw a map."

As if she hadn't said anything, Enid started talking the instant they started down the road. "Homer Simpson and Leroy Petty worked together on building the church. Both of them thought the church should have their name on the sign. Idiotic, if you ask me. The church belongs to Possum Bottom, not any one person. Anyway, one day they were both deep into moonshine and started fighting. No one knows who threw the first punch. They've been enemies ever since and have drawn the rest of us into their squabble. You be careful visiting either one of their wives. Say the wrong thing, and they'll consider you're playing favorites."

"Luke manages."

"That's because he's the teacher and has to be impartial. He's the local peacekeeper and the closest we got to the law. People respect him, they listen to him." She tossed a sly glance over her shoulder. "It would do you good to latch onto a man like him."

"I'm focusing on my career."

"Famous last words of any spinster. What you need is a love charm."

⌒

"Gentlemen, please." Luke held up his hands. "I didn't come to cause trouble. I'm only making sure the children will be attending school." He'd come across the two hardheaded fools arguing in the middle of the road over what side of the classroom they wanted their children to sit on, of all things. "I'm sorting the students by grade level and reading ability this year."

"I won't have my Ruby sitting next to his spawn." Homer Simpson poked Leroy Petty in the chest with his forefinger.

"Then I'll make sure another child sits between them. What the two of you need is your heads knocked together." Luke exhaled sharply through his nose.

"If you was any other man, we'd pound you into the dirt," Homer said.

"Then at least the two of you would be working together on something." He refused to back down from such childishness.

"My oldest, Sam, won't be attending this year. Neither will Johnny. Sam's a man full grown, and I need the two of 'em at home," Leroy said. "Besides, Johnny's busy buildin' his own place for when he finds a wife."

"Ain't no good woman goin' to hitch her wagon to that lazy boy of yours." Homer spit tobacco at the other man's feet. "Maybelle won't attend either. The rest will be there until harvesttime."

"Hold on." Luke shook his head. "Why don't the two of you head home and mind your own business."

"Sure, Teacher. Midwife is coming." Homer swung up onto a sway-backed horse.

"Bet she comes to my place first," Leroy said.

Did everything have to be a competition with these two? Luke suspected they'd pummel anyone who said something bad about the other. Only the two of them were allowed that luxury. They might profess to be enemies, but they'd been friends since childhood from what he'd heard. If he were a betting man, he'd think they were the best of friends and didn't know how to get past their petty argument.

He turned at the sound of a hoof striking a rock to see Enid, followed by Phoebe, rounding the corner. "Good morning, ladies. So we did bump into each other again."

Phoebe's cheeks flushed a pretty shade of pink. "So we did. Gentlemen." She nodded at the other men.

"Ma'am." Homer touched the brim of his straw hat. "I reckon

you'll go to my place first."

"Nope. She's going to mine." Leroy scowled.

"Whose house is the closest?" Phoebe tilted her head.

"Never mind that," Enid said. "Have the two fools flip a coin."

"I ain't got a coin," Leroy said.

"I do." Homer grinned, revealing a missing front tooth.

"We can't use your coin. It's biased."

"Oh, for crying out loud." Phoebe pulled a coin from her pocket. "You two squabble more than any baby I've ever delivered. To prevent further argument, Mr. Simpson has heads, Mr. Petty tails, and I'll hear no more about it." She tossed the coin to Luke.

Luke hadn't had this much fun in a long time. Once again, he felt strongly that Phoebe Hudson would fit right into Possum Bottom. He tossed the coin and caught it in his hand. "Heads."

Homer whooped. "My house is closest anyway. See ya there, Midwife." He grinned at Leroy, then rode away whistling.

Leroy shrugged. "Fair's fair." He turned his horse and ambled away.

"Bravo." Luke clapped. "I was about to wring a couple of necks."

"I think if we treat them as the children they act like, we'll get along." Phoebe glanced up at him.

"Mind if I ride with you? I've still a few families to visit."

She smiled. "We'd love your company, wouldn't we, Enid?"

She reached over and plucked a strand of hair from Luke's head. "Sure enough."

"Ouch!" He frowned. "What are you up to?"

"One more." She plucked one from Phoebe as well. "I'm ready." She wrapped the hairs in a hankie and clucked to her donkey.

Phoebe glanced at Luke, who shrugged. "Only God knows

what these people do sometimes." He climbed onto Ole Blue and followed the women, admiring the way Phoebe sat on Daisy Mae. Back straight, head high, she rode the mule as if it were a fine thoroughbred from a rich man's stables.

Even full of admiration for the young midwife, he couldn't help but wonder how long it would take a well-bred high-society woman to grow bored with the simple life on the mountain. "If you thought the McGee cabin was bad, prepare yourself for the Simpsons'."

Phoebe glanced over her shoulder. "It's worse?"

"Nah." He laughed. "I'm just teasing you. Alice keeps the place so clean you could eat off the floor. She's obsessed with dirt."

"Oh, good. Should make the circumstances better for her baby."

"It ain't Alice's baby," Enid said. "It's that loose daughter of hers, Maybelle. Sixteen, pregnant, and refuses to say who the daddy is. But we'll find out soon enough."

"Don't fill Phoebe full of superstitions," Luke warned.

"I'm at a loss." Phoebe sighed and faced forward.

"Whatever man's name she yells out during the birthing is the daddy," Enid said. "We've had a lot of shotgun weddings happen that way."

Phoebe laughed, then clamped a hand over her mouth. "Oh, you're serious."

Luke chuckled. "This is one folktale that's usually correct."

"I try not to form any preconceived ideas about a person. What they've done is none of my concern. I'm here to deliver a healthy baby and help a mother, not form prejudices."

Luke laughed again at the scandalized look Enid gave her. "You're not the norm for these parts, Phoebe."

"I hope to change that."

He wanted to remind her not to force her thoughts but rather to lead by example, suggesting and showing ways to improve the hill people's lifestyle. He didn't think she'd listen. Life would have to teach her by example and experience or by the sharp words of Enid. Poor Phoebe. All Luke could do was be there to pick up the pieces.

Chapter 5

Phoebe slid from the mule and waved at Luke, who continued up the trail. She unhooked her bag from the animal and followed Enid to where a tall, rail-thin woman with pursed lips swept a porch that ran the front length of the house.

"Alice Simpson, this is the new midwife, Phoebe Hudson. She's here to look at Maybelle."

The woman frowned. "She's young, not much older than my girl. I thought you were going to take care of my child."

"I assure you I'm certified and very capable." Phoebe forced a smile.

"I'm getting too old to spend hours at a birthing bed." Enid crossed her arms. "I ain't seen Phoebe deliver an infant yet, but she did right fine by Mrs. McGee, last I heard. Twins."

"Lord have mercy on us all if Maybelle has more than one." She propped the broom against the wall. "Might as well come on in."

"Thank you." Phoebe smiled at Enid.

"I said I'd help you." She marched up the steps and into the house, leaving Phoebe to follow.

A young, pretty, very pregnant girl sat in a rocking chair,

knitting on a pair of baby booties. She glanced up, curiosity on her face. "You a doctor?" Her gaze flicked to Phoebe's bag.

"Midwife."

"My pa know you're here?"

"He does indeed. Is there somewhere private we can go so I can examine you and make sure the baby is fine?"

"I reckon you can use our room." Alice led them to a small room with a double-sized bed. "I'll be right here making sure you don't do anything strange to my girl."

Phoebe sighed. "I assure you I won't. Maybelle, please lie on the bed."

False modesty, whining, and a multitude of questions about everything Phoebe did, no matter how small, caused the examination to last much longer than necessary. Finally, Phoebe lowered her stethoscope and said, "Everything seems to be progressing along as it should. With your young age, labor can go on for quite some time. Send for me when pains are coming hard and regular. If your baby doesn't arrive before next week, I'll come see you again."

"I've heard tell you and Mr. Morris have been keeping time together," Maybelle said, getting to her feet. "I once thought I would marry him, but he didn't seem interested in me."

"Most likely because of your age, and we aren't keeping time together. Mr. Morris has simply been showing me around and introducing me to the people of Possum Bottom."

Maybelle shook her head. "You went to church with him. That's a big thing around here, ain't it, Ma?"

"Yes, it sure is. We'd like our teacher to settle down. Then young girls like Maybelle won't get their heads full of nonsense." She left the room with promises of coffee.

Phoebe put her tools back in her bag and joined the others in the front room. She could have sworn she'd interrupted a discussion on charms, but Alice and Enid stopped talking the moment they spotted her.

"Make yourself comfortable," Alice said. "I've got sugar lumps and fresh cream. Maybelle, get the cookies off the shelf."

"My feet hurt."

"More than that will hurt if you don't do as I say."

With an exaggerated groan, Maybelle stood from her rocker and pulled a tin from a shelf on the wall. She dropped it onto the table with a loud thud, then returned to her seat.

"Her attitude will change quick enough when there's a baby to care for," Enid said, scowling at the girl. "Nothing takes the focus off oneself like an infant."

Phoebe agreed. She'd seen it with the young mothers who came to the school to allow the training midwives to deliver their babies. Few things made a girl grow up faster than giving birth.

"How old are you, Phoebe?" Alice poured coffee into a solid white mug.

"Nineteen."

"You should be married by now." Her brow lowered. "You're practically an old maid. Why aren't you hitched and having young'uns of your own?"

"I want to focus on my career." Phoebe added cream and sugar.

"Nonsense. Get hitched, have your babies, then be a midwife when your children are grown. That's the way things are done." Alice sat across from her and exchanged a conspiratorial glance with Enid.

"I've a lot to teach Phoebe," Enid said. "Thanks for the coffee, but we've got to go visit Dorcas."

"Give her my regards, bless her heart, having a baby at her age." Alice shook her head. "I don't know what I'd do with myself. Cry, most likely."

"How old is she?" Phoebe glanced from one woman to the next.

"Thirty-five, I reckon. Past her prime, that's for certain." Alice exhaled heavily. "We were best friends until our husbands turned into empty-headed fools."

Phoebe didn't think she'd let a husband of hers dictate whom she could be friends with, but that was a subject best left alone.

Another hour's ride had them at a cabin as different from the Simpsons' cabin as it could be. Where Alice was clean, Dorcas was not. Perhaps it was because she clearly felt unwell, judging by the pallor of her skin. Phoebe glanced around at children ranging in age from four to a young man around her age. Plenty old enough to help his mother.

The son leered at her, tipped his hat, and left when Phoebe asked for privacy.

"Bad seed," Enid muttered.

Phoebe transferred her attention to the woman in front of her and introduced herself. "You look a bit peaked, Miss Petty. Please sit down."

"I was in the middle of making a tonic." Despite her protests, she lowered herself into a rickety chair.

"What kind of tonic?" Phoebe glanced at the stove.

"I sent one of the children out after angelica root. I thought perhaps if I chewed it and drank some tea, it would help with the ever-present upset in my stomach."

Enid lifted the ladle from the pot and sniffed. "This ain't angelica root. Tell me you haven't drunk any."

"Not yet."

"Has anyone else?" Enid paled.

"What is it?" Phoebe asked, dread coursing through her.

"Water hemlock, I think. Dorcas?"

"I had Junior taste it for me to see if it needed sugar." She gasped.

"How long ago?"

"Just before you arrived."

"Where is your son, Mrs. Petty?" Phoebe made for the door.

"I sent him out to gather eggs."

Phoebe dashed into the yard, sliding to a stop at the welcome sight of Luke riding up. "I need you." She whirled and raced for the chicken coop.

⌒

Luke jumped from Ole Blue and sprinted after Phoebe, glancing toward the cabin at the sound of a woman screeching. "What's wrong?"

"We need to find Junior. He's ingested a poison."

"I see him." Luke vaulted over the fence to the chicken coop and scooped the groggy seven-year-old boy off the ground and into his arms. "What do we do?"

"Make him vomit. As much as possible. I'll fetch some water."

With his heart threatening to beat from his chest, Luke stuck his finger down the boy's throat. "Come on. Don't go to sleep on me."

Junior's dark eyes started to drift closed, then shot open as he released the contents of his stomach. Luke repeated the procedure again until nothing more came up.

"Bring him to the house." Phoebe carried a bucket, water

sloshing with each hurried step she took.

"My boy." Dorcas reached out for him.

"I am not a medical physician, ma'am, but I will do all I can to save your son. You must stay out of the way. Enid, if you know of any remedies, now is the time to let me know. Luke, keep him sitting up. I'll force water down him if I need to."

Luke sat in a chair, the boy in his lap. "Help me out, Junior. Drink this cool water."

"Throat. . .hurts." His head lolled.

"I'm sure it does." He met Phoebe's frightened gaze.

"Dorcas, do you have any milk?" Enid looked into a crock.

"The blue one." She wrung her hands in her apron. "The doctor is too far away."

"Get Sam to ride for him. Go!" Enid waved her hands.

Dorcas waddled from the house, screaming for her oldest son.

They managed to get a few spoonfuls of milk down Junior's throat. His breathing grew labored.

"How long for the doctor?" Phoebe asked, her voice resigned.

"Nightfall at the earliest." Luke looked into the pale face of one of his youngest students. "He isn't going to make it, is he?"

"I don't think so, but I won't give up." She poured more milk onto the spoon. "Open your mouth, sweetie."

"You should have gone to medical school."

She shrugged. "Midwifery was difficult enough with the world's mindset."

"Here." Enid thrust a wet rag at her. "Make him comfortable. Mr. Morris, lay him on the bed. This young one will be seeing his Lord soon."

Dorcas wailed and reached for the ladle in the pot on the stove.

"I'll stay with my baby. I want to be the last face he sees on earth and the first he sees in heaven."

Shoving Junior into Phoebe's arms, Luke slapped the ladle from his mother's hands and grabbed the pot. "Are you insane? You've a babe in your belly and other children who need you. Go sit down." He marched outside and tossed the poison into the bushes before rinsing the pot with water from the pump.

He returned to the house and froze at the sight of Dorcas doubled over in pain, a puddle of water at her feet. "The baby?"

"I'm afraid the stress brought on the labor." Phoebe led Dorcas to the bed where her son lay. She held out her hand to Luke. "Help me."

"What do you want me to do?" He took her hand. "I'll do anything."

"Give me strength. Pray." Tears ran down her face. "I'm afraid."

He wrapped his arms around her and pulled her close. "Lean on me. Take a minute. Let Enid get Dorcas ready." He led her to the table.

"But Junior—"

"There's nothing more you can do." The boy's harsh breathing joined his mother's groans.

"I'm glad you're here." She leaned her forehead against his chest and took a deep, ragged breath. "I'm okay now. I'll fall apart when this is over."

"I'll boil water and make a fresh pot of coffee. Where are the other children?"

"I don't know."

"They're in the field with their pa," Dorcas said. "Could you tell them to stay away until this baby is born?"

The sadness in her eyes broke Luke's heart. He set water on the stove to boil, then headed to the field behind the house.

Leroy approached when he spotted Luke. "We done talked today."

"Dorcas is in labor. She's asked that you keep the children here until it's born."

"What are you not tellin' me?" Leroy stiffened. "I see a shadow on your face."

"Junior ingested water hemlock. The midwife, Enid, and I did all we could. We've sent Sam for the doctor, but he won't arrive in time to save Junior."

Leroy's gaze remained locked on Luke's for several minutes. "Tell me Dorcas will be all right."

"I think so, but she's feeling pretty poorly. The women are with her right now." Luke placed a hand on the man's shoulder. "Gather your children and pray."

"I want to look on my boy one last time." Luke headed back to the house to do whatever was in his power to help without getting in the way. Boil water, make coffee, prepare a simple meal, those were things he could do. He tried to ignore Junior's ragged breathing and Dorcas's cries. While he prepared bread and cheese to take to Leroy and the children, he prayed.

He prayed for a peaceful passing for Junior, for safety and health for Dorcas and her infant, and for Dorcas to be able to forgive herself. He'd seen in her eyes the blame she took for mistaking the water hemlock for angelica root.

Hooves thundered into the yard.

Junior took his last breath.

A newborn's cry filled the room.

Chapter 6

The days passed despite the tragic death of Junior Petty. Phoebe continued making her rounds, sometimes with Enid, sometimes alone. Today she rode alone to the Petty house to check on baby Isaiah.

The oldest son, Sam, leaned against the porch railing, a blade of straw dangling from his lips. "Mornin'."

"Good morning." Phoebe tethered Daisy Mae near the only patch of grass in the yard. "How is your mother?"

"Melancholy. You got something in your bag for that?" He spat out the straw.

"I can make some sassafras tea."

"Baby's colicky too. Ma ain't gettin' much sleep."

"I've something for that too. Excuse me," she said when he blocked the doorway.

He laughed. "I reckon a smart woman like you most likely has a cure for everything. I'd like to come courtin' iffen you're agreeable."

Phoebe opened and closed her mouth several times before she was able to speak past the shock. "I don't intend to get married, but I am honored."

"I'll change yore mind." He hopped off the porch and headed into the woods.

Heavens. Phoebe pushed the front door open. "Dorcas?"

"I'm here," she said over the baby's crying. A cigarette dangled from her lips. In her hand, she held a spoonful of milk. Removing the cigarette from her mouth, she blew a whiff of smoke into the milk.

"What are you doing?"

"Curing the colic." She dribbled the milk into Isaiah's mouth. "Works like a charm."

"I've something better for the baby, Dorcas." Doing her best not to show how much the woman's actions had upset her, Phoebe dug into her bag and pulled out a calamus root. "If you've got some more milk to give me, I'll scrape some of this into it. That will take care of little Isaiah."

"I reckon, but we won't know for sure what cures him, will we? The old way or your new way."

Dorcas was right. An old and true method passed down from generation to generation or one approved by the medical association. "As long as the baby is calmed, it won't matter." She turned with a smile. "I'll make you some tea for your sadness."

"Add some whiskey. That'll do the trick." Dorcas put the baby against her shoulder and patted his back. "My Sam said he wants to get hitched. It'll be nice to have a midwife in the family."

"I've told Sam I don't intend to get married." Phoebe mixed the herbs for sassafras tea.

"I guess a fancy woman like you would prefer someone like the teacher. My Sam tends to lean on the lazy side of things." With the baby eased, she laid him in a wooden bassinet. "You can look him over now."

Phoebe weighed Isaiah with a sling-style scale, then listened to his heart and lungs. "He's doing just fine, Dorcas. A healthy little boy."

"Of course he is. Junior's spirit is in him. I saw it right when Isaiah took his first breath and Junior his last. Knowing that is what keeps me going. God must have had a reason." She relit her cigarette. "I'm thinkin' this one would have died if not for Junior's spirit. It ain't good for a mother to mourn during birth."

Phoebe managed to bite her tongue, but she made a point of being at the schoolhouse at dismissal time. She smiled as the doors burst open and children ran yelling down the stairs and off in the direction of home.

"This is a welcome surprise." Luke exited last. "Is everything all right?"

She nodded. "I'd like to talk, if you've the time."

"Of course." He stepped aside so she could enter.

She sat behind a desk, leaving him to do the same. "I've just come from the Pettys'."

"How are Dorcas and the baby?"

"Fine. Oh Luke, I'm at my wits' end. I held my thoughts to myself, but she mixed cigarette smoke with milk to cure the baby's colic." Her eyes widened and locked with his. "She also thinks Junior's spirit resides inside the baby. This kind of superstition is wrong and dangerous."

"It's always been this way."

"That doesn't make it right. Some of the hill folk live in squalor. I want to show them how to live a better life." Was that so wrong? "Cleanliness and less superstition could add years to their lives."

"I admire your passion, Phoebe, but you'll have to lead by example."

"What if I get Enid to think as I do?"

"It would help." He took a deep breath. "Maybe one or two days a month, the two of you could hold classes here and teach the women safer ways to doctor their families. You could also show them ways to be cleaner, hopefully without wounding their pride."

"Alice Simpson is clean."

"Alice Simpson didn't arrive in these hills until Homer brought her home from the war. That's the difference."

"I'll speak with Enid." She stood. "I thank you for listening, even if you don't agree."

"I didn't say I didn't agree." He got to his feet. "I'm saying to be careful how you approach them."

"You've said that before. I've been careful, but when it comes to the death of a child. . ."

"Other people have made the same mistake with water hemlock."

Phoebe knew what she'd do. "I'll have my father send books with pictures that show different medicinal plants. You can use them here, in the school. The children will take them home. The parents will see them. Everyone will learn."

"That's a wonderful idea. You're figuring out how to deal with these people. If you'll give me a few minutes to lock up, I'll escort you home."

"There's no need, Luke. You live behind the school."

Luke smiled. "I don't mind. I enjoy your company." He glanced past her to see Sam Petty slouched against a tree. The way the man watched them made him more reluctant to let Phoebe head home alone.

Phoebe followed his gaze. "He's infatuated with me."

"He is?" That didn't bode well at all.

She nodded. "I've explained to him and his mother that I don't want to get married. My career is my life, at least at the moment. Do you think he'll be a problem?"

"He might be." Luke led her to her mule and helped her up. "Stay here while I get Ole Blue. I'm escorting you home. No arguments." A few minutes later, they rode side by side up the mountain toward Phoebe's cabin.

Occasionally, Luke would catch a glimpse of Sam flitting in and out between the trees, but he didn't say anything. Worrying Phoebe wouldn't accomplish anything.

As they neared her cabin and Sam continued to follow them, Luke wasn't sure how to keep a watch on Phoebe without frightening her. It might do well to speak with the young man's father.

"Why isn't he already married?" Phoebe slid from the mule. "His younger brother is building his own cabin, yet Sam doesn't seem to have any such aspirations."

"He works the farm with his father, and far as I can tell, the plan is for him to stay. The younger brother is free to build but needs to stay close. Women move from their parents' home far more than men do." He cast another glance at the tree line. "I don't like you here alone."

"He won't harm me."

Luke wasn't so sure. He'd seen the man react violently before when he didn't get what he wanted. "Perhaps I should speak to him."

"And tell him what?" She planted her hands on her hips. "Stay away from the midwife or else?"

"Yes. You're a valuable member of this community. Your safety is of utmost priority."

She patted Ole Blue's neck. "Good luck with that. Have a good evening."

Stubborn woman. Once she had safely entered her house, Luke rode to where Sam stood, not bothering to hide anymore. "Do you need something, Sam?"

"Just keeping an eye on my woman." He stuck a plug of tobacco behind his lip.

"I wasn't aware Miss Hudson kept company with anyone."

"She does now." He stepped from the shadows. "I staked my claim today and don't take kindly to you spending time with her."

"We're often in each other's company due to our jobs."

"I reckon." He spit. "Just know I'll be keeping an eye on you, Teacher." He turned and marched away.

Convinced the man was no danger to Phoebe as of yet, Luke turned Ole Blue home. Halfway there, he made a detour and stopped at Enid's.

"Howdy, Luke." She straightened from her gardening. "You needing some doctoring?"

"No, just a few words, if you've got the time." No one knew the hill folk better than Enid.

"Time is something I have a lot of until the good Lord calls me home. Come in for some coffee." Without waiting for an answer, she ducked inside the house built into the side of the mountain.

Luke always found her place fascinating despite the dim light. He felt wrapped in the smell of earth and herbs. Drying plants hung from the ceiling. Jars lined the shelves. A partially finished quilt lay draped over a rack. He smiled and breathed deep.

"How about you stop staring at my things and tell me what's on your mind?" Enid arched a brow.

He pulled a chair away from the table and told her of Phoebe's concerns. "I'm hoping you can help her. The two of you work together."

"We disagree on several things." She stirred something on the stove, sending a foul odor he didn't recognize to mingle with the others. "But I like her right fine."

Luke sincerely hoped it was a stew or soup. "Perhaps you agree on more than you disagree?"

"I'll pay her a visit and discuss it." She ladled some of the stuff from the pot into a bowl.

"What is that?"

"A love charm."

"For Sam Petty?"

"Why in the world would I make one for him?" She tilted her head.

"I thought he might want to give it to Phoebe since he's under the delusion he's going to marry her."

Enid made a noise in her throat. "I can make something to counteract that."

"I don't think Phoebe would want to be mixed up in witchcraft, inadvertently or not."

"This is not witchcraft!" She waved the spoon at him. "I'm a God-fearing woman, Luke Morris."

"My apologies." Even after all the years he'd lived in Possum Bottom, there were times he slipped and said something best left unsaid. Despite their strange beliefs, the hill people fiercely loved and feared God.

Enid poured him a cup of coffee and plopped it in front of him. "How do you expect to discourage that no-good Sam Petty? He's like a fly that won't go away."

Luke shrugged. "I'll think of something. Until then, Phoebe's strong enough to keep him at bay." He hoped. "I thought you might have more advice than to just make a charm."

"I'll speak with his mother. He'll listen to her." She resumed her potion making.

"Sounds like you'll be busy with the Pettys and Phoebe." Luke grinned and sipped his drink. "I appreciate your help."

"What I'm working on will take time to simmer." She tossed him a wink. "You keep on watching over that pretty Miss Phoebe and let me handle the rest. I'll bring her to the schoolhouse tomorrow afternoon so we all can discuss the classes."

Luke's neck prickled as he rode home. He wasn't sure whether it was because of the potential trouble Sam could cause or the fact that Enid was up to something.

Chapter 7

Phoebe's apron held three eggs. The first her chickens had given her. Grinning, she turned and came face-to-face with Sam Petty. Startled, she almost dropped the eggs. "Mr. Petty! I'd take a broom to you if you made me break these."

"I'd be right glad to share them with you."

"I'm afraid not. It wouldn't be proper to allow you into my cabin unchaperoned."

He grinned. "It won't matter to folks, us being betrothed and all."

Phoebe rolled her eyes. "We are not betrothed."

"I reckon you need some convincin' is all." He turned at the sound of a hoof clanking against a stone. "You've a visitor." He touched the brim of his tattered felt hat and sauntered past Enid.

"Go home and stay there," she called after him. "The midwife ain't for the no-good likes of you."

Phoebe agreed, but didn't see any reason for Enid to be rude. "He wasn't doing any harm. Breakfast?"

"Iffen you got enough." Enid slid from the mule. "I promised to take you by the schoolhouse later."

"Quite a bit later, considering the time." Phoebe smiled and led her guest into the cabin.

Enid glanced around. "Who patched the holes in your wall and roof with mud?"

"I did." Phoebe set a pan on the stove.

"Why not let Luke help you?"

"I'm quite capable, thank you."

"A woman ain't meant to do such things." Enid plopped into a chair and drummed her fingers on the table. "This might be harder than I thought."

"What might?" Phoebe glanced over her shoulder.

"Nothing." Enid waved a hand to turn Phoebe's attention back to breakfast.

"Besides," Phoebe continued, "there's nothing wrong with a woman caring for herself. Widows do. You do." Why would things need to be different with her? "I need to go see Maybelle Simpson today. Her time is getting very close."

"I reckon it might foil our plans for seeing Luke later, iffen my hunch is right. It usually is."

"You switched from the schoolhouse to the Simpsons mighty fast." Phoebe cracked the eggs into the hot pan.

" 'Cause I got an inkling when you mentioned Maybelle's name. I reckon we might know the baby's father by nightfall."

Phoebe shook her head and smiled. Luke was right. The mountain people's superstitions were harmless for the most part. She'd focus her attention on promoting cleanliness and improving their quality of life. She raised her gaze heavenward. That was what God had called her to Possum Bottom to do, after all. Wasn't it?

Why else would she have left home to travel so far? Not that she regretted her decision. Not at all. She'd discovered she quite liked the simpler life and was rather good at midwifery and simple doctoring.

"I need to pay a short visit to Mrs. Wilson too."

"I'll wait outside on that one. She don't like me much. That's why I sit in the back during church. Uppity woman says my ways are wrong." She crossed her arms and glared.

"Don't be mad at me. I like you just fine." Phoebe scooped eggs onto a plate and set it in front of Enid. "Help yourself to bread and jam."

"Where'd you get the muscadine jam?" Enid's eyes widened.

"One of my patients. I'd never had any before, but I'm in love with the taste." Phoebe filled her own plate and joined her friend at the table. She'd barely had a bite before Luke appeared in the doorway.

"Ruby Simpson stopped me this morning on my way to the school and said Maybelle is crying like a baby." He grinned. "Could you two hop over there and make sure she's fine?"

Enid nodded. "See? I told you we'd know the name of the father before nightfall."

"Eat up. Luke, are you hungry?" Phoebe stood.

"No, but thank you. I'd best get the school opened. I'll bring Ruby home after to see if you need my assistance." He touched his fingers to his hat and left them to finish eating.

"That man is easy on the eyes." Enid grinned around her fork. "If I was thirty years younger, I'd set my cap for him."

"He is very handsome."

"Much better than Sam Petty."

"That isn't hard to do." Phoebe sat back down. "Don't try to be a matchmaker. I didn't come here to get married." Heaven forbid. Her mother would have a conniption if Phoebe brought home a man from the hills, even one as handsome and educated as Luke.

"We'll see." Enid grinned and quickly finished eating. "God has a mighty way of changing plans on a person."

Phoebe finished eating, checked her medical bag, and then headed for the Simpson house. Since this was Maybelle's first, she didn't expect the labor to go quickly, and Luke hadn't seemed frantic when delivering the news. Mrs. Wilson would have to wait until the next day.

They heard the girl's cries before the house came into sight. Had they made an error in not rushing? Phoebe slid from Daisy Mae and grabbed her bag.

"Don't fret," Enid said. "The girl is very dramatic. You'll see."

Regardless, Phoebe raced for the house. "Midwife," she called.

"Thank goodness." Alice wiped her hands on a towel as Phoebe entered. "Give her something to make her sleep before we all lose our minds."

"If we knew who the father was we could put his hat on her head," Enid said. "That speeds the delivery."

That was a first for Phoebe. "Has she eaten or drunk anything?"

"Not since I gave her some Mason's nes' tea. I had a real hard time finding a dirt dauber nest too. I usually knock them down."

Phoebe shot Enid a glance. "To help speed the delivery," the other woman said as if Phoebe's medical knowledge had flown out the front door.

After examining the pretty young woman with coal-black hair and eyes the same color, Phoebe planted her hands on her hips. "I'm afraid things are progressing slowly and are not to the point to warrant such cries."

"You mean they're going to get worse?" The girl's eyes widened. "I'm going to die!"

"You are not. The baby is in position, and I don't see any foreseeable complications."

"I'm going to strangle Johnny with my bare hands. Oh!" She screamed and pulled a pillow over her face.

Phoebe grinned. "At least we have a father's name."

"I'll send someone for him and the preacher," Alice said. "I won't have my first grandchild born on the wrong side of the blanket."

⌒

"I need you to come with me."

Luke glanced up from grading papers to see Homer Simpson in the doorway, a shotgun cradled in his arms. "I'd be glad to. Where are we going?"

"To fetch Johnny Petty. He's got to marry my girl right now, and I need you with me so I don't shoot him."

Luke didn't have to be told twice. He grabbed his hat and darted after the man. "She admitted he's the father?"

"Just as good as." He swung onto the back of his horse. "I cain't believe my grandbaby will have Petty blood. It's a sad day for sure."

When they fetched the preacher and the boy and arrived at the Simpson home to the sound of Maybelle's screams, Johnny looked as pale as cotton. "Is she dying?"

"No, but you will iffen you don't get hitched right now." Homer glared. "Now we all know why it's you building a cabin and not Sam." He waved his shotgun in the direction of the house.

"I'd a married Maybelle a year ago iffen you and my pa weren't so thickheaded." Color returned to Johnny's face. "Let's go, Preacher Wilson." Back straight, the boy marched toward the house.

Luke immediately searched the room for Phoebe upon entering. Some hair had pulled free of her bun and hung in wisps around her frazzled-looking face. Relief flooded her features when she spotted him. She smiled and bent over to listen to Maybelle's baby.

"We're progressing nicely," she said. "If you want to get married, I suggest you do so soon."

She made her way to Luke's side. "Such a strange wedding. In a cabin, in the throes of labor, surrounded by people. I'll never cease to be amazed at the strength yet strangeness of these people." Her hand slipped into Luke's.

Surprised but pleased, he entwined their fingers. When he looked away from Phoebe, he frowned at a glowing Enid. "What?"

"Nothing." Her smile widened. "Absolutely nothing."

"She's up to something," Phoebe said, slipping free. "She's been toying with something in her pocket all day."

"Yesterday I arrived at her home to see her making a charm."

Phoebe's eyes widened. "People still do that?"

He nodded. "Around here they do."

Preacher Wilson called everyone to attention and started the ceremony. When he got to the part where he said, "You may kiss your bride," Homer snorted.

"Looks like he's already done that, Preacher."

Phoebe laughed, her eyes sparkling as she glanced up at Luke. "Will you take the men out now so we can get this baby born?"

"Do you need anything?" He lowered his voice.

"No. We have it covered. Thank you."

"Anything, Phoebe." He smiled as her face flushed, then

turned and followed the other men outside, pulling the door closed behind him.

"My brother ain't going to take kindly to the way you looked at the midwife," Johnny said, "or the way she looked back."

"We're just friends." Luke sat on the top step, wanting very much to be more than friends with the stubborn, career-minded woman.

"Sam's got his eye on the midwife?" Homer's brows rose. "She won't look at the likes of him. He didn't get past the fifth grade."

Johnny shrugged. "Said he's going to marry her."

Homer pulled a knife from his pocket and picked up a fist-sized piece of oak from the porch and started whittling. "Fool. I'll knock some sense into him. Everyone around here knows Teacher and the midwife will get hitched."

Luke jerked. "Why so?"

"There's at least three love charms with y'all's hair that I know of. You don't stand a chance."

Luke glanced back at the house. So that's what Enid had in her pocket. She'd admitted to making one yesterday. "Who else has them?"

"My wife and Dorcas Petty."

"I don't believe in charms."

"Won't matter. When those three put their minds to something, it's best a man just say okay. There's an ice cream social next Sunday at the church and you two have been assigned the task of turning the crank on the cream. Reckon you'll be together most of the time."

"Assigned by the three women?"

"Now you're catching on." Homer spit to his left. "I'll explain it to Sam. He'll realize nothing he does will change a thing and transfer his attention to some other poor girl."

All three men jumped to their feet when an infant's cry drifted through the window. "Go on, Johnny," Homer said. "You should be the first of us to see your baby."

With a whoop, Johnny barged into the house. Seconds later, they heard, "It's a boy!"

Luke entered the house last and, despite the matchmaking intentions of Enid and Alice, made his way to Phoebe's side. "You've done a fine job once again."

"All I do is guide the mother before, during, and after. They do all the work." Still, she seemed pleased with his compliment.

He told her about the ice cream social. "Since we've been assigned the same task, will you allow me to escort you?"

She laughed. "Are you falling for their matchmaking scheme?"

"No, but there isn't anyone else I'd like to take."

"As long as you realize I haven't changed my mind about focusing on my career."

How could he not realize that when she shot the subject down if anyone even hinted at marriage?

Chapter 8

Heads turned when Luke and Phoebe entered the church on Sunday morning. As was customary, they chose an empty spot in back. Phoebe couldn't help but think how silly the Simpsons and Pettys were to continue sitting on different sides of the sanctuary considering the families should have been brought together by the marriage of Maybelle and Johnny. She smiled at the happy young parents who also sat in the back row.

"Scoot over." Enid squeezed in, forcing Luke to move closer to Phoebe.

His leg pressed against hers. In order to make room, he put his arm along the back of the pew. This action elicited a very satisfied grin from Enid.

Phoebe narrowed her eyes. She needed to have a serious conversation with her friend as soon as possible. Cutting a quick glance at Luke's profile, she noticed the twitching of his lips. Was it possible he would allow Enid to push them together, knowing how Phoebe felt about marriage right now? She needed to find someone of wisdom to talk to.

Her gaze fell on Mrs. Wilson, who squirmed in her seat.

Perhaps some time spent with the preacher's wife would help.

After yet another sermon on the evils of holding a grudge, Phoebe excused herself from Luke, promising to join him later at their ice cream station, and went in search of Mrs. Wilson. She found the poor woman looking very fatigued and sitting in the shade of a tree, her children running circles around her.

"Are you feeling poorly?" Phoebe peered into her eyes.

"No more than usual for a woman so close to her due date. Please, sit with me for a spell. It will take my mind off the pain in my back." She motioned to a chair next to her.

"How severe is the pain? Does it come and go?" Phoebe sat.

"Same as yesterday. And since you deemed everything progressing as it should, I feel as if you have something else on your mind." Mrs. Wilson crooked a brow.

"I do." She wasn't quite sure how to broach the subject of Enid's meddling to a woman who didn't like her.

"Spit it out, child." Mrs. Wilson leaned her head back and closed her eyes.

"I don't want to marry anyone yet, but I feel as if some of the women here are pushing Luke and me together in hopes of making that happen. Worse, I think they're using love charms."

"Enid." She rolled her head to face Phoebe. "Have you found a charm in your home or among your possessions?"

Phoebe shook her head. "I don't believe in superstitious nonsense. My concern is that Luke will get the wrong impression with us being in constant company."

"Have you spoken to him?"

"I've made my thoughts clear."

"Then what's the problem?"

Phoebe sighed. "I don't think he's trying to dissuade the women from meddling."

"As long as Mr. Morris is not taking their actions seriously, you have nothing to worry about." She patted Phoebe's knee. "Although, I do agree that being married would help your reputation in the community." She held up a hand as Phoebe started to protest. "Oh, the women will use your services, dear, as will I, but they do gossip horribly about the impropriety of an unmarried woman of your age being a midwife. Perhaps you should reconsider. You can still be a midwife if you're married."

Phoebe glanced to where Luke laughed with a group of men. "My parents would never approve."

"I don't believe they approved of your coming here, did they? You have some soul-searching to do. Now, go to that handsome man and make ice cream." She grinned and pulled an envelope from her pocket. "Oh. This was mixed in my mail. I'm so sorry I forgot to give it to you yesterday."

Heavens. Even the preacher's wife agreed Phoebe should get married, to Luke, and soon. She exhaled sharply through her nose and thanked the woman for her time.

Of course Luke was the type of man she'd want to marry. The problem was that she'd not thought past her career in as long as she could remember.

She opened the flap of the envelope and pulled out a letter in her mother's handwriting. She quickly scanned the words. Her parents would be arriving for a visit in the next day or two. Clutching the lace at her throat, she swallowed down the rising panic. What would they think of her life here?

"Is something wrong?" Luke stepped to her side.

"My parents are coming." She raised her eyes. "Where will I put them?"

He smiled. "I'll build a trundle that fits under your bed. That will give all three of you somewhere to sleep."

She gazed into his eyes. "Why are you so nice all the time? Don't you ever get angry, confused, sad? Do you always know exactly what to do at any given moment?"

"I'm full of uncertainty." The huskiness of his voice and the warmth in his eyes told her she was the source of that feeling.

"My parents humored me in letting me come here, hoping I'd grow discouraged and return home. They'll never let me stay." She lowered her gaze and headed to where the table had been set up for ice cream. Saying the words out loud helped her realize how much she did want to stay and how much she'd miss not only the people but Luke if she were to leave.

⌒

Luke stayed up late into the night building the trundle for Phoebe. While he worked, he thought over what he'd said about uncertainty. She wasn't the only one who thought life should be focused on career and not romance. At least that was how he'd felt until she arrived.

Was it wrong of him to enjoy the efforts of the women who tried to match him and Phoebe together? He wouldn't mind spending his life with a woman as brave, determined, beautiful, and caring as she was.

Why wouldn't her parents allow her to stay? Once upon a time, Luke's family had been privileged. He was well educated. He'd make a fine husband.

He slid the trundle into the back of a flatbed wagon, then

tossed a hay-stuffed mattress on top. After hitching Ole Blue to the wagon, he climbed on board and headed toward Phoebe's.

A scream from behind the house as he pulled up to the cabin had him leaping off the driver's seat and sprinting toward the outhouse. "Phoebe!"

"Oh, be careful, Luke," she said from inside. "There's a snake out there."

He froze and glanced around his feet. "I don't see one."

"It's on the roof."

He glanced up to see a rat snake over five feet long. He laughed. "You can come out. It's harmless."

"It's a snake!"

"A rat snake." He knocked on the door. "How'd you get in there if you're so afraid?"

"I didn't see it until I was coming out."

He bit his lip to keep from laughing again. "I have your trundle."

The door opened, and she darted out, not stopping to look back until she was well away from the outbuilding. "I need something I can use to kill those things."

"Your best bet is to leave them alone. It was most likely after your eggs. There are a lot of snakes that are not poisonous. I have a book in the schoolhouse you're free to borrow." He couldn't keep the grin off his face.

"Stop laughing at me." With a swish of her dark blue skirt, she marched away.

He jogged to catch up with her. "Have you made space for the trundle?"

"Are you finished having fun at my expense?"

"Yes." A snort escaped him.

She whirled. "I don't understand why my fear of snakes is so humorous."

"It's more like the place you chose to hide is what I find humor in."

She rolled her eyes and continued into the house where she commenced banging things around. "Please get the trundle."

Thankfully, Mr. McGee arrived with several boxes of supplies Phoebe had ordered and helped Luke carry the trundle into the house where they placed it next to the bed. Then, while the older man carried in the boxes, Luke hauled in the mattress and dropped it on top of the trundle.

"It's on wheels so you can store it out of the way when you don't have need of it." He pushed the trundle with his foot, sending it neatly out of sight.

"I could put up a flyer in the mercantile," Mr. McGee said. "I reckon there are several families out here that would welcome something like that."

"I'm not sure I'd have time for such a venture." Although the idea did have merit. "Perhaps during the times school isn't in session."

"Would the hill folk be able to afford something like this?" Phoebe tilted her head. "I will give you the funds when my parents arrive."

Luke frowned, disturbed by her prejudice. "I'll gladly take in trade if they don't have money. I've already told you that's how things are often done here. This isn't the big city."

Her eyes widened. "The Simpsons paid me with coffee and sugar, which I gratefully accepted. I just thought with something like this. . ."

He raised a brow.

She plopped on the edge of the bed. "I need to think before I speak. Thank you for the delivery, Mr. McGee."

He glanced from her to Luke. "She's new here."

"Not that new." He followed the other man out, knowing he'd have to apologize to Phoebe for his harsh words. So much for always being kind. He went back into the house to see Phoebe still sitting on her bed, head bowed. "I'm sorry. Don't cry." He couldn't bear her tears.

She raised her head. "So am I. I'm not crying—I'm praying for a guard to be placed over my mouth."

"Not on my account, I hope."

"Rather for everyone's sake." She smiled and stood to pull the trundle out. "I'd like to test it and see how many blankets I need in order to make it soft. Have you ever had a feather mattress, Luke? They're so much better. Oh." She clapped a hand over her mouth. "I've done it again, haven't I?"

"Not very much." He chuckled. "There's nothing wrong with liking one form of something better than another. Contrary to recent evidence, I don't get offended that easily."

"Good." She lay down and spread out on the mattress. "Not bad at all."

"Phoebe, why is there a strange man on the porch looking through the window?" A woman's stern voice came from the doorway.

Luke turned to see an older version of Phoebe staring at them.

"And what are you doing lying on a bed with this man standing over you? Frank, fetch whatever they call law enforcement around here." She grabbed a broom and advanced.

Chapter 9

"W ait." Phoebe scrambled from the trundle and stepped between her mother and Luke. "He is not attacking me. This is the schoolteacher, Mr. Luke Morris, who so kindly constructed this trundle in order to give us enough sleeping space."

Her father appeared in the doorway. "Then who was the man peering in your window?"

"That would be Sam Petty, who believes we are to be wed and refuses to take a hint. The man is a menace, following me around everywhere."

Her father glowered. "I forbid you to wed a backward hill person."

"I didn't say I'd agreed." Phoebe drew in a slow, deep breath. "Luke, meet my parents, Mr. and Mrs. Hudson."

Luke thrust out his hand. Her father stared at it for a moment, then returned the shake. Phoebe's mother, on the other hand, propped the broom against the wall and glanced around.

"This entire cabin is smaller than your bedroom back home. However do you manage?" She counted her steps across the room. "Ten steps, Phoebe!"

Embarrassment flooded through Phoebe, heating her face as Luke glanced her way. No doubt he now knew where her snobbishness came from. No matter how much she tried to fit in with the hill folk, her upbringing would always make her an outsider.

"Let me walk you out, Luke," she said softly, brushing past her father. Outside, she said, "I am truly sorry for their behavior."

"It's fine. It isn't the first time I've dealt with their way of thinking." He smiled. "Will you be all right?"

"Of course." She tilted her head. "They'll lecture for a while over cups of coffee, then I'll take them around the area and listen while Mother declares how wild the place is. Then we'll return home to my tiny cabin, I'll fix supper, and we'll go to bed. In the morning, they'll make excuses why they can't stay longer, and peace will return to Possum Bottom." The thought sent an ache through her heart.

"They'll pressure you to leave." His eyes darkened.

"Yes. With their strong views about the people here, their arguments may very well persuade me. I'm one against two." Tears pricked her eyes as she thought of her father's words forbidding her to marry anyone from the hills. Not that she intended to wed, at least not for a few years, but knowing she had no future as a wife and mother if she stayed tugged at her heart.

"Pray long and hard, Phoebe. Regardless of what they think, you do belong here." He climbed into the wagon and clucked to Ole Blue.

With a heavy sigh, Phoebe rejoined her parents in the cabin where her mother had already started a pot of coffee. "Sit, Phoebe. We've much to discuss."

"Wouldn't you rather see the area?" She knew her parents so well.

"Later." Her mother handed her a tin mug.

When they were all seated around the small table, her mother added cream and sugar to her coffee. "At least you have a few luxuries."

"My patients are so grateful for my service, they sacrifice their food and possessions as my payment." She wrapped both hands around her mug.

"We brought you a few things," her father said. "Supplies and the like. No idea where you'll put them."

"I'll have shelves built. We make do up here."

Her mother cleared her throat. "That's what we'd like to talk to you about. Do you remember the Winstons? They had a son just a little older than you named Robert."

"Vaguely." Phoebe frowned. "Why?"

"Because he would like to marry you."

Phoebe leaped to her feet. "I knew you disapproved of my coming here, my occupational choice, but to stoop so low as to ask me to marry a virtual stranger. . . Mother! Papa!" Her throat clogged. "I must take a moment lest I say something disrespectful." She whirled and rushed out the door, not stopping until she reached the edge of the yard.

Although she'd watched him ride away, she hoped for a glimpse of Luke. She'd ask him to take her far away for a while. Anywhere but where she was at the moment. Catching a glimpse of Sam lurking at the edge of the woods, she marched toward him.

"If you don't go away and leave me alone, I'll have you arrested." She lifted her chin.

"I warned the teacher to stay away from you." He crossed his arms. "Who are the fancy people?"

"My parents. They've come to inform me they've betrothed me to someone back home. Thus, I cannot marry you. Good day, sir." *Oh, please take the hint and go away.*

"I reckon as long as you're in Possum Bottom and unwed, I've a chance." He gave a nod and backed into the shadows.

Ugh. Phoebe stomped her foot and returned to the cabin. Was there any place in this country where a woman could make up her own mind about the future?

"Now that you've had your snit," Mother said with a sniff, "I suggest you think about Robert Winston and let us know before we leave."

"Which will be. . . ?"

"We haven't decided." Papa patted her shoulder. "Come and show us around. I'd like to know what it is about this place that has my little girl enamored."

Mother declined, saying the trip had wearied her and she needed a nap. Phoebe led her father outside, pointing out the chicken coop and the lean-to for the mule Luke had brought her.

"Is it this place or the schoolteacher you're in love with?" Papa smiled.

"I'm in love with no one."

"You say his name so many times, I must disagree. Do you know anything about him?"

"Only that he is kind, loves these people, and is well educated. What else would a woman need to know?"

"So you are in love with him." He put his arm around her shoulders.

"Oh Papa." She turned and laid her head on his chest. "I had no plans of falling in love with anyone. I love what I do. What if I was to get married and my husband asked me to give up midwifing?"

"If you love him enough, you'd give up anything."

Luke felt as if he had deserted Phoebe when she needed him. But he'd caught the disdain in her father's words regarding backward hill people. Luke called Possum Bottom home, so that made him one of the very people her parents scorned.

He let Ole Blue loose in the corral and went to wash his face and hands at the pump. Mrs. Hudson had actually counted the steps across Phoebe's cabin. Who did that? He shook his head, flinging water from his hair.

Still shaking his head, this time from unbelief rather than to rid his hair of water, he climbed the steps to his small porch. Leaning against the door was a small calico-wrapped package. He removed the calico to reveal a simple burlap doll, no bigger than his hand, dressed amazingly like the style Phoebe wore. Enid's love charm. With a grin and a prayer, he slipped the doll into his pocket. He knew enough about the actions of these people to know Phoebe would have one dressed like him. Harmless, but the gesture still gave him a thrill of hope.

He glanced heavenward. "Your will be done." Whistling, he entered his house and started preparations for a simple supper. After warming up some beans and corn bread, he took the food onto the porch and settled down. His favorite time of day. The only thing that would make it better in his mind would be to watch the sun set with Phoebe at his side.

A pipe dream. The sooner he accepted that fact, the better.

"Teacher!" One of the older Wilson boys, Joey, rode up on an ancient horse. "Ma's about to have the baby and the midwife ain't home. There's a strange woman asleep in her bed. Where should I look for Miss Phoebe?"

"You go on home. I'll find the midwife and be there as soon as possible." Luke set his bowl on the porch and rushed to fetch his mule. Seconds later, he was thundering down the road toward Phoebe's place.

Once there, he barged into the cabin. "Mrs. Hudson."

The woman sat up from her sleep. "What? Who?"

"The preacher's wife needs Phoebe. Do you know where she is?"

"Out with her father somewhere." She swung her legs over the side of the bed. "Help me up, young man, and we'll find her."

He took her hand and gently pulled her to her feet. "This is a big mountain, ma'am."

"Is the mule here? I heard it braying earlier."

Luke grabbed Phoebe's medical bag from near the door and glanced out the back window. "It's here, which means they couldn't have walked far." Outside, he put two fingers between his lips and let loose a shrill whistle. "Phoebe!"

A few more whistles and she came running from the woods, her skirt hiked above her ankles. "What is it?"

"Cover yourself, dear." Her mother frowned. "Seems someone needs you."

Luke tied the bag to Daisy Mae. "Mrs. Wilson's time has come. Hurry ahead, and I'll show your parents the way." He cupped his hands to help her up, then stepped back as she galloped away.

"We could stay here," Mrs. Hudson said.

"I thought you might like to observe your daughter at work.

She's a very fine midwife." Luke led the way to their rented buggy. "Follow me." His tone left no room for argument. These two people needed to see what their daughter was capable of.

"Very well." Mrs. Hudson accepted her husband's assistance into the buggy.

It took a lot of willpower for Luke to keep Ole Blue's gait slow enough for the buggy to keep up. The occasional rut in the road elicited sharp squeals from Mrs. Hudson, but they continued forward at a steady pace.

"Tell us about the preacher and his wife," Mr. Hudson said.

"Good people. Well-liked in the community, and accepting of most of the old-time superstitions while guiding the people in the Word of God." Luke glanced over his shoulder. "Mrs. Wilson is a mite old to be having a baby, in my opinion, but God knows better."

"How can superstition and God be in the same heart?" Phoebe's mother shook her head. "We're to refrain from all appearances of evil."

"Old ways take awhile to disappear. Don't judge too harshly. That isn't our job."

Mr. Hudson laughed. "Perhaps you should switch from teaching to preaching, Mr. Morris."

"I'd rather leave that to those better equipped." Luke returned the man's smile and led them to the cabin behind the church. "Mr. Hudson, we'll stay out here with the preacher and let Mrs. Hudson join the women inside."

"Who is that woman?" Mrs. Hudson motioned to where Enid hovered at the edge of the property.

"That's Enid. She stood in as midwife until Phoebe arrived.

The preacher's wife doesn't care for her beliefs. Out of respect, Enid stays outside unless needed."

"Which I will be, mark my words." Enid bustled toward them. "This is not her first babe. It should have been born hours ago."

Phoebe stood in the doorway. "Enid, I need you. Mother, you could also be of assistance. Preacher Wilson, Luke, Father, pray." With those words, she stepped back into the house.

The preacher bowed his head, tears dripping onto his folded hands. Without speaking, Luke and Mr. Hudson joined him in silent prayer.

Chapter 10

After several grueling hours of administering chloroform to lessen Mrs. Wilson's pain and working to get the unborn baby turned in the right direction, Phoebe could now get off her feet. She fell into a nearby chair as Preacher Wilson knelt next to his wife and new daughter. If not for Enid's experience, the outcome might have been very different.

"The other woman went home to make a special concoction for Mrs. Wilson." Mother handed her a cup of tea. "You did very well, Daughter. I'm proud of you."

Phoebe jerked her gaze to her mother. "Thank you. That means a lot to me."

"Won't you come home now?"

"To Boston or to my cabin?" Phoebe didn't have the strength for another argument.

Her mother perched on the stool next to the chair. "To the cabin. This is where you belong, at least for now. Perhaps Robert will wait for you."

"I can't marry him. I won't marry for anything less than love when the time is right." Phoebe sighed and took a sip of her tea.

"I will stay here for the night in case there are complications. You and Papa go on. I'll see you in the morning, or rather later today."

"I could stay and help." Weariness lined her mother's face.

"No. This is my job." Phoebe patted her mother's hand, thankful beyond words for her change of heart. "Luke will show you the way."

Periodically throughout the night, Phoebe checked on Mrs. Wilson and the baby. By the time the sun came up, she felt confident enough to leave them in the capable hands of Preacher Wilson. "Don't hesitate to send someone for me if your wife develops a fever. She'll need bed rest for the next few days to build her strength."

"I'll take good care of her." He dropped some coins into her hand. "God bless you, Miss Phoebe."

"Thank you." Phoebe smiled and stepped outside where Luke waited next to her mule. Her heart leaped despite her exhaustion.

"I thought you might like an escort." He grinned and helped her onto Daisy Mae.

"I would enjoy the company. Did my parents get home all right?"

"Yes, and both were sleeping like babies when I left."

"I think I might sleep for three days." Phoebe's shoulders slumped. Her mother would frown at the unladylike posture, but sitting upright took more energy than she had.

"Hold up." Luke reached for Daisy Mae's reins, stopping the mule. "You're falling asleep sitting up." He moved close enough to pull Phoebe onto Ole Blue in front of him. "Put your head back and rest. I've got you."

Her eyes closed and her head lolled back and rested on his

chest almost instantly. The feel of his strong arms around her, keeping her from falling, filled her with a sense of safety. Nothing could harm her with Luke near.

When she opened her eyes, she realized he'd kept the mules' pace slow so as not to wake her. "Aren't you tired too?" she asked.

"I'm fine. I caught a few winks waiting for you. Are you feeling all right?"

She glanced up at him. "Just tired. Why?"

"I'm no expert, not having held many women, but you seem hotter than what should be normal, and your face is flushed. You've been working too hard."

She frowned, trying to ignore the pounding headache behind her eyes. "I've a calling, Luke. There won't always be this many babies born in so short a time."

"I understand that, Phoebe, but you can't take care of your patients if you don't take care of yourself. Let Enid help you more."

She shook her head. "I'm trying to teach these people a better quality of life, not encourage them to stay in the old ways." She and Enid still hadn't managed to bring the women of Possum Bottom together for instructive classes.

"You are a very stubborn woman, Phoebe Hudson." He chuckled and tightened his arms around her as they headed up a hill.

As much as she hated to admit he was right, she could no longer ignore the fact that she felt ill, feverish, and achy. She'd feel much better after a good night's rest. She smiled to herself. Maybe the rest of the day and night would be best. She'd definitely feel refreshed in the morning. Right? She had to. Expectant mothers were counting on her.

She closed her eyes and slept the rest of the way home. As she slid from the mule, her legs buckled, and she grabbed onto Luke for support. "I feel dizzy."

Without a word, he scooped her into his arms and rushed to the cabin. "Help, please, Mrs. Hudson." He laid Phoebe on the trundle and stepped back.

Her mother's eyes widened, and she placed the back of her hand against Phoebe's cheek. "She's burning up. Is there a doctor around here?"

"I just need. . .rest." Phoebe pushed her mother's hand away. "A drink of water."

"She's the only doctor close by other than Enid. I can send for one, but it will take him hours to arrive," Luke said.

"Please be so kind as to bring Enid here." Mother waved her hands. "We need to get Phoebe out of these clothes."

"I'll get out of your way," Papa said, placing a kiss on Phoebe's cheek. "I'm right outside if you need me."

"I'm fine." Phoebe tried to sit up. Dizziness overcame her and she fell back, closing her eyes.

She groaned as her mother struggled to undress her, leaving Phoebe in her shift, before piling on two quilts. "Too hot."

"You must sweat out the fever. Stop being such a baby and drink this water."

Phoebe opened her eyes and sipped the water from the cup her mother held to her lips. "Thank you."

"I'll make some soup. Rest, sweetheart."

Phoebe rolled onto her side. Sleep sounded better than anything she'd heard in the last hour. She fell asleep dreaming of how wonderful she'd felt with Luke's arms wrapped around her.

Luke banged several times on Enid's door before she answered. From her messy hair and wrinkled clothes, he could tell he'd woken her up. "Phoebe has fallen ill. We need you."

"Let me get my things and I'll be right there. Send someone with a fast horse for the doctor." She turned and started tossing items into a satchel.

Luke urged Ole Blue as fast as he could toward the nearest house, the Simpsons'. Spotting Johnny chopping wood outside, he sent him for the doctor and turned back toward Phoebe's cabin. He caught up with Enid halfway there.

"What's wrong with her?" she asked.

"Fever, weak, almost fainted. Would have hit the ground if she hadn't latched onto me."

"Why aren't you in school?"

"I felt as if God wanted me to close for the day. Good thing I did. If I hadn't stopped at the Wilson house to ride back with Phoebe, she might be lying on the side of the road at this minute." The thought terrified him. These hills were full of predators, both four-legged and two.

"Don't fear, Luke. We'll have her to rights in no time." Enid slid from her donkey's back and marched to the cabin door, Luke on her heels. "I'm here, Mrs. Hudson. Let's make some tea."

"Thank goodness. I've been bathing her face and arms with cool water, but it doesn't seem to be doing much good."

Luke didn't care what anyone thought. He sat in the chair next to the trundle and took Phoebe's hand in his. She felt far too hot. He glanced at Enid. "Do something."

"We'll start with sassafras tea and go from there. You might be more useful keeping us supplied with cool water."

"I want to stay."

"This cabin ain't big enough for all of us. You go outside with Mr. Hudson and leave the doctoring to us women."

"Come on, son." Mr. Hudson handed Luke a bucket. "We're of no use here."

On the way to the creek, Luke asked, "Aren't you worried at all? Phoebe could be seriously ill."

"What good will worrying do? It's best to pray, don't you agree? The wife and. . .not sure what to call Enid, will care for her until the doctor arrives." He clapped Luke on the shoulder. "Have faith. My heart tells me Phoebe's work here isn't finished. Did she tell you why she wanted to become a midwife?"

"No." Luke scooped the bucket into the creek.

"She should have had a younger sister, but we lived away from the city. No doctor, no midwife near. A difficult labor with no one to help. The child didn't live more than a few minutes, and my wife was unable to have more children. Phoebe believes that had a midwife been closer, not arriving when it was too late, the baby might have lived. She's wanted this ever since."

"She's a very good midwife." Not wanting to be away any longer than necessary, Luke turned away from the creek. "How do you feel about it?"

"I want my little girl to be happy. I suspect you do as well."

"Am I that transparent?" Luke's eyes widened.

"To me you are. My daughter would be safe with you. If you can convince her that marriage and midwifery can go together, you have my blessing." Mr. Hudson smiled. "I wish you luck. She's quite stubborn."

"I've discovered that." Luke increased his pace. Knowing he had the man's blessing warmed him, but first they needed to get Phoebe back on her feet, and then Luke needed to find a way to convince her to marry him.

He paused on the porch while Mr. Hudson inquired whether it was safe for them to enter with the water. Instead of inviting them in, Enid retrieved the bucket and ordered them to stay outside and give her room. "Phoebe is no better, but she is no worse. I feel she is simply at the point of exhaustion. I've given her an herb to help her sleep a good long while. Let me know when the doctor arrives." She closed the door.

Luke should have learned patience what with all the waiting for Phoebe he'd done since her arrival, but when she was the one needing to be tended to, all that flew out the window. He paced the dirt-packed ground in front of the cabin, marveling how her father could sit on the steps with a peaceful look on his face.

"I do believe you're a godly man, Mr. Morris. Pray and leave the rest to God," Mr. Hudson said. "There's nothing else you can do."

Luke plopped next to him. "I've known that my entire life. This time it's different." He pulled the love charm from his pocket.

"What is that?"

"I believe it's a love charm planted on me by Enid. She and a couple of the other local women took it upon themselves to play matchmaker."

Mr. Hudson laughed. "I saw something like that, only it resembled you, under Phoebe's pillow before you placed her there. It astounds me how there are people who still believe such things."

"These people are simple folk." Luke slid the doll back into his pocket. "I wouldn't choose to live anywhere else."

"What if my daughter chooses to leave?" He tilted his head.

"That's not something I need to worry about right now. I haven't told her of my feelings. Perhaps leaving wouldn't be an issue."

"Perhaps."

The door opened behind them as a man on horseback raced toward the house. "The doc is here," Luke said, getting to his feet.

"It's about time," Mr. Hudson said.

"Dr. Reed." Enid stepped aside and let him in. She shook her head at Luke's unspoken question.

"So, she still sleeps." Luke resumed his seat and wished he'd taken up the task of whittling to pass the time.

He glanced up to see Preacher Wilson and several other members of the community marching toward them. Everyone carried a food item in their hand. Luke stood.

"We heard the midwife was doing poorly," Preacher Wilson said. "When the missus found out, she told me to gather some folks, bring some food, and make a prayer circle. So here we are."

Tears burned Luke's eyes. Yep, he never wanted to live anywhere else.

Chapter 11

Phoebe shoved the cup away. "If you force one more cup of that tea down my throat, I'll scream."

"Well, look who's awake." Enid set the cup on the table. "Doc was here. Left a powder to mix with your tea. Said you have to drink it. Who am I to argue with the doctor?"

"Fine." Phoebe pushed to a sitting position. "It's awfully hot in here." She glanced at the bed where her parents slept. How could they sleep in such heat?

"We can open a window now that your fever has broken." Enid got up and threw open the front window. "How are you feeling?"

"Better. What time is it?"

"The sun's been up for an hour or so." Enid handed her the cup again. "Drink it."

Phoebe did and grimaced at the bitter taste. "I'm sorry to have been such a bother."

"Come here." Enid waved her over to the window. "This is how much of a bother you've been." Her soft tone belied the harshness of her words.

Phoebe slowly got out of bed and glanced out to see a circle of her patients and their families. "How long have they been here?"

"Arrived shortly after the doctor. Been praying for you ever since they found out you were ill. Does a heart good, doesn't it? They refused to leave until they got news you were going to recover." She smiled. "We've also got more vittles than we can possibly eat."

Phoebe's throat burned with unshed tears. "I had no idea they felt this way about me."

"Why not? You're their midwife. You're one of us now."

She'd never heard more beautiful words. She'd had friends in Boston but had never truly felt as if she belonged there. She had truly come home.

"Get back in bed this instant," her mother ordered from behind them.

"I will soon. Enid, my robe, please." Phoebe dropped the blanket wrapped around her and slipped her arms into the sleeves of her robe, tying it tightly around her waist. "I want to thank these people for their kindness." She opened the door and stepped onto the porch.

Heads turned in her direction. Cheers went up. She smiled and held up her hands. "I was merely exhausted. I'll be as good as new by tomorrow. Please, stay and partake of the lovely food you brought."

Luke sprang to her side. "Should you be up?"

"I'll sit right here and enjoy the company of my friends." She lowered herself into a chair her father brought out. "I again owe you my gratitude."

He took her hand and raised it to his lips. "I will always be there to catch you when you fall. I'll help set up the food and then bring you a plate."

"Very little." She glanced up as Luke walked away and her father put a hand on her shoulder.

"That's a fine man."

"Yes, he is."

"He cares for you. What do you say?"

"About what?" She frowned. "I treasure his company and friendship, but you know my views on marriage at this time. I'm still getting my bearings here. Papa, I'm not yet twenty."

"Your mother and I would worry less if you were married."

Phoebe waved her arm. "Look, Papa. These people won't let any harm come to me."

"Of course, but you cannot stop a father from worrying." He kissed the top of her head and went to join the others.

Soon the scene resembled a party, one Phoebe wished very much she could join. While the heavy blanket of exhaustion no longer weighed on her, she didn't want to push her strength. She had a job to return to. Babies to deliver and check on. One day away was more than enough. But she didn't want to overtax herself and make it more.

Luke brought her a plate containing a fried chicken leg and a square of buttered corn bread. "Is this enough?"

"It's perfect." She smiled, her gaze landing on the sight of her mother laughing with Alice Simpson. "I'm actually glad I collapsed. If I hadn't, my parents wouldn't have stayed long enough to get to know these people."

"When are they leaving?"

"In the morning. I'll be heading up the mountain to check on a new patient Enid told me about."

"Would you consider waiting until the school day is over so I can accompany you?" Luke frowned.

"I'll be at the school by then. Enid and I are having our first class. She's telling the women here to spread the word." She put a hand on his arm. "You can't always rearrange your life to babysit me, Luke. I'm a grown woman."

"I've noticed." He grinned. "I especially enjoyed the way you felt in my arms on the ride home."

Her face heated, and not because of a fever. She ducked her head over her plate. "It did feel very nice."

He laughed and transferred his attention to his own plate. "Be stubborn and see your patients alone. I'll be here after school tomorrow to fix you supper."

"Leftovers after today's impromptu party?" She arched a brow.

"Sweetheart, there won't be any leftovers. Not with this crowd."

"There's Sam." Phoebe pointed him out, staying to the tree line. "I haven't seen him in a few days."

"No one has. Leroy said he up and disappeared one day, claiming he was going to build his own cabin up the mountain a ways. I guess he heard you were ill." Luke's expression turned grave. "He won't be happy to hear about the love charms."

Her eyes narrowed. "What love charms?"

He grinned. "The one in my pocket and the one under your pillow. Seems our angels of matchmaking have been busy indeed."

Silly superstition. Still, she couldn't stop the flush from returning to her face.

"Are you feverish again?" Luke felt her head.

She pulled back. "No, I am not." Although his touch seemed to make her feel ten degrees warmer.

Enid stepped out of the cabin and handed her another cup. "Medicine time."

"Again?" Phoebe shook her head. "Too soon."

"I spoke to the doctor, not you." She tapped Luke on the head. "Make her drink it."

"As if I can make her do anything." He grinned and winked.

Phoebe sighed and took her medicine.

For what had to be the hundredth time, Luke reassured his students the next morning that the midwife was just fine and back to doing her job. "She merely got overworked staying up all night with Mrs. Wilson."

"My brother Sam says it's because she's doing something she shouldn't, and God punished her." Lucy Petty didn't bother looking up from her slate board where she practiced her multiplication tables. "Sam says that an unmarried woman shouldn't be doing things so intimate, but should be gettin' hitched and raising babies of her own. He says he's going to remedy that situation."

"I'm going to be a midwife," Ruby Simpson stated. "I'll be younger than Miss Phoebe and ain't gettin' married to no boy."

"That's enough." Luke walked between the two rows of desks. "What Miss Hudson does is no concern of ours."

"Yes, it is," Lucy protested. "Someone told Sam that you and Miss Hudson have love charms. He's right riled about that."

"We shouldn't be gossiping." Luke stopped next to her desk.

The girl glanced up. "I reckon you want her for yourself."

The class erupted in laughter and kissing sounds. Luke clapped his hands. "That's enough. Back to your arithmetic."

Hands clasped behind his back, Luke stood in the open

doorway of the school and stared out into the yard. If Sam was talking to his siblings about Phoebe, he wasn't planning on pushing his ridiculous notion of marrying her aside. Luke needed to convince her not to make her visits alone, but to have Enid go with her.

If he had his way, he'd be by her side the entire time. When he'd told her of the charms, he'd almost mentioned his conversation with her father and the blessing given. That had been shot down with her reaction to the charms. Luke would concentrate on getting her to return his feelings; then he'd think of the next step.

He turned back to the students and instructed them to copy down the spelling words on the blackboard. "You'll receive extra points for every word above your grade level you spell correctly on our test tomorrow."

The rest of the day passed as usual. After seeing the students headed home, Luke returned to his desk to grade the day's work and make note of any supplies running low. They always seemed to need chalk.

He found it hard to concentrate over the worry of what Sam had planned. Building his own cabin showed persistence. The community may have rallied around Phoebe, but Sam was one of their own, born and raised in the hollow. Who would they back if it came down to him or Luke? How could Luke keep Phoebe safe in the wake of the man's increasing insistence he was going to marry her?

Groaning, he tossed down his pencil. There'd be no more work today. Instead, he set to work readying the room for Enid and Phoebe's first class on hygiene and health during and after pregnancy. *God, let the women of the community be receptive.*

He knew they'd show up at first out of curiosity, but if Phoebe hit them hard and fast with her beliefs over theirs, they'd not come back.

"Good afternoon," Phoebe sang as she strolled into the room. She headed straight for his desk and set her bag down with a loud thunk. "May I use the board?"

"Go ahead. The students should have already copied everything down." He watched as she wrote the words *cleanliness, nutrition,* and *infant care* on the board.

"Shouldn't you tackle one subject at a time?" He tilted his head.

"We will. We're starting with cleanliness, but I want the women to know what subjects will follow." She smiled. "I'm quite excited."

He returned her smile. "I can see that. Where's Enid?"

"I'm early. She'll be along." Phoebe sat in his chair, crossed her ankles on top of his desk, and grinned, apparently not caring how unladylike the gesture might be. "I met a delightful young woman today. She lives in the next hollow. Polly Hutchinson. Her husband is working timber over in the next county, leaving her alone and pregnant."

"I've heard of them. No children yet." Luke sat in one of the student desks. "When is she due?"

"Not for several months. She really should come closer to Possum Bottom as her time approaches. It's unfortunate we don't have a home or clinic for women who live farther away to come to."

He chuckled. "One thing at a time. Rome wasn't built in a day."

"That is so true." She let her feet fall to the floor and folded her hands on top of his desk. "My cabin seems so quiet with Mother and Papa gone. They left behind several months' worth of dry staples and fabric for new gowns, so storage is now a definite problem." She laughed.

"I'll build you some more shelves and a tall stool to enable you to reach them. Surely you're enjoying not being cramped."

"Hard to feel cramped when I was confined to bed for most of their visit." The sadness left her face. "The bright spot is Mother now approves of what I do and understands the drive behind it."

"Your father told me of your sister."

She nodded. "I know there will be times I cannot save the mother or child or both, but I cherish the cry of every newborn baby."

"The people of Possum Bottom got very lucky the day they hired you." He stood and glanced out the door to see whether Enid was in sight. No one but the ever-present Sam.

Soft footsteps behind him signaled Phoebe's approach. She stepped next to him and groaned. "However will we get him to leave us alone?"

Luke faced her. "Get married."

Chapter 12

The serious expression on Luke's face told Phoebe that he hadn't tossed out the suggestion willy-nilly. "Luke, we've talked about this."

He nodded, his expression still grave. "I realize that, but Sam won't stop following you unless you're at least betrothed to someone else. We can pretend, then break it off at a later time. You can tell everyone I wanted you to stop being a midwife."

"They would hate you for that." She cupped his cheek. "Knowing you would risk Possum Bottom's approval means a lot to me. May I think about it?" Why couldn't she immediately agree with this dear, sweet man? What was wrong with her?

She turned away before he could see the tears in her eyes. It wasn't that she was afraid of marriage. Far from it, considering she'd grown up wrapped in the love her parents had for each other.

Would she be this determined to focus only on her career if she hadn't witnessed the birth of her stillborn sister? Most midwives were married or widowed. What held Phoebe back from being the same?

"Apologies for being late." Enid bustled into the building and headed straight for the front. "I've brought some things to help get the point across. Things such as herbs and the like. Did you bring the books?"

"Oh. They're on the porch." Phoebe had completely forgotten about the herb pamphlets her father had brought and left with her. She'd looked through a few of them, and hoped he'd also sent ones on cleanliness with lots of pictures for those who couldn't read.

"I'll get them." Luke ducked out, more than likely seeking a reprieve from her stubbornness.

While Enid set out the things she used to help improve the lives of those in the community, Phoebe pulled soap from her bag. She'd noticed the redness of some of the children's skin and hoped the women would consider beeswax rather than lye when bathing their babies.

"Monday is wash and baking bread day," Enid told her. "Just so you don't try to switch up what's always worked."

Phoebe narrowed her eyes. "Why would I do that? I'm not here to change things, only improve them."

"Just so you know."

Luke set the pamphlets on the desk. "Her heart is in the right place."

She exhaled heavily. "Please do not talk about me as if I'm not here. I promise to be subtle and discreet. These women trust me now." Which made his gesture of a pretend marriage that much more of a sacrifice on his part. Rather than meet his gaze, she busied herself setting out the pamphlets.

"I'll be at the back of the room to escort you ladies home afterward."

"What did you say to him?" Enid asked after Luke had walked

away. "The poor man looks as if someone shot his dog."

"He made a proposal it wouldn't be fair to accept." She glanced up as the first of the women arrived. "Let's talk about this later."

"He asked you to marry him?" Her eyes widened.

"Only as a pretense to keep Sam at bay." Phoebe sighed. "Please speak no more about it. It wouldn't be fair to pretend such a thing only to break it off in a few months."

Enid laughed. "Life has a way of working things out. You wait and see. Accept that fake proposal and go along for the ride."

"That would fit right in with your love charm, wouldn't it?"

"Ah, you found it." There was no sign of guilt or remorse on the older woman's face. Instead, she clapped her hands and called the talkative women to order. "I want all y'all to listen with open minds as Phoebe shares her school learnin' with you. What you choose to use is up to you. We're only here to help, not boss y'all around."

Phoebe plastered a smile on her face. "Thank you, Enid." Not exactly the introduction she would have chosen.

Several of the women crossed their arms and glared. Others focused emotionless gazes on Phoebe. None of them looked excited except for the person who least needed her help, Alice Simpson.

"Cleanliness is next to godliness, the Good Book says," Alice said.

"That ain't in the Bible." Mrs. Wilson shook her head. "What it says in Second Corinthians is that we are to cleanse ourselves from every defilement. I reckon that might be different than dirt on the floor. Right, Miss Phoebe?"

"Yes, but we aren't here to—"

"I think dirt would be considered a defilement in my

household." Alice huffed and sat down hard in her chair. "Iffen y'all recall, the youngest McCoy child lost a toe after infection set in. If her ma would've kept her foot clean and wrapped, she might not walk with a limp."

"I poured kerosene on it!" A plump woman in the back bounded to her feet. "We don't have the money for shoes like some people."

The room was quickly spiraling out of control, and the grinning Enid was no help. Phoebe held up her hands. "Please. I've informative pamphlets here that will help all of you. Enid brought ones to show you which herbs would be most helpful to use as medicine. If I could have your attention for a few minutes, I'd like to explain why I thought it best to have these classes." She widened her smile and went on to explain the different types of soaps one could make, the importance of regular washing, and the need for enough light in a home. When she'd finished and no one seemed inclined to ask questions, she stepped back and let Enid explain the use of garden and forest herbs.

Only Alice and Mrs. Wilson took the pamphlets at the end of class. "Don't despair," Mrs. Wilson said. "They'll all come again next week. Over time, they'll realize the truth in what you say."

"Thank you." Phoebe forced the words past the lump in her throat.

Enid packed up her things and left, saying things had gone quite well, considering the riot that almost broke out. "Consider my advice about the other." She jerked her head toward Luke.

Phoebe started putting her items back in her bag. Luke's strong hands took over. He didn't say a word, only helped her clean up before escorting her to Daisy Mae.

"They hated the classes." Phoebe's voice broke once they stepped outside.

"Oh darlin', quite the contrary. They may have sat there like stones, but if they hated the class they would have got up and left." He wished there was something more he could do to ease her distress. He handed her a clean handkerchief from his pocket.

She wiped her eyes and handed it back, her face heating at the term of endearment he'd used. "I could also say something to start an argument. Then they'd come for the entertainment, if nothing else." She stepped into his entwined hands and let him hoist her onto the mule.

Luke glanced around the schoolyard for signs of Sam. Not seeing any, he climbed onto Ole Blue, wanting to get Phoebe home before the sun had fully set.

He wanted to ask Phoebe to marry him again. For real, this time. He wanted the threat of Sam to go away. He wanted Phoebe to relax and realize change would come by example.

Before she'd arrived, life had been peaceful, pretty much the same day after day. Now, he'd found himself immersed into the community more than he'd thought possible. As schoolteacher, he thought he'd been driven in like a stake. Showing Phoebe around, even attending some birthings, had made him realize he'd been hanging on the outskirts rather than really joining the crowd. He didn't want to go back to being on the outside.

If she accepted his proposal, then broke it off in a month or so, he'd be further on the outside than before. Still, he'd do it to keep her safe. He'd do almost anything for Phoebe.

He laughed to himself, remembering the time he'd wanted the

same thing she did. To focus on his career and serve the people of Possum Bottom.

"Please share what is so humorous," she said. "I could use a bit of cheering up."

"I was thinking of when I arrived here, stars in my eyes, and a giant desire to improve the lives of these people."

Her eyes flashed. "You were making fun of me?"

"No. Just reflecting on when I had the same strong desire."

"You don't have that desire anymore?"

"Of course I do. I brought you here, didn't I? I prefer to do things more behind the scenes now."

"Where I want to face the bull head-on." A smile teased her lips. "You do have a knack for pulling me out of my well of self-pity."

"Glad to be of service." He gave a mock bow, his heart rejoicing when she laughed.

"You're right. I shouldn't put so much stock in one class. Perhaps next week Mrs. Wilson will let me borrow her baby to use for a demonstration. I think it best to use an impartial woman's child, don't you?"

As Phoebe continued to lay out her plans for the next class, Luke kept his eyes peeled for signs of Sam following them. The raised hair on the nape of his neck alerted him to the fact they weren't alone. It could be a wild animal, but he'd stake Ole Blue that it wasn't.

"Would you like a cup of coffee?" Phoebe offered when they arrived at her cabin. "It's a lovely evening, and I'm too wound up to retire yet."

"I'd love one. While you do that, I'll put Daisy Mae away." He tethered Old Blue, then led Daisy Mae to the lean-to. He patted the space between the animal's ears. "I wonder if Phoebe knows how rare a female mule is?" He should tell her. That fact alone should show her how strongly the people of these hills wanted a midwife.

He returned to the cabin and sat on the top step. Phoebe could do with a larger porch and a couple of rocking chairs, something he could work on when school broke for the summer. He turned as Phoebe joined him, and took the cup she offered.

She sat on the step next to him. "Spring here is wonderful. I can hardly wait to experience the rest of the seasons."

"Summer isn't bad, fall is beautiful, winter can be brutal. Make sure you have proper footwear and a warm cloak." He blew into his coffee, then told her about Daisy Mae's rarity.

"Thank you for telling me. It means a lot to know these people wanted me before laying eyes on me." She laughed. "They were a bit shocked, though, upon first look at me."

He joined in with her laughter. "That they were."

"No more than you." She bumped him playfully, then rested her head on his shoulder. "I did some thinking on the ride home."

"About?" He closed his eyes and breathed deep of the fragrant soap she used in her hair.

"Your proposal."

His heart skipped a beat. "And?"

"I hate for you to make such a sacrifice on my account." She straightened and faced him. "Enid thinks I should say yes, but she also believes in charms."

He grinned. "I think you should say yes."

"What if. . .I can't break it off?" Her eyes glistened.

"Would that be so bad?"

"Maybe."

"Oh, my sweet Phoebe." He set his mug down and cupped her face. When she didn't pull back, he gave her a lingering kiss. When she didn't push him away, he deepened the kiss.

Hot coffee landed in his lap. He jumped up with a howl.

"I'm so sorry." Phoebe put a hand over her mouth in a futile attempt to stifle a laugh. "Really, it was an accident." Her giggles grew infectious.

He reached out for her, pulling her close. "You owe me now, Miss Hudson."

"Very well. I accept your temporary proposal, Mr. Morris."

He kissed her again.

Chapter 13

Phoebe hummed as she headed up the mountain the next morning. She'd spent far too much time dwelling on Luke's kisses after he left. Temporary or not, accepting his proposal would not be a hardship in the least.

She paid visits to Maybelle, Mrs. Petty, and Mrs. Wilson before heading farther up the mountain. She had no deliveries that needed tending to, but there were still families scattered around the hills that she had yet to meet.

Most of them greeted her warily until finding out who she was. "Oh, Enid told us you'd be by," they'd say before inviting her in for a cup of coffee or tea. By midday every nerve in her body twanged.

She stopped next to a babbling brook and pulled a simple lunch of bread and cheese from her bag. As she ate, she marveled at the beauty and peace of living such a simple life. Boston was wonderful, but her heart had quickly grown roots in the Ozark Mountains.

A twig snapped.

"Hello?"

When no one answered, she decided a curious animal had

gotten closer to take a look. The second snap of a twig had her packing up and moving on. An unarmed woman would be no challenge for a bear or mountain lion.

She called an end to her day as suppertime neared, and turned Daisy Mae for home. Once upon a time, she'd have found spending all day with little human interaction lonely. Now, she welcomed the quiet times between patients, especially after her bout of exhaustion.

"Midwife." Sam stepped from the trees and planted himself in front of Daisy Mae.

"Good afternoon, Sam. Is your cabin near here?" Her heart skipped a beat. She glanced around as if curious to know the answer to her question. Instead, her mind scrambled for a way of escape.

"I reckon you'll know where it's at when we're hitched." He spat a wad of tobacco into the dirt.

"I'm sure you've heard I'm betrothed to Mr. Morris."

His eyes narrowed. "You get around, Miss Phoebe. First that guy in Boston, now the schoolteacher. Since you haven't said your vows to either of them, I reckon you won't mind coming with me." He grabbed the mule's reins. "I can lead you or ride up there with you. Your choice."

She tried to yank the reins from his hands. "What are your intentions?"

"I done told you. I aim to marry you." He swung effortlessly onto the mule, wrapped his arms around Phoebe in order to gain control of the reins, and turned them into the woods. "Iffen word gets out you spent the night with me unchaperoned, you'll have no choice but to save your reputation by marrying me."

"No one will believe that fabrication!"

"Folks already gossip about you and the teacher."

"We've done nothing immoral."

"That's right. I've been watching. The two of you always leave the door open. Ain't no one around to check on us, though."

The man was insane. "Surely there's a woman around here willing to be your wife."

"I don't want one of them." His hold on her tightened. "You've turned my whole family against me. Ma warned me to stay away from you. The only way they'll let me back in is with you."

"Your delusions are not my problem, Sam. Your mother sees reason—why don't you? They haven't turned against you; they just don't approve of your actions."

She doubted even marrying him would lessen his mother's disapproval of his behavior. She'd bide her time and find a way to escape. Rather than argue with a man incapable of seeing reason, she spent the time traveling in prayer. She said a quick "amen" when Sam pulled back on the reins and slid to the ground.

"Don't be telling me what my family thinks. I know them better than you." He reached up and helped Phoebe down, then, with a tight grip on her arm, led her to a half-finished cabin roughly the same size as hers. He grabbed a bucket from beside a water pump and thrust it at her. "Fill this up. Don't try runnin' off. I'll shoot you in the foot. I don't mind you being crippled. As long as nothin' messes up that pretty face and comely figure, I'll be happy."

She stared as he marched to where a few boards nailed to two trees provided a hastily erected lean-to. He put Daisy Mae in next to a bay horse. When he turned and scowled, Phoebe filled the bucket.

"When you're done there, you can fix me supper. I've some ham and beans inside. Hurry up. It gets dark quick up here and there's a panther that lurks around each night."

"My mule."

"She'll bray good and loud if it comes around. I'll deal with it then." He jerked his thumb toward the cabin door.

Phoebe squared her shoulders and entered the cabin. A large fireplace took up most of one wall. A single cot sat against another. A chair, a pile of blankets, a trunk, and that was pretty much all that the cabin held.

Thankfully, the beans had been left simmering. Phoebe made coffee and corn bread and cut up the ham to add to the beans. Once the food was finished, she handed Sam a battered tin plate and took her seat on the floor. She wouldn't sit on the bed, and he had already made himself comfortable in the chair.

"I like a woman who doesn't talk much."

"I wish the same could be said about you."

He threw his spoon across the room, narrowly missing her head. "I don't like a woman with a smart mouth."

Phoebe hadn't expected Sam to resort to violence. All he'd done so far was follow her around the mountain. Now that she knew he would physically put her in her place, she clamped her lips shut and ate in order to keep up her strength. She planned on leaving the moment he fell asleep.

After they ate, she cleaned up the dishes and curled up in the corner with a blanket. She glared at Sam from across the room.

He sighed and reached into the trunk to pull out a length of rope. "I can see in your eyes what you're plannin'. Let me help you stay out of trouble." He picked her up, plopped her into the chair, and secured her with the rope.

⌒

Luke arrived at Phoebe's the next morning armed with wood he planned to use for building more storage shelves. The chickens clucked from their pen. No smoke drifted from the chimney, unusual for so early on a Saturday morning. Had she been called to a birthing during the night?

He leaned the boards against the wall and opened the front door. The cabin had a lonely, empty feeling to it, the bed made with not a wrinkle in the quilt. A sense of dread trickled down Luke's spine.

One glance out the window to see no sign of the mule in the small corral told him Phoebe had left. She'd gone up the mountain to visit patients, but which ones? Folks were scattered here and there among the thick woods. Finding one woman would be near impossible unless he knew the path she'd taken. Still, he had to try.

First stop, Enid's. She wasn't home either. Luke rode hard for McGee's Mercantile. Not bothering to loop Ole Blue's reins around the hitching post, he barged into the shop. "Have you seen Miss Hudson or Enid?"

The man glanced up from his ledger. "Not since yesterday. Something wrong?"

"I have a terrible feeling Miss Hudson didn't make it home yesterday. Anyone due to have a baby around this time?" All community news filtered through the mercantile.

McGee's face wrinkled as he thought. "Not that I can recall. Not for a month or two at least. Where was Miss Hudson headed?"

Luke sighed. "Up the mountain. Where does the young woman live whose husband is off working? Hutchins?"

"Hutchinson. Lives in the next hollow. Follow the creek due east. From what I can tell, you can't miss it. It's a ways past the Petty homestead, but you can make it there in an hour or two at the most. I'll let Enid know you're looking for her iffen she stops by."

"Much obliged." Luke darted back outside and headed Ole Blue toward the Petty place.

About an hour later he stopped next to the clothesline, where Dorcas was hanging baby nappies, and asked after Phoebe.

"She rode by here yesterday," Dorcas said, "but other than a wave, we didn't talk."

Luke scanned the house and yard. "The menfolk all gone?"

"Working the fields, except for Sam. Ain't seen him in days. He's building a cabin up past the lumber mill."

Good. Having the man away worked in Phoebe's favor if she were lost on the mountain. "If you see Miss Hudson, please tell her I'm looking for her, and I'll meet her back at her cabin."

Dorcas grinned. "Iffen you can't keep track of the woman you plan on marrying, you're in for a heap of trouble."

He laughed. "I reckon I am." His smile faded as he urged the mule on with no sign of Phoebe or Daisy Mae.

Dear God, please don't let her be injured or worse. Don't let her be lost and frightened. The mountain is a very big place for a little woman.

Once he found her, he'd kiss her. Then, if she'd frightened him unnecessarily, he'd give her a good shaking, then kiss her again. He couldn't remember being this scared before in his life.

The Hutchinson cabin had been built on a small rise above the creek. Tall pine and oak trees shaded it. A coon hound napped on the porch next to a young black woman rocking and knitting on the porch. She glanced up, startled.

Luke stopped a few feet away. "Don't be alarmed, ma'am. I'm looking for the midwife, Miss Hudson."

"Ain't seen her since yesterday afternoon. She said I was her last visit, and she was goin' home." She set down her knitting. "She missin'?"

"I'm not sure. Do you know of anyone expecting a baby last night?"

"No one lives this far up but us." Her dark eyes widened. "Want me to send for my husband, Hank? He can be here in a day. He's a good tracker, or you can use Beau here iffen you got something of hers he can sniff."

He pulled the handkerchief Phoebe had used from his pocket. "Will this do?"

"We can pray." She took the handkerchief. "Find, boy." The dog's eyes opened and he sniffed the square of white muslin. "You'll have to get off that mule and run to keep up with him, mister. He goes where nothing big can." She stepped back and waved her hand. "Go, Beau."

With a howl, the dog lumbered down the steps and into the woods. Luke touched his finger to the brim of his hat and slid from Old Blue, pulling his shotgun from the strap holding it in place on the mule's back. It wasn't wise to go in unarmed with bears and wild hogs roaming around. "Thank you." He sprinted after the dog.

Thank goodness the braying and crashing through the underbrush made it easy enough to know where the animal went. "Hold up, Beau." Why hadn't he thought to put a rope on the dog?

They forded creeks and went up and down hills, but still headed down the mountain for the most part. Then Beau stopped sudden enough that Luke almost stumbled over him. The dog circled an area of the road, brayed, and took off through the trees and back up the mountain.

What if Mrs. Hutchinson was wrong about her dog's ability to track? The handkerchief could have had too much of Luke's scent and not enough of Phoebe's. Or—an icy fist clenched his heart—something had happened to make her turn around.

Chapter 14

Phoebe's wrists were rubbed raw by the time Sam stopped his snoring and untied her. She glared and flexed her fingers. "I need the outhouse."

"I'll be coming with you." He grinned and snapped his suspenders over a stained shirt. "Then I've got work to do while you fix us breakfast. After that, well, we'll head to the mercantile and let it slip that we spent the night together. Maybe we'll even seal our union so there's no question in folks' minds."

"No one will believe your story." She marched past him and headed for the tiny structure behind the house. With another glare, she slammed the door closed.

With him watching her so closely, she wasn't sure how she could escape. There had to be a way. She chewed her fingernail. Short of assaulting him when his back was turned, something she might actually enjoy, she couldn't think of a single thing.

She wasn't too terrified of being alone in the woods, except at dark. She rode Daisy Mae everywhere. Which meant she needed to escape during daylight, taking the mule with her.

"Hurry up." Sam banged on the door.

After completing her business, she exited and marched to the nearby creek to wash. She glanced around for a rock or branch she could use as a weapon. She found one possible stick as big as her wrist, but had no way of retrieving it without Hawkeye seeing her.

Sam gripped her arm and yanked her to her feet. "I'm hungry." He gave her a shove toward the cabin.

"Keep your hands off me." She tossed her hair away from her face and headed for the house, trying her best to reform the bun that had come loose during the night. The last thing she wanted was to look wanton when they rode into town.

She stood in the cabin, hands on her hips, and glanced around for something to prepare. "What are you expecting me to cook? Your shelves are virtually empty."

"There's beans still and flour for biscuits. You're the woman. Figure it out." He grabbed an ax from the mantel. "Holler when it's done." Whistling as if he'd achieved something great, he strolled back outside.

Phoebe would fix breakfast only in order to keep up her strength, but had no intention of serving Sam. She heated up beans, quickly ate a bowl full, and grabbed the skillet from next to the fireplace. She placed her back against the wall next to the door and called Sam in to eat.

When he came through the door, she took a deep breath and swung the skillet as hard as she could at his head. The man crumpled to the floor. Without a backward glance, she darted to the lean-to to retrieve Daisy Mae. Using a sawed-off tree stump, she climbed onto the mule's back and sent her rocketing into the forest as Sam's curses rose.

"Thank You, God, that I didn't kill the fool." No one could call her a coward who wouldn't take chances to keep herself safe. She bent low over the mule's head to escape low-hanging branches.

"You won't get far!" Sam's yells grew fainter. He was right though. His horse could go faster than Daisy Mae, and Sam knew the woods better than Phoebe.

The braying of a dog spurred her on. Dogs meant people and help. "Come on, Daisy Mae. We must go faster."

The mule yanked against the reins and plodded forward. They splashed across the creek that flowed to Sam's cabin, then picked up the pace when they arrived on the poor excuse for a trail. At least the grass was trampled, and the trees had been cut down for building and firewood, thus providing a clearer train of sight. The bad thing was that it would also allow Sam to see her better.

"I could almost go faster on foot." Phoebe flicked the reins. "Don't you understand the urgency?" The mule pulled her head again, then stopped to graze.

Something crashed in the brush behind them.

Phoebe slid to the ground, hiked up her skirt, and ran into the trees on the opposite side of the trail. Daisy Mae would have to find her own way home.

Using branches and roots, Phoebe half slid, half climbed down the mountain into the next hollow. She should be getting close to the Hutchinson homestead. She could find respite there.

"Laws mercy, Miss Phoebe." Mrs. Hutchinson waddled toward her as Phoebe stepped into the clearing. "A man was here looking for you. Was right worried."

"Clean shaven or bearded?" Phoebe leaned against a tree to catch her breath.

"Clean. I sent him with Beau to find you. His mule is right behind the house."

"Don't tell anyone you've seen me." Phoebe ran for Ole Blue. She couldn't risk harm coming to the expectant mother by her staying.

The other woman followed. "At least take something to eat and a flask of water. I'll be quick." She hurried into the house, returning with half a loaf of bread and some water. "I promise not to tell anyone but the nice man who owns the mule that I've seen you."

"Thank you. Which way did he go?"

Mrs. Hutchinson pointed down the path. "You'll hear my dog before see him."

Phoebe's shoulders slumped. She'd been so close to rescue only to head in the wrong direction. She'd beat herself up later. With a flick of the reins, she sent Ole Blue after Luke.

The sun rose above the trees. Occasionally, Phoebe could hear the far-off howl of the dog and the yells of Sam. The sounds bounced off the mountain until she didn't know which way to turn.

"We'd best head home, Blue, and hope Luke shows up there. Wandering aimlessly isn't helping either of us."

"Phoebe!"

She gasped and turned as Luke stepped from the trees. Without a second thought, she jumped from the mule and ran into his arms. "Sam's after me, Luke. We've got to go."

Luke glanced back the way she'd come. "He'll follow the mule's tracks. Go home, Beau." He slapped Blue on the rear, then pulled Phoebe back into the trees.

⌒

Anger rolled through Luke. Phoebe was dirty and her shirt ripped in several places. He'd strangle Sam Petty when he saw him. "Are you all right?" He cut Phoebe a glance.

"He didn't hurt me, but he'll be sporting a knot on the head from me hitting him with a skillet." She grinned.

"That's my girl." He kept a firm grasp of her hand and increased their pace. "We'll be at the mercantile soon, and I'll telegraph the county sheriff. Sam won't bother you anymore."

"He most certainly will, if he catches us. He's on horseback."

They came across Enid a couple of miles from the mercantile. She straightened from digging herbs and frowned. "What in tarnation has happened to the two of you? You look like you've been through a war."

"Sam abducted Phoebe, she escaped, and now he's after her," Luke said.

"I reckon I can stall him iffen he comes this way. You two go on." She smiled, glancing at their clasped hands. "I'm guessin' my charm worked."

Luke smiled down at Phoebe. "More like God's blessing than a superstition."

Enid laughed. "You're right, but it sure was fun." Her smile faded at the sound of something heavy coming their way. "Go."

"I don't think you should be—"

"Don't argue with your elders. Sam won't hurt me or his pa would skin him alive. Go!"

Luke pulled Phoebe after him. They stepped from the trees and onto the dirt road. They'd be in the open, but he didn't think Sam would try anything when someone could pass by at any minute.

The tension in his body eased when the mercantile came into sight. "Almost there, sweetheart."

"Thank the good Lord. I've got blisters, and I'm pretty sure one of them has busted." Phoebe limped at his side.

"I'll take care of you." He slung the rifle strap over his shoulder and scooped her into his arms. "I'm so proud of you. You're even stronger and braver than I imagined."

She rested her head against his shoulder. "Right now I'm tired and sore. I'll be angry later."

Luke carried her into the mercantile and set her on a chair next to the counter. "McGee, I need you to fetch the sheriff. I'm going to doctor some of Miss Hudson's wounds. Put it on my tab."

"No need. On the house. Your order is on the counter, Miss Hudson." The man rushed to the back of the store.

After handing Phoebe the box of medicines she'd ordered, Luke pulled the supplies he would need from the shelves while she opened the box and riffled through the contents. He lifted Phoebe's hands. His vision filled with red at the raw skin around her wrists. "He tied you up?"

She smiled. "I kept trying to escape." She hissed as he pressed a cool cloth with antiseptic against the skin. When tears appeared in her eyes, he handed her the handkerchief he'd gripped in his hand during his search.

Once he'd finished cleaning the scrapes, he wrapped her wrists in clean gauze, then bent to remove her boots. A blister on her left heel had burst and started to bleed. How she'd managed to keep up with her dash to freedom was miraculous.

"Phoebe." He tilted her face to his. "I don't want a temporary engagement. I want to marry you for real. This minute, if we could. You can be a midwife for as long as you want. I won't stand in the way of your dreams. When I thought you were lost. . ."

"Oh Luke." She cupped his face. "All I could think about was getting home to you. Yes, I'll marry you."

Luke pressed his lips against hers and thanked God for bringing her back to him. "I'm the luckiest man—"

"You'll be the deadest iffen you don't step back from my woman."

Luke glanced over to see Sam holding a knife to Enid's throat. "We've called the sheriff. Don't make this worse than it already is."

"I reckon no one will miss an old woman."

"Fine, Sam," Phoebe said. "I'll go with you, but please, let me have something to drink first. A wife dead of thirst is of less use than Enid. Let me grab a few of my medical supplies and I'll come." She slipped her hand into the box of medical supplies and grimaced as she stood on her sore feet. "I know when I've lost the battle." She put a restraining hand on Luke when he moved to stop her. "We both know this is how it has to be, Luke." She peered up into his face and winked.

What was this wonderful woman up to now? While Sam's attention was on Phoebe, Luke slowly started moving his shotgun into position in front of him. Where was McGee?

"Let Enid go." Phoebe stopped a few feet from Sam.

"You can't boss me, woman." Sam thrust Enid away from him. "Let's go." He motioned his head toward the door.

Phoebe stepped forward and pressed the handkerchief of chloroform against his nose as hard as she could, then stepped back at Luke's order. He slammed the butt of his shotgun against Sam's forehead.

Sam's eyes widened, then he folded to the floor.

"Let's tie him up this time, shall we?" Phoebe smiled and knelt, keeping the cloth to Sam's nose.

"I got some twine." McGee came running from the back. "I'd have been here sooner but was trying to find my shotgun. The missus is always taking it hunting and leaving me without. Can't complain. It puts food on the table."

Luke laughed and put an arm around Phoebe, pulling her into a one-armed hug. "Marriage to you will be a new adventure every day. I love you, Phoebe Hudson."

"I love you, Luke Morris." She leaned against him. "I look forward to our adventures."

Epilogue

I am going to miss you." Tears shimmered in Phoebe's mother's eyes. "But I don't think I've ever seen a more beautiful bride."

"Since this room doesn't have a mirror, I'll have to take your word for it." Phoebe smiled and smoothed her hands down the cream-colored gown that her mother had married her father in. "It fits."

"Of course it fits. We're built the same." She reached for the door of the small room at the back of the church. "I'll send your father in, then take my seat. I do believe the entire county is here to hear you say your vows."

Phoebe peered through the slightly opened door. The small church was packed to capacity. "The Simpsons and the Pettys are no longer sitting on separate sides." Instead, the wives chatted and laughed, while the men hovered at the back talking. "No doubt Enid would say she'd given them charms of peace or something." She laughed.

"I think it more likely that Mr. Petty was so outraged at his oldest son's behavior that he approached Mr. Simpson with an apology. At least that's what I heard." Her mother smiled, then stepped out, closing the door behind her.

Seconds later, Phoebe's father entered. He crooked his arm. "There's a very nervous young man waiting for you, but you look at peace."

"I'm marrying the country's most wonderful man. He'll let me continue to work, and these people have accepted me as one of their own. God is good. Of course I'm at peace."

"God does know what's best for us when He pulls us from our place of comfort and leads us to somewhere new." He patted her hand. "You remind me of your mother on our wedding day." He placed a kiss on Phoebe's cheek.

"Promise you and Mother will come visit often."

"The train goes both ways, my dear."

She laughed. "But babies don't wait on a train schedule."

The organ started the processional music. Phoebe's heart rate increased. She took a deep breath as someone threw open the door. With a smile on her face, she moved down the aisle toward the man destined to be her husband.

Her father placed her hand in Luke's. "Take care of my little girl."

Luke pressed his lips to her hand. "With my very life."

Preacher Wilson began, "Dearly beloved. . ."

Cynthia Hickey grew up in a family of storytellers and moved around the country a lot as an army brat. Her desire is to write about real and flawed characters in a wholesome way that her seven children and nine grandchildren can all be proud of. She and her husband live in Arizona where Cynthia is a full-time writer.

Love's Rebirth

by Darlene Franklin

Chapter 1

Auraria, Colorado
1871

Dr. Asa had promised help would come.

Maia Cybele Brownstone—or MC, as she preferred to be called—wished the second doctor would hurry up and arrive. Her latest client was a young girl who claimed to be sixteen and looked like she was fourteen.

The girl had no business requiring the services of a midwife. She should be at school, learning, imagining the man of her dreams. Instead of giving her body to men at the brothel.

An oft-told story, but one that never failed to infuriate MC. Asa provided services for those who couldn't pay, although the funds that made it possible came from the same men who took advantage of these unfortunates. But as Dr. Asa said, it was good they received help, however it was achieved.

Dr. Asa was close to a saint in MC's eyes, but he was away on a three-month honeymoon in Europe after his Easter wedding. He had promised that an old army buddy would take his place but hadn't given his name.

The new doctor hadn't arrived on time. Perhaps the stage-coach was delayed. That happened fairly often, even in the clement spring weather.

Doctor or no doctor, the coming baby wouldn't wait, and it was breech. Although MC had assisted with breech births many times, she always preferred to have a doctor present.

She sent up a prayer to the Lord, who was the true Healer, and made young Gail as comfortable as possible. Someone rang the front doorbell.

A man filled the doorway, his arms full of a writhing pregnant woman—and a black doctor's bag at his feet.

Was this the new doctor? He was older than she'd expected, close to her age. She'd expected a younger man when she heard he had just finished medical school. Now she would guess he had served during the war before starting, the weight of all he had seen evident in his bearing.

"Come in," she said.

They appraised each other for a short time. "You must be MC Brownstone, the assistant Asa promised." He sounded surprised.

Interesting that Dr. Asa hadn't revealed her gender. She straightened her back. "I am. The young lady can use this room." She pointed through an open door. "I will help you when I can, but there's a child in that room having a breech birth." She clenched her teeth and said the words she didn't like to admit. "I could use your help."

Gail cried out at that moment as if to emphasize MC's point.

She abandoned the doctor to return to her patient. "The new doctor is here." She checked Gail's progress then reassured her. "You're coming along splendidly. We have a wee bit of time. The doctor brought a patient in with him. Can you be brave for a few more minutes?"

Gail relaxed as the pain passed. "I can. God bless you."

The doctor had already started examining the patient who had come in with him. Had he noticed how conveniently the medical supplies were laid out, or did he expect it as a matter of course?

"How may I help?" she asked when he didn't acknowledge her presence.

"I will let you know." His voice was muffled beneath the tent he had placed over the woman's lower body. She appreciated his concern for his patient's privacy, at least.

The woman's eyes fluttered open. "You're an angel."

"It's just the sunlight on my hair," MC joked. "But God did send me here to serve you." She wrung a rag in the basin of water she'd prepared fresh that morning and wiped the sweat rolling off the woman's face. "I believe she has a fever, Doctor."

"Of course she does."

"You'll have to forgive him, Nurse." The familiarity in the woman's voice made MC wonder if she could possibly be the doctor's wife. "My brother's always got a temper when things don't go his way." This woman was his sister? Where was her husband?

A contraction hit the woman, and Gail cried out at the same time. The doctor brushed the hair from his sister's forehead.

MC took a step toward Gail's room. "Doctor?"

Go," he said.

She bit her lip. Gail needed his help now, but MC's training kept her from protesting his decision.

"Where's the doctor?" Gail said as MC entered the room. "I thought he came in."

"He's with another patient." When the contraction passed— they weren't long yet—MC turned to the door.

"Don't leave me," Gail said, panicked.

"I'm going for the doctor."

Of course the new doctor was worried about his sister. Fever in childbirth was always a dangerous thing. But MC knew how to treat a fever. Gail needed the doctor.

In the ten years since she became a midwife, MC had kept a record of every mother who died, every babe. Each one was a personal failure. But with God's help, that wouldn't happen today.

She crossed the room and stood at the doorway. "Doctor, I'll stay with your sister while you check on our other patient. Her name is Gail."

He reluctantly left his sister's bedside. MC explained Gail's situation when she passed her at the door. "She's but sixteen years old, and small of frame. She'll not have breech birth easily."

His nostrils flared but he nodded. "My sister's name is Belinda. We thought she was a month out, but she went into labor while we were on the train." He hesitated. "She's not married."

"Most of my patients aren't," MC said prosaically. "I'll take good care of her."

The doctor's sister appeared to be a healthy woman in her midtwenties. Pity washed over MC for the woman who had been lured into passion, then left alone with its consequences.

MC heard Gail go into another contraction. Belinda smiled weakly. "Maybe we won't give birth at the same time after all. My pains are coming less often, as if they're as uncertain about birthing this baby as I am."

MC smothered the laugh that rose up inside of her. If that were true, half the babies born here would never see the light of day. She patted Belinda's hand. "You've been strong enough to bring this child to term. He or she will be born strong and healthy, and you will be fine as well."

Belinda laughed. "I like you. I think we shall be friends."

"By the way, your brother told me your name is Belinda, but I still don't know his name."

"Oh, he's Dr. Vaughn Strahan."

Pride rang through Belinda's voice, but MC could hardly pay attention. Vaughn Strahan. Sister named Belinda. Fought in the war. Aimee's age. Could it be? Oh no, oh no, oh no. But she wouldn't say a word until she could get home tonight and confirm what she suspected.

Vaughn Strahan knew the value of a good nurse. He had met Clara Barton in person, and the capped nurses were beacons of hope on the field, when many feared only death. In the camp where he had been kept prisoner, several of those nurses were slaves, fiercely proud in their work.

He just wished his friend Asa had warned him that "MC" Brownstone was, in fact, female.

The nurse was right. This young girl would have a hard time with a breech birth. Her body simply wasn't developed enough.

Someone arrived to greet incoming patients, Asa's mother, probably. He reached a decision about Gail. Laying his hand on her forehead, he said, "Rest while you can. I'll be back in a few moments." He stepped outside in search of MC.

He found her sitting near the doorway to Belinda's room, perhaps to see if any new patients entered. "Does my sister require your immediate attention?"

She blinked rapidly, as if drawing her attention back from a distant object. "No."

"Then I need your help."

They stepped into the office to talk privately. "I agree with you," Vaughn said. "It's doubtful Gail can manage a breech birth." Her correct assessment had increased his confidence in her abilities.

"There are things that can be done. . . ," MC said. "Sir."

"I need your help to turn the babe to its normal position. That's best done with two of us."

The nurse relaxed, although something else was on her mind, something new after her time with his sister. "Yes, sir."

MC stayed with him through the tedious and painful process. Her steady hands made success possible.

An hour later, Gail gave birth to a baby boy. He was small, and rather ugly as babies go.

"He's just perfect." Gail couldn't take her eyes off him.

"You rest up while I look your son over." The child's small size worried Vaughn.

MC looked up from her chair inside his sister's room as Vaughn walked by. The question in her eyes turned to joy when the baby wriggled and let out a soft cry. She came to the doorway.

"Safely delivered, mother and son," he said.

MC reached for the bundle. "You go on ahead—see to your sister. I'll take care of this little fellow."

He frowned. "I want to examine him further, but you can hold him still for me. No danger of cold at this time of year."

After the examination, MC gathered baby bunting to wrap up the infant. "Is he sound, Doctor, aside from being so small? Gail will be devastated if she loses this child."

"He should be fine if he has a proper home to grow up in." Vaughn grunted. "From what Asa told me, she probably works in a brothel?" The smoky, boozy atmosphere of such places was not a good environment, not at all, morals aside.

"Well." MC drew in her breath. "We do our best."

The rest of the afternoon sped by. He met Mrs. Smith, Asa's mother. He stepped in to see Belinda as often as possible. The nurse's ministrations had brought her fever down, but her labor wasn't progressing. He feared it would wear her out.

Vaughn went in search of MC, to send her home, when he noticed a little girl in the waiting room talking with Mrs. Smith. The girl was holding the new baby.

Vaughn frowned. A child that young—she looked like she had barely started school—had no business holding such a young baby. He headed in her direction.

"You cute boy, you. Your mother loves you so much." Baby talk streamed from the little girl's mouth. "God loves you too, but I bet you know that." She looked up when Vaughn entered the room.

Columbine-blue eyes focused on him, flooding him with memories of another set of eyes that color. He could forgive her almost anything at that moment.

The girl gave the baby to Mrs. Smith and jumped to her feet. "You must be the new doctor. I'm Aimee. What's your name?"

"I am Dr. Strahan, but you may call me Dr. Vaughn, if you prefer." Who was this child, and how did she know about him? "And who are you?"

"She's my daughter." MC came out of Belinda's room and removed her nursing apron. She spoke to her child. "What have I told you about talking to strange men?" Fear edged her reprimand,

and Vaughn wondered what he had done to frighten her.

The girl's eyes turned a stormy purple. "But he's not a stranger, Ma. He's the new doc, isn't he?" She smiled at Vaughn, and his heart melted again.

MC glanced at him apologetically. "Let's take young Bill here back to his mother. She's had a good rest and he'll be getting hungry."

Vaughn waited until they'd left the room, then asked Mrs. Smith, "How often is that child at the clinic?"

"She comes here every day after school. I keep an eye on her."

He shook his head. As progressive as he was regarding female education, as much as he believed children needed to learn the facts of life, this girl did not need to be in this environment.

Mrs. Smith pursed her lips. "Don't you judge MC before you get to know her. She's a good Christian, a widow. My son prizes her services highly. Did you know she's the one who hired him? She recognized her limitations as a midwife and searched for some time before they met. She inspired him to his life's work." She looked him straight on. "Do you share their passion?"

What kind of question was that? He'd accepted the position, hadn't he? Although he hoped to also work among nearby Denver's more well-to-do women, if only to supplement the clinic's income.

But he hadn't expected MC Brownstone. Women who cared so passionately about the world's troubles often put themselves in dangerous situations, like his beloved Sara.

MC and her daughter returned. "Let me make proper introductions. As you know, I'm Dr. Asa's midwife-nurse, MC Brownstone. I've been working in these mining camps almost from the beginning, and I was blessed when Dr. Asa joined me. And this young lady here is my daughter, Aimee. Aimee, this is Dr. Strahan. He's come to help us."

The girl curtsied. How out of place it seemed for the setting.

"Pleased to meet you, Dr. Vaughn." She glanced at her mother. "He asked me to call him that."

He couldn't resist her charm. Dropping to one knee, he said, "I'm pleased to make your acquaintance."

She giggled but extended her hand in a very businesslike manner.

What an unusual child. He accepted the handshake. "And what shall I call you? Miss Brownstone?"

She giggled again. "Call me Aimee, of course."

He tore his attention away from the girl to speak to her mother. "And what am I to call you?"

"Will you think it odd of me if I ask you to call me Nurse here in the office?"

He slowly smiled. "I think that's a grand idea."

"I'm ready to leave for the day, but send a messenger if you need my help with your sister."

She left before he could ask what he should call her outside of hours. He had a feeling that he would have to earn the right to call her MC. Besides, that was no kind of name for a woman. He had to find out her given name.

Chapter 2

Her suspicions about the new doctor warred with exhaustion, and MC attempted to set both aside to spend time with Aimee. She was lucky that Dr. Asa allowed his mother to take care of her there in the office. Otherwise she might not see Aimee from dawn until dusk.

MC would rather quit working than not have time with her daughter every day. She'd seen the condemnation in Dr. Vaughn's eyes when he'd seen Aimee at the office. But MC had never blamed the girls she helped, and she didn't want her daughter to feel any shame in her mother's chosen work.

People assumed Aimee was the daughter of one of "those girls" because she was adopted. Better that Dr. Vaughn believe that than to learn the truth. At least if what she suspected was the truth. Yes, Aimee had been born at the clinic, but her birth mother was a far cry from a prostitute.

Aimee's bedtime prayer lasted longer than usual. In addition to mentioning what happened at school and the birth of Gail's baby, she talked about her friend, the new doctor.

Ordinarily MC delighted in every word. But this time she

joined her daughter with her own private prayer. *What do I do if what I suspect is true?*

At last her precious child was sleeping, under her roof, as she had every night since her mother died when she was only hours old. MC could finally verify if her suspicions were correct. She'd kept a careful record of everything Aimee's mother, Sara, had told her. She had set the papers aside, waiting until Aimee got older to share the full story. Meeting Dr. Vaughn today reminded MC of what was written in the diary. If she was upset with his arrival, she had reason to be. If she guessed correctly, she faced a dilemma greater than even King Solomon could have solved.

After Aimee fell asleep, MC went to the attic. She knew exactly where she had stored her most precious memories.

She brought the locked box downstairs, where she could spread things out. At the top of the box, she found the letter she had received from Sara's sister-in-law after nearly a year of trying to locate any living family. Bitterness was evident in the statement that Sara's husband had been missing in action since the Battle of Westport and was presumed dead. The letter writer made no offer to take in the child.

When time passed without any further contact, MC assumed both of Aimee's parents were dead. It became easier to say Aimee was her daughter. To MC, Aimee was the child she had lost in pregnancy, before her own husband had died in battle.

It was a match made in heaven. MC was a woman without husband or child. Aimee was a child without mother or father. Their family was designed by God if not by birth.

Next, MC reread the journal, noticing how her tears had smudged some of the writing. She had cried easily in those days, before she learned to laugh again.

She had remembered correctly. Sara's husband was Vaughn Strahan, Captain in the Grand Army of the Republic. Of course, the fact they shared the same name didn't guarantee the new doctor was Sara's husband. She'd been married to a simple Missouri farmer.

She read the entries again, looking for further clues. Sara Everett had married Vaughn Strahan in Hawthorne, Missouri, on February 14, 1861, the last Valentine's Day before the firing on Fort Sumter had broken the simmering rebellion into open war.

The records in Sara's box indicated her husband had enlisted in the army early in 1862. He was thirty-one years old at the time. Today he would be forty.

Aimee's birth certificate listed mother as deceased and father as missing in action.

Tears blurred the letters on the missive Sara had received from her husband's family, but MC could make out the initial "B" before the Strahan. B for Belinda?

Nothing proved that Sara's Vaughn and Dr. Vaughn had anything more in common than their names, and a sister whose name began with "B." She held on to a slender hope that her suspicion was unfounded.

MC reached for a locket at the bottom of the box. Behind the portrait of Sara, the left side held a lock of Aimee's white newborn hair and her mother's dark auburn tresses. A miniature of Sara's husband filled the other side.

MC knew exactly where she had seen that strong chin, those piercing eyes, those jutting eyebrows before. If Sara's Vaughn and the new Dr. Vaughn weren't the same man, they looked like twins.

Anger welled in MC's breast. Renewed anger at the toll and losses of the recent war. Anger at Vaughn for not coming to Auraria as soon as he was released from wherever he was held, to claim his child.

Dr. Asa had indicated the new doctor was a widower. He didn't mention children.

Was it possible Dr. Vaughn didn't know he had a child? Any more than she hadn't known he had lived?

But what would he do now if he learned he had a child? No, she couldn't consider the possibility. Aimee was her child. She refused to think of it any other way.

She should pray about it, but what if she didn't like God's answer? God's will would be perfect and good—in theory. She had experienced it, many times, in ways she didn't understand.

She glanced at the ceiling. "I guess that's where the Holy Spirit comes in. He'll put my feelings into sensible words." *But please, God, don't take away my daughter.*

For now, she wouldn't say anything. No need to face it until she had to.

⁓

By midnight, Vaughn would have welcomed MC's help. Belinda's labor had progressed to its final stages, but she was weak.

So was he, as well as tired and hungry. He went in search of the food Mrs. Smith had left for him. At least one of them needed to be fully alert.

The coffee was cold, but it was better than a shot of whiskey. He'd seen too many men go the wrong road that way. And as Mrs. Smith had promised, he found a box of crackers in one of the cabinets in the small office. "I tell my son that this is the most important healing tool in the office," she'd said.

When he returned, Belinda was gasping for breath, in the throes of another contraction. "I never knew it could be this hard."

"Just focus on your breathing, even when the pains come." He'd found out the hard way, when he was imprisoned, that he could ignore a lot of pain and misery if he just focused on breathing in and out.

"Easy for you to say." Another cry ripped through her.

Two more hours passed before he laid her daughter in her arms. A good-sized baby, conceived a week before her wedding, before her fiancé died in a hunting accident. He couldn't find it in his heart to blame her when he came home after finishing medical school. The neighbors had shunned her, the house was bare of food, and Belinda was four months pregnant.

He changed his mind about staying in Kansas after the way they treated his sister. Denver appealed to Belinda, and so Vaughn had accepted his friend Asa's offer. He still wondered if he should have gone somewhere he could make more money.

He examined the infant, fully formed, from the soft downy hair on her head to the toenails on her feet. "She's perfect. Just like her mama."

"Little Lizzie Mae." Belinda had decided to name the baby for their mother.

What name had his Sara chosen for their child? Was it a girl or boy?

He gave Lizzie a quick, gentle bath. Someone—MC?—had put a large kettle on the stove for him to use as needed and had assembled a pile of clean rags. He wrapped his niece in warm material and laid her on her mother's lap while he attended to the afterbirth. Time enough to dress the baby in the dressing gown Belinda had made for the occasion when they both had rested from the birth.

He changed the bed linens and made Belinda as comfortable as he could.

"Thank you," she said. She brought the baby to her breast. "I love you, little Lizzie Mae."

Vaughn watched them, admiring the miracle of birth, until they had fallen asleep. He refilled the kettle and found his way to the cot they kept in the office.

He had hardly closed his eyes when he heard a rattling at the door. Outside the window he could see the first rays of sunlight. He threw on his shirt and rushed to answer, wondering if a woman had arrived in need of help.

MC had entered the main room, her daughter with her. Hearty smells wafted through the air from the basket the little girl was carrying.

"We thought you might be ready for a warm breakfast," she said. "And Belinda as well, if she has given birth."

He hesitated, again wondering about the wisdom of speaking so plainly in front of a child. "About two and a half hours ago."

"Is it a girl or a boy?" Aimee asked.

"A girl." Belinda had shuffled to the doorway, her baby in her arms. "I named her Lizzie Mae, after my mother."

"Then we have something in common." Aimee beamed. "My name is Aimee Mae. I think Mae was my grandmother's name." She put down the basket and held out her arms. "Let me hold little Lizzie while you eat something."

Vaughn cleared his throat, and MC turned to him. "Unless there is a reason she shouldn't eat this morning, Doctor? I'm sorry, I should have asked."

Vaughn relaxed and shook his head. He told himself to be glad he had a nurse who would rise before dawn to come in and take care of her patients. Not to mention himself. Most mornings he managed a meal of cold biscuits and coffee. She'd brought crisp bacon, fluffy eggs, buttery toast, and tasty hot oatmeal, with fresh milk.

"I noticed yesterday that you like coffee. I'll get some started." She looked at the baby in Aimee's arms. "She's beautiful."

He couldn't agree more. The baby reminded him of the day his sister was born.

Maybe it wasn't so bad that young Aimee be exposed to a newborn like this.

He had eaten nothing but broth and crackers for the past twenty-four hours. Suddenly ravenous, he ate all his portion and barely kept himself from grabbing the unfinished items from his sister's tray. She was falling back asleep.

"Let's get you back to bed," MC said. She placed Belinda's arm around her shoulder and headed for the room. She looked back at Vaughn, inviting him to follow her. While he'd been eating, she'd cleaned up Belinda's room a bit more. It was as fresh as a bedroom in his own home. He helped Belinda settle in bed, and MC made her comfortable. They laid Lizzie beside her.

"Take it easy, dear Belinda. You and Lizzie need this time to get to know each other." MC glanced around the still-empty waiting room. "Seeing as there is no one here yet, do you mind if I get Aimee to school and take my things home with me? I'll be back before the first scheduled appointment. It's at ten this morning."

He almost laughed. "I believe I can take care of myself and any stray patients for a few hours unattended."

"Good." She nodded. "I'm glad you found the cot in the office."

She disappeared without any additional warning, as she had on the previous evening. He'd have to move quickly to get her attention.

Chapter 3

A few weeks later, MC arrived at the clinic an hour after it had opened, an arrangement she had made with Dr. Asa when they first opened the doors six years ago. Once a week she walked Aimee to school and talked with her teacher.

"Good, you're here." Belinda appeared in the doorway, hugging Lizzie to her shoulder. "Things have been quiet so far this morning. Give me a few minutes to get Lizzie settled, and I'll be back out."

Belinda had shown herself adept at handling reception duties, so Mrs. Smith had decided to take the opportunity to get away for a bit. "It's for the best," she'd told MC. "Too many cooks in one kitchen spoil the broth. Besides, I've been wanting to visit my daughter."

Dr. Vaughn had already ingrained himself in the practice. MC hadn't asked him yet about Aimee, and as time passed, she told herself it was best if he never knew.

MC hung the picture Aimee had drawn for her on the wall behind the desk. According to the appointment book, Gail was due for a follow-up visit. She had missed once. If she didn't show up today, MC would go by the place where the young mother lived and worked.

139

She set out new reading material, provided by Aimee's teacher. *Godey's Lady's Book* tended to disappear as quickly as it was supplied, but MC didn't mind.

Since Belinda's arrival, they'd added a few books as well.

There had been no clinic when she first started working in Auraria, of course. During the war, she'd been responsible for all but a few births in the community. In the process, she'd learned how to do many things commonly left to physicians—and had learned enough to recognize her limitations.

The women in her care needed a doctor, and God put her together with Dr. Asa. For a month now, though, her dear friend had been on his honeymoon.

In the other room, Lizzie cooed while Belinda talked to her. MC had been blessed to have raised Aimee from infancy, to share those precious early memories.

Aimee. MC still hadn't found a way to ask Dr. Vaughn about Sara. The longer she waited, the harder it became. The longer she waited, the more she realized what a good man Dr. Vaughn was, in ways that had little to do with being a doctor. It showed in his tenderness toward his unmarried sister. He also had accepted MC's role in the practice more easily than most doctors she had met.

Belinda returned to the desk. "She's asleep. Oh, my brother asked me to send you to the study when you came in. I'm sorry, I forgot earlier."

MC knocked and entered the study. Dr. Vaughn had the ledger books open, poring over the accounts. That was rarely a good sign. Had he decided they could no longer afford her services?

"Nurse—Mrs. Brownstone—" He spread his hands.

"MC," she reminded him. "I'm listening."

"Asa and I would like to free the clinic from our sponsors. Several are heavily invested in the brothels that house most of our clients. While we feel compassion for the women, we fear we are identified as part of the problem."

Asa and I. Apparently Asa had neglected to mention that the building belonged to *her.* But she would table that discussion. What he said about their sponsors had always been true. "Has something changed?"

"The brothel owners came to me, asking me to provide services I am unwilling to perform. I know Asa has refused in the past. They're threatening to stop their support if we continue to refuse."

MC could guess the kind of services he meant. Illegal and immoral methods to prevent or end pregnancy.

He continued. "Perhaps they will leave me alone once I prove I am steadfast in my principles. However, it wouldn't hurt if we had a secondary location, with a different clientele."

MC nodded. "I'm afraid you're right. Ladies with means won't come to a clinic that caters to women of the street. But the cost of renting a second location would be prohibitive, would it not?"

"What if I told you we could open a second clinic, rent free?" Dr. Vaughn wriggled his eyebrows.

MC's jaw dropped. "Do you have a place in mind?"

"One of the larger Denver churches has invited us to hold a clinic twice a month. We can keep all monies earned as long as we agree to help a local orphanage when needed."

His eyes twinkled, as if he knew how much that would appeal to her. "That's where you come in. Are you available to work with me, as my nurse, not necessarily a midwife, two Saturday mornings a month? Belinda has said she's willing to take care of your daughter while we travel and work."

It sounded wonderful, except Saturday was the day of the week she set aside for Aimee. But— "Tell me more. What will you do when they need your help at other hours?"

Vaughn drew a deep breath when MC asked for more information. His plan would only succeed with her help, and it involved flexibility.

"The clinic at the church will be open to whatever ailments our patients bring to us. If a woman goes into labor and we're busy with another case, a doctor in town has agreed to help. But the new clinic will mean longer hours than we've had previously." He had observed firsthand the long hours MC worked when needed, which she balanced by taking time when business was slow. "Asa has telegraphed me that we can offer you a small increase in salary."

Her head snapped back, and he wondered if he had offended her sense of pride. "My salary isn't the issue."

"Do you object to my sister looking after your daughter?" The question dangled between them.

Vaughn had expected an immediate denial. Instead, she hesitated a second too long to answer.

"I thought you got along well with Belinda." He fought to keep anger from his voice.

MC sat up straight as a washboard. "I'm not concerned with Belinda's qualifications. Unless I'm assisting at a birth, I spend Saturday mornings with my daughter. I'm loath to give up that time."

"Would another day of the week be preferable?"

"No, Saturday is the best day." She concentrated for a moment. "I will bring Aimee with me. We don't get into Denver as often as

I would like. This is our opportunity." She nodded, a smile lighting her face.

"Do you accept my offer, then?" he asked.

"Yes, I do." She extended a hand. "I'm praising God with you for making this possible. I'll be praying that people will come."

Vaughn didn't just want patients. They needed a clientele who could afford their services. Without an increase in income, he didn't know how long the clinic could continue to operate.

"Something else is troubling you," she said. "What is it?"

His desire to protect his coworkers—especially a woman—fought with her right to know. "I'd like to see us free of those men altogether. A one-day clinic is a drop in the bucket. We need more."

MC looked out the curtained windows, her eyes focused in the distance. "God has provided for us this far. He will continue to provide." A too-bright smile lit her face when she turned back to Vaughn. "The new clinic is only the beginning. There'll be more. You'll see."

Saturday morning, Belinda and Lizzie Mae accompanied him to the clinic. First they stopped by MC's house, a modest two-story building.

Aimee greeted them at the door. With ribbons in her hair, she looked dressed for a day in the city. What treat did MC have in mind for her daughter after the clinic? He didn't know all the amenities Denver had to offer, not yet.

"Dr. Vaughn, Miss Belinda, come in. Ma is cleaning up from breakfast. She'll be ready right fast."

She led them to the front drawing room, where Belinda laid

Lizzie in Aimee's arms. The infant wiggled and blew bubbles while Aimee laughed. The girl's abundant joy said a lot about MC's abilities as a mother. Was there anything the woman didn't do well?

Watching mother and child reminded Vaughn of the cruelties of war, of the loss of the family he and Sara had dreamed of. But he wouldn't let that pain destroy today's opportunities.

MC's home surprised him in its warm mixture of yellow, peach, and pink, a contrast to her work attire of somber gray, dark blue, and lavender.

"Sorry I'm late." MC came into the room. Underneath her starched apron she wore a deep rose dress with intricate designs. It heightened the rose in her cheeks and shaved years from her age.

Belinda cleared her throat, and he realized he must be staring. "You are looking well today, Nurse," he said.

MC's blush matched her dress. "Since we're not in the clinic, you may call me MC."

"MC." His lips formed the letters. "No, I won't do it. I cannot address a lady as lovely as yourself by her initials. What kind of name do they conceal? Magnificent Constantina? Mercy Charity? Morgan of Camelot?" he teased.

She blushed again. Her daughter came to her rescue. "Her name is Maia Cybele Brownstone. I think it's perfectly lovely." Aimee drew out the syllables as if they were poetry.

"Maia." The syllables lingered on his tongue like honey. "Your name suits you."

Maia's cheeks turned even redder as she scowled. "If you do not wish to call me MC, then Mrs. Brownstone suits me fine. And it's time for us to be leaving. Come, Aimee, let's get our things."

On the other side of the doorway he heard the mother

remonstrating her daughter. He turned to Belinda in a silent appeal.

His sister was standing with her mouth open. She noticed his attention, closed her mouth, and quickly bundled Lizzie Mae into her basket. "Respect her wishes, brother. She must have a reason."

His sister's words rebuked him gently. Vaughn must have taken a false step somehow. That didn't surprise him. He'd never been a ladies' man, and time hadn't changed him.

Maia smiled as if nothing had happened when Vaughn helped her into the carriage. Once they were seated, he said, "I meant no disrespect. I admire you as a nurse, and today I saw the beauty of the woman behind the uniform. Please accept my appreciation. I will attempt to curb my tongue in the future."

He would call her MC in conversation. But in his thoughts, she'd taken on a new identity: the lovely Maia Cybele.

Chapter 4

During the ride, MC fought to bring her thoughts under control. "MC Brownstone" had a certain anonymity. She'd written to Belinda Strahan about Aimee, using her maiden name, Maia C. Beachley. She'd seen Belinda's change of attitude when she heard her full name. She hoped against hope that the doctor's sister didn't put Maia C. Beachley and Maia Cybele Brownstone together.

They arrived at the church with fifteen minutes to spare. Someone had arranged a room into the semblance of a clinic, complete with room dividers and an abundance of supplies. She would have little need of the things she'd brought with her.

MC made a point of thanking Pastor Atwood and his wife when they arrived. Mrs. Atwood had done some nursing during the war, which explained the well-prepared clinic.

"If everything is arranged to your satisfaction, there's a client who would like to speak to you before others arrive." The pastor smiled anxiously, but Vaughn agreed readily. They were both eager to begin.

Their client walked with heavy steps, her face lined with

exhaustion. The child she carried must be taking a toll on her body. MC estimated her age as close to her own—thirty-two—until she sat down. Her face relaxed enough to suggest she was in her early twenties. She looked vaguely familiar, but MC couldn't place her.

"Thank you for agreeing to see me. My husband doesn't know I'm here." The patient initiated the conversation without preamble.

Vaughn's left eyebrow shot up, but he waited for MC to take the lead, as she often did with new patients. "We'll be as quick as we can. What brought you here today?"

The woman glanced around as if to see if anyone else could hear before looking at MC. "You did. I heard the doctor was bringing a nurse-midwife with him, and I knew I had to see you."

MC glanced at Dr. Vaughn. A small nod gave permission for her to continue. "We'll be glad to help, if we can." Dr. Vaughn scooted his chair back, giving them the illusion of privacy. MC took the woman's hands between her own and waited for her to continue.

"You see, my husband feels I should give birth at home with the aid of his mother. She had twelve children, and they dropped out of her as easily as an apple falling from a tree."

MC smothered a laugh at her turn of phrase. "But you fear it won't be like that for you. Especially with a first child."

The woman's mouth twisted in a wry smile. "I know it won't be like that. I've had four daughters, all of them at home, and every birth has been difficult."

Four children already? She didn't look older than twenty-two or twenty-three.

The woman must have read the expression on MC's face. "My husband is"—she turned a delicate shade of pink—"enthusiastic about his marital responsibilities. I was thrilled with my first pregnancy; we both were. But I thought I would die when I gave birth to our first daughter." She paused. "I was in labor for three days. I was barely eighteen."

"And then you fell in love with the baby," MC said.

"She more than made up for the agony of her birth. But when I discovered I was with child again three months later, I was more frightened than at any other time of my life."

Dr. Vaughn had taken out a notepad.

"It's been five years. I've had four live births, all girls, and one miscarriage. Our son."

MC grimaced. Sometimes a man's pride suffered when his wife gave him only daughters.

"I got pregnant again a month after my third daughter was born. My husband's mother blamed me for not taking care of myself. Is it a sin that I wasn't very upset when I lost that child, glad that he left me alone for a month and that I went six blessed months before conceiving again?"

Blast the man for treating his wife like a brood mare. "I would say you were thanking the good Lord for giving you time to heal," MC said gently.

"Yes!" She didn't speak for a minute. "The last pregnancy was relatively easy, and the labor was almost bearable. But when I gave birth to yet another daughter, he could hardly bear to look at her. He simply said, 'We'll have a son, someday soon.'"

The woman wasn't her husband's only victim, if he only valued sons.

"I put that out of my mind, recovered quickly, enjoyed the new baby who looks just like her father. But he came to me when she was but a week old."

Tears formed in her eyes as she looked at MC. "That was five and a half months ago. I was with child within a month."

Dr. Vaughn released a sharp breath.

MC said simply, "And that was too soon."

"If he had given me time to heal, to recover, I might have welcomed another chance to produce a son. But this pregnancy has been as difficult as my first. I'm convinced it is a boy. He rides differently within the womb. I'm afraid. . ." Her voiced trailed away.

MC filled in the blank. Afraid she would miscarry, and of her husband's reaction. Afraid of childbirth for a baby she was too worn to bear. Afraid for her daughters, if something should happen to her.

Dr. Vaughn leaned forward. "May I ask a few questions?" His voice was gentle as a spring rain.

The woman nodded.

"Do you need anything today to ease your pregnancy at home?"

"I have some recipes I've used with patients before," MC suggested. "For meals that keep you strong."

"I'd appreciate that."

Dr. Vaughn inched his chair forward. "You were wise to come today. You and that baby, be it boy or girl, need a physician's care to arrive at a successful birth. Our job is to get you strong and healthy. You should also plan to have us with you when you give birth, in case there are any complications."

She paled a little at that statement, as if she were unwilling to confront her husband.

MC looked through her bag for the promised recipes. "If you don't have one already, ask your husband to get you a cast iron frying pan, and then cook all your meals in it. Eat meat as often as possible." She tapped the recipe cards on her knees. "Tell him you want to fix him special food. He doesn't have to know it's for your health."

The woman dried the tears from her face. "You make me feel better already."

"Come back in two weeks, if you can," Dr. Vaughn said. "A month, at the very latest."

Five minutes later, the woman was gone.

MC prayed the woman would be able to return.

⌒

"We still don't know her name," Maia said. "I'm surprised you didn't ask."

"Maia." Vaughn whispered her name, thinking again how it reflected the midwife's sturdy beauty.

"That's 'Nurse' while we're in the clinic." Maia scowled at him.

"Sorry." He shook himself. He didn't want to antagonize the woman who charmed him more and more as they worked together. "We can ask when she returns. Or we can ask Pastor Atwood." He lowered his voice, although there was no one to overhear. "At least the camp women know how to take rudimentary precautions against pregnancy. I've never understood why some men treat their wives like breeding stock."

When Maia didn't respond, he asked, "Did I shock you?"

She shook her head. "No two marriages are alike. Not everyone conceives with ease, and not everyone struggles so with childbirth."

He'd known Maia was a widow, because of Aimee. Her comments raised questions in his mind. Had it been a difficult marriage? Childbirth? There was some kind of story behind her words.

He wouldn't pry, but he knew the question would remain in his mind.

Mrs. Atwood knocked on the door and entered. "Thanks for seeing Mrs. Ferguson early. Other patients have arrived, if you're ready for them."

Vaughn grinned. Mrs. Atwood had supplied their patient's name. "Send the next one in, unless you need something, Nurse?"

Maia shook her head. "You set up everything so well, Mrs. Atwood. There is very little else we need."

The pastor's wife blushed. "Here is the list of patients who are waiting." Seven names appeared on the list, with a brief note beside each name. "I took the liberty of asking them why they wanted to see you, Doctor."

Maia laughed. "With Mrs. Atwood's help, you might not need my services."

The list included not only the patients' names, but also their ages and what Mrs. Atwood knew about their complaint. His eyebrows rose. "You've done half my work. Thank you." He scanned the information. "Please bring young Jeremy in first."

Once Mrs. Atwood closed the door, Vaughn spoke to Maia. "I will always need your assistance. You have a gift in patient care that is rare. Your rapport with the patients makes you invaluable." He hoped his smile conveyed his sincerity. "I may know medical terms that you don't, but—"

She turned her head away, as if unwilling to accept his praise.

He continued, determined to make his point. "—but you know things I don't know. I consider us partners."

He opened the door, looking for Jeremy. It came as no surprise that a young boy with his arm in a sling was talking with Aimee.

Who could blame him? The little girl was pretty, outgoing, and smart. Give her ten years, and every lad on the front range would come calling.

He didn't envy Maia the job of keeping them away. Or maybe he did. If his child had lived, if it had been a girl, she'd have been about Aimee's age. A fierce sense of loss swept over him.

He shook his head to clear it and called out, "Jeremy? Jeremy Fisher?"

Aimee helped Jeremy to his feet. His left foot turned slightly inward, and his right arm was in a sling. "This is Dr. Vaughn. He's oh so nice."

Maia shook her head. "Remember, you should introduce the child to the adult first."

Oh yes, the rules of etiquette. "I don't mind. I'm pleased to meet you, Jeremy. Why don't you come into my office? Do you have anyone with you?" He glanced around the office but didn't see anyone prepared to join them.

"I know—" Aimee began.

Maia frowned, and Aimee stopped speaking. "Dr. Vaughn, please excuse me while I speak with my daughter." Aimee's shoulders fell as they made their way to a far corner.

Jeremy looked crestfallen. "I hope she's not in trouble. We were just talking." He beckoned for Vaughn to bend down and whispered in his ear, "She sure is pretty."

"Yes, she is," Vaughn said, but his eyes were on Maia.

Vaughn asked the boy a few questions before Maia returned. The broken arm was the result of a fall from a tree, a common enough boyhood experience. He made a slight adjustment to the sling. If only someone was there to ask about the leg. Mrs.

Atwood's notes didn't mention it. A second read-through showed something else he had missed at first glance.

"Jeremy, please wait here while I consult with my nurse." Vaughn led Maia some distance away. "He's from the children's home."

"I know. Aimee told me."

Maybe that time in the corner wasn't a scolding.

"Aimee is often my secret weapon when it comes to treating children. We encounter too many broken bones." She raised her head high. "A child will often tell another child things they are afraid to tell adults."

Aimee did have an open face that invited people to tell her anything, just like his beloved Sara.

"Mrs. Atwood intended to come in with Jeremy," Maia continued, pulling Vaughn's thoughts away from his wife. "But she was called away suddenly."

Vaughn glanced across the room, where his sister was reading a book to several children. He took out the patient list: four of the seven were children from the home. "They shouldn't send the children here unsupervised. I would like to speak with someone about that boy's leg."

"The children also told Aimee their caretaker will be back within an hour and that they all hope to have a chance to see the doctor. Apparently she's unwilling to linger here long."

"Very well. Let's finish with Jeremy first." But when he asked the boy about his leg, the lad didn't remember when it was injured.

By the time they were finished with Jeremy, the children's worker had arrived. When he called for one of the girls, she brought in three children and nodded to Maia. "Hello, Mrs. Brownstone."

Then she turned to Vaughn. "They are all suffering from the same malady. There is no need to take time for individual visits."

Each child was running a slight fever. Vaughn wanted to scold her for bringing them into a place where they could pass on their contagion. "If you had sent word, I would have come to the home. It's best not to bring children out when they are sick like this."

"I'll send word next time."

He recommended willow bark tea and consulted with the worker about a healthy environment. "I have questions about Jeremy's leg."

"I don't have time for that today. I must get back."

Vaughn drew a deep breath, prepared to argue.

"Take this with you, then." Maia handed the harried woman a piece of paper.

Vaughn stared at her. What was she doing? Didn't she understand he needed to talk to the woman?

Chapter 5

MC had anticipated Dr. Vaughn's displeasure. "I simply wrote down what you said about Jeremy's leg, and I made a copy."

"I can't believe she wouldn't stay long enough to listen," he huffed. But as he glanced through the notes she handed him, he didn't voice any objections.

He was so cute when he was exasperated.

Where had that thought come from?

Flustered, she moved on to a more comfortable subject. "I can guess why she didn't want to stay. Delphine's one of my former clients. Perhaps she didn't want me bringing it up."

Dr. Vaughn's mouth formed an O. "We need to schedule another clinic as soon as possible." He frowned. "We're only supposed to come here once a month, but that might not be enough." He wiped a hand across his forehead. "I didn't intend to make this a second practice."

Secretly she agreed, but neither one of them could say no when people needed help.

The last three patients were all adults with common complaints.

After the last one left, Belinda joined them. "I've been talking with Mrs. Atwood."

"Please don't tell me we have more patients," Dr. Vaughn said with a groan.

Belinda laughed. "Nothing like that. Next time, she'll set up a separate area for children. I'll sit with them. I'm already watching over Aimee and Lizzie, so it seems like the logical thing to do."

MC and Dr. Vaughn exchanged glances. "We were talking about going to the children's home instead," he said. "Maybe the church will allow us to hold clinic there one Saturday a month."

"That's a good idea." Belinda nodded. "But people will bring their children here, now that they've met you both. Not to mention Aimee—she's bragged about both of you."

"Only because it's true. Dr. Vaughn's the greatest. Ma says so." Aimee came up at the last of the conversation. "Isn't that so, Ma?"

Belinda and Dr. Vaughn both shook their heads. Why did he leave her feeling so much more flustered than anyone else she'd worked with?

"There's no shame in speaking the truth." MC had waited a moment too long to respond. When Belinda hid a smile, MC allowed herself to smile with her. "I can't fault the child for repeating what she heard."

"I tend to be blunt myself," Dr. Vaughn said, bending over so he could look Aimee in the eyes. "Don't ever change. And thank you for the compliment." He winked at MC.

It was a precious moment, altogether too like a father-daughter moment, one that warmed her heart. Then MC remembered all she stood to lose if the doctor ever discovered her secret. "However, a woman needs discretion if she is to make it in this world, Doctor."

She hated the chill in her voice. He drew back into himself, his openness already a thing of the past. "Discretion, but not subterfuge, Nurse."

She almost wished he'd used her name.

They had planned on spending the afternoon in the city, but a messenger arrived from their clinic. "We need you to come right away. Young Gail attempted suicide."

Dr. Vaughn and MC sprang into action and were out the door within two minutes. Gail's baby had died during the night. MC understood her grief, and despaired over the feeling of helplessness it created.

Mrs. Atwood ran behind them with a lunch pail. "Perhaps you can eat on your way."

"Let's go straight to Gail," MC suggested, and Dr. Vaughn agreed.

"You'd best grab a spare bag, in case you used up anything this morning. You can drop me and Aimee at the clinic and pick up the bag," Belinda suggested.

"Excellent idea," MC said. Bless Belinda. MC didn't always have child care available on such short notice.

They made quick progress, but with each hoofbeat, MC sensed Gail's life ebbing away. They couldn't get there quickly enough.

Twenty minutes later, they reached the brothel where Gail worked. Anna, a girl just about Gail's age, fell into MC's arms.

"Are we too late?" MC's face grew cold as blood fled from her cheeks.

"Nurse Brownstone, you're here, and you've brought the doctor. Thank you." Candy, the madame of the house, welcomed them at the door. "Gail cut herself with a dull knife. She lives still, but she needs help."

The girl lay in restraints, the cuts on her wrists bound tightly by dirty bed linens. If loss of blood didn't kill her, infection might.

MC snapped into action. "Anna, please get us some boiled rags. These sheets will be the death of your friend."

Gail's limp, bandaged body hurtled MC to another day, some five years past, when she came upon a client for whom help came too late.

Not this time, she promised herself. She refused to let Gail give in to the demons that plagued her. She'd get her out of the brothel if she had to take her under her own roof. She'd done it before, but not since Aimee had grown old enough to understand the girls' situations. Not all her girls wanted to be rescued. Others were riddled with addiction and couldn't shake free.

Gail wasn't like that, although at the moment she reeked of alcohol. She'd sought consolation for her grief. During her pregnancy, she'd kept herself dry, and all for naught.

The owners of the brothels seemed to agree with Scrooge, that such children might as well die and decrease the surplus population. But MC had observed such love for the innocent, untouched children of the women. When a child died—as happened far too often—the mother often lost hope.

She coordinated seamlessly with Dr. Vaughn even better than she did with Dr. Asa. It was as if they'd never had that small disagreement after the morning clinic.

Once again she could admire Dr. Vaughn at work.

❦

As long as they were working with a patient, Vaughn mused, he and Maia made an excellent team. Dinnertime approached before he finally sat down. He gestured for Maia to do the same.

"She has to get out of this place. Do you agree?" He kept his voice low to prevent the girls keeping vigil from overhearing.

Maia hesitated for a second before nodding. "We don't have a choice."

Her voice lacked confidence, but they could talk that out later. "She's well enough to be moved. Will they try to stop us?"

Their eyes locked, and a common purpose grew between them without words. They finished their meal in silence, then made their way back to Gail's room where Maia searched for a suitable gown for Gail to wear during the ride. As she slipped it on the girl, she whispered, "We're taking you away from here."

Gail nodded. Vaughn scooped her in his arms and headed for the door.

Anna's eyes widened when she saw what was happening. She glanced at the far door on the corridor. "Be careful."

The carriage was only twenty feet away, out the door and down the steps.

They had almost reached the door when a voice boomed behind them. "I appreciate all you've done for my girls, but we can take care of her from here."

"That's Jude Hackett, the one who leaves money with Dr. Asa." Maia's lips thinned in disgust.

Dr. Vaughn didn't break stride. He nodded for MC to open the door and descended the steps as quickly as possible.

Hackett ran after them, gun in hand, but he didn't raise it to shoot. "Tell Asa Smith he'll have to look for alternate funding. He'll get no more from me."

Vaughn drew his lips into a sharp line and eased Gail into the back seat of the carriage.

"I'll ride back here with her," Maia said.

Vaughn guided the horses as carefully as possible, to minimize the jostling. Even so, Gail cried out in pain and roused to wakefulness.

She struggled to sit up and stared down at her hands and moaned. "Why did you have to stop me? I have nothing to live for."

"That's what you think now, but you'll find something new. You never have to go back to that place, ever again," Maia soothed her.

Gail looked around wildly. "Where are you taking me? He'll never let me go."

"You're not his slave. And if you signed some sort of contract, a good lawyer can break it," Vaughn called over his back. "But for now, focus on healing."

"I'd rather be dead," Gail said.

Belinda greeted them at the door.

"We have company." Vaughn emphasized the last word. He carried Gail into the house.

Belinda's eyes registered recognition. Maia said, "Gail's son died last night. She tried to join him."

Belinda's eyes immediately softened in concern. "Oh, the poor girl. That wee boy was the one thing that gave her a reason to go on."

Was his sister speaking of her discussions with Gail while they both recuperated from childbirth—or was she speaking of herself and Lizzie?

Vaughn carried Gail to one of their beds and checked that she hadn't suffered any ill effects from their rapid journey. What had happened to Maia? He could use her help in giving the girl a good bath. Surely she hadn't gone home without letting him know.

He found her deep in discussion with his sister.

"Who decided to bring Gail back?" Belinda was speaking.

"It was your brother's idea." Maia chuckled. "He walked out of there like her guardian angel." There was admiration in her voice.

Vaughn decided to make his presence known. "Talking about me behind my back, hmm?" He smiled to take away the sting.

"I'm glad to see you working together so well. It bodes for a good future," Belinda said. "The two of you make a good team because you respect each other." She turned back to Maia. "We can continue our discussion another time. I had another idea. Would it comfort Gail to hold my Lizzie? Perhaps even to nurse her, if she's in discomfort?"

"Let me get a look at my favorite niece first," Vaughn said. It was a joy to see Lizzie growing healthy and well. "She's doing fine. You ladies can join me when you're ready." He returned to Gail's room to discover she was awake—and frightened. How could he help her understand she had no need to fear?

"We're not letting you return to that place. You are young, and you have your future ahead of you."

"But I've no place to go." Gail began to cry. "Without the baby, I have no reason to try."

Maia came in and held Gail, rocking her, as if she understood the pain in the girl's heart.

"You'll stay with me." Belinda came in with Lizzie in her arms. "She's fussing for a feeding, and I'm all worn out. Would you be willing to feed her for me?"

Gail hesitated a moment, then nodded. "Iffen I can help."

"And then us unwed mothers will figure how to make a new

life for ourselves together," Belinda said candidly.

Belinda had mentioned some such harebrained scheme to Vaughn earlier. Trust her to make the decision on the spur of the moment. What they would do, and how they would accomplish it, was a different matter.

It was a good thing his sister had come west with him. This was one of those times he wouldn't know what to say.

But when he considered the practice Maia had built, he realized perhaps it wasn't so impossible after all. She had made a life for herself and her daughter out of little more than hopes and dreams.

Chapter 6

The glow of Gail's rescue stayed with MC all through the coming week. Each day she praised the Lord for making her dreams a reality. Vaughn—she couldn't think of him as Dr. Vaughn anymore, not after the past twenty-four hours—had given her the courage—and the muscle—to do what she had long wanted to do. Get the girls out of the system that was killing them.

No one was happier than she when Anna arrived at the clinic early Saturday morning, seeking refuge.

But when Maia arrived at the clinic on Monday morning, reality set in. Dale Rathbone was waiting in the office, talking with Vaughn. The lawyer's presence was never a good sign.

MC had met Rathbone shortly after she arrived in Denver a decade ago. She had begun calling herself "MC Brownstone" instead of "Maia C." at his suggestion. He said that using her initials would give the illusion that she was male, which might open doors for her. He'd been right. The ruse had succeeded. Still today, there were people who didn't realize "MC Brownstone" was a woman.

When Rathbone caught sight of her, he shook his head. She

could guess why he was in her office. Gail.

"What were the two of you thinking, poking the hornet's nest like you did?" He shook his head again.

Vaughn jutted his chin forward. "We couldn't let Gail stay in that place."

"Taking Anna in as well sealed your fate." Rathbone pulled his glasses to the tip of his nose and peered at Vaughn over their tops. "No one applauds your sentiments more than I do. That's why I helped Mrs. Brownstone set up this clinic in the first place."

Vaughn looked puzzled.

Rathbone chuckled. "You don't know, do you? The building, the clinic—they're both in Mrs. Brownstone's name. She's the owner."

Vaughn looked to MC for confirmation.

"It's true." She nodded. "From the beginning, I recognized the need for a place where women could come to discuss their problems away from the. . .milieu"—she wrinkled her nose—"they live in."

He nodded, but he still didn't know the whole story.

"I bought this house and lived upstairs. At first I was on my own, and then Dr. Asa joined the clinic after Aimee was born. I wanted to raise her away from the clinic, so he moved upstairs, and Aimee and I found another place."

"I don't blame you." Vaughn shook his head in disbelief. "I never guessed this was your business."

"I like to keep it as private as possible. The owners think Dr. Asa is the owner, and I'd like to keep it that way," MC emphasized.

"We're straying from the central problem." Rathbone brought them back to the issue at hand. "When you took out the loan, you agreed to accept certain limitations. You're expected to keep the

girls healthy, free from disease, and to deliver their children safely."
Here he winked and put a finger to the side of his nose. "Since you
were unwilling to help them get rid of their babies."

Vaughn's mouth twisted into a grimace. "I have never—"

"Nor have we, or will we, on any condition." MC shuddered at
the thought.

"But you also were prohibited from attacking their businesses.
As awful as it sounds, I think they would prefer for Gail to die
than for her to escape. Her attempt gives the other girls the idea
they can get away as well. And without the girls, they have no
business." He shook his finger at them. "Gail's suicide attempt and
your spiriting her away was bad for morale. And then their fears
were realized when Anna came to you for help. Mr. Hackett is
determined to make you pay."

"Let him try," Vaughn growled.

A part of MC applauded her knight in shining armor. But MC
the business owner guessed what was coming. "Perhaps you should
explain what the consequences will be."

"He's calling in the note, to be paid in full at the end of the
current lease period."

Vaughn was following closely. "And that means?"

"He wants payment in full for the house by August 1, or else
the title will revert to his name." Rathbone took off his glasses.
"I'm so sorry, Mrs. Brownstone."

MC knew how impossible that would be, and so did Vaughn.
She had used up what extra capital she had earned when she hired
on the new doctor.

She bit her lip for a few seconds. "Is there any room for nego-
tiation?" She wouldn't come right out and say *if we send Gail back.*

Rathbone shook his head. "The damage is done. They look at it as a business risk that didn't pay off. I'm sorry. I truly am."

He picked through his papers and handed over a crisp sheet of stationery. "Here is the official notice." He dug through his briefcase again. "And here are the terms of the original mortgage. Just in case you can't find your copy easily."

MC's hand brushed Vaughn's as they reached for the papers at the same time. He took the copy of the mortgage, while she retrieved the notice they had been served. She wrinkled her nose. Time hadn't increased her fondness for legal mumbo-jumbo, but the intent was perfectly clear. They had the tenancy free and clear until the last day of July 1871. Unless the holder of the mortgage received payment in full on the remainder due, the title would revert to the seller.

She did the mental calculations. That meant they had a little more than fifty days to find the money—or to find another place to do business.

"At least we have a little time to get the money together." She injected her words with a note of confidence. "It took a miracle to obtain the first loan. God will provide again, I'm sure of it."

A small voice suggested she shouldn't pester God for a second miracle after she had already received one when they successfully rescued Gail.

Vaughn set down the papers he had been reading. "You're absolutely right," he agreed. "This original document is incredible. God may have been at work behind the scenes, but you clearly have a gift for the law, Mr. Rathbone. I thank you for safeguarding the clinic in so very many ways."

"Thank you, but your praise is unwarranted." The lawyer smiled weakly. "Unfortunately, I was unable to prevent a catch-all phrase from being included that the owner demanded."

"Where it says we're to provide women's hygiene care and 'other services as requested.'" Vaughn nodded. "I did see that."

The clause MC had known would come back to haunt them.

Rathbone held out his hands, palms up. "He hasn't tried to hold you to those terms, because what he'd like you to do is mostly illegal."

"Is it legal to force girls to stay in their employ?" The question burning in Vaughn's heart burst out.

Rathbone and Maia looked at each other. "Did Gail sign a contract?" Maia asked.

Rathbone nodded. "And like all such contracts, it's designed to keep her bound in perpetuity. The owners and managers of the brothels charge exorbitant fees for food and lodging and even the medical services you provide." He dug in his briefcase. "This is the current balance on Gail's account. They even charged her for your services after her failed attempt to end her life."

Maia's lips had drawn into a tight line, but steel glinted from her eyes. "Perhaps it's for the best. We've broken our deal with the devil. I don't know how we'll manage it, but at last we'll be free from the taint of evil that has hung about our clinic for too long. We shall be in touch, Mr. Rathbone, as soon as we determine our plan of action."

"God be with you," Mr. Rathbone said, and left by the side door.

She kept her chin up and her face forward, but Vaughn saw the muscles working in her neck. No wonder Maia had such a take-charge attitude when it came to the clinic. "Do I have a say in what happens?"

She glared at him. "I don't know whether to celebrate the fact we've made the break I've longed to make—or to be angry with myself for agreeing with you to take Gail, and thus making it impossible to continue our work."

He searched his soul for twinges of regret but could find none, only a deepening conviction. "It was that kind of thinking that allowed slavery to persist for so long in our great nation." He paused before adding, "I lost everything I had to fight for freedom. I prefer this kind of fight."

Maia's lips thinned. "But what if we lose?"

"It's a single battle in a long war. If we lose on this front, we'll fight a different way." His conviction grew with every word.

The angry flames faded from her cheeks. "We acted in the best interest of Gail and took necessary steps. But now I'm thinking about all the others involved and wonder if we were too hasty. There's Dr. Asa, his mother, and his new bride. And—my daughter. Not to mention Belinda and Lizzie Mae, and now there's Gail and Anna as well."

Vaughn's shoulders stiffened. If she wanted to play the family card. . .

"But both of us lost family during the war, and we kept on going. I shouldn't live in fear of what might happen—although I confess I do worry about providing for my daughter." She rubbed the tears away from her eyes.

Indignation seeped out of Vaughn. "Women and children should never be at the forefront of war. I'm sorry you are in that position, but sometimes the battle finds us whether we choose it or not."

She nodded. "We built this clinic on a fortress of prayer. If God removes the safety of this castle, surely He has a better place for us somewhere else."

Vaughn could only hope so. "I already know there's not enough money in the books to pay the entire amount. We were prepared to pay the annual installment, but this. . . It's exorbitant interest."

Maia's ears turned pink. "Banks did not think kindly of a woman owning a business, especially given the nature of our clients. They always considered it high risk." She drew out a shaky laugh. "I guess we proved them right."

"Nonsense." Vaughn frowned. "If anyone was irresponsible, it was me. Acting on impulse, bringing Gail back."

"But I agreed with your action. Also, my name's on the paper, not yours." She offered a weak smile. "And even if you were, do you have the means to pay for the difference?"

He shook his head. He had some money, but not enough.

"Think on the bright side. We've made a start with the clinic at the church. We made twenty dollars on Saturday, and we're bound to make more as time goes on."

Even if they doubled that income, they wouldn't make enough.

Her smile sparkled. "We have some time before the deadline." Her smile turned mischievous. "In fact, I propose a party—celebrating Gail's, and our, freedom from those monsters."

Curiosity replaced the cold fear growing in his insides. "Tell me more."

Chapter 7

N ot just a party." MC rubbed her hands together, twining her fingers over each other as the thoughts formed in her mind. "Perhaps we could have a basket raffle, with each one of us preparing a basket with food and other things. We could highlight our success stories: Delphine from the orphanage, Gail, a few others I know."

"What if—" Vaughn interrupted.

"If they're willing, of course." She swept past his interruption. "But we already have an ideal spokesperson, although her situation is far different. Belinda."

"No." Vaughn's lips formed a straight line. "Parade my own sister around as if she were a common prostitute? Never."

The door opened as he said the words, and Belinda stampeded in. "You should be careful how loudly you speak behind closed doors, Brother. I heard every word." Her color heightened. "I am aware I'm a fallen woman, which, in the opinion of many, is no better than a prostitute. Unlike unfortunates like Gail and Anna, I was blessed with options."

MC applauded. "You have a strong mind and will. That's why I think you should be the spokesperson at our efforts to raise money.

We hope to continue the clinic, free from interference by the brothel owners."

Belinda tilted her head. "Intriguing."

"You've already expressed an interest in helping unwed mothers find meaningful employment that will support them and their children. Our interests lie on a similar path."

Belinda nodded. "I agree. But why now?"

Vaughn placed his hands on his knees. "Because we have to pay our mortgage in full by July 31, or else we no longer have a home or a clinic." Bitterness dripped from his words.

Belinda's mouth formed a perfect O. "Then we must get to work. Call it a Freedom Festival, perhaps, and hold a series of events in July."

MC's hunch about Belinda proved accurate as ideas spewed from her like a tilting windmill. "Before we do any specific planning, however, we need to speak with the pastor."

MC brushed away a niggling sense of worry. "Even if he objects, we can still continue our plans."

Belinda and Vaughn turned to her with identical expressions on their faces, their relationship plainly stamped on their features. "If he doesn't agree, perhaps I should bend over and write in the sand," Vaughn said.

MC allowed herself a chuckle. "That's hardly fair. From everything I've heard and observed, Pastor Atwood is indeed above reproach." Unlike a few she could name. Thank God most of them no longer pastored churches.

Belinda smiled sweetly. "Better yet, if several churches are involved. Let's go to pastors known for denouncing lives of sin and ask for their help."

Her enthusiasm was contagious. MC felt much happier about the future of the clinic than she had earlier. Before long they heard a bell ringing in the other room.

"Oh, it's time to get to work." Belinda headed out the door.

MC frowned. She had one last unpleasant task to finish. "Tell them it will be about twenty minutes, please."

Vaughn nodded. "Unless it's an emergency, of course."

After the door closed softly behind Belinda, Vaughn looked at MC. "Which one of us will write to Asa to tell him what has happened?"

Of course, they'd both thought of their business partner. "I wish we could wait, but. . ." MC's voice trailed off.

"Agreed. He must be told. Should we send a cable?"

After discussion, they decided a letter was sufficient. From what she knew of Dr. Asa, he might return on the next ship. "We'd best tell him what we have planned. I'd bet money on his being in town before July."

They each wrote a letter. MC wrote in detail about the legal matters Rathbone had brought to them. Vaughn described his sister's plans. After MC explained the situation, she debated about how to close the missive.

I hate to interrupt your honeymoon bliss. But I cannot in good conscience allow you to return home to a business that no longer exists, without explaining the situation. My fervent belief and prayer is that God will show us favor in our plans.

After they read each other's letters, they placed them in separate envelopes. Gail offered to take them to the postal carrier.

MC hesitated. "I worry that Hackett or one of his henchmen will take you back by force. Until that danger has passed, I'd like for you to have an escort."

"I can go with her while you're seeing patients," Belinda said.

Her brother agreed, and they left. He joined MC at the window, where they could see the pair at the street corner.

"I hope we didn't make a mistake." Vaughn voiced their common concern.

MC wanted to dismiss the question, but she couldn't. "It's risky. But if we don't show faith in Gail, how will she learn to have faith in herself?" She touched the file drawer. "If anything happens to the letters, we have copies we can send."

Vaughn nodded. "I suspect that Asa will leave Europe as soon as he receives word. What terrible timing."

MC's thoughts had followed the same path. "There would never be a good time for this to happen. But God promises to equip us for battle, doesn't He?"

"I'm tired of fighting," was his only answer. "Come, let's fight the battle we're best equipped for, the lives of our expectant mothers."

The drawing room had filled while they wrote their letters, driving home the possible consequences. Everyone in the waiting room had seen Gail leave, free as a bird. Someone was certain to report back to the owners. They would retaliate, sooner or later, and he blamed himself for most of it.

Vaughn sent up a quick prayer, the best protection he could offer. He had to close his mind to fear. When he was a prisoner of war, he had learned the art of shifting his focus to something pleasant. Otherwise he would have gone crazy every time a prisoner was beaten for some meaningless offense.

The same God who kept him alive and in sound mind through those days would take care of those he cared for today.

Today's crowd included several faces he'd never seen before. Any worries he had that Hackett would forbid his girls to use their services disappeared. Perhaps curiosity had brought in more clients.

They worked steadily throughout the morning. Vaughn breathed a deep sigh of relief when Belinda slid back behind the desk in the waiting room. Her nod told him everything had gone well, and she would give a full account during their lunch break.

Due to the volume of clients, they ate in snatches between visits. In fact, Vaughn and Maia had to see patients separately to make sure everyone was helped.

If anyone had told him before he arrived in Auraria that he would be comfortable leaving the care of his patients to a nurse-midwife, he didn't think he would have believed it. But he trusted Maia's care absolutely, knowing that if she needed his help, she would call for it.

The pace continued unabated until midafternoon, when most of the girls had to go to "work." Aimee arrived from school in time for the late-afternoon tea Gail prepared after the last patient left.

"I'm so thankful we have Gail here." Belinda echoed his thoughts as she closed the desk. "Otherwise I'm not sure how I would take care of Lizzie Mae."

Yes, God was working everything out. At least for today, and that was all he had to think about. God would take care of tomorrow when it came.

Vaughn was eager to discuss the day's events with everyone, but Maia headed home with Aimee. They seemed so much part of the family, he sometimes forgot she had a life apart from the clinic.

The rest of the week sped by. Client numbers remained high at the clinic, and Gail took a larger role with each passing day.

He discussed the numbers with Maia on Friday morning. The office was empty, since Belinda had taken the day to drum up support for their fundraising. "Is this kind of fluctuation in patients normal? We've had several new clients this week."

Maia shook her head. "No. I alternate between gratitude and premonition. When is the other shoe going to drop?"

Vaughn pulled in his lips. "It's almost as if Hackett has given the clinic a green light. I'm thankful he hasn't come after Gail since she's been here—"

"She's a walking billboard, advertising what we hope to do."

"Why doesn't he keep his girls away?" he asked.

"I'm not sure. They're curious, but cautious too. No one except Anna has asked for similar help, although both Belinda and Gail keep offering."

Anna stayed hidden away. She didn't want to show her face yet, and no one blamed her.

Vaughn nodded. They had decided their primary responsibility was to their clients' health. They had no business interfering further in their living circumstances until they had a better alternative. Gail's presence at the clinic was a silent testimony to the possibilities.

Would the peace last until the deadline? How would the owners respond if Maia succeeded in paying the note?

"It's a lull in the hostilities, but not the end, I'm sure. But until they come after us again, we take care of our patients to the best of our ability," Maia said.

She had a lot of wisdom. When they closed shop at the end

of the day, Belinda hadn't returned from her fundraising errands. Worried and restless, Vaughn blurted out, "Maia, would you and Aimee join me for supper?"

A slow smile spread across her face. "We can do that, but we can't stay long."

The warmth of her response surprised him. What would it be like to enjoy a meal with her at a nice restaurant, without family or clients present?

He couldn't mislead her. "The truth is, I'm worried about my sister. I'd appreciate company while I wait."

Her smile disappeared at his words. Was she frightened of dining alone with him?

"I appreciate the invitation. Now I have a reason to be here when Belinda returns home safe and sound. I'll go help Gail with supper, since she wasn't expecting company."

Vaughn stayed in the office, going over the books one more time. They had made as much this week as they had in the previous fortnight. But even if they made that much money every week, they still wouldn't have enough money come July 31. He couldn't wait to hear what Belinda had learned today.

His sister returned shortly after six, her arms full of food and with three girls in tow. "Hello! Set aside whatever you have for supper. I brought company with me, and we decided to bring our food with us." Her guests spread out a loaf of bread and slices of meat, together with a pie. "And I'm glad you're still here, MC. You can hear the news firsthand."

Maia looked at Vaughn with an unspoken question. "Reinforcements?" she whispered.

He shrugged. He was sure his sister had an amazing tale.

Chapter 8

Their dinner guests both surprised and delighted MC. Belinda had enlisted the help of not only Delphine from the orphanage, but also another former patient. Olive had found a job as a seamstress when an accident left her disfigured and ill-suited for her former work. Maia greeted them each with a hug and warm words of welcome.

The third guest surprised MC the most: Mrs. Ferguson, their first patient at the church clinic. When MC reached for her hands, Mrs. Ferguson smiled widely. "I bet you're surprised to see me. When we met at the church, I could tell you didn't recognize me."

MC searched her memory. "You've never been a patient here."

"Imagine me when I was fourteen, and not pregnant."

MC closed her eyes. Slowly a picture emerged of a skinny, quiet teenager who kept in the background when MC was at the brothel. "You're Candy's daughter!" *Think, MC.* "You're Fran."

"That's me," she said. "Ma didn't want me getting into the life, so when my husband began courting me, she encouraged an early marriage." Fran raised her head in pride. "Whatever you think of my mother, I'll always be thankful of what she sacrificed for me. I would give anything if she could get out of the life herself."

MC's heart softened. "A mother's love is a powerful thing. She made sure you would have a better life."

"Well, yes. But she knew something of my husband's appetites. Sometimes it doesn't feel much different than the exchange in most brothels."

MC's heart broke at the sadness in her tone.

Fran rallied and a smile broke through. "But it's definitely better being the mistress of my own home! When I heard about what Belinda was trying to do, I wanted to help." Her smile widened. "And best of all, my husband supports my decision. That tells me his heart is in the right place."

"I'm glad to hear it."

Belinda came out, baby Lizzie in tow. The infant had reached the age where she frequently smiled. She was the picture of her mother, adorable.

MC remembered how much fun Aimee was at that age. She would have liked a half dozen children just like her, but such was not to be. She treasured her daughter and relived the joy in her patients' new babies.

Tears formed in her eyes. "You ladies are so amazing. You have overcome so much, and you're putting yourselves at risk for others."

"None of us would be here if someone hadn't helped us." The seamstress hadn't spoken until now. "You gave a good word to Miss Tillie for me. Otherwise she never would have given me the job."

Everyone in the group nodded. "You've helped all of us at one time or another," Delphine said. "You can't imagine what this clinic means to women in our position. It can't close, and we won't let it. Surely God is on our side."

Her enthusiasm was contagious.

"This is just the beginning," Belinda said. "We're going to hold the fundraiser at the orphanage hall. Neutral ground, we hope, and maybe folks will consider adopting a child while they visit."

MC felt more hopeful than she had in weeks. "God has given us a plan and a venue. What will come next?"

The next three weeks sped by. Belinda engaged the interest of both the *Denver Tribune* and the *Rocky Mountain News* in their efforts at reform.

Dr. Asa arrived in Denver with his bride on the same day that the first article ran in the *Rocky Mountain News*. He made it his job to engage the help of the medical community. In the same way, Mrs. Atwood enlisted the aid of ladies' societies across the state.

MC watched with delight when people offered financial support. Many also volunteered to work during the four-day Freedom Festival, which pleased her even more. Their plan for a one-day festival expanded to four days, since Independence Day fell on a Tuesday.

They closed the clinic early on the last day of June. Aimee spent the day at the orphanage, helping with the final decorations. The effect was as sparkling and vivacious as Delphine herself. The children they had met at the first clinic at the church had become familiar friends. Aimee would want to invite every one of them to her next birthday party.

Vaughn was already at the orphanage when MC and Aimee arrived early Saturday morning. By God's grace, he'd arranged a police presence throughout the festival, in case Hackett decided to interfere. So far nothing had happened, but that didn't mean nothing would.

On Saturday the first, they opened a free clinic at the orphanage to a line of waiting patients. Everyone had agreed the days needed to start with a free clinic. "Let people know the quality of care they will receive if they come to you," was how Mrs. Atwood put it. They saw everything from a premature infant to an elderly gentleman with a bad case of rheumatoid arthritis.

They slated contests for every day, beginning with a pie-eating contest on Saturday. Women lined up to pay a nickel for a raffle ticket. Seamstress Olive was offering an amazing grand prize: a ready-made dress. She offered to stitch dresses made-to-order for five runners-up, asking only that the women pay for the cost of material.

In the afternoon, MC taught a class on child care. The two doctors planned to take turns teaching over the next three days.

Vaughn insisted—with MC's backing—that everyone on the planning committee should share their experiences at evening rallies. Pastor Atwood would moderate. The last presentation would include a question and answer session.

Despite everything the Lord had done to bless the festival, MC still feared interference. Nothing happened on Saturday. The few prostitutes who braved the crowds received warm welcomes.

People flooded the festival on the fourth. Half the women in Denver waited to hear who'd win Olive's services, and the men wanted to try the pie-eating contest. The evening would end with a question and answer presentation involving all of the festival founders.

Before MC entered the hall on Tuesday evening, Belinda

pulled her aside. "Hackett's here, with half a dozen other owners. I expect he wants to intimidate our ladies and keep them from speaking the truth, since the police prevented them from taking direct action."

MC glanced around the curtain that been erected in the hall. The brothel owners filled the front row. Her heart clenched in her chest. Could the police do anything? She looked for Vaughn.

⌒

Vaughn went in search of the police as soon as he saw Hackett arrive. "Can we get them to leave?"

The look on the patrol officer's face gave his answer. "I'm here protecting your right to assemble. They have the same right to assemble as long as they don't disturb the peace."

Vaughn bit back the protest on his tongue. Their very presence disturbed the peace, in his opinion. But silent intimidation wasn't illegal, just immoral.

He said a quick prayer for courage. Not just for the speakers. They had already shown more bravery than some generals he'd seen on the battlefield, and he doubted today would be any different.

In fact, he had come to appreciate the strength it took for women to enjoy the same freedom of movement men enjoyed. Pride coursed through him for his sister's bold spirit.

Most of all, Maia continued to win his admiration. Her desire to help prostitutes went beyond a calling. For some reason he couldn't fathom, she identified with them, and their plight, completely. They wouldn't find a more steadfast advocate.

Pastor Atwood broke into his thoughts by calling everyone to join him in a prayer circle. "You've been an amazing army in this war for the souls of women caught in prostitution. Today is our biggest battle yet. The enemy is prepared to engage in open warfare."

He locked gazes with each of them, one by one. "Let us pray that we will go forth boldly, in the name of the Lord, trusting in His power to move mountains and change hearts."

The pastor's prayer would have left most men shaking in their boots, but would it touch the sin-hardened hearts of the owners?

When they opened the curtains, a few more owners had joined the original group, until they filled the front row. Vaughn reminded himself he wasn't depending on human power. God opened and closed human hearts.

God hardened Pharaoh's heart against Moses. Was that what was happening here? Had God hardened the hearts of these men so that His glory would shine more brightly?

Either way, it would be a harrowing ride.

Before they could walk onto the stage, a messenger arrived from the dormitory and whispered in Delphine's ear. "I'll be back as soon as possible," she said before following him out a side door.

"We'll pray," Pastor Atwood said.

They walked out proudly. The three women together with Maia and Belinda followed the pastor. Vaughn took the last seat, next to Maia.

Vaughn kept himself from staring at the front row. Surely they wouldn't be callous enough. No, forget callous. They wouldn't be foolish enough to harm anyone with so many witnesses around.

Pastor Atwood had closed his eyes in a brief prayer. "Delphine will join us when she returns. I'll get started."

As the pastor greeted their guests, Vaughn allowed his eyes to roam over the audience. Once he unglued his gaze from the front row, he realized how many people had come out, and what a variety they had attracted. He recognized several couples—some had even dared to bring their families—from the church. He also recognized shopkeepers from Auraria. Several had indicated a willingness to hire a girl wishing to make a break from life in the brothel.

Here and there, in recesses where they were almost hidden—as Belinda and Maia had planned—he spotted a few familiar faces from the clinic, women brave enough to risk the brothel owners' ire, and his heart swelled in gratitude.

The pastor finished his remarks, and it was Vaughn's turn. He had once been called charming, and he drew on the graces of the drawing room, almost forgotten in the dregs of war. He spoke of his recent arrival to the clinic and how impressed he was by Asa's and Maia's dedication to their work, and how proud he was to work with them.

Asa chose to remain in the audience because he wasn't involved in the decision to take in Gail and Anna. He completely agreed with their actions, but they all thought it best if he kept a low profile.

Delphine still hadn't made an appearance, although it was her turn to speak. With a glance and a nod, Maia took her place. "Miss Delphine Plante, the headmistress of the orphanage, has been detained. I welcome you in her stead to the Loving Care Home for Children. Delphine began working at the home shortly after she left her work in the cribs, an environment even harsher than the brothels. . ." She told the story simply, but Vaughn could sense the waves of emotion sweeping over the room.

Olive, the seamstress, spoke next. She compared herself to

Dorcas, privileged to make clothes for those who needed them, grateful for the skill to work in a trade.

Gail's fear was palpable. Maia placed her arm around her shoulder and whispered in her ear.

They walked to the podium arm in arm. Gail's steps were steady if slow. She kept her gaze ahead, not seeking the anonymity of the floor. Her hand clung tightly to her prepared speech.

Tension crackled across the room. The police at the exits promised peace. Short of firing a weapon, the owners couldn't touch her, physically. But they could still touch her spirit.

The moment Gail stood at the podium, six men on the front row stood and pulled their chairs to the edge of the stage, where they could ogle her ankles. They didn't speak a word, but the force of their presence could have knocked the glass out of the windows.

Gail didn't flinch. She cleared her throat.

Before she could speak, Hackett raised a whiskey bottle high before smashing it to the floor, and the stench filled Vaughn's nostrils. Someone else poured a cheap perfume; another dropped a cigar. The foul air swept across the hall. Coughs and sneezes erupted, and a dozen handkerchiefs emerged.

Gail continued speaking, but few could hear her.

The police headed for the men responsible. As they placed restraints on Hackett, he said, "You'll never escape the stench. You're tainted for life, all of you."

Vaughn exchanged glances with Maia. She stood and tapped Gail on the shoulder. "If I may say a word?"

Gail nodded and stepped aside.

"Thank you, Gail, for sharing your story. Also, a word of thanks to the police who helped us today."

Light applause broke out.

"Under the circumstances, I believe we will enjoy the rest of the meeting more if we retire to the dining hall to continue," Maia said.

Delphine walked down the aisle as Maia was speaking. "That's not possible." Despair had replaced her confidence. Had the men done something to harm the children?

Surely God wouldn't let that happen.

Delphine stepped up to the platform and used a schoolmarm's voice. "I am sorry to announce we have to cancel the rest of this evening's festivities. Several of our children have come down with the measles. I suggest you all leave immediately and take the necessary precautions."

Chapter 9

By Saturday morning, MC was bone tired. When they weren't taking care of the sick children, they were finishing up festival business—all of it outside of clinic hours. But there was good news. Three of their new patients at the clinic had expressed interest in escaping—"someday."

If they'd hoped for a lull on Saturday morning, they were disappointed. Double the number of usual patients arrived for their clinic. MC recognized women from the festival, ones who had come for several of their classes. Their reputation was spreading.

She began to have hope for the deadline, although it was too soon to tell.

She had intended to part ways with Vaughn and Belinda after the clinic until they discovered they all planned on doing some shopping in the city. They rode together in the carriage to Denver's biggest store.

The women headed for the section for infants and children. "I know that nappies are easy to sew," Belinda said. "But the store-made ones are thicker and have stronger edges, in my experience."

"I agree." MC nodded. "I buy most of Aimee's clothes. I

prefer to spend my time away from work enjoying my daughter, rather than sewing. Of course, that often means doing household tasks together. We especially enjoy cooking."

Aimee grinned. "I'm good at scrambled eggs and biscuits."

"Perhaps you could cook for me sometime." Belinda sighed. "I'm not a very good cook. I wish my mother had taught me."

"I'm cooking tonight—Ma promised." Aimee twirled in excitement. "You and Lizzie and Dr. Vaughn can come if you like."

Maia sensed the hesitation in Belinda, the same she felt. *She knows about Aimee; I know she does.* The thought sent shivers down her spine.

"Of course we'll come," Belinda said.

Aimee stopped in front of a row of baby rattles. Her hands hovered over one painted with delicate pink hearts. It was beautiful, but the girl put it down and reached for a cloth rattle instead.

"I won't betray you, you know," Belinda said in a low voice. "Although I think you should tell him."

Panic seized MC's throat. Instead of words, she hugged her friend.

"What's the special occasion?" Vaughn returned from the men's section where he had gone for socks.

"You're coming to our house for scrambled eggs and biscuits tonight," Aimee told him.

"If that's okay with you," Belinda said.

"I'd like that very much." Vaughn accepted the invitation with grace. "Breakfast for supper is one of my favorite meals."

MC couldn't uninvite him now, could she?

A part of her looked forward to having him as her guest. It had been a long time since she had cooked for a man, even if they were serving breakfast, and her daughter would do most of the cooking. Maia would add her own twist to the meal.

Aimee decided on a pink-and-white gingham rattle that made a cheerful sound. After MC approved her choice, she took it to the teller to pay for it. Belinda also went to make her purchases, leaving MC alone with Vaughn.

"What have you bought for yourself?" he asked cheerfully.

Nothing. "I have no need of anything from this section."

Vaughn studied her closely. "You were going to leave this magnificent establishment without purchasing anything for yourself. I bet you haven't bought anything for yourself in a long time."

She shrugged. "It's a common fault with parents. We spend any spare money on our children."

Sadness passed over his features. "Since I have no children to spend money on, will you allow me to buy something for you? I wish to thank you for your help at the church this morning."

She would be paid for her time, but that wasn't what he meant, and she knew it.

The thought made her uncomfortable. No one had taken her shopping since her husband's death. "There is no need."

She doubted that would stop him.

⌒

Vaughn didn't wait for Maia's permission to buy her something. He guided her in the right direction, afraid she might bolt if he spoke aloud. They had to pass unmentionables on the way.

He found what he was searching for on a lady's vanity. He'd love to see her brush her glorious hair, not that he expected to ever observe it.

"What are you doing?" She held back.

He pulled her forward. "I've seen the brush you use on Aimee's hair. It's a fine, serviceable brush, but it's not the kind my mother liked to use."

His hand roamed over the hairbrushes on display, studying several before choosing one he thought most suitable. "The bristles on this brush should be well suited for nightly hair combing through thick hair on a tender head."

He felt an unexpected urge to stroke her hair but refrained. "With a pretty mother-of-pearl handle to make it pleasant to look upon and to hold. This set provides a brush for both you and your daughter."

Tears brimmed in Maia's pretty brown eyes. "It's a lovely gift. It's completely unnecessary, of course, but I won't dishonor you by refusing it."

By the time he finished paying for his purchase, Belinda and Aimee had returned.

"And this is for you, young lady." Aimee squealed and hugged Vaughn around the middle. "Thanks, Dr. Vaughn."

As he looked into her beautiful eyes, a realization clicked in his mind. Aimee looked nothing like her mother, from her blue eyes and blond hair to her broad nose and dimpled cheeks.

"Aimee's adopted, isn't she?" The words spilled out of his mouth before he could think about their impact.

Deep red ran across Maia's face and neck. "She has been in my care from the moment she entered the world. She has never had another mother."

"Except for the woman who gave her birth," he said.

"Vaughn, stop pestering her." Belinda tucked Aimee's present into Lizzie's basket. "I need to find a quiet corner. Will you come with me, MC?"

Aimee stayed behind with Vaughn. "Can you help me brush my hair? It's such a pretty brush."

He obliged. Her hair was thick and curly, springy to the touch. Maia kept it tangle-free, but Vaughn's mind wandered back to the days when he combed Sara's long hair. For the brief year they'd had together before war called him away, he'd brushed it for her, a hundred strokes every night. A tremor passed through his limbs as he remembered the sweet lovemaking that often followed.

Aimee's hair was a different color than Sara's though, less auburn and more golden. More like his own during a long summer.

If their child had lived, she might look like Aimee.

The thought struck him so abruptly that he sat on top of a nearby barrel.

It couldn't be. Or could it? She was the right age, the right coloring. One question could eliminate the hope springing up in his heart. "Aimee, when is your birthday?"

"April 2. And I'm seven."

She was born in 1864. That meant her life started nine months earlier, in late June or early July of 1863.

"We'll have a spring baby," Sara had told him in the last letter he'd received from her. Thoughts of his child had kept him alive during the long months he had spent in the prisoner of war camp, before the war ended and he could finally make his way home.

By the time he was released from the prison camp, Sara had long since left, headed for Denver, searching for him. His sister had sold the family home and moved away. The few people he knew who remained informed him that Sara had died, and her baby with her.

But if all that was a lie? Possibilities swirled in his head. Wishful thinking made him string coincidences together. He couldn't confront Maia with speculation.

When the ladies returned, Maia repeated her dinner invitation. She looked younger by at least five years. Had the attention he paid to her earlier put that glow in her cheeks? He regretted it now.

"I'm afraid I can't tonight. I've remembered a previous engagement." His answer stopped short of being curt.

Maia looked from him to Aimee and back. What had happened between them? Had he figured out her secret? Maia hid her hurt well, although the bloom faded from her cheeks. "Very well. Instead, Aimee and I will enjoy a matinee while we're in town. If you'd drop us off, we'll find our own way home."

Vaughn found the theater easily, and from there it was a straight shot home.

To his surprise, Belinda remained quiet during the drive. At first he found the silence soothing, but soon her distress became evident. When they came to a complete stop in front of the clinic, he saw tears cascading down her cheeks.

"What's troubling you?"

Her mouth fluttered open and shut, like a baby bird seeking food and not finding it. "Let's get inside. Lizzie needs to nurse."

The baby cried as if on cue. Perhaps his harsh words had stirred her discomfort. "I'm sorry," he whispered to his niece. "You've had a long day."

Even after Belinda settled herself in the drawing room, she struggled to tell him what was troubling her.

"Come now, we've never had secrets from each other."

"You don't know everything." She shook her head. "There's

something I should have told you a long time ago." She drew a deep breath. "It's about Sara."

"Sara?" Tremors passed down Vaughn's arms. "What about Sara?" It took every ounce of his control not to raise his voice.

Belinda sighed and spoke in a low voice. "About the time the war ended, I received a letter from a Maia C. Beachley saying Sara had died. She had written a year earlier, but she sent it to your old address. Someone there sent it to our parents, but they had died. By the time I received it, I was struggling to make it on my own. I was only sixteen, Vaughn. I didn't know if you were alive or dead either, and I decided your child would be better off with the woman who had chosen her out of love. Then when you came home, alive from the dead, I couldn't find a way to tell you."

He had a child? *Maia?* The confusion came out in a single word. "Aimee?"

"Aimee is Sara's child. Your child. I've suspected it ever since I learned MC's name was Maia Cybele, but I only confirmed it today."

"Why didn't you tell me right away?" He had to punch down the anger rising in his heart. "What changed?"

"I—I told Maia I would never betray her secret, and she didn't deny it." More tears threatened. "And what's the first thing I do after I made that promise? I've told you about it."

"You should have told me first!"

Vaughn's anger subsided when he saw how frightened Belinda seemed. He fought to see things from her point of view. "I'm sorry. You were put in an impossible situation."

"I couldn't tell you before. I didn't have any proof. I didn't even have her letter." Belinda choked back a sob. "Please don't make me cry. It will upset Lizzie."

Vaughn stood abruptly. "I can't talk about this now." He touched his niece on the cheek. "You're right. I don't want to upset this child."

He left the house and set off at a brisk pace. Anger surged through him at Belinda's deception, at Maia's deception. He could barely understand how things had happened as they did. But to keep the truth from him, after he returned from the camp? To let him see his daughter day after day, without telling him? Denying a father his right to know his own child?

One other person might know more of the story. *Asa.* Vaughn headed to his friend's house, in spite of his promise to himself that he wouldn't bother the honeymooners. In fact, he had forbidden Asa to take part in the Saturday clinic for another month.

Asa opened the door at his urgent knock. "Welcome to my home!" He peered at Vaughn's face. "Something's troubling you. Come into my drawing room and tell me what's happened."

"What do you know about Maia's daughter?" he asked.

Asa took a long look at his friend. "I think you'd better tell me what's happened."

Vaughn's account of the day's discoveries was shortly told. "When did you first meet Maia?"

Asa shook his head. "Not soon enough to answer your questions. By the time we met and discussed our partnership, Aimee was at least six months old. I knew she was adopted, but nothing about the circumstances. I swear it. I never would have kept it secret from you."

Asa's wife, Sherry, brought out tea and cookies. "If anything, I think this calls for us to praise our God. Who else could have brought you through that horrible war and reunited you with your daughter?"

Asa patted his wife's hand. "That's true. Think of the remarkable string of events that brought the two of you together. God's hand was in it, for sure."

"Or He could have prevented it in the first place." Vaughn wasn't easily convinced. "And you're forgetting the bigger problem. Maia considers Aimee her daughter. She won't let me take over without a fight."

"Is that what you want?" Sherry asked.

"I want my daughter, yes." Conviction stronger than the tensions that had led to war stirred in Vaughn's soul. "I'm afraid she won't want me."

"Oh Vaughn. God already has it worked out," Sherry said. "You'll see."

No wonder Asa loved this woman of rock-solid faith.

When Vaughn made it home that night, he didn't see signs of Gail or Anna. They were probably already asleep, and he wasn't ready to explain the day to anyone. He had to prepare to confront Maia in the morning.

Chapter 10

The day that had started out with such promise had ended in disaster. Even Aimee had felt the pressure, although she didn't complain when Vaughn backed out of their dinner invitation.

Her only complaint was being tired, nothing a good night's sleep couldn't cure. MC settled in for the nightly ritual of brushing Aimee's hair. The sight of the new brushes filled MC with dread. But Aimee would be disappointed if she didn't use them.

MC forced herself to touch the brush, to accept the fact Vaughn had guessed her secret, although she didn't know how.

The brush slid easily through Aimee's hair. "I'm surprised your hair is so soft tonight, after the day we've had."

"Dr. Vaughn brushed it when we were at the store. He has nice hands. We had such a lovely talk."

Fear tightened MC's insides. "What did you talk about?"

"He asked me about my birthday. He's oh so nice, and I can tell he likes you too. Don't you think so?"

Her birthday. That might be how he guessed. Regret soured MC's heart. "He's a very nice man, but not for me."

After Aimee fell asleep, MC wrestled with her problem.

Vaughn was sterling material for a father and a husband. She'd seen it in the way he took care of Belinda when they'd first arrived. He'd impressed her in his dealings with Aimee.

In the way he'd treated her, as well, although that might change now that he knew the truth.

What should she do? If she told him the truth now, she'd lose everything: her beloved child, her job, and the man she had grown to admire.

If she didn't tell the truth, she'd lose all of that as well as her self-respect. She should have told him as soon as she figured it out.

If necessary, she could start over again. She'd done it before. But why did life have to be so hard?

A thunderstorm in her heart kept her awake. God would help her do what she must. A respite of peace followed her acceptance of that ultimate truth, and she was able to catch a few hours of sleep.

She awoke early, her mind set on seeing Vaughn as soon as possible. Her presence at the clinic, which also served as his residence, was rare on a Sunday. He didn't even know where she and Aimee went to church. However, today she would head there before going anywhere else.

Aimee would stay behind. MC prayed that God would help them find a way to tell Aimee the truth, together, that Vaughn would recognize her well-being should take priority.

Before Aimee started school, MC's neighbor, Rosie Danforth, had taken care of her. She still did when there was a need. MC tapped on Rosie's door. "I have an urgent situation that needs my attention this morning."

"I'll be glad to help with Aimee." Rosie reached for her sewing basket. "Let me tell Don, and I'll be right over."

Five minutes later she was at MC's doorstep. "Thank you for coming on such short notice," MC said.

"Nonsense. Babies don't arrive on a schedule."

If Rosie knew the nature of MC's errand, she might not feel so generous.

"If you're not back when she wakes, I'll take her to my place. My children have missed seeing her."

MC apologized for neglecting her friend before she left. If only an apology would solve the problem with Vaughn. Would she ever see the clinic in the same way again? She owned the building for now, but she had come to depend on her team.

The door to the apartment opened to her knock. Sunlight framed Vaughn's silhouette. It put streaks of gold in his hair, just like Aimee's. She hadn't noticed the resemblance before. She swallowed her pain.

"We need to talk," she said.

"I've been expecting you," he said. "Come in."

In an effort to fight her rising panic, MC made note of the changes Belinda had made to the apartment. She was fixing breakfast. "We thought you might come. I made extra."

Vaughn escorted her to the table and drew back a chair. MC didn't think she could eat a bite, but when Belinda insisted, she accepted a spoonful of eggs and a sweet muffin with a cup of steaming hot coffee.

She said a word of prayer with each bite.

Vaughn prayed for God's guidance in his blessing, then cut into his sausage as if nothing had happened. MC forced herself to eat the eggs, but the muffin crumbled dry in her parched throat, and she poured herself a glass of water. "I cannot eat before I speak."

When Vaughn left half his sausage uneaten, MC knew he was no more comfortable with the situation than she was.

"Belinda told me about your letter, but I want to hear it from you. How did you meet Sara?"

His voice was gentler than when they had parted yesterday afternoon, as if he were holding back. She took courage and began her tale.

"Sara had gone to your Nebraska family. As far as they knew, your unit had joined up with troops in Colorado. She came to Denver hoping to find you, or at least to wait for you." MC hesitated. "She mentioned the danger she'd been in in Missouri, with her husband in the Grand Army of the Republic, in a community of Southern sympathizers. She felt Denver was a safer place to wait as her pregnancy advanced. Neither one of us heard what happened to your parents. I'm so sorry."

MC took a deep breath before she added the painful conclusion. "I attended her childbirth. Her search had weakened her, and her impression you had died disheartened her. She only survived childbirth by twelve hours, and she begged me to take care of her daughter after she died."

Memories of that night brought on tears, which she struggled to control. "Aimee was that baby, as you have guessed. I've taken care of her from the hour she was born. When I couldn't locate you or Sara's family, I considered her my daughter."

A thousand emotions flooded Vaughn's mind at her words, primarily gratitude. Thankful for Sara's foresight to leave Missouri before the attack came. Grateful to Maia for taking in their baby instead of turning her over to a children's home. At least his daughter had survived the massacre.

Belinda took up the story. "I was at the pastor's house the night the raiders came. They killed our parents and burned our house." Belinda had paled, but her voice was steady. "The pastor made sure I got to our family in Nebraska, but I lost contact with Sara in the process."

Vaughn closed his mind to the horrors of what might have been. "Whatever frustration I feel, Maia, I will be thankful for the aid you gave my wife and daughter." He looked her straight in the eye. "As difficult as things are right now, as difficult as the situation is."

He spread his hands, trying to pull himself together. "Without your intervention, the lie I was presented with would be truth. My wife and child would both be dead." Angry hurt still rankled in his heart, but he hoped Maia would accept the olive branch.

She shook her head, her agitation increasing with each nod. "I'm not Maia. Not anymore. I may have the name MC for business reasons, but I've become her. And now I've given up any right to softness and kindness when I took your daughter from you. Call me MC."

Had she not heard a word he'd said? "Maia suits you. I've thought of you as Maia ever since I first heard your name." He offered a small smile. "You'll always be Maia to me."

She didn't repeat her protest. "Do you have any other questions?"

"I want to know everything. Denver's a fair-sized city, and Auraria's outside of town. How did you meet Sara?"

Maia flushed. "I'd rather not say."

Tension built in his arms and shoulders when she avoided his question.

Belinda spoke next. "Asa's mother mentioned you worked as a midwife in the red light district before you opened the clinic. Is that where you met Sara? In the brothels?"

Maia refused to meet his eyes when she nodded.

"Sara would never!" Vaughn exploded.

Half a minute ticked by before Maia spoke again. When at last she lifted her head, her eyes snapped with fire. "You're right. She never did what you are suggesting, but she was desperate to find you. She thought you might have gone there, because you had in the past, before your marriage. You had confessed it to her."

"Will I never be rid of one foolish, youthful mistake? Sin, to call it by the right name?" Vaughn sank against the chair back, stunned and ashamed. "I repented and never repeated my transgression."

"Desperation took her there." Maia paused. "By the time I met her, her time was approaching. I offered her shelter while she continued her search, and my services when needed."

Belinda laughed, and Vaughn snapped his head up, ready to growl.

"You look just like a child with his hand caught in the cookie jar." His sister's smile dimmed a sparkle at his frown. "We're both women of the world. I'm sure Maia thinks no less of you than I do. You were a young man sowing his wild oats."

Maia nodded in agreement, and Vaughn struggled to let go of the guilt. "That's how she met you and why you were with her when she gave birth."

Belinda stood. "I need to take care of Lizzie. Be nice to each other."

Maia's face creased with grief again. "It is always difficult to lose a mother in childbirth. Doubly so with Sara. We had become close friends. When she knew her time was short, she pressed her personal possessions on me, including the only address she had for you and your family. I was glad to give her peace by agreeing to help."

She turned her head aside, as if unwilling to share her grief—or perhaps she didn't want to see his.

"I never should have left her," he groaned.

Maia's head shot up. "Never say that. She never once blamed you. You were fighting to heal the bad blood between brothers across this nation, to bring an end to an evil in our country, to find peace at last. You were her shining hero who could do no wrong."

If Vaughn had known of Sara's death while he was in the prisoner of war camp, he would have given up and died. Her belief in him had kept him going.

A small part of him blamed Maia for his wife's death. But no. He should praise her for her big heart, taking in his child when she had no one.

But God help him, he couldn't, not yet, in spite of his own experiences of watching patients die. Her story brought back the grief he thought he had set aside years ago.

Maia's eyes, frightened yet hopeful, reminded him of Sara. He put his hands in front of his face. "I know I'm wrong, but my heart sees you as the woman who killed my wife and stole my child." He heaved a sob. "Time—and God—will have to heal this wound. I know I'm not thinking straight."

Maia straightened her shoulders. "I shall not bother you in your apartment again. But this building belongs to me, as you well know. I can and must return to do my work. Speaking of which. Is Gail here?"

"No, we haven't seen her—"

"Make no mistake. Aimee is my daughter in every way that matters." She stood. "I'll be on my way after I see Gail."

Two minutes later, she returned to the kitchen. "Gail's drunk. I've never seen her this bad. A long, slow form of suicide."

Belinda paced down the hall, seeking to keep Lizzie at peace with the tension around her. She had just caught the news about Gail. "She didn't get the job she offered for this morning. I didn't know she'd take it to heart."

The noon hour approached, and Vaughn knew Maia was anxious to get home. "Why don't you go on home. If you want, you might come back later this afternoon to check on Gail."

"Very well." She grabbed her coat and prepared to leave, but when she put her hand on the doorknob, someone knocked.

She peeked through the windowpane. "It's Jimmy, my neighbor's son. She's been taking care of Aimee this morning." Maia opened the door, Vaughn half a step behind. She asked, "What is it? Has something happened?"

"What's wrong, boy?" Vaughn said as the urchin slipped farther away from him and crept closer to Maia.

"Aimee's got those measles spots, and Ma thinks Mrs. Brownstone had best come."

Oh, what change a few words made. When Aimee hadn't gotten sick at the same time as the orphanage children, Vaughn had hoped she'd be spared.

He had been prepared to send Maia home and stay with Gail by himself. Not now. He could not, he would not, be left out of his daughter's care when there was a need.

Maia took a step down, then stopped. Her shoulders drooped as she turned to look at him. "One of us should stay with Gail."

He prepared to protest, but she had climbed back one step.

"Because of the situation, because Aimee might need a doctor, and you're the best doctor I know." She coughed. "For that reason, I will stay here while you go with Jimmy. I can easily attend to Gail's needs, but Aimee might need your expertise more." Her shoulders shook. "God help me if anything happens to her and I'm not there."

What sacrifice lay behind those words.

"Go on! She needs you now."

He grabbed the supplies he needed from the office and followed Jimmy onto the street. In his eagerness, he lengthened his strides, and the boy trotted to keep pace. Vaughn quizzed him about Aimee's illness. What did the red spots look like? Had he seen anything inside her cheeks? Of course not, he wasn't looking in her mouth. When did they first appear?

The questions poured out faster than Jimmy could answer. He stopped running, puffing in between answers. "I don't know no more, Doctor. Can't you wait till we get there?"

Vaughn bit back the impatience he felt. "I'm sorry. I was rushing. I'm worried about Aimee, you see."

The kid grinned. "We're only three blocks away now. See you there!"

He sprinted away in the direction of Maia's house. Vaughn followed, his legs taking long strides, eating up the yards. The boy went to the house next to Maia's.

A woman about Belinda's age stood in the doorway. "Are you

the doctor?" She didn't let him in immediately.

"Mrs. Brownstone asked me to come in her place. There's a sick woman at the office."

"Come in, then. I'm Mrs. Danforth." The puzzled look on her face told Vaughn she couldn't understand why Maia had sent the doctor instead of coming herself.

He wasn't going to enlighten her. "Where is Aimee?"

Mrs. Danforth tilted her head. "Upstairs." She led him up the steps. "I've been giving her plenty to drink and applying cold compresses. Aimee says the light's bothering her, although her bed is away from the window."

She stood in front of the door, a scowl on her face. "Do you know when Mrs. Brownstone will be coming?"

He'd had enough. "You don't know me, Mrs. Danforth, but there's a lot going on here that you know nothing about. I care for Aimee as if"—he forced himself to add those words—"she was my own. Mrs. Brownstone knows this, and asked me to come, because I know more about cures for childhood diseases than she does."

Mrs. Danforth's mouth fell open and closed without saying anything.

Before Vaughn went into Aimee's room, he spoke with Jimmy. "If you'll stay nearby so I can send word back to Mrs. Brownstone, there's a dime in it for you."

"Yes, sir." The boy plopped down on the floor beside the door and prepared to wait.

His mother followed Vaughn into the bedroom. She'd laid Aimee on a bed in a quiet corner. Aimee was restless. Her breathing was labored, and those hideous red dots covered her wherever he could see. She also appeared to be running a fever.

His thoughts ran rampant while he checked her over. Had taking her to the clinic yesterday—was it only yesterday?—exposed her to a virulent illness? Nonsense. She was in contact with the disease at the orphanage, during the festival. They just thought the danger period had passed.

How things had changed with the knowledge Aimee was his daughter. If she belonged to someone else, he knew exactly what he would do. But knowing that his child's life lay in his own hands made him question every move, every decision. And Maia trusted him to take care of her in her place.

He'd never known what a difference being a parent could make.

Chapter 11

MC grew restless as the day dragged on. Belinda did more good for Gail than she did. When MC brought in broth, Gail was sobbing in Belinda's arms.

How would Vaughn handle all the tears? Would he think they threatened the return of morbid thoughts? Or would he realize tears helped Gail let go of her loss and face her future, one teardrop at a time?

MC stayed at the office because she'd promised she would. As the hours crept by, she became convinced Gail hadn't suffered any lasting harm from the previous night. The less she worried about Gail, the more MC worried about her daughter.

Their daughter, she reminded herself. If Aimee was too ill for Vaughn to leave her side, then MC should be there. She was wasting her time with a patient whom Belinda was nursing better than she could.

At five o'clock, MC fixed a simple meal of seasoned beans with chunks of corn bread. Gail accepted a small portion. After they ate, she checked the girl's physical condition—it had returned to normal. She decided to head home as soon as she finished with the dishes.

Someone knocked on the door. When she saw Jimmy Danforth standing outside, she told Belinda, "I need to leave. Gail is stable for now."

"Oh yes." Belinda smiled. Helping the girl had revived her spirits as well. "I pray everything is well with Aimee."

MC saddled up the clinic's second horse. Thoughts of reaching Aimee as soon as possible pounded in her chest.

"I'll see you at the house," she told Jimmy, and took off.

He called after her, but noises from the street made it impossible to hear his words.

Five minutes later she was at the Danforth home. Surprise blossomed on Rosie's face. "The doctor's not here. Didn't Jim tell you?"

"He tried to, but I was in a hurry. Where is he? Where's my Aimee?" MC's temples pulsed with an urgency to see her daughter.

"He said something about a house," Rosie ventured. "He took Aimee and left in a bit of a rush, and I wasn't paying as close attention as I should."

MC clamped her mouth shut to avoid accusing her friend of not keeping Aimee in her house. But Rosie had no way of knowing the worries flooding MC's heart. Vaughn had taken off with his daughter, and she didn't know where they had gone.

He couldn't have meant his house, because she would have seen him on the way. Besides, why would he send Jimmy if he was coming himself?

She looked out the window at her home, where she longed to be. Oh, for an ordinary Sunday, when she would spend long hours with her daughter! Tears blurred her eyes as she looked at the house she'd purchased as a home for the two of them. It was as worthless as a shack if she lived there alone.

Lights swam before her eyes. She brushed away her tears, but the lights still bothered her.

The lights came from her house.

Of course!

What a fool she was. "I'm going home," she told Rosie.

"I'll be praying," her friend said.

MC led the horse to her stable and entered the house by the back door. Meaty smells came from the kitchen. Through the grate in the ceiling, she heard Vaughn's deep voice. "I was a very good friend of the woman who gave birth to you. I happen to know she was very excited about her baby. She was hoping for a girl, you know."

Was he telling Aimee the story without her being there? MC dashed upstairs. Vaughn met her at the door to Aimee's room. "Be quiet now, or she'll wake up. I just got her to eat a bite of your fine mutton stew. Sleep is the best thing for her right now."

Had he been speaking to a sleeping child? MC glared at him but tiptoed into the room.

The battle waged against the illness was evident. Measles peppered Aimee's skin like a pincushion. Her hair hung in clumps around her shoulders and her bedclothes were twisted. MC took comfort from the gentle rhythm of her breathing.

MC sank into her chair with relief. Aimee lived. She kissed her daughter on her forehead before placing a small soft rag doll in her arms.

Minutes ticked by while Aimee slept. Vaughn's snore betrayed his exhaustion. MC removed her shoes, shifted Aimee gently to one side, and climbed into bed beside her.

When next she awoke, darkness ruled the night. Vaughn no

longer sat in the doorway, but his bag remained.

Consternation coursed through her veins. Of course Vaughn wanted to continue the vigil until he knew his daughter was well. Neither one of them would leave, no matter how many women went into labor, unless Dr. Asa was overwhelmed.

Aimee shifted restlessly in her sleep and sweat soaked her nightdress. MC's dress was also dampened, but that could wait. The first order of business was to cool down Aimee.

MC lit the candle next to the bed and checked the water basin. It was full, the water gently cool. Vaughn must have refilled it when he awoke. He would make a good nurse. Her lips curved at the thought.

⌒

Vaughn heard the movement overhead from the spot he had found to sleep in the library.

Aimee. His muscles sprang to attention, ready to dash upstairs before he remembered Maia was already there, in the bed with his daughter.

After the past twenty-four hours, he knew two things beyond a doubt. He cared deeply for his daughter, the child of his body. And Maia cared just as deeply for the child she'd claimed as her own for seven years.

They would both fight for the privilege of keeping her. Vaughn recognized Maia's claim, but he would not give in. His place took precedence.

The noises didn't settle down, and Vaughn grew concerned for Aimee. He reached for his bag, then remembered he had left it upstairs.

He climbed the steps slowly, making small noises as he moved, to warn Maia of his approach.

When he knocked on the door, she whirled around. Instead of anger, he saw worry, and he crossed the floor to Aimee's side in two long steps. Maia had changed Aimee's nightgown and had placed a cool cloth on her forehead.

Her breathing had grown ragged. Vaughn took out his stethoscope. The slow crackle of fluids in her lungs concerned him.

When he looked at Maia closely, he recognized her disheveled state. She was as damp as Aimee's discarded clothes and, frankly, smelled a little dank. "Maia, you must take care of yourself. You'll do Aimee no good if you get sick."

She glanced at her own soaked dress, colored, and clutched her arms around her as if to ward off disease. "I'll go change," she said.

"And bathe yourself," he said. "You know the precautions you need to take." He heard the harshness in his voice and added, "Our daughter needs both of us."

Her eyes opened wide at his use of "our," but she didn't protest. He wasn't sure why he had used it. It slipped out naturally.

He placed another pillow beneath Aimee's head. He had the makings in his bag for a compression for her chest, and warm tea might open her nasal passages and get air to her lungs. The willow bark would also aid in lowering her persistent fever. He headed down to the kitchen.

Maia returned before he did. She saw the items in his hands, including the pitcher with steam rising from the top. "Hot water?" she asked.

"For her chest," he explained.

She nodded. "I'll give her the tea. I suggest you take a bath yourself." She blushed slightly. "I laid out a suit for you in my bedroom. It belonged to my husband, but I think it'll work in an emergency."

It did fit, just barely. Maia's husband must have been a little shorter and rounder than Vaughn was. After he cinched up the slacks with a belt, the cuffs rode above his ankles. They didn't fit well enough for a wedding or funeral, but they were more than suitable for today's need.

Maia was a good mother, despite his initial misgivings when he'd seen Aimee at the clinic that first day. Last night he had checked out the house, telling himself he had the responsibility to see the circumstances in which his daughter had been raised.

The house sang of warmth and love. The furnishings, some used, some new, all welcomed a child, a friend, a confidante. The library held Shakespeare's works, early American classics from Cooper, Hawthorne, Thoreau, and Emerson, as well as recent best sellers like *Uncle Tom's Cabin* and *Little Women*. He also spotted numerous books on midwifery and childbirth, as well as several well-thumbed books of devotions and prayers.

In the drawing room, a hymnbook sat on an upright piano, suggesting Maia had a passing knowledge of the instrument. He saw a well-stocked sewing basket in the corner. He found the greatest varieties of delights in Aimee's room. They weren't extravagant—the child wasn't spoiled—but from child-sized journals to picture books to dolls to a planter by her windowsill, Aimee was encouraged to explore, have fun, and learn.

Given the alternative of his daughter growing up in Delphine's orphanage or growing up as Maia's daughter, Maia had been a heaven-sent angel.

But in spite of appreciating everything Maia had done, he

couldn't forgive her for keeping Aimee's identity a secret from him for so long. It was his right to know his daughter. But above all, it was Aimee's right to know her parents.

For that matter, why hadn't Belinda told him his child lived, when at last he came home? Even worse, she had kept his relationship with Aimee a secret, even after she guessed the truth.

It still wasn't the time to deal with his questions. Aimee had survived the night, but she was far from well.

He sat in front of Maia's vanity. Hair caught in the bristles of the new brush set attested to its use. He pulled a few strands of Aimee's golden hair from the brush, chiding himself for the whimsy as he did so.

He used a different comb to run over his own hair, loosening a few strands so like Aimee's. He had done his best. He returned to his daughter's bedroom.

Chapter 12

MC couldn't help comparing Vaughn's appearance with that of her first husband. The love of her youth welcomed everyone with his smile, a father figure who had appealed to her younger self. She had prospered under his gentle tutelage while he prepared her to live without him, as if he sensed he would die before his time.

If he had lived, they would have changed together. Losing him had made her who she was now.

Vaughn was a different sort of man, more assertive and direct. Whatever differences she had with Vaughn, he cut a fine figure of a man. Like her husband, he preferred agreement over dictatorship, although he was decisive when the need called for it.

Something subtle had altered over the past twenty-four hours. Vaughn had taken root in this house, in Aimee's life. Once planted, he would be impossible to uproot. Step by step, she'd acted in Aimee's best interests, and now she had to face the consequences of her actions.

Her daughter's health improved throughout the day. Medically speaking, she didn't need the presence of both a nurse and a doctor.

MC had to speak her mind.

She fixed a simple meal of beans and called Vaughn to supper. Nothing fancy, but plain food filled the body and often was healthier. Vaughn ate without comment or complaint.

When they finished, she suggested they pray. They both asked for Aimee's healing, but neither one of them asked for God's guidance about the future.

"Aimee is much better, don't you think?" MC asked brightly.

"Thank the Lord." Vaughn started to get up from the table.

"Sit down."

It worked like a charm with children. Not so easily with grown men, but he responded to the steel in her tone just the same.

She drew a deep breath. "There is no need for both of us to remain here today. If Aimee takes a turn for the worse, I will, of course, send word."

He didn't blink. "Or I could stay, and you could go."

He wanted to fight. She'd expected as much.

"That's not proper. We've exceeded the bounds of propriety as is. Especially since there is no need today. People are waiting for you at the clinic."

"Let them wait. There is every need for me to be here. I will not abandon my daughter when she is recovering. If you say it's improper for me to stay here, then so be it. I'll take her with me. She'll be comfortable enough at the clinic."

He headed for the staircase.

MC blocked the bottom step, the swirls of her skirt filling the stairwell. "She doesn't need a clinic. She needs to be surrounded by her own things in her own home!"

The mouser MC kept around the house meowed loudly and

disappeared under a chair. Upstairs Aimee began crying. MC turned on her heels and dashed up the stairs, Vaughn a step behind her.

Aimee was wide awake. "I heard you shouting and I woke up. Why are you arguing? Did I do something wrong?"

MC put her arms around her daughter, as if her physical presence could protect her from the coming revelations.

Vaughn claimed the foot of the bed, announcing his right to be part of this conference.

"What's going on?" Aimee's voice rose into a wail as she grew agitated in MC's arms. Gentle rocking didn't calm her as it usually did.

"We'd better explain," Vaughn said. "If you don't, I will. Before she makes herself ill again."

He was right. "Let me get something. Promise me you won't move?"

He sat in a chair. "I'm not going anywhere."

She went to the library, where she had last left the box with Aimee's history, and brought it to her daughter's room.

She addressed Vaughn first. "Aimee knows some of the story. Please let me explain what's happened my way. I promise to speak nothing but the truth."

Aimee looked from one to the other in puzzlement.

When he didn't answer right away, MC spoke again. "You'll have your chance to speak. But let me go first."

When he nodded, she turned her full attention to their daughter.

"I thought you would be a little older when I shared this with you." She held the box tight in her hands. "You know that you're my own special girl, the best of all God's wonderful gifts He's given to me."

"I know I'm 'dopted. You told me when I asked you why my eyes were blue and yours were brown. You said I had my mother's eyes."

"That's right. And I told you we're alike on the inside, where it counts. That God made us a family."

"Like God 'dopts us into His family," Aimee said. "Because He loves us so."

"Yes. Your mama asked me to look after you when she died. I was sad, but I was happy too. I had my own little girl to love and care for. But now the time has come for you to see this."

"This is a picture of your mother." She opened the locket, keeping her thumb over Vaughn's image. "She was beautiful, like you. Her name before she got married was Sara Amanda Haden. And she fell in love with a handsome young farmer."

"My daddy!" Aimee squealed. "But he died in the war, before I was born." She looked at MC's box. "Do you have a picture of my daddy too?"

Proceed with caution. "Before I show you his picture, let me tell you a little more about his story." She closed the locket so Aimee couldn't see it yet. "It's a sad story. That's why I've waited so long to tell you."

"Of course it's sad. He died." Aimee crossed her arms. "I'm ready."

"Some things are worse than death." The words, coming from Vaughn, startled MC. His eyes begged him to let him tell his story his own way. It was his right.

"Aimee, I—knew your father." Vaughn's throat tightened as he said the words. "He fought with many brave men in several battles. He watched men die. He saw good nurses, like your mother, help others. But he lived, and he dreamed of the day he could go home to Missouri, to his Sara and to their baby."

Vaughn fought to hold back tears. When he was sure his voice was steady, he continued. "But then one day the enemy—"

"Johnny Reb."

Vaughn choked back a laugh at Aimee's choice of words, but he'd heard them called worse. "Johnny Reb captured him and took him a prisoner for over a year, until the war ended."

"April 9, 1865."

"That's right. You were a year old by then. He was so sick and weak, the Grand Army of the Republic took him to a hospital. He made a friend while he was there. You know him."

Aimee's forehead furrowed. "You?" she asked doubtfully.

Vaughn shook his head, biting back the words.

"Dr. Asa?" Maia suggested.

"That's right. Dr. Asa helped him get well. All he wanted to do was to get home to his dear Sara and their child. He left the hospital in June and rushed home to Missouri."

"But Mama was dead. In Denver."

"He didn't know that yet. Not until he went home and learned his parents were dead. Some very bad men—not Johnny Rebs, but outlaws who thought they were fighting for them—had killed them both. Only his sister escaped. She told him your mother had died giving birth, and that her baby also died."

He couldn't bring himself to say the final words, to finish the story. *I'm your father.*

Aimee shook her head. "That is very, very sad." She pushed against the bed. "But it's not true. I'm alive."

"He had no way of knowing that." Tears clogged his throat, and he coughed. "He didn't want to be a farmer anymore, so he went to medical school and tried to forget about his wife and their baby. But he never could forget them, not for a single day."

Maia held Aimee in her arms. A heartbeat passed, five. When Vaughn didn't continue speaking, Maia said, "Dr. Vaughn's story has a happy ending. Aimee, I have a picture of your father. Take a look." She held out the open locket.

Aimee frowned. "But that's not my father. That's Dr. Vaughn."

He knelt on the opposite side of the bed and reached for her hands. "Yes, that's true. Both things are true. I married the most wonderful woman in the world and our daughter is just like her."

Aimee looked at him, at Maia, and back at Vaughn. "You're my father?"

"I am!" His arms slid around her shoulders, and he felt her weight shift to himself, although she didn't let go of Maia.

"I promise you, I never stopped loving you. Every time I helped a baby into the world, I wondered if they were anything like my own child—not knowing I met you the day I arrived in Denver."

"Now I have a father and a mother." Aimee's smile quickly reverted to a frown. "Why were you arguing?"

Vaughn arm's tightened just the slightest bit around Aimee. Now that he'd found her, against all hope and possibility, he knew one thing for certain. He'd never let her go.

He felt an equal pressure from the other side. Maia would fight for her daughter with the fierceness of a mountain bear.

"Your father thought you should go to the clinic until you're all better. I told him that's not necessary. You can stay right here at home and he can visit you every day." Maia's words held no anger, but she wouldn't change her mind.

"And I want you with me so I can be sure you're getting better. I can't see you from the clinic, can I?" He was skirting the true question—what would happen once Aimee was better?

He saw Maia clinging to Aimee, but didn't realize his own grip on her arm was tightening until Aimee cried out in pain.

Vaughn let go first, and Maia laid their daughter against the bed, where she thrashed from side to side, looking daggers at both parents.

"Leave," she said. "I don't want to see you right now."

"We can't leave you alone," Maia said.

Both adults had moved inches back from the bed.

"I'm scared of both of you. Leave me alone." Hysteria scratched Aimee's voice.

Guilt paralyzed Vaughn. Someone had to stay with Aimee. He looked to Maia for help.

Fear, hurt, and pain stampeded across her face in successive order, each one leaving her more irresolute than before. An eternity passed—it might have been ninety seconds—before the backbone returned. "Very well. I will leave, but you cannot be alone. Your father will stay."

She paused at the door, looked over her shoulder. "I love you with all my heart. Always remember that." She shut the door softly behind her.

Aimee regarded Vaughn with stormy blue eyes. "Aren't you leaving too?"

Oh, for water to help unglue his tongue from the top of his fear-parched throat! He swallowed hard instead. "You're too young to be left alone. But I'll go sit by the door after you do two things for me."

She eyed him suspiciously.

"Drink some water." He'd rather give her broth, but right now he needed to build her trust.

"That's easy."

He placed his elbows on his knees and leaned forward so he could speak with her eye to eye. "And promise me you'll never, ever, talk to your mother like that again."

Aimee sipped the water. Slowly her face returned to its normal color. In a small voice, she said, "Does she still love me? Does she still want to be my mother?"

What had prompted that question? "She'll love you forever. But you hurt her badly. You should say you're sorry when you see her again."

He kissed her cheek and stood to go to the door, as he had promised.

"You can stay, if you want."

"I will, if you promise to rest."

She rolled on her side and closed her eyes. One eyelid popped open. "You know, if you married Ma, you wouldn't have to worry about where I would live." She closed her eye and fell asleep.

Chapter 13

Marry Maia. Aimee had put into words a notion that had been brewing in Vaughn's mind for the past several days. Marriage was the simplest answer, and the best thing for Aimee, bringing her parents together in one family. But was that enough to build a marriage on? Could he imagine spending the rest of his life with Maia at his side—perhaps even having children together?

He studied Aimee on the bed. She looked like Sara, and she had her same sweet spirit. But her comportment reflected the woman who raised her. She was fearless and outgoing, smart and compassionate.

The same qualities he admired in Maia. Things he. . .yes, he would admit it to himself. . .things he loved about her. Things he wished to protect and nurture.

Aimee's suggestion wasn't just a good idea. It was the best idea, and what he wanted. But how would Maia feel about it, especially after this morning? He never should have threatened to take Aimee to the clinic.

He checked Aimee again to make sure she was breathing easily, then slipped downstairs. Maia met him at the bottom of the stairs.

"You stayed." He wasn't surprised.

"I couldn't leave." She shrugged. "If any harm should come to Aimee because of our argument—"

"Shh. She's doing fine."

Worry traveled across Maia's features. "I'm glad to hear it. While I've been waiting, I had a most ingenious idea."

Was she about to propose marriage to him?

"Come into the drawing room with me." She tugged on his hand, and he followed willingly. "It answers both your desire for constant access to Aimee and our need for an alternative clinic site if we fail to raise the necessary funds." She flashed a smile at him, lighter in spirit than he had seen her in days.

Curiouser and curiouser. He followed her down the hall to the front of the house, where the library sat on one side and the drawing room on the other. She pointed out the two doors in the drawing room, which opened to smaller rooms.

"The pantry is through that wall." Maia nodded in the other direction. "It would be easy enough to build a connecting door. It would be a good place to house medical supplies."

Vaughn shook his head. "Why would you want to do that?"

"If we lose our current location—if we haven't raised enough money—we can move the clinic to my house. The house is in my name. Hackett can't touch it. Of course, we'd need to find new housing for you and Belinda, but that wouldn't be as hard as finding another location for the clinic."

She smiled widely, as if she had found the perfect solution. "And you'd be here every day, and able to see Aimee whenever you liked."

Vaughn mentally scratched his head. Maia's solution would

allow them to leave things at the current status quo. But he wanted more than that. It was time to swallow his pride and fear and expose his heart.

"I like your creativity, but I prefer my solution." They settled on a brocaded armchair and settee in the drawing room.

"And what is that?" she asked with good humor.

His heart hammered in his chest. "A small tweak to your proposal. I was waiting until this morning to mention it to you." He was making it sound like a business deal, and Maia deserved romance.

He shook his head. "What I'm trying to say is, what's happened these last few days has caused me to do some soul-searching."

It still wasn't coming out right.

"Maia Cybele Brownstone."

She fidgeted at his use of her complete name.

"Our daughter suggested it first. I've given it some thought, and I couldn't agree more."

"Aimee is good at solving problems." Maia smiled indulgently.

"She said we should get married. That way, we'd all be in the same house. We can adapt the first floor for a clinic, but understand this: I want to marry you even if we have to live in a tent on the open prairie."

Maia's hand was at her throat, and she sank back against the settee cushion.

He had left out the most important part. He slid out of the armchair onto his knees. "But I'm not asking for your hand in marriage because of Aimee, or because of the clinic. I'm asking you because I admire you. Because I appreciate you, and yes, I have come to love you over these past months." His mouth twisted in a crooked grin. "Part of what I love about Aimee is how much she's like her mother."

Maia made a small choking sound. "I'm nothing like your Sara."

Vaughn wrapped his hands around hers. "I don't mean Sara. I mean you, Aimee's mother. Besides, I don't want another Sara. She was the love of my youth, but I'm a different man. I want you, Maia Cybele Brownstone. A hardworking woman with high ideals and plenty of compassion. A woman who will raise our children to be kind to strangers. A woman who keeps her head in an emergency. A woman who was willing to sacrifice what she valued most for what was best. When you left Aimee in my care."

His fingers clung to hers, and he felt the cold metal of her wedding ring. "I may not measure up to your first husband, but I pledge myself to you with everything I am and have."

Maia laughed and cried, but she left her hands in his.

"Answer me, please." Her silence left him in agonizing doubt.

Maia removed one of her hands from his and wiped away her tears. Keeping her eyes fixed on his, she slowly, deliberately removed her wedding ring from her ring finger. "Graham was a wonderful man. But like you, I've changed. He wouldn't approve of the work I've undertaken, but you see the value in it." Her voice wavered a little. "You make me feel important."

"You are. I d–do." He stammered to a finish. "Does that mean you'll have me?" He wanted to climb to the top of Lookout Mountain and shout it to all of Denver.

❦

Maia couldn't believe what she was hearing. Only hours had passed since they had shared ultimatums. Now he was proposing?

He was suggesting the solution she hadn't dared to dream of. Her heart catapulted in her chest, spreading delight through her body.

When she felt able to speak, she said, "A few hours ago, my heart was breaking. I was worried about Aimee, yes. But I was also heartsick because I had lost your esteem and goodwill. That hurt more than I thought possible."

She looked at the ring she had taken off her finger. "This ring represents a past that no longer fits who I am today." She set it on the lamp table. "Vaughn, you do me the greatest honor in the world. Yes, I accept, and not only because of Aimee."

He took her hand again and together they stood to their feet. "I'm sorry, I don't have a ring. A fact I intend to remedy at my earliest convenience."

"I have a better idea," Maia said, not believing her daring. "If you want to make our engagement official, why not do it the old-fashioned way? Seal it with a kiss."

"Nothing would please me more." He leaned in, his mouth gently brushing hers, then meeting with an intensity that shook them both. When they broke the kiss, he put his hands on her shoulders. "Officially sealed. Shall we go tell our daughter that we took her advice?"

"Yes." She released his hands and ran for the stairs, Vaughn on her heels.

"We're going to wake her up." He laughed when they reached the top of the stairs.

"Let's." Maia felt giddy with relief. "Seeing us together might cure her illness overnight."

"Ma? Pa?"

Aimee stood in the doorway to her room, holding her doll, puzzlement written on her face.

"I took your advice," Vaughn said. "I asked this wonderful woman who is your mother to be my wife."

"Hurrah!" Aimee looked at her mother, waiting for her response.

"And I said yes." Maia and Vaughn moved as one, lifting their daughter so she was cradled between them.

Aimee put her arms on their shoulders and looked from one to the other. The pink in her cheeks came from happiness, not fever, and her joy was contagious. "I've wanted a father all my life, and now I'll have one." She kissed Maia on her cheek first, then Vaughn. "When are you getting married? So Pa can move in here?"

"What do you say, Maia?" Vaughn asked. "I want you to be my wife so we can face Hackett as one on August 1. Could we be married next week?"

"I should say that's too soon." Maia giggled. "But next week sounds perfect."

"After church on Sunday."

"I'll be counting every minute," Maia said in a low whisper.

Aimee hugged them both around their necks, a twenty-four-carat smile on her face. "We'll be the best family ever."

Bestselling author **Darlene Franklin**'s greatest claim to fame is that she writes full-time from a nursing home. She lives in Oklahoma, near her son and his family, and continues her interests in playing the piano and singing, books, good fellowship, and reality TV in addition to writing. She is an active member of Oklahoma City Christian Fiction Writers, American Christian Fiction Writers, and the Christian Authors Network. She has written over fifty books and more than 250 devotionals. Her historical fiction ranges from the Revolutionary War to World War II, from Texas to Vermont. You can find Darlene online at: facebook.com/darlene.franklin.3

If Not for Grace

by Patty Smith Hall

Dedication

To my brother, Glen Darby,
and my sister, Rosalind.
I love being your big sister.

Dear Friends,
  I hope you enjoy Grace and Patrick's story in If Not for Grace. When I started writing this novella, I didn't know it would take me to some dark places. But as Grace and Patrick learn, only in darkness can one truly appreciate the Light.
  I'd love to hear from you. Visit me at https://www.facebook.com/authorpattysmithhall.

Blessings,
Patty

Prologue

Park Avenue, New York City
Spring 1885

Candlelight glittered off the crystal sconces, casting the ball-room in a luminous glow. Stringed musicians filled the air with music, the fashionably dressed dancers circling the room in a romantic waltz. In the corner nearest the gardens, a line of New York's society waited to greet their host and hostess. Grace pressed her face between the wrought iron posts of the staircase. "Isn't Mama the most beautiful lady at the ball?"

Matilda Stephenson—Tilly—snorted beside her. "My mother is just as pretty as yours, Grace Sullivan, and she's graceful too." Leaning back, she looked at Grace. "Did you know she's second cousin to the Earl of Sandringham?"

"Yes, Tilly, you tell me that every time there's a ball." Grace continued watching the dancers. "Then can we agree that my mother is the most beautiful lady giving a ball?"

Tilly nodded. "So it's agreed. Our mothers are the most beautiful ladies here."

The gals giggled, then instantly went still when Grace's nanny gave them the eye.

"We'll have to be quiet or Old Parker will make us go to the nursery with the children," Grace whispered.

"Really, Grace. Why do you still have a nanny?" Tilly rolled her eyes heavenward. "It's embarrassing. We'll be fourteen on our next birthday."

Grace couldn't tell her the truth, that she didn't mind having a nanny. She worried where the crotchety old nanny would go if Papa let her go. Despite her nanny's stern personality, Grace had a soft spot for the woman who'd cared for her almost since birth. Still, if she wanted to watch the evening's festivities, she'd have to be quiet.

She turned her attention back to the dancers. "I can't wait until my first ball. Mama says I'm to have a dance teacher later this spring."

"Why? It's just a bunch of circling around and stuff," a decidedly male voice croaked.

Turning from her view of the ballroom, Grace rose as Patrick Mosby walked toward them. Recently, an awkward tension had hung between the two of them, but she hoped to smooth things out tonight. After all, he was her dearest friend in the world.

"What would you know about dancing?" Tilly asked, straightening her dress as she stood.

"Ma is forcing me to take lessons." He smirked as if the idea of promenading around the floor was worse than death. "Not that I'm ever going to use them."

"I won't marry a man who doesn't know how to dance," Grace said as they moved farther down the hall, away from Nanny Parker's prying eyes. "I haven't done it much, but I'm certain I'll enjoy it."

"Won't you need to know how when you decide it's time to marry?" Tilly asked Patrick.

"I have no intention of marrying."

Grace burst out laughing, which drew another sharp look from Nanny. "I thought you said you were going to marry me."

Tilly's gaze snapped between the two of them. "When was this decided?"

Patrick shook his head. "After I almost got her killed sliding down the staircase. But we were children then." He glanced at Grace. "You survived."

"It was just a deathbed promise to you? I should be rude and hold you to it, but I won't." Grace gave him a gentle push. "What are you going to do, all by yourself?"

"Go west. My grandfather has a silver mine in Colorado. Maybe I'll go work for him for a while." Patrick glanced toward the crowded ballroom. "Anything but what my father does."

Grace understood. Over the past year, Patrick's arguments with his father had become more frequent and their daily scrimmages about Mr. Mosby's long absences and the smell of spirits on his breath had almost become physical. She had listened to Patrick's worries even when she didn't understand them, and she prayed every night for his safety.

"Maybe those girls out west like to dance too," Tilly suggested. "What will you do then?"

Patrick caught Grace's gaze and smiled. "Should we show her?"

She took his outstretched hand. As the strains of the next song cleared the balcony, Patrick settled his hand on her waist and led her into the first turn of a waltz. A girlish thrill ran through her. Her very first dance, and with a boy as handsome as Patrick.

"You've been practicing!" Tilly squealed, clapping and bouncing on her feet.

Grace's skirts swished around her calves as Patrick led her into another turn. It had taken the good part of a month, but she'd finally convinced him to teach her, and was she ever so glad! She couldn't imagine dancing her first waltz with anyone but him.

As the last notes of the music drifted away, they slowly came to a stop and Grace dropped into a deep curtsy. Patrick bowed over her hand, brushing a kiss above her fingers. It was the most wonderful dance of her life.

Patrick pulled her up. "Not bad, Gracie. Much better than the last time we practiced."

"That's your fault," she answered with a smile. "You were too interested in the new horse your grandfather bought to pay any attention to me."

"The horse is more fun," he teased as they rejoined Tilly by the railing. He turned to their friend. "What are you looking at that's so interesting?"

"I don't know."

Grace glanced over the railing. "Who is that? Whoever he is, he's not dressed for a ball."

"I don't think he's here for that." Tilly pointed to two police officers in the foyer. "He came in with them."

They watched as the man perused the ballroom, then, finding the object of his search, set out across the room.

Patrick's face grew taut. "Why is he talking to my father?"

Suddenly the two officers grabbed Mr. Mosby by the arms and wrestled him into the foyer, the attendees following along as if the scene was part of the night's festivities.

Grace turned around, but Patrick was gone. Glancing down the hallway, she saw him at the top of the stairs. She started toward him. "I'll go with you."

"No, you stay here. I'm just going to check on things, then I'll be back."

"Patrick. . ." But he didn't wait, taking the steps two at a time until he reached the foyer. She couldn't abandon him, not when he might need her. She started for the stairs.

"Miss Grace."

She turned in time to see Nanny storming toward her. "You and Miss Tilly are to go to the nursery this instant."

Grace had seen the shock on Patrick's face. She couldn't abandon him—she wouldn't. "I'm going downstairs to check on Patrick."

"Mr. Patrick can take care of himself." Nanny waved them into the nursery, closing the door behind them.

As Grace stepped deeper into the room, she suddenly got the feeling she might not see Patrick again for a very, very long time.

Chapter 1

Lower Manhattan
Late Fall 1895

Just one more push, Leonia." Grace Sullivan met the woman's pained gaze as she held the slippery cord away from the babe's neck, fearful the veins that had given him life would strangle it out of him. "One more push to deliver the shoulders and your baby will be here."

"But I'm so tired." The young girl, barely old enough to be out of the schoolroom, fell back against the pillows, her face ruddy from hours of exertion, a fine sheen of perspiration soaking her body. "Just a few minutes. Please?"

Grace exchanged a glance with her friend and fellow midwife, Nia Shoemaker, who shook her head. The child needed to be born now or they risked losing it.

The woman had to push. "Leonia?"

She opened her eyes to meet Grace's. "Yes."

"The baby is in trouble, but once he or she is born, it won't be a problem anymore," Grace said slowly, not wanting to alarm her. "One more push, and you'll get to hold your child."

"All right." Leonia grabbed hold of the linen ropes tied to the bedposts and pulled herself up, bearing down as hard as she could.

Grace glanced down just as one shoulder, then the other appeared. Within seconds, the baby's limp body slid onto the bed linens, Grace's fingers still holding the umbilical cord away from his neck. "It's a boy."

"A boy." Joy and awe filled Leonia's voice as she fell back onto the bed. "Me Thomas will be beside himself. He said he didn't care whether it be a boy or a girl, but I knew he wanted a son."

Nia held out a length of toweling, and Grace took it, using it to give the boy a vigorous rubdown. He should be breathing on his own by now. Grace glanced up at Nia, whose expression mirrored her own worry. *Please, dear Lord! Help this child!*

It was a whimper at first, and then a throaty cry filled the room. The babe's deathly white pallor turned a healthy shade of pink. Grace drew in a deep breath, then whispered, "Thank You, sweet Lord."

"Let me take this gentleman and get him cleaned up," Nia murmured, holding a thick blanket open. Grace gently placed the raven-haired boy in the folds, then stood. Nia smiled at her. "You did a good job."

"Thank you, but you did all the work."

"He's dark-haired, just like his da," Leonia said, her eyes transfixed on her son. There was laughter in her voice when she turned to Grace. "Does he have all his fingers and all his toes?"

"I didn't get the chance to count them." Truth was she hadn't noticed. Grace helped the new mother into a fresh shift, then stripped the soiled sheets, replacing them with clean ones.

"Yes, my dear," Nia answered as she carried the baby back to the bed. "Your son is perfectly normal, and from the sounds he's making, very hungry."

"Of course he is." Loosening the ties on her shift, Leonia bared her breast, then held out her arms. "He comes from a long line of men who are hearty eaters."

Nia laid the boy in his mother's arms. Instinctively, he turned his head toward her breast, his mouth open in search of nourishment.

There was a loud banging at the door. "Is everything all right?"

The slight panic in the young man's voice made Grace smile. "Are we ready for Thomas to meet his son?"

Leonia nodded, her deep green eyes sparkling with joy as she gazed lovingly at her son. "Yes, please."

Grace hurried to the door. A pale-faced man a few years younger than herself greeted her, his worried blue eyes darting around the room before coming to rest on his wife. "Is the babe. . . ?"

She took his arm and led him deeper into the room. "I was just coming to get you."

"I heard a cry and then. . ." His voice trailed off as his gaze settled on his child. "The bairn. . ."

"You have a bonny son, Thomas."

"A boy," he whispered as he sank down in a chair next to his wife. "And you, Leonia dearest, are you all right?"

"I'm fine, my love." She glanced down at the child. "Isn't he the most beautiful thing in the world?"

"No."

Leonia met her husband's gaze. "No?"

Thomas reached out and took her hand. "He's a close second behind his mother."

The young woman blushed. "Would you like to hold your son?"

The worried look was back in Thomas's eyes. "Are you sure? I've never held a wee one before." Yet even as he asked the question, he held out his arms to receive his son.

Grace's heart burst with joy. This was why she'd turned her back on all the things her late parents' money could give her. Instead, she'd dedicated her life to helping the poor and poverty-stricken. Helping those who had no possibility of helping themselves.

Her joy dimmed. To pay for her past mistakes.

Nia walked up to her, wiping her hands with a towel. "It looks like our work here is done."

"Not yet." Grace shook her head. "I've still got to give their apartment a good cleaning."

"A lot of good that will do," Nia huffed as she walked into the parlor with Grace. "Eight people live with them in a room no bigger than a thumbprint, and McCleary refuses to put in proper ventilation and plumbing despite the building codes." She took the soiled linen and balled it up. "They're still going to take their baby home to filth and dirty water."

It was something Grace didn't want to think about. "Have we got an apartment available?" She glanced around at the room they'd made into a makeshift delivery room. "Maybe they could stay here. We could set this up—"

Her friend's hand on her arm stopped her. "We need two delivery rooms."

"Do we? It wouldn't be for long. Just until I can secure another building and have it renovated."

"Grace." Nia's steady voice cut through her thoughts. "You can't take in all of Manhattan. It's just not possible."

She hated that Nia spoke logically, just as she despised the thought of sending Leonia and Thomas back to that filthy pit they called home. She glanced around. There had to be a way to provide clean and affordable housing to these people. She just hadn't stumbled across it yet.

Maybe it was time to approach Mr. McCleary again. "I'm going to have my lawyers draw up a proposal for the building next door. Maybe McCleary is ready to sell."

Nia glanced toward the room where the couple and their son were, then back. "Let's give them some privacy."

Grace knew what that meant. A good talking-to about how she couldn't save all of Manhattan or even Mulberry Street where they lived. They were doing good work here at Sullivan House, the four-story tenement Grace had purchased after her friend Tilly's death four years ago, and that was all they could do.

Yet Grace didn't believe any of that. She knew there was more she could do to help these people. Just the thought of another woman losing her child or her life in one of McCleary's flophouses sent a chill down her spine. No matter what Nia's argument might be this time, Grace would not be moved. She would secure another apartment building and help young families grow in an affordable, safe place.

For Tilly.

Grace followed Nia into the hallway, then through another parlor until they reached their office at the front of the building. Nia deposited the linens into a laundry chute then sat down in a nearby chair. "You look ready to drop."

Grace couldn't argue with her. Leonia had labored for almost an entire day and night before finally delivering her son. Taking a seat across from her friend, she stretched her neck from one side to the other. "Why don't you want me to buy the building next door?"

Nia drew in a deep breath. "McCleary and the other land-lords aren't too happy about the money you're taking out of their pockets."

Grace's head snapped up. "You know as well as I do I'm not making a cent from this. All I want is for children and their families to have a better start in life."

"I understand that. But people like McCleary aren't much into noble causes." She hesitated. "To him, you're a threat."

Grace chuckled. "That's utter nonsense."

"No, it's not," came another voice from the doorway.

Both of them turned to find Rosie, Grace's maid, standing there. "Men like McCleary don't understand common decency. All they want is to make coin on the backs of others."

"You sound as if you've had personal experience with the man," Nia said.

Rosie nodded. "My da lived in one of his apartments. Twelve people to a room not much bigger than this office. When Da died, McCleary shoved his body into the corner then charged me a death tax for his inconvenience." Her lips pressed into a stern line. "He rented out Da's place before he was even cold."

Nia went to her and wrapped her arm around the woman's waist. "Oh Rosie, I am so sorry."

Grace wasn't surprised. McCleary and the other landlords along Mulberry Street handed out tax bills like the mint printed money. Even orphaned children, some as young as four or five, had to pay to sit over the grates to stay warm at night. Well, she'd had enough of it. Every man, woman, and child deserved a clean, safe place to call home. She would find a way to make it happen.

She owed it to Tilly.

"I'm still going to make inquires. If I can find another building close by, just think of how many young families we can help."

Nia gave a resigned sigh. "Would you at least take someone with you when you go on your rounds?"

"That would be too much of a bother. You've got to remember that most of the men working here are doing the jobs of two or three people. They don't have time for me."

"They will make time. McCleary's been known to drag people he wants to 'talk' to off the streets." She thought for another moment. "And no more going out after the lamps have been lit."

That made Grace sit up. "But our patients might need me."

"Then take someone with you." Leaning on her elbows, Nia templed her fingers. "You can't be out on the streets alone."

Grace blinked, then glared at Nia. Her friend was serious. "Babies don't wait until daylight to be born. You know that."

"Then the mothers can come here." Nia waved her hand to the hall that led to the birthing rooms. "We have plenty of room."

Of course they did. Grace had seen to it. Still, there were those who felt more comfortable elsewhere. "Some women prefer to birth their children in their own beds, and I respect that."

"I don't know why," Rosie said.

Grace glanced back over her shoulder at her. "Why would you say that?"

"I don't mean to be rude, Miss Grace," Rosie said, "but no woman would want to birth a child in a filthy place like one of these tenements. Not me, nor any of my family."

"Do your people still live in these tenements?"

"Yes, my niece and nephew. Kasey has a suitor, a really nice gentleman, who talks marriage sometimes. If she had a child. . ." She drew in a sharp intake of air. "I'd bring her here. No question about it."

Another one who needed a place to stay, two really. Rosalind's niece and nephew. "You know your family is welcome at any time."

"Miss Grace, that's very kind of you, but they can't afford a fine place like this."

Oh dear. Had she embarrassed the woman? That was never her intention. "No, Rosie. What I mean is, they can come live here. We don't charge family."

"We won't be taking any handouts." Rosie sniffed. "We'll pay our rent just like everyone else."

"Of course." Grace nodded. Pride was a difficult thing to overcome. "This is the same offer I extend to all my renters. They would pay as they always have." She thought for a moment. "What about my rooms?"

"Grace!" Nia exclaimed.

"Miss Grace, I can't allow you to do that," Rosie said. "Where would you sleep?"

Grace glanced around. "I could bunk down in here until a space opens up. I stay in here a great deal of the time anyway."

"I couldn't ask that of you, not after you kept me on after your parents passed away."

"You're not asking me to do anything." Grace reached out and took the older woman's hand. "And it's I who should be grateful. You stayed by me during those difficult days. The least I can do is ease your mind concerning your family."

Rosie studied her for a long minute. "If you're certain."

"I've never been more certain about anything."

The woman broke into a happy smile. "God bless you, Miss Gracie. You've got such a good heart." She glanced down at the watch pinned to her bodice. "If I hurry, I can have them here by this afternoon."

"Then go," Nia said, the tone of her voice one of resignation. "I don't want any of us out after dark."

Rosie started for the door, then turned, walking back to Grace. Bending down, she enveloped her in a long hug. "Thank you so much, Miss Gracie. You'll never know how much this means to me."

Satisfaction warmed Grace's heart at the thought of helping a dear friend. It was always like this when she helped someone, the sense of purpose she felt until she realized how much more work she needed to do. If only she'd learned from her mistakes earlier. Maybe then she would have known how to help Tilly. If she had, Tilly and her baby would have lived.

When the door clicked shut, Nia turned to her. "You realize you're going to be sleeping in here tonight."

"Yes, I know that." Grace glanced around at the accommodations. Would she be able to fit a mattress in here? "But did you see the look on Rosie's face? She was so relieved at the thought of having her niece and nephew nearby."

"I understand that, but now you're delegated to the floor."

"I'll have a bed brought in," she replied, rounding out her back to get the kinks out. "Besides, it's not for long."

Nia massaged her forehead. "So you didn't hear a word I said about McCleary."

"Of course I did." She met her friend's gaze and held it. "I won't be scared away from what is right. Mr. McCleary has a price, and once we figure out what it is, we can get started on renovations."

The room went silent; then Nia spoke. "It wasn't your fault, you know. About Tilly."

Even now, the thought of losing her friend sucked the air out of her lungs. Grace smoothed her hands over her skirts. "I have to take some share of the blame. She could have had her child at my home under a doctor's care."

Nia scoffed. "As if a doctor would treat someone who married so far beneath her."

Her friend had a point. In the two years since she'd moved to lower Manhattan, Grace could count a handful of times she'd seen a doctor south of Mulberry. It was one of the reasons she'd studied to be a midwife. Without their presence to care for the pregnant mothers and newborns, there would be no one to help when things went wrong.

It was one of the reasons she dropped out of society and moved her household to Mulberry Street. She was determined to help those like Tilly who died in childbirth along with her daughter. With every baby safely delivered, Grace got a piece of her heart back.

"I'm going to wire my lawyer later in the day and have him come up with a proposal for Mr. McCleary."

"I give up." Nia tilted her head back to look at the ceiling. "You're going to do what you want to do anyway."

"Not always. I wasn't sold on this wallpaper, but you seemed to like it," Grace teased.

"There is that." Nia's face softened. "But I do want you to be careful, Grace. I never had any children, but I like to think if I'd had a daughter, she'd be a lot like you."

Grace reached out and touched Nia's hand. "You've been a great comfort to me since my parents. . ." Her eyes began to burn from unshed tears. "You know."

"It's all right, dearest. You've had a rough time between Tilly and your parents. Then, right away, you began renovating this place while learning how to be a midwife. It's a bit overwhelming."

"I'm all right. Really. Nothing that a short nap won't take care of." She settled back in her chair. "And I promise I'll find someone to walk me to my appointments every evening so you won't have to wonder if I'm dead or alive."

"Thank you," Nia replied. "That will make me feel more at ease."

"Then it's settled." Grace drew a deep breath in an effort to clear away the cobwebs in her head. Thoughts of Tilly and her parents' untimely deaths were never far from her mind but felt particularly close when she was tired. A long nap would put her to rights. "I'm going to lie down for a bit."

"I think I will too. Do you want me to tell Rosie, or will you?"

She glanced at her friend's tired face. "You go ahead. I'll tell her."

"Thank you." Nia stood, then walked over to her and gave her shoulder an encouraging squeeze. "Things will get better, my dear. I promise."

"I know," Grace answered, not quite trusting her friend's assurances. "Sleep well."

"You too."

She watched as Nia opened the door and let herself out. Grace's life had been in shambles when she'd met the midwife and begged her to take her on as an apprentice. Nia had refused Grace at first. She recognized the brokenness of Grace's life and questioned her intentions. Neither of them had expected Grace to hound the poor woman until she grudgingly gave in. Over the last two years, they had become dear friends.

But not best friends. Never best friends. Tilly's sudden death in childbirth along with Grace's parents' accident had been too much to bear. She'd never open herself up to that kind of pain again.

Grace stood and left the office, heading for the kitchen. A light snack might help her sleep. She'd have Cook prepare a tray for Nia too, just in case. As she entered the dining hall, the aroma of crisp bacon and buttered toast made her stomach growl.

"Miss Grace?"

She sighed, then turned to see Melly, one of her former house-maids, rushing toward her. Usually the girl announced the arrival of a mother in labor, but today Grace saw something worrisome in the woman's expression. "Is something wrong?"

"There was a man at the door." Melly handed her a cream-colored sealed envelope. "He told me to give you this."

Uneasiness churned in Grace's stomach as she took the missive. Probably another threat from McCleary, though those usually came in the form of a rock through a window or a missed coal delivery. "Did he say who it was from?"

Melly shook her silvery-blond head. "Nor did he wait for a reply."

Grace tore open the envelope, pulled the scrap of paper out, and read it. Then she went over it again, slowly this time, to make certain she'd read it correctly.

Dear heavens.

"What is it, Miss Grace? You've gone white as a sheet."

"I'm fine," she answered, going over the page once more. What did the letter mean, they were practicing without a license? Midwives had been assisting new mothers for hundreds of years. Why were they being singled out? She handed the note to Melly. "Someone has lodged a complaint with the city council. They want to shut down Sullivan House."

Chapter 2

This was not how he'd intended to spend his morning.

Patrick Mosby leaned back in his leather chair and studied the small crowd that had assembled for this morning's emergency council meeting. Generally, these affairs were brief and usually in front of an empty room. Granted, there was the occasional disgruntled resident who bent the council's ear about one problem or another, but never this kind of crowd.

The men—no ladies had graced the council's offices in the three years since Patrick had been elected—were stylishly dressed and carried themselves well. Not like the society types he'd known as a boy, but somewhere just beneath them. There was an urgency about them. As if the outcome of this meeting had a direct effect on them.

"Please come to order." Chairman Wendell Hodges tapped his wooden gavel on his desk. "I'd like to get this business expedited as quickly as possible."

Patrick glanced down at the meeting's agenda. What business was the chairman talking about? He raised his hand and was recognized by Hodges. "Sir, what is this important issue that's robbed the council members of a morning's work? Couldn't this have waited for our regular meeting?"

"No, sir, it could not. It is a matter of life and death."

Patrick turned his attention to the man standing at the visitor's podium. He had an owlish look about him, with his slicked-back hair, prominent ears, and wire-rimmed spectacles pushed up his long nose.

"Dr. Zimmerman." Hodges nodded. "You may begin."

"Thank you, Mr. Chairman." The man leaned forward, clutching the edges of the podium. "I and my fellow physicians are constantly on the lookout for situations that could be a public health risk. It is our calling, and we take it very seriously."

"The people of New York City thank you and your colleagues for your unwavering diligence," the chairman said. "I take it you have identified such a risk."

"Yes, sir." The doctor preened like a peacock.

Patrick leaned forward, his irritation at the man growing. "Well, get on with it."

"Councilman Mosby, this gentleman is my guest." Hodges gave him a reproachful stare. "It would do you well to remember that."

In other words, these men were lining Hodges's pockets. Still, it wouldn't do any good alienating his constituents. Patrick faced the crowd. "I beg pardon, sir. I'm just a little surprised by this health risk you speak of. Is there another outbreak of typhus or something?"

The man glanced back at his colleagues, many who gave him an encouraging nod, then turned back to the commissioners. "As you may be aware, until recently, physicians were scarce in the city, which has resulted in other, untrained individuals being left to care for. . ." He cleared his throat. "Certain ailments. In many cases, it continues today."

Good heavens, this would take all day if the man didn't get on with it. Patrick swallowed his frustration, then spoke. "What exactly are you trying to tell us, Dr. Zimmerman?"

The man glared at him. "We would like for the council to close down the practice of midwifing."

Patrick blinked. Had he heard the man correctly? "I don't understand. Midwives are for the most part women. Who better to attend a woman in a delicate condition but another woman?"

Zimmerman gave a little sniff. "Women have no formal training or experience in the matter. Why, anyone can put up a shingle and call herself a midwife."

Patrick glanced down the table at his fellow commissioners and saw the same confusion in their expressions that he felt. "And has that been a problem?"

"Yes, sir." The physician stood a bit straighter. "Some of these so-called practitioners are going so far as to offer pre- and postnatal care." He huffed. "As if there were such things."

"There is, and we've found it helps ensure both a healthy mother and a healthy baby."

That voice. There was a familiarity to it. It was slightly deeper now, with tones that reminded him of the girl he'd considered one of his dearest friends in the years before his father's arrest and death. And as she moved through the throng of men and made her way to the podium, all remaining doubt was wiped away. It was her.

Grace Sullivan.

Patrick sat back, a tightness in his chest. Grace Sullivan, all grown up and standing in front of him. How many times had he thought to call on her, to find out how she was and maybe even renew their childhood friendship? She probably wouldn't have seen him anyway, not after the disgrace his father brought to their family. Besides, he had a reputation to build, a business to run, as well as his seat on the city council. There had been no time.

"Who might you be?" The chairman's harsh words broke through Patrick's thoughts. "Why are you disrupting this meeting?"

Grace went to stand at the podium, and Patrick took a closer look. Tall like her father, she held herself with a regal air that only old money could give. Pale blond hair was caught up in a service-able chignon at the nape of her neck. Her dress was not what one would consider the height of fashion, nor were the dark smudges under her eyes.

Patrick took a breath. Something had happened to his old friend, but he had no clue what it could be.

"My name is Grace Sullivan, and I run the Sullivan House on Mulberry Street in lower Manhattan. We offer an expectant mother care before, during, and after the birth of her child."

"You're a midwife?"

She nodded. "Yes, I am."

Grace, a midwife? In lower Manhattan? "What are you doing in the tenements?" The question slipped out before he could stop it.

Her head swiveled toward him, and her gaze met his for one brief moment before her eyes widened. "Patrick Mosby?"

"You know Councilman Mosby?" Hodges asked, his gaze going to Patrick, then back to Grace.

"We were childhood friends," Patrick answered. "But we haven't seen each other in years." Not since the day his father had been arrested for swindling most of the families in their social circle. Had Grace's family been affected? Was that why she worked in the tenements now?

"Miss Sullivan," the chairman continued. "Are you trained in midwifery?"

"Yes, sir. I received my training from Nia Shoemaker. Since completing it, I have delivered close to a hundred babies, all of whom have survived."

"Who owns this house, Miss Sullivan? Who pays you to run it?" one of the other councilmen asked.

"I own it."

To own an apartment building, even on the lower east side, would have cost Grace a pretty penny. With that kind of money, she could have set herself up nicely, even had her choice of possible beaus to court her.

That thought unsettled him.

Other questions came to mind. Why had she done this? What did she hope to accomplish in the middle of an area run by McCleary's Irish gangs? And why would her parents allow her to do such a cockeyed thing in the first place?

"Sullivan," Hodges mused for a moment, studying her. "You wouldn't be related to the Park Avenue Sullivans, would you?"

She stiffened. "They are. . ." She stumbled over the words. "They were my parents."

The Sullivans were gone? When? The news stole the breath from Patrick's lungs. Her parents had been like family to him, their mothers as close as sisters. Until his father, by one selfish act, had as much as confessed to his crimes against their friends.

Still, he knew how close Grace had been to her parents. Their loss must have affected her greatly. Patrick leaned forward, hoping to catch her gaze. "I'm so sorry, Grace."

She lifted her eyes to meet his, and in that brief moment, they mourned the loss together. "Thank you." She cleared her throat and was businesslike again. "I was informed that this meeting would decide whether to shut down a vital part of our mission, which is the health and welfare of women and their children."

A hum of disgruntled male voices settled over the room. Finally, Dr. Zimmerman took to the podium once more. "This woman," he bit out, "advertises herself as a medical professional, which she most certainly is not. Her kind is giving our profession a bad name it does not deserve."

Or, more than likely, taking money out of the doctors' pockets, though Patrick doubted any of these men would venture to the lower east side to deliver a child of an immigrant.

"Miss Sullivan, how do you respond to this?"

She glanced back at the crowd, then turned to face the council, her eyes a vivid blue despite the dark smudges beneath them. "I have never advertised nor declared myself to be a medical professional. Just as midwives have for centuries, I care for women at the most vulnerable moment in their lives. I won't apologize for that." She looked at Zimmerman then. "I do have one question to ask the physician."

The man glared at her as if she were wasting his time. "What might that be?"

"If you and your colleagues are so concerned about the loss of life, why haven't you extended your practices to include the lower Manhattan borough?"

A roar rose up in the room. Patrick sat back in his chair, fighting hard to contain a grin. Grace had always spoken her mind. It was good to see she hadn't lost that ability. But as he looked at the chairman's livid face, he knew she hadn't done herself any favors. The doctors formed a powerful coalition, one that even Grace with all of her wealth couldn't take down.

Still, she had a point. The poor and immigrant families deserved basic creature comforts—clean water, a safe place to lay their heads at night, and jobs to support their families. Families that Grace helped every day despite the dangers she faced.

But why, when she could live a life of leisure as one of the darlings of society?

It was a question that needed answering, and who better to ask than Grace herself?

Chapter 3

S hall we take this to a vote? All in favor of outlawing the practice of midwifery. . ."

The words drifted around her, not quite making sense to her
exhausted mind. The chairman, a Mr. Hodges, held his gavel
upraised, as if prepared to render a verdict. Why couldn't these
men realize they were in effect giving a death sentence to women
and children who without her and Nia would never survive?

"Mr. Chairman, I believe we shouldn't be so rash. Miss Sullivan raises a valid question concerning our residents of the lower
east side. I would like to hear the doctors' recommendations to
correct it."

Grace glanced up as Patrick finished speaking. His presence
had been an unexpected surprise. The last she'd heard, he'd gone
out west to rebuild his family's fortune after that nasty scandal
with his father. She hadn't seen him since the evening the swindling charges had been filed and his father was arrested. Patrick
had disappeared from her world in a heartbeat, leaving her confused and angered by his abandonment.

Now here he was, and speaking out in her defense.

Grace scoffed. She didn't need his help, though if he could get an answer out of Zimmerman, she would appreciate it. If he couldn't, she already suspected the true reasons behind Zimmerman and his colleagues' attack on midwives.

The doctor beside her fidgeted with his sleeves, a fine sheen covering his too-pale face. "Councilman Mosby, you are talking about our livelihood. We have a reputation to uphold."

"So according to you and your colleagues, the people who inhabit that area aren't worthy of your expertise?" Patrick asked, his voice calm and methodical.

Zimmerman at least had the decency to look uncomfortable. "That's rather a simplistic way of looking at the situation, sir."

"Sometimes, Doctor, it's easier to look at things that way." He turned to the chairman. "Mr. Hodges, I would suggest we study the matter until the next council meeting so that we serve all the citizens of New York." He turned his gaze out to the crowd. "Not just the wealthy ones."

"How dare you!" Dr. Zimmerman's cheeks flamed red. "You know good and well a reputable physician won't go to lower Manhattan. Why, it would be the end of his career."

Closing her eyes, Grace drew in a long, slow breath. The medical community astounded her. Called to serve, yet only the people they saw fit. They should have been ashamed of themselves.

You weren't much better. She placed gloved fingers to her temple as shame raced through her. Her best friend in the entire world had needed her help, but she'd been too concerned about what her peers would think of her and how her reputation would suffer. Tilly's quiet resignation still haunted her, and Grace would spend the rest of her life making up for her selfishness.

If the city didn't shut her down.

"Then we need a plan to help the poor." Patrick met her gaze, and her heart did a strange little flutter in her chest. "As Miss Sullivan has spent time among these people, I think she needs to be included in the conversation."

"I agree," the chairman replied. "Would you look into this for the council, Mr. Mosby? Maybe follow her around and see what she does to care for these families? As you are already acquainted, you seem the most obvious choice."

Grace wasn't sure how she felt about Patrick tagging along as she went on her appointments, interviewed families for apartments, and carried out all the other daily chores that went into running the house. He had no place in the world she'd built for herself. She stepped forward. "I'm not certain my patients will feel comfortable in Mr. Mosby's presence."

Hodges stared back at her. "Well, if we can't verify your assertions, then all there is left to do is vote on the matter."

One glance at the councilmen convinced her this was a battle she would lose. "Very well. I will make myself available to Mr. Mosby for however long is necessary."

"Good." The chairman looked to Patrick. "What about you?"

"I graciously accept, Mr. Chairman." He gave her a brief smile then grabbed the leather-bound book in front of him and flipped it open. "I will give my report to the council six weeks from today."

"Then we stand adjourned." Mr. Hodges hammered his gavel on the table.

"This isn't over, Miss Sullivan." Dr. Zimmerman tugged at the sleeves of his coat. "We will fight until midwifery is outlawed throughout the state, and then the country."

Her pulse flared. It sounded like war had been declared and the doctors had fired their first round. She slumped slightly, the weight of the morning bearing down on her. Of course things looked bleak. They always did when a person was as tired and hungry as she was.

A light touch to her arm made her turn around. Patrick. He'd always had a particularly irritating habit of sneaking up on her when she was deep in thought. Grace straightened. "Hello, Patrick. I never expected to see you here."

Was that a ghost of a smile she detected? "I could say the same for you."

"How long have you been back in New York?"

He seemed puzzled by the question. "How did you know I'd left the city?"

Another annoying habit of his, answering a question with a question. Well, she couldn't very well tell the man she'd kept tabs on him after his family had been shunned by their social circle. "I must have heard it somewhere."

"I guess it was news, wasn't it? The son of a known swindler heading west to make his mark probably didn't sit well with our old friends." The soft smile that had lit his features straightened into a hard line. "That would have been fodder for the gossips for weeks."

"That's not what I . . ." The words died on her lips. She was too tired to argue with him over something so ridiculous. Instead, they needed to focus on the needs of the people in lower Manhattan. "Thank you for helping me with Dr. Zimmerman and the rest of the council. This was not how I pictured my morning going."

"You weren't given notice about the meeting?"

She met his gaze. He seemed genuinely surprised. "A man came to the apartment building early this morning with a notice about the meeting. I had to hurry just to get here in time."

"Do you still get up before the sun rises?"

Her breath caught. Patrick always caught her off guard. "You remember our early morning rides in Central Park?"

His eyes softened at the memory. "Remember when your mother's maid caught us climbing down the trellis outside the kitchen? What was her name?"

"Rosalind, but she prefers Rosie most of the time," Grace replied. "She came to work with me at Sullivan House after Mama and—" Grace swallowed hard. One day, this would come easier, but not today. "Mama and Papa were killed in a carriage accident two years ago."

His touch felt warm and familiar when he took her hand. "I'm so sorry, Gracie. Your parents were good people. I know it had to be hard on you to lose them, you were so close."

"Yes, we were." For some reason, she felt comfortable talking to Patrick about her parents. Maybe because he'd known them as she had. As a child, Patrick had spent his mornings at her house while their mothers had their daily visits. Even after the scandal broke, Mama had tried to visit Mrs. Mosby, to no avail. Her mother's heart had broken when her friend cast her aside.

Grace's heart had broken too. Just thirteen, she'd imagined herself in love with Patrick, silly child that she was.

Now, her future depended on him. "What time would you like to get started with your tour?"

"Tour?"

"Of Sullivan House." She bit back her frustration at his

confused expression. "Isn't that what you wanted? To get an idea about the needs of the poor and immigrants living in the lower east side? I can show you what we're doing to provide housing, education, and basic medical needs for our renters."

Patrick eyed her skeptically. "You make them pay for your services? I thought this was your mission."

Did he always believe the worst about people? "It is a mission, but these are proud people. They want to earn their keep. Charity is not something they'd easily accept, not even if their lives depended on it. So I charge a small fee for a three-room apartment and use it for the upkeep of the place. Believe me when I say that it doesn't cover much, nor have I ever expected that it would."

"I see." Yet he didn't look convinced. "I guess I'll find out more once you show me around."

She stiffened at his words. "I can provide my books so you can see how I spend the money."

A pained look crossed his face. "I've insulted you."

"Well, yes." She fidgeted a bit, uncomfortable that he could still read her so well.

His gaze met hers. "I'm sorry, Grace. Truly, I am, but if we want to have any hope of defeating the doctors, I'll need as much information as you can give me."

"You want to help me?"

With a soft smile that could curl the toes of any red-blooded woman, he nodded. "I've been concerned about the people in the lower east side for some time now. It's my hope that this report will finally get the council moving on some remedies to help them."

There was a sincerity in Patrick's voice that spoke to her own worries for the people she served. Allowing him to help might be the answer she'd been praying for these last two years. Whatever childish feelings she'd felt for him were in the past, as was their friendship. He was simply a man who wanted to meet the needs of his constituents.

She closed her eyes for a moment, her legs and arms heavy. It would be nice to have someone to lighten the load. She finally opened her eyes to find him watching her. "What time would you like to come tomorrow?"

"Why not this afternoon? My carriage is waiting outside."

Her muscles throbbed with exhaustion, and she swayed before righting herself. "Not today."

He gently grasped her by the shoulders, his steady hands sending tiny flames of warmth down her arms. "Are you all right?"

Grace swallowed hard, the events of the morning finally catching up with her. "It's just I was up most of the night delivering a baby, and I'm tired and hungry and want nothing more than to climb into my bed and sleep the rest of the day away."

"Then let me take you home."

She shook her head. "You don't have to do that. I can walk."

Dissatisfaction plowed his brow. "Your family used to have a carriage house full of horses and every means of transportation ever developed. Are you telling me you no longer have them?"

"I had no need for them, so I sold them." Grace swallowed against a wave of nausea. "I only kept a small buggy and my mare."

"You still have Duchess? She was older than dirt when we were children." He eyed her suspiciously. "Is that why you walked? Because you didn't want to strain poor Duchess?"

It seemed Patrick still had the ability to find her soft spots. "I need to go if I want to get some rest this afternoon."

She started for the exit, but Patrick hurried by and stepped in front of her. "Which is why you're going to let me take you home. I have a carriage right outside."

"I don't want to be an imposition."

He gave her a sober shake of his head. "You would never be an imposition to me, Gracie."

She wasn't sure if it was the exhaustion or the lovely way he spoke her name, but she truly believed him. Their friendship still meant something to him. She nodded. "All right, then."

With a triumphant gleam in his eye, Patrick took her arm and led her out of the room.

Chapter 4

He hated to wake her.

Patrick glanced over at Grace. She had held out longer than he expected before the exhaustion that seemed to weigh her down like an anchor finally pulled her under. Her exhaustion gave him an opportunity to notice the changes in his childhood friend. She still had a pert little nose that turned up at the tip, but her features had softened. Her eyes were still that icy shade of blue, though now he'd found a gentleness there that was appealing.

The carriage turned, and Grace's head swayed. Not wanting to disturb her, he moved to sit beside her, gently wrapping his arm around her, offering his shoulder as a pillow. She snuggled closer until her head rested beneath his chin.

Patrick glanced once more at her, then turned to look out the window. At one time, he'd thought to marry Grace. Of course, he was fourteen then, and she was just a child. Yet even then she'd been a kindred spirit, the one person he could talk to about anything. He could see a life with her.

Until his father had made that all but impossible. Patrick

leaned his cheek on the top of her head. His childish dreams had died along with Papa, and there was no going back.

But he could help Grace. If she'd found a way to fulfill the needs of her renters, maybe they could duplicate it throughout lower Manhattan. Instead of gangs, disease, and early death, the Italians, Irish, Scottish, and Russian immigrants pouring onto their shores could find a way to be productive and prosperous American citizens.

The carriage hit a pothole. Grace lifted her head, blinking a couple of times before looking up at him. Her eyes still full of her dreams, she smiled. "Patrick."

His breath grew ragged, every inclination screaming at him to sit her on his lap and kiss her. But this was Gracie, someone he hadn't known until today that he still cared about. He gently disentangled himself and moved back to his seat.

Grace straightened, blinking away what was left of her slumber. "Are we there yet?"

The carriage jerked to a halt in response. Patrick opened the window and unlatched the door, putting down the steps. He stepped out then leaned back in, holding his hand out. "Miss Sullivan."

Pausing a moment, she slid her gloved hand into his. She came down the stairs, then hesitated slightly as if getting her bearings. Then she turned to him, a soft smile so full of joy gracing her lips, he wondered if he'd ever felt such an emotion.

She nodded toward the building behind him. "Welcome to Sullivan House."

He turned, shock resonating through him at the sight of the dilapidated four-story structure.

Sullivan House looked to be on the verge of coming down around her ears.

Patrick had never been good at hiding his thoughts, and it was pretty obvious what he thought of her home. Grace pressed her lips together for fear she'd fly off the handle at him, but really, what had the man expected? Compared to the other buildings in the area, it was passable. It was the interior that mattered. At least, that was what she told herself.

"Come." Grace tugged his arm. Patrick followed reluctantly, his gaze falling on the broken cobblestones that made an uneven path to the front door.

"Grace, this looks. . ." He seemed to reach for a word. "It's awful, Grace. The shutters are broken, the shingles uneven, and the paint is peeling off the sides of the house." He glanced around at the other buildings. "It's worse than I remember."

He had memories of this place? Was it through his position as city councilman, or something else? But he didn't elaborate, and she felt too peeved by his assessment to ask. "If you come inside, you'll see most of the renovations were done on the interior. After all, a person can't live under a shutter."

"You sure the roof won't fall in on us?"

She whirled around to face him. "I've worked hard to make this place a home for these people, and I won't have you bad-mouthing it. Is that clear?"

He crossed his arms over his chest and studied her. "You never had much of a temper as a girl, but I have to say, it suits you."

Grace shook her head, every nerve in her body vibrating. "You are the most frustrating—"

"I'm sorry." There was laughter in his voice. "You're just rather lovely when you're in a temper."

Grace went still. Compliments, particularly from men, were uncommon for her. Patrick must be teasing her again. "Stop it."

"Stop what? Complimenting you?" He cocked his head to one side. "The Grace I knew loved receiving them."

"Well, that girl was vain and snobbish and only thought of herself." She took a shaky breath. "I should hope the woman is different."

Patrick nodded, a concerned look in his eyes. "It was just a compliment, Gracie."

She dropped her chin to her chest. She'd blown a simple statement out of proportion for no reason at all. "I'm sorry, Patrick. I'm just so tired and worried about this thing with the council. It's an excuse, I know, but I promise you, I'm not usually like this."

"It's all right, Gracie. I'd just forgotten how much I loved teasing you. I've truly missed it." He reached around her and pulled on the door handle.

And what about me? Did you miss me too? The questions reverberated in her mind as she walked into her small foyer. Why should she think he'd thought about her at all these past years? They'd been mere children when he'd disappeared from her life. He had his life to get on with and so did she.

Grace unbuttoned her coat, then felt surprised when Patrick helped her out of it and hung it on a nearby peg. A simple courtesy, one she hadn't realized she missed. Once he'd hung up his coat and hat, she led him into the larger of the two parlors.

Turning to face him, she clasped her hands in front of her. "This is where we greet our families. We have a small area where the children can play or read a book while we talk."

"You have an interview process, then?"

"To a point. We want to make certain our families feel safe in their own homes, so we don't allow people who have had a run-in with the law. We also don't allow spirits or tobacco in the building."

He cocked an eyebrow as she sat down and gestured to the chair across from her. "I can understand turning away the felons and spirits. But really, Grace, a man needs a good cigar after a hard week at work."

"They can enjoy tobacco outside, then," she replied, relaxing back into the cushions. The nap in the carriage had helped, but after so many hours without sleep, she felt herself waning. "There are also lanterns in each room because I won't allow candles. It's too much of a fire risk."

"And if one of these tenements catches fire, it would burn down the whole neighborhood."

She nodded. "One of the buildings a couple of blocks over caught fire last summer and took the two buildings next to it before they got it under control." Her head lolled back against the cushion. "It's something I worry about."

"Anything else?"

She cupped her cheek in one hand. "You mean besides getting supplies for our school and keeping food on the table? Oh, and the deliveries. We can't forget about them."

"Sounds like you have a lot of responsibility."

Her lids grew heavy and she closed her eyes. "I've never looked at it like that. For me"—in spite of herself, she heard her voice growing softer—"it's about helping those less fortunate. Someone like me but who's lost it all and has no one else to turn to."

"Grace?" Boots clicked across the floor before meeting the rug. She forced her eyes open long enough to see Nia standing there, looking every bit concerned. Nia glanced from Patrick to Grace.

"Nia, this is Patrick Mosby, an old friend from my childhood. He's on the city council and is going to decide whether we can continue to practice midwifery or not." She gave a little nod to him. "Patrick, Miss Nia Shoemaker, my friend and fellow midwife."

Patrick stood and took Nia's outstretched hand. "It's a pleasure, ma'am."

"Likewise." Nia turned her attention back to Grace. "You look terrible. Weren't you able to sleep?"

She shook her head and yawned. Why had no one told her how comfortable this couch was before? "Something came up."

"Something's always coming up, dear." Nia's voice held that tone her mother always used when Grace misbehaved. "It's time to get you to bed."

Grace shook her head, then felt strong arms lift her up. When she opened her eyes, she was staring into Patrick's handsome face. "What are you doing?"

"You're falling asleep." He shifted her weight, and she instinctively looped her arms around his neck. "That's much better, now isn't it?"

Despite being dead on her feet, Grace felt herself blush.

"Don't be embarrassed, Gracie. You know how much I love to tease you," he whispered before lifting his head. "Where are her rooms?" he asked Nia.

"I'll show you."

Grace tightened her grip around his neck and shoulder. He was more muscular than she remembered, but then again, he'd only been a boy of fourteen, not the man she'd met today. This Patrick was confident and self-assured, taller than she remembered, and handsomer than a man had a right to be.

And he was carrying her in his arms. Grace relaxed and let her head fall to his shoulder.

Might as well enjoy it while she could.

Chapter 5

S he sleeps here?"

Miss Shoemaker pushed a chair out of the way to clear a path for Patrick. "We had a young couple deliver their first child this morning who didn't have anywhere to go. Grace, being Grace, rented them her apartment."

He bypassed the small desk and headed for the clean tick mattress sitting low to the floor. Kneeling down, he gently placed Grace on her back, then covered her with the serviceable quilt at the foot of the bed. Dragging the blanket up over her shoulder, she turned to her side, her breathing already slow and even.

Patrick followed Miss Shoemaker outside then waited until she clicked the door shut before asking his question. "Is Grace planning on living in her office for long?"

"Who knows?" She shrugged as if this kind of thing was a normal occurrence. "She has a mind of her own."

He didn't need anyone to tell him that. Even as a girl, Grace wasn't easily swayed into mischief. Her soft heart didn't help matters either. These people weren't the only ones who needed his help.

As they walked through to the parlor, Patrick took a more

detailed look around. The walls and ceilings, though old, had been patched and given a fresh coat of paint. The floors had been either replaced or sanded down and were buffed to a soft shine. Comfortable chairs on plush rugs were gathered into groups so that the renters could converse and even play a game of chess or checkers. There was a warmth to the place, a hominess that reminded him of the Sullivans' Park Avenue home.

"You and Grace have done a remarkable job with this place," Patrick said as he sat down across from Miss Shoemaker.

The older woman glanced around. "Grace wanted to give her renters a feeling of home, though I'm quite sure this is nicer than any place any of us have ever seen before, much less lived in."

"It reminds me of her mother."

"Ah." Miss Shoemaker sighed. "That makes sense. Grace adored her parents."

Patrick scooted to the edge of his chair. "Grace said they were in a carriage accident."

She studied him for a long moment, then gave a slight nod. "Just before Grace's twenty-first birthday. Her father passed instantly. Her mother died on Grace's birthday a few days later. Grace says her mother gave up because she couldn't face a life without her husband."

Patrick could see that. Even as a boy, he could see the love the Sullivans shared for each other. "That must have devastated her."

"Well, yes. That and. . ." She stared at him. "Mr. Mosby. . ."

"Please, call me Patrick."

"Then you must call me Nia." She started again. "Patrick, do you truly want to help Grace?"

"Well, yes. Her and all the midwives really. That's what the city council sent me here to investigate." He leaned forward, resting his forearms on his knees. "The people here are just as much a part of this city as those on the upper east side and should have the same opportunities. I want to see how the council can work to achieve that."

"You won't make very many friends doing that."

Patrick studied the woman's stoic features. Usually, he was good at reading people—it proved helpful in his position on the council—but this woman held her cards close to her chest. "Do you speak from experience?"

Nia glanced around, then leaned closer. "As you may know, McCleary runs Mulberry Street."

"Yes, I've met the man several times, but I was under the impression he ran legitimate businesses."

"Legitimate, my eye." She sat back as if his assessment of the man had pushed her away. "He's a gangster, Mr. Mosby, plain and simple."

That sounded nothing like the polished man he'd met at Chairman Hodges's recent fundraiser. "What makes you say that?"

"Have you ever seen the tenements run by Mr. McCleary? Eight people to one room, sometimes ten or twelve with no ventilation or running water. Trash piled up in the streets around them. The rooms so filthy that the rats would rather roam the streets than stay there." She caught her breath. "He even rents the heat grates outside of his buildings to the orphans who don't have a place to stay."

Patrick swallowed hard. He'd known the situation in the tenements was tenuous the few years he'd lived there, but McCleary hadn't been in control then. Still, the man could do whatever he liked with his property. "I'm not sure there's anything I can do. . ."

"He's threatening Grace."

Anger sparked in his blood. "What do you mean, he's threatening Grace? What has he done?"

"So far it's just spoiled milk at the back door, missing coal deliveries, and last week, one of his gang put a rock through the front window. But she's got this idea in her head that she needs another building." Worry creased her brow as she dug into the pocket of her dress. "Then there's this."

He took the crinkled scrap of paper she held out to him and read it. His heart slammed against his rib cage at the vile words. The missive wasn't a threat so much as a promise of violence against her. He jerked his head up. "Grace can't stay here."

"She won't leave." Nia sighed and sat back. "I've tried to tell her she could do just as much good for these people if she went back to her friends and made them aware of the need. But she won't listen. She thinks it's her calling to serve them."

Stubborn woman. He gave Nia the note. "Does she know about this?"

She shook her head. "It came while she was at the council meeting, and she was in no state to read it when she came home." Her body tensed as she leaned toward him. "You're an old friend of hers. Surely you can talk some sense into her."

Patrick wanted to help, but he wasn't sure how much good it would do. "I haven't seen Grace in almost ten years. I'm not certain what I could do."

Nia's mouth thinned into a stern line. "She needs protection."

"What kind of—"

"Grace visits expectant mothers in some of McCleary's

buildings in the evening after they get home from work," Nia interrupted. "If you could accompany her. . ."

Patrick sat back and thought for a moment. If he tagged along on Grace's visits, he could keep an eye on her while gathering information for his report. He could also check out McCleary. If the Irishman was behind the threatening note, the police needed to be notified.

"When does Grace start her rounds?"

Chapter 6

G race eyed the clock. Five thirty. Too late in the day for polite callers. Most people were settling down after a day of work or enjoying a meal with their families. She was in the clear.

Patrick wouldn't come today.

She brushed the wrinkles out of the sheet, then pulled the corners tight before tucking it under the mattress. Not that she should expect him to come. She'd fallen asleep before they could arrange a day or time for him to have a proper viewing of the house.

Still, he could have sent a note around to let her know he'd been held up or that he'd changed his mind. Grace punched the pillow. Why did it matter so much to her if he changed his mind anyway?

Stupid, stupid girl.

She didn't have time for this. There were rounds to make and her bag still needed to be prepared. Placing the pillow on the bed, Grace gathered the soiled linen and headed toward her office.

A half hour later, she was ready. Her heavy bag of medical supplies and patient files securely on her shoulder, she cut through the large parlor on her way to the front door.

"You're a little early this evening, aren't you?" Nia called out from the door leading to the kitchen.

She glanced at the clock. "Just a few minutes. I thought I'd get an early start."

"Some of our patients might not be home yet."

Grace crossed her arms. Nia had never complained about her leaving early before. "Is there a problem?"

"No, I just—"

A knock at the door interrupted her. Nia hurried across the room to the front door. What could have her friend moving so quickly? Unless it was someone in labor. Grace mentally went through their patients. No one was due for another two weeks, but that didn't mean anything. Babies came when they were good and ready.

Adjusting her bag, she headed for the foyer where Nia and their guest. . . "Patrick? I wasn't expecting you." Not exactly the truth, but why was he here now, just as she was leaving?

Patrick glanced at Nia, then took a tentative step toward her. "Miss Shoemaker was kind enough to tell me that you make nightly rounds in the neighborhood. She thought it might be a good place for me to start my research." He gave her an uneasy smile. "That is, if it's all right with you."

Grace's heart did a tiny leap. Spend the entire evening with Patrick? Maybe she could find out why he'd disappeared from her life the way he had. "That would be lovely."

He held out his arm to her. "Then, if you're ready."

"Of course." She scurried toward him, telling herself she was in a hurry to see her patients, then took his arm. Sinewy muscles flexed beneath her fingers, and her stomach fluttered. She drew in a silent breath as he made his farewell to Nia then led her into the foyer.

"You're quiet this evening," he said as he took her bag from her shoulder. "Is something bothering you?"

"No," she replied a bit too quickly. "Not at all. I just wasn't expecting you this late in the day."

"I'm sorry. Would you rather I come back tomorrow?"

Would she? The answer surprised her. She grabbed her coat from the peg on the wall and put it on. "No, Patrick, you can stay. You need to know how desperate the need is here."

"Of course." Putting the bag down, he took her coat and helped her with it. She held her breath when he gently freed her low chignon.

They quietly walked out into the cold. Night had barely fallen, but the ominous clouds overhead stole the last drops of sunlight, making the streets almost pitch black.

"What time do the lamplighters come by here?" Patrick's hand covered hers, giving her a sense of comfort.

"We don't have lamplighters, at least not at this end of the street." She tugged him over to a nearby table and grabbed her lit lantern she'd brought. "Maybe you can fix that."

"That should be easy to do." He took the lantern. "But why is just this street without lamplighters?"

She hesitated. Mr. McCleary was known to have several politicians in his pocket. What if Patrick was one of them? Still, what harm would it do to tell him the truth? "Nia thinks Mr. McCleary is behind it."

"From what I've learned recently, it sounds like something he would do."

She breathed a slight sigh of relief. "Thank heavens. I thought. . ." Her doubts questioned Patrick's character, news he might not be too happy to hear. "It's just known around the neighborhood that McCleary has some influence over some of the local politicians."

"And you thought I was one of them?"

"No, not really. It's hard not to be a little cynical when you've seen the worst in people." She leaned into him. "Can you forgive me?"

He tilted his head toward hers, the light hint of bay rum teasing her senses. "There's nothing to forgive, though maybe you could answer a question for me."

As they reached the street, she pulled him to the left. "Ask away."

"Why are you here?"

Grace stumbled but righted herself quickly. To answer that would be to reveal the worst parts about herself. If Patrick knew what she had done, how she'd refused to help Tilly, how she'd turned her away, he'd never speak to her again. *Father, I've already lost one friend. Do I have to lose Patrick too?*

"Gracie?"

She drew in a deep breath. "After Mama and Papa died, I sort of floundered for a bit. Sullivan House gave me a mission to focus on. It was something I thought they would be proud of."

"I'm sure they would be, but don't you think they'd want to know you're safe and away from—what was it you called it?—the worst in people."

"You sound like Nia."

"That's because she's worried about you." She felt the tension in his body heighten. "You're putting yourself in danger down here."

She stared into the darkness, anger bubbling in her veins. "It sounds like you and Nia had a long talk after I went to bed yesterday."

"You didn't go to bed. I carried you, because you would have fallen on that pretty face of yours."

Grace blinked. "You think I'm pretty?"

"Are you asking for a compliment?" Anger still smoldered in his dark eyes, but something else shone there too. Attraction? Butterflies fluttered in her stomach. "You're a beautiful woman, Grace, for all the good it will do you," he muttered.

"What does that mean?"

He stopped and turned to face her. "It means you should be married with children of your own, helping these people by sharing their plight with others." His lips pulled into a disgruntled line. "Not down here trying to save them all by yourself."

Her temper snapped. "How would you know what I'm trying to do? It's not like you've asked me or tried to understand how important this is to me." Glancing around, she lowered her voice. "Don't you see—I need these people as much as they need me!"

His eyes bored into her. "What? Why do you need them?"

To answer him was more than she could bear at the moment. Withdrawing her arm from his, she reached for her bag. "Go away, Patrick."

"What?"

Grace threw the bag over her shoulder. "Go away. Back to the house. Nia can supply you with all the information you need."

He took her by the shoulders. "I'm not going back to the house."

"Go home, then." The words stumbled on the knot in her throat. She couldn't tell him the real reason she'd given up her life on Park Avenue and come to the slums to live. The truth would send him away.

And Grace was quickly realizing she wanted Patrick to stay.

But that was impossible. She'd chosen her life's course, and it didn't include Patrick Mosby. Spinning on her heels, she turned and ran into the darkness.

Stubborn woman.

Patrick walked by another building, searching each window for Grace's silhouette edged against the curtains. She'd taken off so quickly, he hadn't been able to recover fast enough to see which direction she'd gone.

Maybe he should call out her name. Surely someone in these buildings would know where to find her. As he continued down the street, shadows moved around him, and it wasn't until he was almost upon him that he noticed the little boy.

"Are you all right, son?"

"I'm not your son." Moonlight glimmered off the blade the boy thrust at him. "Now give me your money."

He glared at the child. "I don't have time for this."

The boy brought the knife a little closer, aiming at Patrick's stomach. "Then just give me your money and you can go."

Why, the brat couldn't be more than seven or eight years old. Patrick crossed his arms over his chest. "No."

The child's eyes widened. "Don't you see I can cut you?"

There was a tremor in his voice. Whoever he was, he hadn't been at this for long. "I think I can take you."

"Mr. McCleary wouldn't be too pleased."

"Is that who you work for, Robert McCleary?"

The boy gave him a stiff nod. "I'm the man of the family now with Pa gone. Mr. McCleary told me that if I bring in enough coin, he won't throw us out of our apartment." He rubbed his nose against the worn sleeve of his jacket. "Ma and the baby depend on me."

"Darby!"

They both looked back to see Grace coming out of the shadows toward them, her cheeks rosy pink from her exertions. As she neared, she rested her hand on the boy's shoulder as if to comfort him. Her gaze clashed with Patrick's over the boy's towhead. "I thought you were going home."

She should have known he would never leave things like that between them, but he wasn't going to rehash it right now. He glanced down at the child. "I was too busy being accosted by this knife-wielding br—boy."

"Hmm," she muttered, then dropped down beside the boy. She held out her hand to him. "I thought we talked about this, Darby O'Hern. You are not to try to rob people for that man again."

"How am I supposed to support Ma and Caroline, then, Miss Grace?" He relinquished the blade to her. "I promised Pa I'd keep a roof over our heads and food on the table."

Such a heavy responsibility for a boy. It seemed unfair for one so young to be left to bear the burden. But if Patrick had learned anything, it was that life was rarely fair.

"We'll find you an honest job, not one that could get you in trouble." Grace glanced over the child's head to look at Patrick. "Or worse."

No, if McCleary had no qualms about sending a young boy

out on the street to rob, it wasn't hard to imagine what he'd do if the child failed. The concerns Patrick had for the neighborhood bloomed.

"When?" The boy sounded frantic. "We owe rent and Mr. McCleary wants it now."

Patrick knew that feeling, always wondering if you were going to have a roof over your head or food to eat. Many a night he'd gone to bed hungry when the rent was due. If he could keep another person from experiencing that need, he'd do it. "I've got a job for you."

"You do?" Grace studied him with watchful eyes. "What kind of job?"

Patrick shuffled through the files of people who worked for him until he finally found a vacancy. "I'm in need of a footman."

"I don't know. That's a big job for such a small boy," Grace replied.

"I can do it," Darby piped up, then tilted his head to look up at Patrick. "What does a footman do?"

Patrick should know this; he had three of them. "Well, you'll sit with the driver and let down the steps for me and my guests. You'll also be in charge of cleaning the carriages as well as learn how to take care of the horses." He looked down at the boy. "Does this sound like something you'd like to do?"

The boy eyed him suspiciously. "That depends. How much are you going to pay me?"

Smart kid. He'd do well for himself one of these days. "More than enough to pay rent and keep your family fed and clothed." Patrick held out his hand. "What do you say?"

Darby looked at Grace, who nodded, then broke into a smile

as he took Patrick's outstretched hand. "I'll work harder than any man you have."

Patrick suspected he would. The boy had more gumption than most men. "I'll come around and collect you in the morning, then. And no more thieving. Is that understood?"

"Yes, sir." But instead of leaving, Darby stood there, a worried look on his young face. "What am I going to tell Mr. McCleary? He's not going to like that I'm coming to work for you."

Grace stood up, her eyes meeting Patrick's. "He's right, Patrick. McCleary might try something once he learns you've hired Darby."

"Is there any way we could move them into Sullivan House?"

"Maybe." She nibbled at her lower lip like she always had when she was thinking. "We'll have to move some things around, but I don't think it will be a problem."

"Miss Grace, we can't afford a place in your building," the child exclaimed. "And we won't be taking charity."

"Darby." Grace answered calmly as she placed her hands on his shoulders. "My apartments don't cost as much as Mr. McCleary's, so we shouldn't have a problem. But we do need to move you quickly."

"Son, go home and tell your mother what has happened." Patrick held the boy's gaze. "Get everything you own packed up. I'll be by to get you all in an hour. Is that understood?"

"Yes, sir!" The boy rocked from heel to toe as if he were about to burst with excitement. "I can't wait to tell Ma."

"Then go."

The boy took off like a firecracker on the Fourth of July, running down the street, skipping and laughing until he finally reached the corner. Turning toward them, he gave them a big wave. "Thank you!"

They watched Darby disappear into the apartment building; then Grace swirled around to face him. "That was a very nice thing for you to do."

His ears went hot. It wasn't often he was called out for a good deed. "There was nothing nice about it. I had a need, and Darby fit the bill."

She turned, then started slowly down the street. "Are you coming?"

He smiled to himself. Grace had never been able to carry a grudge for long. Even when he'd talked her into sliding down the banister and she'd broken her arm, she hadn't stayed mad long. He caught up with her. "Where are we going?"

"I have one more patient to look in on." She shifted her velvet bag to her other hand to allow him room. "Miss Van Dyke is due in about a month, but she's had a rough time of it. I want to see how she's feeling and make sure everything is in place."

"Why doesn't she come to Sullivan House and have her child?" He took her bag and threw it over his shoulder.

"It's very complicated, but in the end, she decided to have her baby at home."

"You're just full of secrets." He'd hoped for a more playful tone, but the words had come out flat instead. He decided to change the subject. "You should have waited on me. We had plans to do your rounds together."

"You and Nia made plans." There was an edge to her tone. "I was supposed to merely go along with them without one thought for my opinion."

She was right. She may have been threatened, but that didn't mean she shouldn't have a say in the matter. "I'm sorry."

Grace shook her head. "Don't be. I know Nia shared her concerns with you and that she's worried. I just want to be able to care for my patients when they need me."

"I understand that." Patrick hesitated. He needed to choose his next words wisely. "But I want you to think about this. If something happened to you, what would these people do then? Isn't it in their best interest to keep you safe?"

"I never thought of it like that."

Good, he had her thinking. Maybe if she knew about the note Nia received, she might understand their concerns. "Did Nia tell you about the note?"

Grace jerked her head up. "What note?"

Patrick took her arm and led her to a lighted street corner. "Nia got a note this morning while you were at the council meeting. It was from McCleary."

Even in the dull light, he could see her face pale. "What did he say?"

He dreaded telling her, but he had no other choice. "He wants you to drop the idea of buying another apartment or there will be consequences."

"Consequences," she mimicked, then stared up at him. "You never get used to them, the threats."

Fury coursed through Patrick. "How many times has he threatened you?"

"Once or twice. But I refuse to let that bully stop me from helping these people. I don't care how many threats he makes."

"Grace." He glanced around. It was only then that he recognized where they were. No signs marked the avenue, but he knew the markings on the buildings, the path that led up behind the second apartment to the right, the stairs that creaked.

"Patrick? What's wrong?"

He swallowed hard. Grace wasn't the only one keeping secrets. He pointed to the place he'd spent the last ten years trying to forget.

"That's where Pa killed himself."

Chapter 7

T hat's where Pa killed himself."

The way he said it, the pain still so palpable, lanced straight through her. Moving closer, she felt his breath against her palm as she cupped his cheek. "Oh Patrick."

He covered her hand with his. "I told myself I wouldn't let it bother me. Pa made the decision to—" He stumbled on the word. "Do what he did. But I was the one left to comfort Ma and Katie. We still had to pick up our lives after the mess he made."

Slipping her hand into his, Grace led him to a couple of wooden boxes where they sat down. "What happened that night when your father was arrested?"

His eyes locked with hers when he lifted his head. "You know about that?"

"I was going through my eavesdropping phase then." She gave him a gentle smile. "Remember?"

He nodded. "I wish you hadn't overheard that particular piece of news."

"Why don't you tell me about what happened?" Resting her hand on his back, she rubbed tiny comforting circles. "That is, if you want to talk about it."

Grace waited for several minutes; then, just as she was about to stand, Patrick spoke. "My father wasn't always wealthy. Da worked his way here on a ship in the mechanic room, then used the skills he'd learned to get a job working in the press room at the *Times*."

"You never told me that."

He glanced up at her. "I didn't know myself until Da was arrested. He made up much of his life."

How horrible, to not truly know who your father was. But then, who knew the true heart of a person or what led them to behave a certain way except the Lord Himself? "I'm sorry."

"Anyway, Da met my mother at some gathering at the newspaper. As you know, Grandpa Emerson owned an ironworks factory over the state line in New Jersey and was one of the paper's largest advertisers." Patrick shook his head. "Da always said it was love at first sight."

Knowing the late Mr. Mosby's penchant for lying, Grace wondered if it was love of Miss Emerson's dowry rather than affection for the woman herself. "I'm surprised your grandfather allowed the marriage."

"He didn't. Da kidnapped my mother."

She sucked in a breath. "Kidnapped her?"

Patrick gave her an easy smile. "You should see the look on your face. It's priceless."

She gave him a gentle shove. "So it wasn't a kidnapping."

"Oh yes." He lowered his head again. "But Ma was a willing captive. When they came back to the city, Grandpa had Da jailed, but after a month they released him."

"Why?"

The tips of Patrick's ears went pink. "I was on my way."

She felt her cheeks go hot. "Oh."

"Grandpa decided the best way to handle the situation was to help Da get settled into a position. For the marriage, Da not only got my mother's dowry, but Grandpa bought out a competitor's company and gave it to my father."

"That was extraordinarily generous."

Patrick rubbed his forehead with the tips of his fingers. "Yes, and what did my father do? He lost it all. That was when he decided to swindle all of our friends out of their money like he had my grandfather."

"Oh Patrick." What a terrible thing for his father to do! Patrick probably felt like he could never show his face in polite society again. Yet she still had one unanswered question. "How did you end up here?"

"After Da died, Grandfather released the rest of Ma's dowry." He turned his head and glanced at her. "He probably figured something like this could happen. Ma decided she couldn't let Da's victims suffer, so she paid them back as much as she could." Their eyes met and held. "We didn't have anywhere else to go."

"Oh Patrick. I didn't know how bad things were. If I had. . ." She stopped. What could she have done? The only thing she had to offer back then was her friendship, and he already had that. "Mama tried to contact your mother after your father's arrest, but your mother never responded."

Patrick took her free hand in his and gently stroked her knuckles. "Ma was too ashamed. She'd been duped by the man she married. She didn't leave the apartment much back in those days."

"And Katie?"

"She's happily married and living in Philadelphia with her husband." For the first time since he'd started talking, he smiled. "I'm the uncle to the most adorable little girl."

Grace returned his smile. "What's her name?"

"Isabella." Grace dropped her hand from Patrick's back as he straightened. "She's my little Izzy Bear."

"You sound like a doting uncle."

"She makes it easy to spoil her. She truly is the most precious child in the world."

"Spoken like a true uncle." She glanced down at the watch pinned to her bodice. "We should be getting back. It's getting late, and my last patient sent word she was working late tonight. Besides, Nia will worry." Grace rolled her eyes. "Like she always does."

"Grace." The somber way he spoke her name drew her attention back to him. He stood and then, holding her hand, helped her to her feet. "Please promise me you'll be extra careful."

Really, this argument was getting old. Why didn't anyone think she could take care of herself? "I'm always careful."

"And you won't go on rounds unless I can go with you?"

"But. . ."

"No buts. You won't go on rounds without me." He stroked his thumb across her knuckles, leaving her slightly breathless. "I can't risk losing you again."

Grace swallowed against the onslaught of emotions. She didn't want to lose him either. She nodded. "I promise."

Chapter 8

"Grace, we have a problem."

Two whole weeks without a problem. Grace was surprised it had been that long. She made a final notation in her account book, then lifted her head to find Nia and Rosie hovering in the doorway, worry etched on their faces. "It can't be that bad."

"I'm afraid it is." Nia stepped forward and handed her a folded sheet of paper.

Grace cringed. Folded papers bore the worst news. She took the paper and read it. Dear heavens, it was bad. She glanced back at the women. "This is a mistake. The funds are drawn out of my accounts and delivered on the first of each month."

"They say we owe additional funds."

Grace read the letter again. "I don't understand. We've paid everything the water department has asked for."

"They don't agree. In fact. . ." Nia and Rosie glanced at each other before turning back to her. "They've turned the water off until they're paid in full."

"What?" This was more than a problem. It was a catastrophe. "When did this happen?"

"I'm not sure. The water was on when I washed the dishes last night," Rosie replied, wringing her hands together until they turned a pale pink. "But this morning, Mr. McDaniel from the fourth floor came down around six to ask about the water."

Which meant it was turned off in the middle of the night. "This make no sense. The water department wouldn't send someone out here in the night to do this."

"Maybe." Nia shrugged. "Or maybe not. Depends on if someone in the department is working for McCleary on the side."

McCleary again. The man couldn't possibly make this much mischief. "Or maybe it's just a mistake." Grace pushed her chair back and stood. "I'll go to the water department and get this all cleared up."

"Get what all cleared up?"

Patrick. A wave of relief flooded through her. His presence these last two weeks had comforted her in a way she hadn't known she needed. She was extremely glad to see him. She handed him the note. "There's a problem with the water department, and they've cut off the water."

He read the paper, then glanced up at her. "You've paid them, haven't you?"

"Of course I have," she answered, a bit irritated he'd even ask. "You've seen the bank drafts."

He nodded. "Then I know some people we can talk to about this." He met her gaze. "I've got my carriage right outside."

We. Patrick said that word a lot when referring to Sullivan House business, and though it should have annoyed her, Grace found she rather liked the sound of it. As if they were partners in this mission. Grace grabbed her accounting book and circled her desk. "I'm ready."

"That's what I like, a woman who doesn't keep you waiting." His soft smile made her heart skip a beat.

Yet Grace wished she had taken the time to fix her hair or put on a different dress than the serviceable blue wool she wore. Not that it mattered in her world.

As she approached the women, they stepped to one side. Nia whispered, "I'll be praying everything turns out okay."

Grace took her friend's hand. "We need every prayer we can get."

"You ready?" Patrick held out his arm to her.

She nodded, taking his arm.

Several minutes later, Patrick helped her into the carriage and took the seat beside her. Once they were under way, he turned to her. "That note wasn't from the water department."

What worry she'd had intensified. "I don't understand."

He pulled the note from his coat pocket and opened it. "See the letterhead? It almost matches the city's, but it's a bit off-center. And the ink is lighter, a navy blue rather than black."

She took the letter and studied it. Patrick was right. "Why didn't I see that?"

"I see city correspondence all the time in my work, so I wouldn't expect anyone outside of city hall to notice it."

She sank back into the cushions. "I must be the most naive person in the world."

Patrick took her hand between his and leaned close. "I like you that way."

She lifted her gaze to meet his. "Really?"

"Really." He stroked his thumb over her knuckles. "It's kind of nice to take care of you."

She should be insulted. For the last two years, she'd done a pretty good job of taking care of herself. Yet there was something lovely in knowing Patrick was there to lean on. She squeezed his fingers. "I like to take care of you too."

"You mean like when you climbed the trellis outside my window with a sack of books?" he teased.

"Your mother wouldn't let me in."

"I had scarlet fever, you sweet idiot."

Grace felt a smile on her lips. "I didn't catch it, did I?"

"No, you didn't, but if you had, I would have felt terrible." He turned serious. "You were my friend, and I wouldn't want anything bad to ever happen to you."

Grace stilled. She understood that feeling. It was the same way she'd felt when Tilly's parents had disowned their daughter for marrying one of their footmen. Only Grace had failed to keep Tilly safe, to help her when she was at her most vulnerable.

She slid her hand out of his grasp. "Why would someone send me a letter like that? They had to know I'd contact the water department. How did they turn off the water?"

If he noticed her change of demeanor, he didn't show it. "They probably have someone with the city, maybe a pipe fitter, working with them."

"You think it's McCleary."

"Maybe." He rested back against the seat. "Or it could be someone who saw what you were doing with Sullivan House and decided to make some easy money off of you." He tilted his head toward her. "Still, I want to check with my friend James Tyler and make sure your accounts are up to date. He's director of the city's waterworks."

The carriage slowed to a stop. Patrick had just started for the door when it flew open. Darby, dressed in an oversized livery coat and dark pants, stuck his head inside. "Mr. Patrick, you've got to let me do my job." He glanced over to her. "Miss Grace! Look at my coat. Don't I look spiffy?"

"You look very handsome indeed." She watched the towheaded boy let down the steps. "And it looks like you're settling into your new job."

"I'm trying, but this one"—Darby nodded to Patrick—"he's always trying to beat me to it."

"It's an old habit." Patrick hurried down the steps before turning back to Grace. "I worked as a footman for my grandfather for a few years."

"So that's why you're so good at it," the boy replied.

And another part of Patrick's life she'd not known about. Every day for the last two weeks, she'd learned something new about him. How he'd sold newspapers to put food on his mother's table. The years he'd spent out west, building and repairing the rail lines. How a prayer meeting had led to his salvation. Each story had given her a clearer view of the man Patrick had become, a man she could respect and maybe even love.

Yet marriage wasn't in her plans. Sullivan House and the work she did there were her life's focus.

Grace took his hand, the warmth of his touch causing all her good intentions to blur. Their gazes met, and she knew he felt it too, this indescribable pull like a magnet to iron. She hurried down the steps, letting go of him as soon as her foot touched the ground.

Patrick followed her to the door and opened it for her. "James should be back from lunch by now. If anyone can find out what's going on, it's him."

They had just passed through the foyer when someone waved Patrick down. Grace couldn't help but notice that people were studying her, measuring her up against. . . She stilled. Was there another woman in Patrick's life? The thought made her heartsick.

As they stood waiting for an elevator, she had a question. "Do you know everyone at city hall?"

"Of course I do." Patrick answered her with a smile. "I wouldn't be much of a councilman if I didn't."

"Have you ever brought anyone else here, like a lady friend or a fiancée?"

He turned to her, blocking everyone's view of them. "Are you concerned that I have?"

"No," she answered a bit too quickly. With his attention focused on her, she felt her insides squirm. "Well, maybe."

As the elevator door opened, he helped her inside, then secured the gate. When the door closed, Patrick pulled her into his arms. "I've never done this at city hall."

Grace caught her breath as he tilted her head back and pressed a kiss to her cheek. She closed her eyes, enjoying the sweetness of the moment when he pressed his lips against hers. She'd only been kissed once before, when she'd decided she just wanted to get her first kiss over with. Patrick had been an unwilling partner, and things between them had been awkward for a few days. Then they'd slipped back into their normal routine of being friends and all was forgotten.

Grace would never forget this kiss.

He lifted his head for a brief second, and she mourned the loss. But then, as if the first one wasn't enough, he kissed her again. She threw her arms around his neck, holding him close.

The bell that announced their arrival dinged, and Grace jumped back. What was she thinking, kissing Patrick where anyone might see them? Why was she kissing him at all? She ran a shaky hand over her skirts, her body still tingling from Patrick's kisses.

The elevator stopped, and he opened the gate. She walked past him, not daring to meet his gaze. How was she supposed to make her case to the water department when all she could think about were those few moments in the elevator with Patrick?

She was being silly. It was just a kiss between friends. Nothing to feel awkward about, yet she couldn't make the feeling go away. She had to focus on the business at hand. "Patrick, what if your friend can't help us? We have to have water for our renters."

He rested his hand at the small of her back as he opened the door. "Jim can get it turned back on and maybe find the person who cut it off. If we know who he is, we might find out who our letter writer is."

Walking into the cramped space, she immediately found herself in front of the desk of a young man wearing spectacles and a three-piece suit. He glanced up at them, wearing a polite smile. "Mr. Mosby. How are you today?"

"Fine, Mr. Nelson. I'd like to introduce Miss Grace Sullivan."

The man bowed his head slightly. "Ma'am."

"Mr. Nelson."

With introductions finished, Patrick got right to the point. "Is James in?"

"He's in, but he's not available now." The man looked over the rim of his glasses. "He's working on the budget."

"Would you tell him Patrick's here? I'm sure he'll want to see me."

"Mr. Mosby, you know as well as I do that I can't—"

"It's an emergency."

Nelson glanced from Patrick to Grace; then, as if satisfied by what he saw in their expressions, he rose and walked to an interior office.

As the door clicked shut behind him, Grace closed her eyes. "Why did you tell him it was an emergency?"

"It's going to get us in, isn't it? And it is an emergency. You've got an apartment building full of people with no way to cook or wash clothes."

"But I don't want to get on the man's wrong side either."

Patrick turned to her. "Do you need water in your building?"

How had she never noticed that he had a tiny scar over his right eye or that he had shades of ginger in his dark brown hair? Or how his lips against hers could be so soft and firm at the same time?

This had to stop. She squared her shoulders. "Of course we need water."

He smiled at her. "Then it's an emergency."

Mr. Nelson stuck his head out the door. "Mr. Tyler will see you now."

Grace entered the office with Patrick close behind her. From the newspaper articles she'd read, she knew that the last director of the water department had been a personal appointment by the mayor. He had chosen a man with opulent taste that could rival Rockefeller's. Rather than earn his money honestly, the man had plunged the department into scandal with a variety of bribes and blackmail that now saw him doing time in jail.

James Tyler was the exact opposite. The sparse office held a large desk with two chairs in front of it and no pictures on the walls. Grace liked him instantly.

"Jimmy." Patrick walked the short distance to the desk and reached across to take his friend's outstretched hand. "I see you finally got rid of the Remington painting."

"Donated it to a museum uptown." He shook Patrick's hand. "Figured those uppity types might want to stare at the ugly thing for a while. What's so important that you had to disturb me?"

"If you were a gentleman, you'd see I've brought company with me." Patrick turned then, holding his hand out to Grace. "Jim, I'd like you to meet Miss Grace Sullivan."

The man wiped his hand against his pant leg then extended it to her. "I'm sorry, ma'am. I've been working on this budget all morning, and usually when Paddy shows up, it's to bug me about one thing or another."

Grace stole a look at Patrick. "I can understand that."

"Grace owns an apartment building on Mulberry Street and is having some problems with the water."

"Mulberry Street." Mr. Tyler eyed her for a long moment. "Are you a landlord or something?"

She knew she liked him. The man didn't mince words. "I am the landlady, but I also live there."

"Grace is a midwife." Patrick rested his hand against her lower back. "She provides housing for families with small children."

"Geez, you could knock me over with a feather." Mr. Tyler raked his gaze over her, then shifted his attention back to Patrick. "She looks like she belongs on Park Avenue rather than in lower Manhattan."

"That's because she does. We grew up together."

"Then that makes sense." He motioned to the two chairs in front of his desk. "What exactly brings you here today?"

"This." Patrick pulled out the bill and handed it to Mr. Tyler. "I think it's fake, but we thought we'd better check with you first."

The man glanced over it. "This isn't one of ours."

Grace exchanged a look with Patrick. Then it was McCleary. Who else could it be? He was the only one who'd ever given her any trouble in the past. But how—

Her thoughts were interrupted by Mr. Tyler's question. "Have you run into trouble with any of the neighboring families?"

Patrick spoke before she could answer. "McCleary's been giving her problems. Spoiled milk, missed coal deliveries, a rock through the window, stuff like that." Almost as an afterthought he said, "He threatened her."

Grace glanced up at him. "There wasn't any reason to tell him that."

His expression tightened. "There's every reason to tell him. He needs to know what we're dealing with here."

"Why? I have no intentions of letting the man bully me."

"Grace. . ."

Patrick looked ready to explain when Mr. Tyler butted in. "I'm sorry if I'm interrupting a lovers' quarrel, but I've got work do to here." Once he had their attention, he started again. "So we know that McCleary has bothered Miss Sullivan in the past. But why would he escalate things now? Has anything changed?"

Grace got a sinking sensation in her stomach. "I put in an offer on another apartment building in the area."

Patrick gawked at her. "Why did you do that?"

"Because we need more rooms." Frustration flared in her chest. "Every day I have to turn families away because we don't have any more apartments available. I'm tired of doing that. I feel like I'm letting these people down when I have the means to take care of it."

The men exchanged a look; then Mr. Tyler spoke. "McCleary is putting you on notice."

Grace blinked. "That's ridiculous."

"Miss Sullivan," Mr. Tyler said, "Robert McCleary makes his money from his many tenements on the lower east side. Nobody cares if he follows the building codes or overcharges his renters for a measly one-room apartment, because he's got half of the city's government officials in his back pocket. Now you've come in, buying up apartment buildings, and he can't help but feel threatened. He thinks you're horning in on his territory."

"But there is no territory, and I'm certainly not horning in on it." Irritation laced her voice. "I'm simply providing a safe place for people to raise their children."

"I know." Patrick took her arm and turned her to face him. "But those families used to pay rent to McCleary. You're taking money out of his pocket."

She jerked her arm out of his loose grip. "You've seen those slums. Nine to ten people to a room. No fresh air or sunshine. Rats as long as my arm." She turned her head to glare at Mr. Tyler. "What are the other half of the city officials, the ones who are not on McCleary's payroll, doing about it?"

Mr. Tyler's stern expression warned her that she had gone too far. "Miss Sullivan, I will have a man out there within the hour to turn your water back on. But let me give you a little piece of advice."

"What would that be?"

"Go back to Park Avenue." He leaned across the desk as if to make a point. "You're going to get yourself killed down there if you don't watch it."

Anger flowed through her veins. She'd been wrong. She did not like this man. "What about the families under my care? Am I supposed to abandon them?"

"Gracie, you're not responsible for them."

Patrick's words hurt. Of the few people she trusted, she thought he understood how much Sullivan House meant to her, what it meant to the community. Yet now at the first sign of trouble, he'd have her run back to her Park Avenue townhouse.

Grace straightened, her heart a stone in her chest, her world weighing heavy on her. "Thank you, Mr. Tyler. I appreciate all your help in this matter."

Without another word, she turned and walked out.

Chapter 9

Stubborn, stubborn woman!

Patrick knew he'd hurt her feelings. But he'd rather that than see her broken and beaten by McCleary's thugs. Or, Lord help them, worse.

"I can see why you care about her," Jimmy said as he sat down. "She's got spunk."

"Shut up." He stalked to the door, then back to his friend's desk. "You'll have someone out there to get the water back on?"

Jimmy gave a curt nod. "Just like I told the lady. Within the hour."

"Good." Patrick hurried to the door, then through the outer office. If he could catch her before she got on the elevator, he might get a chance to explain. As he rounded the corner, he caught himself. Grace stood at the window, discouragement weighing down her shoulders. She dabbed at her eyes, a small hiccup breaking the silence.

"Grace."

She turned, and once again, he was struck by her unassuming beauty. He took one tentative step, then another, until he stood in front of her. Lifting his hand to her face, he brushed his thumb against her wet cheek. "I'm sorry."

"I thought you believed in what I do." She sniffled. "But it sounded like you'd rather I go home."

Patrick pulled a clean handkerchief from his vest pocket and handed it to her. "It's not that." She gave him a stern look. "All right, it is that, but hear me out."

Stepping away from him, she blew her nose. "All right, then. What is it you want to say?"

His mind went blank. What could he say to her? That he feared for her life every moment he was away from her? That the thought of something happening to her kept him awake all night?

"Grace, McCleary threatened your life."

Wide blue eyes met his. "What are you talking about?"

"The note." Even now, he wanted to punch McCleary for the things written. "What I didn't tell you is that he listed ways he planned to hurt you unless you gave up the idea of buying another apartment."

"Dear heavens." She took a shuddering breath, then glanced at him. "Is that why you made me promise not to go on rounds without you? Because you don't think I can take care of myself?"

He was quickly losing his temper. "Yes, Grace. You're not safe with a man like Robert McCleary around. But that's not why I made you promise."

"Then why?"

"Because. . ." *I care for you.* Patrick shook his head. Of course he cared for her. "You're my dearest friend. I worry about you."

Something akin to hope died in her eyes. She shifted away, putting some distance between them. "I appreciate your concern, really I do. But Sullivan House is my life now, and when the next building is purchased and renovated, Mr. McCleary will see that I have no intention of taking over his 'territory.'"

He wanted to shake the obstinacy out of her. "Don't you see? McCleary doesn't want to share. He wants it all, including Sullivan House, and if that note is anything to go by, he'll do whatever it takes to achieve that."

Grace walked over to the elevator and pushed the call button. "I'm going to walk home."

"Let me take you home. Please, Gracie."

She shook her head as the elevator arrived. "I'll be fine."

As she reached for the gate, he stopped her. "Grace, use your head. Walking home makes you an easy target for McCleary."

She glared at him. "In the middle of the day?"

Grace was so sweetly naive. She was a lamb in a world full of wolves, and until he convinced her to give up the idea of another tenement, he intended to stay close. "I'll go with you."

"What?"

"I'm going to walk with you."

"You are the most irritating man in all of New York," she mumbled as she closed her eyes.

"And you're the most stubborn woman." His mouth tugged up into a half smile as he opened the gate for her. "We make a perfect couple."

She hurried into the corner of the elevator. "I'm not speaking to you."

He followed her inside, taking the place beside her. "There's that stubbornness I was talking about. I don't remember you being so obstinate when we were younger."

She didn't answer, nor did either of them speak as they walked through the building and out onto the street. Crowds bustled along the sidewalks, men in derby hats and three-piece suits hurrying to business meetings, women clustered together as they strolled down the street.

After waving off his carriage, Patrick caught up with Grace. "Are we still not speaking to one another?"

"I do have one more question." She didn't look at him but continued looking straight forward. "I just want to know why. Why did you kiss me?"

He wasn't sure what to tell her. When she'd asked him about other women and he'd realized she was a little jealous, his heart had just about jumped out of his chest. The thought that his kind, beautiful friend could have feelings toward him had made him feel. . . He couldn't describe it.

And he'd kissed her, not once but twice, and enjoyed every second of it.

How did he explain that to her? He leaned down slightly so that only she could hear him. "I just wanted to kiss you."

Her eyes widened, but still, she refused to look at him. "Do you kiss every woman you want to kiss?"

"No," Patrick almost shouted. The disapproving stares of two well-dressed matrons reminded him of where they were, and he lowered his voice. "No, I don't go around kissing just anyone."

"Yet you kissed me."

Yes, and if he had the chance, he'd do it again in a heartbeat. But he couldn't tell her that either. "Grace, can't we just forget it?"

"I think that's an excellent idea." She finally glanced at him, the soft smile playing on her lips irritating. "It's completely forgotten."

"Good."

"Good." Yet from where Patrick stood, there was nothing good about this situation at all. If Grace wouldn't take the situation with McCleary seriously, he had no other choice.

He'd have to talk to McCleary himself.

Chapter 10

Grace lay staring at the ceiling. A damp chill in the air had her pulling up the quilts to burrow under them. Sleep had come in fits last night and she'd found herself staring into the darkness more than once.

Why did Patrick have to kiss her? She pulled her pillow over her head and groaned. How was she supposed to forget the feel of his arms around her, the way his lips tenderly touched hers before deepening the kiss, searing it into her bones? She'd felt like she was soaring, only to plunge to earth when he'd sided against her at the water department and then told her to forget what had happened in the elevator.

Drat the man!

Somewhere in the early morning hours, she'd grudgingly realized the truth in Patrick's concerns. What good would she be to the people of Mulberry Street if she was beaten into submission, or worse? Still, the thought of abandoning them went against everything she believed in. How could she reconcile the two? Continue her work here at Sullivan House while holding McCleary at bay?

Throwing the covers to the side, Grace stood then turned to

straighten her bed before beginning her daily toilette. After she finished, she walked to the chair and picked up the gown she'd picked out the previous evening. The gray wool matched her mood. Quickly, she threw the dress over her head and worked the buttons into place.

She glanced in the mirror as she walked to the door. Grace never would have worn such a drab gown in the old days. Her armoire had been full of the latest fashions in the loveliest shades of lavender, pale pink, and mint green. Laces and silks, walking dresses and elaborate ball gowns. More than one person could possibly wear. And the shoes! Leather ladies' boots and satin dancing slippers in every conceivable cut and color graced her closet.

But what did all those things matter without the people you loved? Without some kind of purpose that got you out of bed every morning?

Her parents' deaths had taught her that. Grace glanced at the lithograph that held a place of importance on her desk. At their memorial service, dozens of people had told her about the many acts of service her parents had performed over the course of their marriage. As the minister said, they had served in silence as God had intended, gaining their rewards in heaven rather than in this human existence.

Tilly's death had given Grace the purpose she had sought. A healthy twenty-one-year-old woman shouldn't die in childbirth for lack of health care. If only she'd offered to help, at least called a doctor, maybe Tilly and her child would have had a chance.

Could she give up her life's purpose now, when she was finally making a difference?

A knock at the door interrupted her thoughts. "Miss Gracie?"

Rosie, probably wanting to go over their maintenance list for the day. She hurried around the desk to the door, then opened it. "I'm sorry. I'm running late this morning. Do sit down."

"You haven't even dressed your hair." Taking Grace's hand, Rosie led her over to one of the two chairs and gently pushed her into the seat. "I'll work on it while we go over the list."

"You don't have to do that."

"But I want to." She gathered the hairbrush and pins beside the washbasin and brought them over to the desk. "Some of my best memories are of getting your mother all dressed up for some ball or whatnot." She grew quiet for a moment. "I miss her."

"I do too."

Rosie slid the brush through Grace's hair, and she had to bite back a moan. "I'd forgotten how good it feels to have someone brush my hair."

"Then I'll have to do it more often." Rosie brushed Grace's hair upward, then worked to secure each length with pins. "Your mother, she would have been right proud of you, doing all of this."

"It's not that much."

"Maybe not to you, but to the people in this building, it's everything." She opened a pin with the tip of her tooth, then secured it. "It's like she always said. You can't expect a person to understand the love of Christ when they're worried about where their next meal will come from or where they'll sleep tonight."

"Mama and her sayings." Yet as Grace thought about it, she realized each one held a biblical truth. "I don't think she would have been very proud of the way I treated Tilly."

"Everyone makes mistakes, little one." Rosie curled another long section of hair and pinned it. "You had no way of knowing what would happen."

"Maybe not, but still." She dropped her gaze to her lap. "She looked so frail the last time I saw her, as if she didn't have the energy to draw her next breath. I did nothing to ease her burden."

"Neither did I. But I'm not sure Tilly would have wanted our help anyway." Rosie wrestled the last pin into place, then stepped back. "I blame her parents. They made it impossible for her to come to them for help. To my way of thinking, they should be the ones ashamed of themselves, not you." Tilting her head to the side, she smiled. "I believe I've outdone myself. Go look."

Grace rose and went to the mirror. Instead of the low chignon at the nape of her neck, Rosie had shifted it to the top of her head, loosening it so that it appeared to float on a cloud of curls. "You've made me a regular Gibson Girl. But why go to all that fuss?"

"There's nothing wrong with looking nice, is there?" Rosie returned the hairbrush and remaining pins to the crate by Grace's bed. "And we never know when Mr. Mosby might drop in for a visit."

Grace's smile deflated. "I'm not sure Mr. Mosby will come around anymore."

"Why's that?" Hands on her hips, Rosie searched Grace's face. Then she scowled. "You didn't argue, did you?"

"He doesn't believe in what I'm doing here, Rosie." Which wasn't quite true, but she wasn't ready to concede yet. "He feels I'm in too much danger, and that I would do better sharing these people's plight with my society friends."

The older woman stood silent for a moment, then said, "I think he's right."

Grace jerked around to face her. "Rosie!"

"I'm sorry, little one, but Mr. Mosby has a point." She walked over to where Grace stood and took her hand. "When you bought this apartment building, I didn't worry so much, but then, I didn't know about men like Mr. McCleary." She squeezed Grace's hand. "But I've heard stories about him from some of the people who live here. He's a cruel man, and not someone you want to make angry."

"I know. But I can't just walk away. These people need me."

"There are other ways to help besides being here."

"Patrick said the same thing yesterday, but I don't know." Grace shook her head. "I just hate the thought of giving in."

"Maybe you and Mr. Mosby could work together." Rosie gave her a knowing glace. "Seems a man like him with all his political aspirations would be looking for a wife to help him along the way."

Grace dropped Rosie's hand and stepped around the desk to the door. "Patrick is a friend, Rosie. It's not like he's calling on me."

"But he could be." Rosie followed her out of the office, waiting as Grace locked the door. "I seem to remember you favored each other's company when you were children."

"That was a long time ago. People change."

"Yes, I know. They grow up." Rosie stepped in front of her, much like Mama used to when Grace was on a tear. "It seems that you have even more in common now, wanting to serve the people of this city and everything."

Maybe. "I never saw Patrick as someone interested in politics."

"Oh, I did." Rosie chuckled. "That boy could charm the birds out of the trees. Remember when he talked you into sliding down the staircase on that old rug from your mama's room?"

She'd forgotten about that. Grace laughed softly. "We had

finished reading *The Thousand and One Nights* and Patrick got this idea in his head that we could fly just like Aladdin did in the book."

"He had a time of talking you into it."

"I knew it couldn't work, but he made it sound like so much fun, I finally gave in." Grace grimaced. "We hit the marble floor so hard, I felt it in every one of my bones."

"Ah, that was when Mr. Mosby dislocated his shoulder."

Grace stopped and looked at her. "I didn't know that."

"Remember, he threw himself in front of you as you hit the floor. Your mother was certain he'd broken his arm, but the doctor saw that it was his shoulder and put it back into place. Mr. Mosby wanted to protect you."

Grace let that sink in. Was that why he'd helped her at the water department and volunteered to go with her on her rounds? "He's always been protective of me."

"Of course he has, and I reckon he always will be, seeing as how he's in love with you and everything," Rosie said matter-of-factly.

"He doesn't love me." Yet he'd kissed her as if he felt something more than friendship toward her. A tiny kernel of hope sprouted in her heart. That kiss, she'd realized this morning, had meant more to her than just a kiss between friends.

But then he'd told her to forget it, and she'd been left hurt and confused. Maybe he was as confused about his feelings as she was. He hadn't meant to hurt her at all.

For some reason, that made her feel better. "You ready to get started today?"

"The way your mind moves from one subject to another." Rosie shook her head. "It makes my head spin."

Grace laughed, probably the first real laugh she'd had in a long time. It felt lovely and light, and she decided to savor it while it lasted.

"Grace!"

Grace turned and saw Nia, breathless and wild-eyed, running toward them. There was a large dark stain at the hem of her skirts as if she'd been splattered with mud, but then Grace noticed the drops of crimson on her friend's apron.

"It's the Fitzwilliam girl," Nia blurted out between breaths. "I can't get the bleeding stopped."

Grace grabbed her by the arm and pulled her toward the delivery room. "How long has she been in labor?"

"An hour, but she just showed up here about fifteen minutes ago."

There was an edge to her voice that scared Grace. Nia was a veteran midwife, having practiced for over twenty years. If she was worried, then there was need to be.

Then Grace remembered why. "Didn't she lose a child earlier this year?"

Nia nodded. "It was an early delivery then too. The baby was too early to survive. We almost lost them both."

"I remember." Patrice Fitzwilliam worked in one of McCleary's brothels, earning her keep while supporting her two younger brothers. Still just a child herself, she'd flatly refused Grace's offer to leave McCleary's employment and come stay at Sullivan House. Grace feared her pride would eventually leave her brothers homeless. "How is she otherwise?"

"She's banged up pretty bad. A bit flushed like she's running a fever."

This wasn't good news. "Does she need a doctor?"

"You know of one who will leave the likes of Park Avenue to

tend a prostitute in Manhattan?" Nia scoffed.

The truth of the answer bothered Grace. "No, but the girl still needs one."

"Let's look at her together before we go making rash decisions," her friend answered as she opened the door to the delivery room. "It could be something simple that I've missed."

Grace doubted it. Nia was meticulous when it came to their patients.

The rustle of skirts behind her made Grace turn around. Rosie and Patrick were heading toward them. He must have sensed the worry in her expression, because he quickened his pace. "What is it?"

No hello or anything? Simply quick and to the point. Grace smiled to herself. The old Grace would have been caught up in all the social proprieties, but this Grace was forever grateful. "We have a patient who may need a doctor."

"I'll fetch one, then."

Of course he would. Hadn't he always done everything he could to make her life, and the lives of all those around him, better? He started for the door, but Grace grabbed his arm. "Let me check on her first. It might not be anything, and I don't want to take the chance of getting a doctor here for nothing."

"All right." He nodded. "I'll do whatever you need me to do. I just want to help."

She could have kissed him. Instead, she focused on her patient. "There is one thing you need to know." She shuffled her feet. How could she explain something as indelicate as Patrice's profession? Warmth infused her cheeks. "Patrice works for Mr. McCleary in one of his. . .brothels."

His jaw tightened, and there was a dangerous look in his eyes. "What has that got to do with anything? She's someone who still needs a doctor, isn't she?"

She was, but Grace knew better than most what doctors thought of the tenements. "Yes, but—"

"Don't worry, Gracie." The corner of his mouth tipped up into a crooked smile. "The good doctor doesn't need to know anything about your patient until he gets here."

"But I need to examine her. . . ." She followed him down the hallway.

Patrick grabbed his coat and hat, then turned to her. "Then the doctor can help you with the delivery, sweetheart." He cupped her cheek in his palm. "You know you want him there."

He was right. She would feel better if a physician was in attendance. Grace nodded. "Hurry, please. With her being so young, I'm not sure what to expect."

"I believe in you, Grace." Patrick pressed a soft kiss to her forehead, then opened the door. "I'll be back before you know it."

The door clicked shut behind him.

⌒

Grace's heart fluttered as she rushed down the hall to evaluate her patient. Knowing Patrick was there, and that he valued her work, made her fall a little bit more in love with him. Since the night he told her about his father and everything that happened to his family, there had been a shift in their relationship, at least for her. Her heart beat a little faster when his name was mentioned, and she felt a joy she'd never known. She didn't just care for him as a friend. She could see a life with him.

"Grace!"

She had barely opened the door to the room when Patrice let out a terrifying scream. In an instant, blood pooled on the sheets beneath her. Grace hurried toward the linen cabinet and pulled down every towel they had. By the time she made it to the bedside, Patrice had mercifully passed out.

"I shouldn't have left her." Nia hurried to the foot of the bed and pushed the girl's legs up. "She's going to bleed to death."

"We're not going to let that happen." Grace refused to give up. She shoved the towels beneath Patrice's hips. "We need to elevate her legs."

Nia pulled the pillow from beneath Patrice's head and pushed it under her knees. What are we going to do if this doesn't work?"

"It's going to work," Grace answered. *Please, God. Let it work!*

"There doesn't seem to be as much blood." Nia glanced over Patrice's belly. "How did you know to do that?"

"I read it somewhere." Grace went to the door and called to Rosie. Once she'd sent her off to find more towels and linens, she came back to the bed. "Did the baby. . . ?"

Nia laid a clean pillowcase in the bassinet beside her, then lifted the tiny child from the bed, her fragile body barely big enough to fit in Nia's two hands. As she laid the child down and began rubbing her with the edges of the pillowcase, a small mew rose up from her, and the purplish-blue tinge to her skin disappeared, turning it pink and rosy. "She's alive."

"A miracle," Grace whispered. "So fearfully and wonderfully made."

"My baby." A weak whisper rose from the bed. Grace bent down with her ear close to Patrice's lips. "Tell her her ma loved her."

Grace took the girl's cold hand in hers, rubbing her chilled fingers to generate some warmth. "It's all right, darling girl. We've stopped the bleeding. You'll be up and holding your daughter soon."

The girl licked her lips. "I'll never hold my little girl. I'm paying for my sins." She opened her eyes. "Don't ever tell my brothers what I'd become."

Tears blurred Grace's vision. Maybe if she gave the girl something to live for, a hope for the future. "Will you come and live here with the children?"

"I don't know." Her face turned a paler shade of white. "I want to pay my own way."

"We'll work something out. Maybe you could care for the younger children while their parents are at work."

"I'd like that." Her face tightened. "Would I have to go back to—"

"Never!" Grace bit out, then worked to keep the tears at bay. "There'd be no reason to."

"I'd like that." Her eyes drifted shut again. Grace heard a breath, then another.

Then the young girl went deathly still.

Chapter 11

I should have you arrested, dragging me down here to this god-forsaken place."

Patrick ignored the rotund man sitting across from him. He'd mistakenly revealed their destination to the first two doctors he'd approached only to have the door slammed in his face. He'd only shared their location with this one once the carriage was under way and a large amount of money had been agreed upon.

The portly man glanced outside. "Will I be safe?"

"Not if you don't stop complaining, Dr. Moore." Patrick gave a snort. "Aren't doctors sworn to help those in distress?"

The man had the nerve to look offended. "I have saved many lives in my years of practice and served some of the most affluent families in the city." He huffed, glaring out the window as if he were descending into Hades itself. "My reputation will be ruined after this."

Patrick wanted to knock that smug look off his face, but Grace needed the old windbag. "If it helps matters, you'll be aiding Miss Grace Sullivan of the Park Avenue Sullivans."

"Miss Grace. . ." The man coughed, his eyes going wide. "That woman from the council meeting?" He smirked. "I thought we'd scared her away with that note."

Bounding from his seat, Patrick caught the doctor across the throat with his forearm. "What note?"

"I. . ." The man breathed in short puffs. "I can't. . ."

Patrick eased the pressure at the doctor's neck. "What note, Dr. Moore?"

He swallowed. "Dr. Zimmerman thought if Miss Sullivan was threatened, she might abandon her midwife practice, so he had one of McCleary's men deliver it to her right after the council meeting. He thought with her living in the tenements, she would never trace the note back to us."

Patrick shoved him back against the seat. "And turning off the water to Sullivan House, was that Dr. Zimmerman's idea too?"

Dr. Moore nodded as he shifted away from Patrick. "Zimmerman thought if we kept up the pressure, she'd eventually pick up her skirts and run, and McCleary was happy to oblige." Moore drew in a deep breath. "We only meant to frighten her."

Patrick grabbed the man by his lapels and jerked him upright. "I'm certain my friend, the chief of police, will be very interested in you and your colleagues' scare tactics. I'm certain Sing Sing is in need of a physician or two."

He tossed Moore back into his seat, then took his own. There would be a price to pay for this, possibly his council seat, but at the moment, he didn't care. Grace, who'd never asked for anything from anybody, needed his help, and he'd move heaven and earth to provide it.

So it wasn't only McCleary involved. What other plans did the doctors have for her? "Is there anything else?"

Moore's nervous gaze met his. "I don't know what you mean."

Patrick inched forward, sending the man cowering into the corner. "Do you and your fellow physicians have any other plans to terrorize Miss Sullivan?"

He shook his head. "Not that I'm aware of." He hesitated, then continued, "Please understand. I never wanted—"

"Don't." Patrick turned from him, knowing that if he didn't, he'd plant a facer in the man's snub nose. "In fact, it might be best if you stop talking."

A few minutes later, the carriage slowed to a stop outside Sullivan House. Patrick reached for the door, but it flew open and Darby let down the steps.

Patrick jumped out, then turned and ruffled the boy's hair. "Have I told you what an excellent job you're doing, Darby?"

The boy's face lit up. "You mean when you let me do my job."

"I may need your help." He nodded to the man huddled inside the carriage. "I may need a little help with this one. Do you know anyone who could guard him after he's done with Miss Grace?"

"There's Mr. Pipitone. He's a butcher down in the meat district."

Patrick fished out a gold piece and handed it to the boy. "If you'll have him meet me in the parlor, I'll give him double that."

Darby stared at the money in his palm, then back at Patrick as he hurried down the sidewalk. "Thank you, sir."

Patrick turned his attention back to Dr. Moore. "Well, are you coming or am I going to have to drag you out of there?"

That sent the doctor into motion. He grabbed his medical bag and exited the carriage. Patrick gripped his arm just in case he decided to make a run for it.

Rosie met them at the door. "Thank heavens you're back." She motioned to the hallway. "Second door on the right."

From the breathless urgency in the woman's voice, there was no time to waste. Propelling the man across the parlor, Patrick turned down the hall. Women lined the walls, some holding babies, their expressions full of worry and fear. One bowed her head, her lips moving in silent prayer.

Patrick knocked on the door. "Grace? The doctor is here."

The door swung open, and his heart twisted in his chest. Grace stood there, disheveled, tiny wisps of her hair framing her pale face. The sleeves of the gray gown were rolled up, revealing capable arms. Her apron, once a snowy white, now was speckled with flecks of crimson. Pride filled him. She was the most beautiful woman he'd ever known.

And he loved her.

"Doctor, I'm so glad you could come." Grace held out her hand, as if they were in a Park Avenue parlor rather than the slums of the lower east side. "We could certainly use your help."

The physician pushed past her. Patrick took a step to go after him, but the look on Grace's face stopped him. Whatever was going on inside the room was much worse than she was letting on. She rested her hand on his chest, and he captured it in his, giving her all the strength he could through a simple touch.

She straightened then gave the women present a smile before going back into the room and closing the door.

"It must be bad for Miss Grace to call for a doctor," a woman across from him said, a small babe snuggled close to her breast. "She's only done that once since I've been here."

"Though why she did it for Patrice Fitzwilliam is beyond me," snapped another woman, heavy with child. "That child would rather be dead than go back to the life she had."

"Don't judge the girl," a young woman answered. "You would have done the same thing if you had two wee brothers at home who depended on you."

Curiosity got the better of him. "How old is Miss Fitzwilliam?"

The women exchanged looks, but no one spoke. Why should they? He hadn't done anything to earn their trust, not like Grace had done. Well, he intended to change that.

"Please, I'd like to know so that I can help."

An older woman glared at him. "We don't need your handouts."

These people had their pride. Patrick began again. "That's not what I mean. There are other ways I can help you, like cleaning up this area and getting people like McCleary out of here."

"And how would you be doing that?"

Patrick walked closer to them. "I'm a city councilman."

The older woman snorted. "A politician."

"Yes, but—" There was only one way to make these people believe him, but he loathed to do it. "I lived just down the street for a few years with my mother and sister after my father killed himself. Pa had swindled most of our friends out of their money and thought death would be easier than prison."

The women stared at him wide-eyed, shock in their expressions. Then the older woman nodded to him. "Maybe you could help with McCleary. He's been a boil on the neighborhood for long enough."

Relief flooded through him. "Tell me about Patrice Fitzwilliam. You say she has two young brothers."

"Aye," the woman beside him answered. "Their parents died a while back from the typhus. Patrice has tried to keep a roof over their heads ever since."

He still didn't understand. "Couldn't the girl find work in the garment district or maybe as a nanny?"

"She's not old enough for that. She's only thirteen."

Thirteen? Still a child herself, and she'd been working in McCleary's brothel, selling herself to pay rent to the man. Bile rose in Patrick's throat. How many others had suffered this same kind of abuse just for a room?

This had to stop. He turned to the older woman. "Would you tell Grace I'll be back as soon as I can?"

"Yes, sir."

He started down the hall, then stopped. "Where can I find the Fitzwilliam brothers?"

Another young woman spoke up. "They're in McCleary's building three blocks east of here. Room 418."

"Thank you." He turned and hurried to the parlor, stopping only to ask Rosie to prepare a tray for Grace and the Fitzwilliam boys.

He had a call to make.

⌒

The distinct sounds of a fiddle and a harmonica grated against Patrick's ears as he stood at the base of the steps of the McCleary house. Unlike McCleary's residence uptown, the four-story building seemed a truer reflection of the man himself than the opulent home on the upper east side. Painted on the outside, yet on further inspection, hard and broken.

Anger sparked in Patrick again as he thought of the Fitzwilliam girl. Her brothers were younger than he thought, three and four at the most. Left alone in a room most likely used as a closet at one time, the boys looked thin for their age and the youngest one could barely stand. Patrick grabbed what little belongings they had and gathered the boys into the carriage, making a quick stop by Sullivan House before moving to the next idea on his list.

A meeting with Robert McCleary.

He was taking a chance the man would be at his establishment today, but it was a risk he'd have to take. Patrick climbed the short staircase then knocked on the door. A panel slid to one side, revealing a pair of dark, world-weary eyes. "May I help you?"

"I need to speak to Mr. McCleary. It's about Patrice Fitzwilliam."

"Patrice!" Worry creased the corners of the woman's eyes. "Is she okay? She looked so bad when she left here this afternoon."

A voice roared behind the oak door. "Get away from there, girl, and get back to work if you know what's good for you."

The young woman was yanked away, replaced by eyes of steely blue. "What do you want?"

Anger sparked in Patrick's belly and he took a deep breath. He'd need a calm head when he talked to McCleary. "I'd like to speak to Mr. McCleary concerning Patrice Fitzwilliam."

"Where is she?" the man snarled. "The silly chit was supposed to be here an hour ago."

Patrick's hands curled into tight fists. "That's why I'm here. If I could just talk to Mr. McCleary."

The man eyed him a moment longer, then slammed the panel shut. "Go away."

Patrick pounded on the door. "I'm not leaving here until I speak to McCleary."

The door opened and a brute of a man came at him, brandishing a thick plank of wood. "You'll leave now if you know what's good for you."

Patrick took a quick inventory of the man. A couple inches taller and a few pounds heavier, the man might have stood a chance any other day. But Patrick had been bruising for a fight ever since Dr. Moore's confession this afternoon, and the sight of the Fitzwilliam boys had only added to his ire.

"You want to fight." Patrick stepped toward him. "Be a man and fight like one."

The plank fell to the floor. "All right, you stuffed shirt. Let's see what you've got."

Behind them, a crowd of scantily clad girls, some as young as the Fitzwilliam girl, gathered at the door. Patrick felt the sting across his knuckles as he planted his fist in the brute's face.

Suddenly the girls parted and the man who'd caused this ruckus stood in the doorway. "Gentry, stand down."

The man backed away, though Patrick could sense the tension coursing through him. "Yes, sir, Mr. McCleary."

The older man turned to Patrick, his smile a little too bright. "Councilman Mosby, so glad to see you this fine evening. Would you like to come in, maybe partake in some refreshments?"

Patrick studied the man in the doorway. Robert McCleary could have passed for anyone's kindly old grandfather with his snowy white hair and ready smile. Of course, the two thugs shadowing him gave him a sinister look that was more in line with a criminal who controlled the Irish tenements. A man he intended to bring to justice.

Patrick stepped forward. "I need to speak to you about Patrice Fitzwilliam."

A slight sneer marred his grandfatherly appearance. "So the councilman has a taste for the young ones."

He ignored the dig. "You mean the thirteen-year-old child you forced to work in this place."

The kind facade ripped loose. "What about her?"

There were so many things Patrick wanted to say, but in this case, it wasn't the time or the place. "She showed up at Sullivan House today in labor. We had to call a doctor to attend to her."

"If you're expecting me to pay—"

"No, I'm expecting you to be a halfway decent human being and let these girls go home where they belong."

McCleary pounded his cane against the hard floor. "They live on my property, Mr. Mosby, and if they can't pay their rent, they must work it off."

Patrick clenched his fists behind his back as bile burned a path up his throat. How could such a man prosper when so many around him barely survived? "How do you live with yourself, McCleary?"

The older man chuckled. "When did you become such a pious saint? Don't forget I knew you when you lived on these streets. I'm certain I could dig up enough dirt on you that no one, not even the Irish, would want you on the city council."

McCleary could try, but Patrick had kept his head down and worked until his grandfather finally hired him on. It would be best to get to the business at hand. "The Fitzwilliamses are moving into Sullivan House as of today, which means Patrice won't be back."

McCleary seemed unmoved. "I wouldn't keep her around, but the men like her."

Depraved animals. Just the thought of someone abusing a child that way made him burn. "I've already moved the boys and retrieved their things."

"And their moving fee? Will you be taking care of that too?"

"A moving fee?"

The man eyed him. "The Fitzwilliamses are leaving me high and dry. I have no one to lease their room to, so until it's rented, there's a few dollars that accumulate every day." He leaned against his cane. "The room will be hard to rent seeing how filthy they left it, but twenty dollars might cover it."

Pulling out his wallet, Patrick counted out the bills and tossed them to the ground. Then on a whim, he tossed down two hundred dollars more. He looked past the older man to the girls behind him. "Go, your rents have been paid for the month. Come by Sullivan House in the next week, and we'll try to find you honest work."

No one moved at first, then one and another filed past McCleary, hurrying past him as if worried they'd be caught and brought back.

McCleary chuckled. "How very heroic of you, Mosby. I wonder what your constituents would feel about their councilman if they knew about your visit here tonight."

"They'd probably think the worst of me," Patrick admitted, not that he cared. His only concern at the moment was Grace's safety.

McCleary stepped toward him. "We could be allies, you know. Why, with my help, you could be governor or maybe a senator." His smile turned Patrick's stomach. "We could do great things together, you and I. Rebuild your family name."

To finally walk away from the stigma of his father's death, but at what price? No, it wasn't worth it. He'd lose whatever pride he had in himself, but most of all, he'd lose Grace. Nothing was worth that. "I want to talk to you about Grace Sullivan."

"What about her?"

"I learned that you and certain members of the medical community have been working together to terrorize her and her renters. I want it stopped now."

Placing both hands on his cane, McCleary leaned forward. "What could possibly entice me to do that?" He glanced down at the cash on the porch floor. "More money?"

"My first act at the next city council meeting will be to introduce a new order to strengthen the housing codes on the books and to instigate strict follow-up." Patrick glanced up at the walls of the tenement. "And this will be the first place I'll send the building inspectors. From the looks of the Fitzwilliamses' room, I'd say a large majority of your buildings will be condemned."

"You might want to tread lightly, boy." McCleary's grandfatherly expression turned cold. "I do have some influence in the city."

"Which will end when your so-called friends learn about your dealings with these children." McCleary's mouth slackened, and an emotion Patrick recognized flickered in his eyes. Fear. "No politician would risk that kind of scandal."

"So if I were threating Miss Sullivan, you'd want me to stop or you'll rain down your personal brand of Hades on me." He sneered at Patrick. "You do know this is blackmail."

"Oh no. You misunderstand me." Patrick stepped closer until he could feel the man's breath on his face. "I plan to do everything I described to you. But if Grace is hurt, if she receives another threat, I'm going to assume it's you and personally escort you to Sing Sing."

McCleary chuckled. "Ah, so that's how it is. You have a tendre for Miss Sullivan. Many men have been brought down by the love of a woman."

"This one won't be."

A rock-hard arm snagged him by the waist and pulled him back. "You aren't being very respectful of Mr. McCleary."

"It's all right, Brutus. This is a free country." McCleary's words held a hint of sarcasm. "Mr. Mosby has the right to his opinion."

"This isn't finished."

"I disagree. You've said all you're going to say." He nodded to his bodyguards. "Boys."

Two men grabbed Patrick by his arms and pulled him out of the house and down the sidewalk, then dumped him in front of his carriage. As he stood, he realized McCleary was right. He was finished, save one last thing.

"McCleary?"

The man standing in the doorway turned and faced him.

"I'll be back," Patrick said. "And when I return, it will be to shut you down."

Chapter 12

Grace wrung out the washrag and gently rubbed Patrice's slender arms. Small bruises blackened the skin around her wrists and shoulders, as if someone had held her forcibly in place. The thought twisted her stomach. What this young girl must have suffered in her thirteen years! What kind of animal would do this to a child?

Never again would she feel such horror. In these last moments, Grace would tenderly wash and prepare her body for burial.

"I'm sorry, Miss Sullivan," Dr. Moore began as he dried his instruments and returned them to his bag. "But this is exactly why physicians should attend to these matters instead of half-crazed heiresses who think a little knowledge makes them an expert on the matter." He poured fresh water into the basin, took a bar of soap, and scrubbed his hands. "Thank God we were able to save the baby. We could have lost her too."

She deserved the doctor's scorn. Grace gently pulled Patrice's tangled hair out of the buttons at the back of her filthy dress. Try as she might, nothing she did had stemmed Patrice's bleeding. In her mind, she'd done nothing less than kill her. It was like Tilly all over again, only this time, her pride and inexperience had led to someone's death.

The buttons undone, she pushed the rag to Patrice's waist and stopped. "Doctor?"

Moore turned from the basin, then moved to stand beside her. He touched the deep purple bruise that covered most of Patrice's abdomen. "Did you notice this when she came in?" the doctor asked.

Grace swallowed. If she'd noticed the bruising, would it have saved Patrice? "Things rapidly deteriorated in the delivery room. There wasn't time to remove her clothes."

"It looks fairly recent." He pushed lightly on Patrice's stomach. "The main injury looks like it occurred here in the area of the spleen."

"What does that mean, Doctor?"

Straightening, he took a deep breath, then glanced at her. "Generally, if the spleen is injured, it has to be removed surgically. A serious operation, but one a person can survive. But if the surgery isn't done in a timely manner, it can lead to profuse bleeding."

"You mean. . ." Grace cleared her throat, tears threatening. "Patrice's death wasn't our fault."

Moore didn't answer at first, then turned toward her, the petulant expression he'd been wearing for most of the evening replaced by one of understanding. "No, Miss Sullivan. Miss Fitzwilliam would have succumbed to her injuries regardless of anything you or I could have done."

Tears sprang to her eyes. "She didn't die because of me."

"No." He dug into his vest pocket and handed her his handkerchief. "With all the facts presented, I can say that you and Miss

Shoemaker did the best anyone could do under the circumstances."

Grace sucked in a breath. "I'm so sorry, Dr. Moore. I didn't mean to fall apart on you like some half-crazed heiress."

He chuckled softly. "I don't blame you for throwing my words back at me. I haven't been. . .the kindest person to you."

Grace pulled the blanket over the young girl's body. "I understand, Dr. Moore. There are many who share your opinion of midwives."

"I fear I owe you an apology for much more." His gaze shifted away from her and he looked decidedly uncomfortable. "You see, I was one of your opponents at the city council meeting last month."

"Oh." Grace wiped her nose, not certain where this conversation was going. "You have the right to your opinion, as I do to mine. I understand that."

"Yes, but some of my colleagues and I didn't understand, and did some things that made it inconvenient for you to do your job." He pressed his lips together, then met her gaze. "I'm sincerely sorry about that. I just. . ." Moore glanced at Patrice. "Before today, I had never been to the lower east side, so these people weren't real to me. They were simply stories I'd heard, and I judged them harshly for it. Now I see who they are, flesh and blood, and I realize how selfish I was to refuse to treat them."

"I understand." Grace laid her hand on his forearm. "I did the very same thing, and my best friend died in childbirth because of it."

"I'm so sorry. Was it someone I would know?"

"Possibly." Grace nodded. "Matilda O'Neill. But she was a Stephenson before she married."

"I was her doctor when she was just a girl." His gray brows

furrowed. "You say she died in childbirth?"

"Yes, a little over two years ago."

Dr. Moore's expression turned somber. "There wasn't anything anyone could have done to save her, Miss Sullivan."

"How can you—" she started, but the doctor shook his head.

"I don't usually discuss my patients, but with Tilly gone, maybe this will help you." He paused for a moment. "I diagnosed a serious heart condition in her when she was eight or nine that would have made it very dangerous for her to carry a child."

"A bad heart?" Grace whispered, then glanced up at him. "She never told me."

"That doesn't surprise me." He sighed. "Tilly struggled with the diagnosis and the restrictions it put on her life. She wanted what she shouldn't have. Marriage, children. It was difficult for her."

Yet she had both, a marriage to the man she loved and a child she longed for. Tilly lived her life the way she'd wanted, and Grace should be happy for her, even if it didn't end the way she would have wanted.

A weight eased off her soul. "Thank you, Dr. Moore. I can never repay you for everything you've done here today."

"No, thank you. At the next council meeting, I will voice my opinion that the city still needs its midwives." He held out his hand to her, and she took it. "I'd also like to discuss the possibility of seeing patients here one day a week."

His offer was everything she'd been praying for in recent months. "Dr. Moore, I accept the generous offer of your time. I'm certain the people of Mulberry Street will feel the same."

"It's something I should have done long ago."

Grace didn't know how to respond. "Would you like to join

me in the parlor? I'm sure Rosie has arranged a tray of coffee and refreshments."

The fatherly smile he gave her warmed her heart. "Yes, I could do with some coffee and a sandwich about now."

Nia was setting out a tray of tea cakes, sandwiches, and cheese when they arrived in the main parlor. Several of the ladies from upstairs were still gathered, softly speaking among themselves.

Grace glanced around for Patrick, disappointed not to find him. Nia walked over to her, a steaming cup of tea in hand. She handed it to her. "Patrick left a little while ago, but he said he'd be back."

Grace took the cup, not realizing how cold she was until she held the tea in her hands. "Do you know where he went?"

"I have some idea, but you're not going to like it."

Nerves caused her stomach to flip. "Where?"

Nia studied her as if weighing whether to tell her or not, then spoke. "He went to see McCleary."

Grace's cup rattled in the saucer. Patrick went to see McCleary? Was the man crazy? Didn't he understand what McCleary was capable of? "Tell me he didn't go alone."

"I wish I could." She stepped closer. "He did manage to get Patrice's brothers out of their rooms without anyone noticing. Rosalind is sitting with them upstairs."

"Where did you put them?"

"In my apartment for now, but we're going to have to figure something out before tonight or we'll have people sleeping on the floor."

"Thank you." Grace's thoughts were miles away. Why had Patrick gone alone to meet with McCleary? Didn't he know he could get hurt or even— "I need to go out for a while."

Nia crossed her arms at her waist. "No."

"I have to find him."

Her friend shook her head. "I don't think that's wise."

"Maybe not, but sitting here wondering if something has happened to him isn't doing me any good either." Grace set her cup down on a nearby table, then turned back to Nia. "Could you see that Dr. Moore gets safely home? Oh, and ask him which day works best for him next week. He's volunteered to see patients here."

Nia stared back at her, a stunned expression on her face. "Well, you could knock me over with a feather. He's going to do that?"

"That's what he says."

"Then we'd better jump on that opportunity while we can." Nia headed across the room to where Dr. Moore sat talking to Liam, who lived there with his wife and four children.

After everything they'd been through today, Grace needed to see Patrick. She hurried out of the parlor to the foyer. As she grabbed her coat from its peg, the door opened, and a cold gust of wind sent a chill up her spine. Whirling around, her heart slammed against her rib cage.

"Patrick."

Without thinking, Grace dropped her coat and hurled herself against his chest. He folded her into his arms, holding her close. "Grace."

Her name on his lips felt like a prayer. She laid her head on his shoulder. "You scared me to death. Why did you even go and see him?"

"You were worried about me." There was a hint of a smile in his voice.

"No," she lied as she attempted to push him away. He caught her hand and pressed it against his chest. She softened into him, loving the feel of him against her. No matter where they were in this world, whether in Manhattan or on Park Avenue, here in his arms was where she would call home.

She tilted her head back a little to meet his gaze. Why had she never noticed how brown his eyes were? "All right, so I was a little worried. I thought you might have gone off and gotten yourself killed."

"You don't have much faith in my ability to take care of myself, do you?" he teased.

"I did give you a black eye once."

He barked with laughter. "Only because you caught me off guard, you little minx. I had trouble explaining that at school the next day."

"I'm sorry," she answered with a smile. It felt so good, the easy to-and-fro between them. It gave rhyme and reason to her day after this terrible afternoon.

"How is Patrice?"

Grace briefed him on the events of the afternoon, including Dr. Moore's heartfelt apology and his offer to work. Patrick listened to her, holding her close as she wept over Patrice and the children who had lost their sister and mother, and over Tilly.

"Tilly had a heart condition she kept from us," she said, snuggling close to his chest. "Dr. Moore assured me that's what caused her death, and not anything I failed to do."

Cupping her chin in his hand, he lifted her head until their gazes met. "Is that why you became a midwife? Because you wanted to help the Tillys of the world?"

"That was a big part of it, but the truth is I needed a purpose in my life. Tilly's death reminded me of how selfish I could be. I want my life to have meaning. I want it to be something that honors the Lord."

"Oh Grace." He leaned his forehead against hers. "I've been so worried about rebuilding my family name that I'd forgotten what it was like to live from hand to mouth. You reminded me of that, and now, I want to do more than just build my reputation. I truly want to help these people and every citizen in this city." He brushed a kiss on her nose. "I need you in my life, Grace. I love you."

Joy sang through her. "I love you too, Patrick."

Lowering his head, he pressed a kiss to her cheek. "Do you remember our first kiss?"

Grace smiled. "We were so awkward afterward. I thought I'd done something wrong."

Patrick kissed the corner of her mouth. "I suspected then that you were the only one for me."

She reached up and kissed his brow. "You never told me that."

"No." He tilted her head back, lowering his head until she felt his breath on her cheek. "But it's true, dearest. Now and for always."

Epilogue

One year later

Grace stood at the top of the majestic staircase, watching the eclectic crowd of Park Avenue society, politicians, and local business leaders gather in the expansive ballroom. Everything was as close to perfect as possible. The food and drink had been picked with their friends in mind, as well as the entertainment.

Tonight, she and Patrick would share their vision for the lower east side and ask their friends and colleagues to share in it with them. She tugged at her gloves, then glanced back at the bedroom. Patrick was usually ready before her.

Walking back to the room, she pushed open the door. Her heart leaped as it always did when she saw her husband. Since their marriage a month ago, she'd found herself staring at him quite a bit, and praising God for allowing Patrick Mosby back into her life.

He must have sensed her presence, for he smiled. "Dearest, could you help me with this tie? I can't seem to get it straight."

Her skirts swirled around her legs as she moved across the room. "I seem to be helping you tie your ties a lot recently."

"That's because you're so good at it." His lips twitched as he wrapped his hands around her waist. "And because it gives me an excuse to be close to you."

"We have a room full of guests downstairs waiting on us." She tugged at the tie, moving it into the correct position. "It would be rude to be late."

"Have I told you how beautiful you look tonight?"

He curled his arm around her and brought her close as she crinkled her nose. "All right. We have to go. Just one kiss then."

Patrick lowered his head, and Grace forgot about the ice carvings and everything else, her only focus this man she adored with all of her heart.

When he lifted his head from hers, he looked as dazed as she felt. "Are you sure we have to go downstairs?"

Grace giggled as she stepped out of his reach. "It's for a good cause, remember?"

"Yes," he answered begrudgingly. "I should be horsewhipped for not taking you away on a honeymoon instead of throwing this party."

"You know we can't get away yet." She took his arm and led him to the door. "Half of Mulberry Street is expecting a baby at any time, and we don't have enough midwives as it is. And you've been busy too, pushing the council for more housing reforms. We'll get away soon, my love. I promise."

He stopped in the doorway and looked down at her. "As long as I'm with you, I don't care where we are."

He gave her another kiss that was over far too quickly, then escorted her out into the corridor. As they came to the top of the stairs, he turned to her. "May I have the pleasure of all your waltzes tonight, Mrs. Mosby?"

Grace smiled up at him. "Tonight and every night, my love."

With one last kiss, they went to greet their guests.

Multi-published author **Patty Smith Hall** lives near the North Georgia mountains with her husband, Danny. When she's not writing on her back porch, she's spending time with her family or working in her vegetable garden.

Between Two Worlds

by Marilyn Turk

Chapter 1

New Orleans
1890

G et out! Leave me alone!"
A shrill female voice escaped the open window from a room somewhere above Camille Duval as she pushed open the heavy iron gate.

Camille froze, staring up at the second floor of the grand home, searching the tall windows framed with black shutters where the voice had come from.

An imposing structure, the home was similar to many of its neighbors in this affluent area outside the busy commercial district of the Vieux Carre. Camille drew in a deep breath, brushed the wrinkles from her gray skirt, and straightened before proceeding toward the mansion constructed in the Italianate style of the Garden District, its veranda and balconies ornamented with intricate black wrought iron, what they called "black lace," a sharp contrast to the pale pink stucco exterior.

Camille climbed the few marble steps to the veranda where double mahogany doors with leaded glass inserts awaited the introduction to her first patient in New Orleans. She knocked, listening for approaching footsteps or another sound of the distraught female voice.

A uniformed doorman opened the door and peered down at her. "Rousseau residence. May I help you, ma'am?" The man's voice was deep but gentle, his ebony skin accentuated by white hair denoting years of service.

"I'm Camille Duval, the midwife Mr. Rousseau hired for his wife."

The man's eyebrows shot up. "You a midwife?" He looked her up and down.

A door closed upstairs, and a man called out. "Joseph, is someone here?"

Lifting his chin, Joseph spoke. "Yes, sir. A Miss Duval."

Heavy footsteps pounded the wooden stairs, and soon their owner came into view as he rounded the landing of the staircase. When he and Camille made eye contact, he smiled.

"Invite her in, Joseph." The man trotted down the remaining steps and approached. "Miss Duval, I'm Vincent Rousseau. Your uncle Claude spoke highly of you."

Joseph stepped aside as Camille entered, her eyes scanning the huge mural on the wall in the foyer depicting a plantation scene before settling on the gentleman in front of her.

She nodded. "Thank you, Mr. Rousseau. It is nice to make your acquaintance."

Vincent Rousseau motioned for her to follow him. "Let's go to the parlor for a few minutes before you meet Adelaide." He turned to the doorman. "Joseph, would you please ask Ida to make us some coffee?" Mr. Rousseau coughed following the question, withdrawing a handkerchief from his pocket to wipe his mouth.

Camille started to protest, since she hadn't developed a taste for the strong beverage of the city, but didn't want to be rude. She followed him into a parlor with ceilings easily twenty feet high. Heavy gold drapes flowed from the arched floor-to-ceiling windows, drawn open to allow light to enter. Gold-and-white brocade wallpaper surrounded the room, stopping only at the fireplace that boasted a gilt-edged mirror above. Despite the splendid furnishings, the odor of cigar smoke lingered, and Camille wished the windows were open.

Mr. Rousseau coughed again as he pointed to a settee and waited for her to sit before he took a seat opposite in a padded velvet armchair. The man was older than she'd expected, perhaps in his late forties, she assumed, based on the silver streaks in his black hair. Uncle Claude had told her that Adelaide was Mr. Rousseau's second wife, his first dying after twenty-five years of marriage. The man wasn't unattractive, but his cough was rather persistent, and he appeared to carry a little too much weight.

"So your uncle tells me you're a trained nurse."

Camille nodded. "That's correct. I trained in nursing school at the New England Hospital for Women and Children in Boston."

Mr. Rousseau studied her, clasping his hands in front of himself. "And you're trained in midwifery as well?"

"Yes, sir. That was part of my training." Joseph arrived carrying a tray with a silver coffeepot and two cups. He set it down on the low table, poured the coffee, then handed a cup to each of them. Camille offered a smile of thanks before the man exited the room, and waited for the coffee to cool, hoping her failure to drink it wouldn't be noticed.

"Have you had any real experience as a midwife?"

"Yes. I've worked in Charleston for the past two years as a nurse and midwife."

"Glad to hear it. I want nothing but the best for my Adelaide. She's young, and this is our first child. Adelaide has a delicate nature; that is, she's not very strong of body." He chuckled. "On the other hand, she more than makes up for it in spirit. She can be pretty willful, when she sets her mind to it. And I must say, being in the family way has not agreed with her constitution."

"She's been ill?"

He nodded. "Yes, quite. She hasn't been able to leave her room for weeks. I hope she won't be this sick the entire time."

"Do you know how far along she is?"

He rubbed his hands together. "I don't keep up with such things, but I don't think she's too far, as she isn't showing any signs that I can see. Then again, she doesn't want to see me lately. I think she's angry with me."

Camille remembered hearing the woman shouting earlier and felt sorry for Mr. Rousseau, not the first to be the target of a woman with child who blamed the father for her discomfort. "Her attitude sounds fairly common, especially in the early stages. Most women feel better as they get further along."

"I certainly hope so." He took a swig of the hot beverage.

"May I see her now?" Camille set down her cup and stood. Even if she liked coffee, the room was entirely too hot for her to drink it.

Mr. Rousseau swallowed more coffee, then stood. "Of course. I suppose now's as good a time as any."

Camille lifted her bag and started toward the door.

"Oh, I forgot to tell you. She doesn't know you're coming."

Camille paused. "She doesn't? Have you not told her I will be her midwife?"

Mr. Rousseau's sheepish expression answered her question. "Adelaide has some notions about who she wants to help her. Have you ever heard of Madame LaFleur?"

"No. Is she a local midwife?"

"Not exactly. But she claims to have many types of powers, healing and otherwise. Adelaide puts a lot of stock in what she says. You'll have to convince her you know more than Madame LaFleur."

Dr. Julian Charbonnet stepped down from the mule-drawn streetcar and looked at the slip of paper. Dr. Bennett had told him the Rousseau house was just two blocks from where the streetcar stopped at St. Charles and First Street. He also said the house would be easy to find, with its pastel exterior and massive size. Although Dr. Bennett had informed Mr. Rousseau that his new partner would be filling in for him, Julian wished he could have been formally introduced first.

The house came into view, its commanding position dominating the corner lot and surrounded by a black iron fence. Huge oak trees and tropical foliage tried to hide the house from the street, but its upper balconies peeked out and confirmed its presence. Julian walked across the street to the house, drew himself up, and approached the front door. On the second knock, the door was opened by a uniformed man.

"Dr. Julian Charbonnet, to see Mr. Vincent Rousseau." Julian handed his card to the doorman.

The man glimpsed the card. "I'll tell him, sir." But as the doorman turned to go, an older gentleman entered the foyer accompanied by a lovely young woman. Could this be Mr. Rousseau's wife?

He'd heard she was several years younger than her husband.

Julian cleared his throat, and the man and woman glanced his way. The man frowned. "And who might you be, sir?"

The doorman handed Julian's card over, and the man scrutinized it, then looked back up at Julian.

"Dr. Charbonnet, is it? Yes, Dr. Bennett told me you'd be calling. Went to Europe, did he? Do come in." He swept his hand to invite him inside.

"Mr. Rousseau, it is an honor to meet you." Julian extended his hand, trying not to stare at the stunning woman beside his host.

Mr. Rousseau shook hands, then turned to the young woman. "Dr. Charbonnet, you're just in time to meet Miss Camille Duval. Miss Duval is my wife's new midwife."

"A midwife, did you say?" Julian noted a tiny frown between Miss Duval's eyes.

Mr. Rousseau nodded. "Hard to believe, isn't it? But she's a nurse too. Even though she's young, I'm sure her nursing skills will make up for that."

Julian attempted to hide his surprise. "Nice to meet you, Miss Duval."

Miss Duval offered a polite smile. "And you as well, Doctor." She glanced up the grand staircase. "Now, if you gentlemen will excuse me, I must go meet my patient."

She turned, lifted her skirt, and began climbing the curved staircase. They watched her part of the way up, then, as if breaking a trance, Mr. Rousseau coughed a few times before speaking. "Let's go into my study."

Julian noted the man's hacking cough and splotchy red skin. Dr. Bennett had described Mr. Rousseau as a powerful man in the city. Would he be a difficult patient?

"Coffee or brandy?" Mr. Rousseau picked up a glass, then poured himself a drink from a crystal decanter.

"Neither, thank you."

"Dr. Bennett said you were a recent graduate from Tulane University."

"Yes, sir. That's correct. May I ask you what you're doing for that cough?"

He lifted his glass. "This works well. After a few glasses, I forget what ailed me." His next swig was followed by coughing. He stood by the fireplace where Julian joined him. Julian set down his medical bag, opened it, and retrieved his stethoscope.

"Would you please remove your coat?"

"If you insist." Rousseau took off his jacket and laid it over the back of a nearby chair. "The vest too?"

"Please, sir."

Rousseau removed the tight-fitting vest as well, revealing his extra weight and the perspiration stains on his shirt.

Julian placed the end of the stethoscope on Rousseau's chest and listened, noting the man's heavy breathing and rattling. "Turn around, please, and lift your arms."

Rousseau obeyed like a petulant child. Julian listened to the man's back as well, confirming his suspicions.

When Rousseau turned around again, his forehead and upper lip were dotted with perspiration. He swigged his brandy. "See, I'm fine." He chuckled, which brought on another cough.

"Your lungs don't sound good. Have you been taking any medicine?"

Rousseau waved him off, then lifted the lid of the humidor on his desk, pulled out a fat cigar, and lit it. "Oh, some nasty-tasting stuff Dr. Bennett gave me. I don't like it."

Julian motioned to the cigar. "That is only making matters worse."

Rousseau shrugged. "But these came straight off the ship from Havana. Won't you have one?"

"No, thank you, and you really shouldn't have one yourself." Julian had never desired sucking in the pungent aroma of cigars, whether through his mouth or his nose, and wondered how anyone else could.

"Dr. Charbonnet, are you going to deny me the pleasures of my life?" Rousseau tapped the cigar on the ashtray, but ashes littered his trousers as well as the floor.

"I'm only trying to help you enjoy life longer, sir."

"Humph. That's a matter of opinion."

Julian glanced at the windows, hearing the muted sound of horse hooves clopping on the street outside. "Perhaps you can open your windows and get some fresh air in here."

"And street dust." Rousseau coughed as if for emphasis.

"Sir, the foliage in your yard keeps most of the dust out. You really should try to get a breeze through here—open several windows for cross-ventilation." Julian glanced up. "At least turn on the ceiling fan." Only people of means could afford the new electric fans.

"All right, fine." Rousseau walked to the center of the room and pulled the chain. Slowly the two-bladed fan came to life, making an awful squeaking sound. "There, you happy? Sounds like a lonely duck, doesn't it?"

Julian smiled, happy to have won one small victory. As he put his stethoscope away, a couple of thumps sounded through the ceiling. Julian looked at Rousseau, who shrugged.

"Miss Duval will have to get used to Adelaide's petulant temper." He winked at Julian. "Aren't you glad you don't have to deal with women's issues?"

"Yes, sir, I am. But I must say, women in the family way aren't the only difficult patients."

Rousseau cut him a glance, then grinned. "Point taken. Perhaps I'll take some of that nasty stuff. I'd rather do that than give this up." He lifted his cigar. "At least I can chase it with some good brandy!" He laughed, then coughed.

Were all of his patients going to be so obstinate? An image of Miss Duval's pretty face entered his mind. He certainly hoped Mrs. Rousseau was more cooperative than her husband.

Chapter 2

"Who are you? What are you doing here?" Adelaide Rousseau lay on her side, a mass of long black curls covering her face. Her ruffled white chiffon peignoir covered the rest of her.

"I'm Camille Duvall. Your husband hired me to take care of you."

"Take care of me? You don't look like a maid." Adelaide pushed herself up to look at Camille, then collapsed back onto the bed, knocking a couple of books off the nightstand in the process. She groaned, then curled into a ball, her porcelain skin matching the white sheets on the four-poster bed.

Camille picked up the books, one of which was a Bible, and returned them to the nightstand beside a crystal beaded rosary. "I know I don't look like a typical midwife, but I'm a nurse as well."

Adelaide's eyes shot open. "Did Vincent hire you to be my midwife? How dare he? I already have a midwife."

Camille remembered Rousseau's warning. "You do?"

"Yes, the best. Madame LaFleur. And I don't need anyone else!"

"I see. Does she come to your house?"

Adelaide shook her head. "No. She's too busy. Besides, Vincent doesn't want her here."

"Then how. . ."

"She sends things by my chambermaid, Sukey."

A tap sounded, and the door opened a crack. "Miss Adelaide?"

"Come in, Sukey."

The black woman stepped inside, glanced at Camille, and frowned. "I'll just empty this for you." She walked over to the chamber pot, picked it up, and carried it back to the door. She looked over her shoulder at Camille before leaving the room.

"See? Sukey's taking care of me, so you don't have to."

Camille scanned the large bedroom with its white provincial furniture and pink velvet tufted chairs. A floral brocade chaise occupied the area by windows that opened onto the balcony high above the street. "I'm not going to live here, at least not during your early stage. But I'll come check on you regularly."

"And do what?"

"Whatever needs to be done. Do you know when you had your last period?"

"Two months ago, and I've been sick ever since."

"So you're perhaps seven or eight weeks. Morning sickness is normal at this stage."

"But I'm sick morning, noon, and night!"

"Have you been able to eat anything?"

"No! I can't even tolerate the smell of food."

"Then we'll have to find something you can keep down. You need to stay healthy so the baby will be healthy."

"Madame LaFleur is going to send over one of her potions. Then I'll be fine. You can tell my husband your services aren't needed."

What kind of potion was the woman sending? What were the contents? Camille needed to see it and make sure it wasn't dangerous for Adelaide to take.

"I'm afraid he insists that I take care of you. He only wants the best care for you."

"Ha. *He* has never been with child. How does he know what's best for me?"

"He asked, and my uncle Claude recommended me. I've been involved in midwifery in Charleston where I used to live."

"And you came all this way for me?"

Camille glanced toward the window, thankfully open to admit some air. "Well, yes. Yes, I did." While she hadn't come to New Orleans specifically to treat Adelaide, she did come to the city to be a nurse-midwife, so she wasn't exactly lying. The young wife should realize her husband's concern for her.

Adelaide tried to sit up again, so Camille hurried to fluff her pillows to help.

"I've never been to Charleston. What's it like?"

"In a way, much like New Orleans, since it's a busy port. But it's not nearly as large as this city. And you seldom hear French spoken."

"You have family there?" Adelaide's questions sounded like those of a curious young girl.

Camille shook her head. "I did, but not anymore. Both of my parents passed away in the last two years."

"I'm sorry. Mine passed too. This used to be our house, but Vincent bought it from my father. I have an older sister and brother who are married and live in Baton Rouge. You know, Vincent's one of the few Frenchmen who lives in the Garden District, and that's only because he bought our house."

Camille's uncle was one of those Frenchman as well, since the Garden District was originally settled by Americans who wanted to live separately from the confines of the busy French Quarter. "Has this always been your bedroom?"

Adelaide gave a feeble nod. "Yes. Vincent and I shared a bedroom before, well, before I got in the family way. But I'm too sick to share a room, much less a bed, now."

"You'll get better with time."

"If I live long enough." A shadow passed over Adelaide's face.

Alarm shot through Camille. "Why would you say that?"

"My mother lost several children and almost died having me."

"Then we have to make sure you're healthy. I'll ask your cook to make you some clear broth."

"I think she can only make rich food like gumbo. She tried to get me to eat some yesterday." Adelaide covered her mouth as if she would retch. The door opened, and Sukey returned with the empty chamber pot and placed it beside the bed.

"Sukey, I'm Camille Duval. I'll be helping Mrs. Rousseau during her pregnancy."

The maid glanced from Camille to Adelaide and back, a surprised, if not frightened, look on her face.

"Don't worry, Sukey. I still want Madame LaFleur's help. Can't have enough good luck."

Sukey nodded, but frowned and seemed worried nonetheless. "Yes, ma'am." She backed out the door.

"You rest," Camille said. "I'm going to ask the cook to make you some broth. If she can't do it, I'll do it myself."

"You can cook?"

Camille smiled. "It was part of my training."

Adelaide closed her eyes, and Camille moved to the door. Something caught her attention at the end of the bed, and she went over to look at it. A small leather pouch was tied around the tall bedpost. Why would such a thing be tied to the bed? What was in it? She reached out to touch it, and a shiver ran down her spine.

Camille closed the door behind her and bumped into Sukey standing outside the room. "Excuse me, I didn't know you were there." Had the woman been listening to her conversation with Adelaide?

Sukey remained silent, her arms crossed, eyeing Camille with suspicion.

"Can you please show me to the kitchen? I'd like to speak with the cook."

"I can answer any questions for you. What do you want to know?"

The maid's abrupt manner caught Camille off guard. What had she done to earn Sukey's annoyance? Perhaps the maid disapproved of someone else taking care of Adelaide.

"I'd like to speak with her myself." Camille had learned to be firm yet polite in her previous experience. She would not let this woman stand in the way of her duty. "If it's not convenient for you to direct me to the kitchen, I'll find it myself. Perhaps Mr. Rousseau won't be opposed to my roaming through his house."

Sukey's eyes darted downstairs; then she uncrossed her arms and huffed. "This way." She proceeded down the open hallway that overlooked the grand foyer and passed other closed doors that Camille assumed were additional bedrooms. At the end of the hallway, she went through a door to a plain staircase, the servants' stairs, and started down. As a midwife, Camille ranked higher than a household servant, yet she wasn't above doing what was necessary if the situation called for it.

The steps ended in the basement. Sukey turned the corner and walked into a large kitchen filled with wonderful aromas and a large black woman stirring a pot on the stove. She looked up at Camille, then glanced at Sukey, who shrugged.

"You must be the nursemaid Mr. Rousseau hired. I's Ida. Is you hungry? I'm fixing Mr. Rousseau his dinner now. Sukey, set another place at the table so this lady can join him."

"Yes, I'm Camille Duval, Miss Adelaide's nurse and midwife. And please, don't go to the trouble of serving me. I won't be staying for dinner."

Her eyebrows rose, but her attention remained on her cooking as she threw some chopped onions into the pot. The onions sizzled and a delicious aroma wafted from the pot as she continued to stir. "No trouble to feed one mo'. I been working here feeding people since Miss Adelaide was a chile." She looked up at Camille, her eyes roving over her. "You have children?"

"No. I'm not married."

Ida rolled her eyes. "Then what you know about having babies?"

"I've helped many women deliver their babies in the past few years." This wasn't the first time Camille's ability and knowledge had been questioned. Until recently, most midwives were older women who had had several children of their own. However, every time the question came up, Camille fought to maintain her composure in defending herself.

"Humph."

"But my job is more than delivering babies. It's providing care for the mother-to-be so she remains healthy and both she and the baby will have a safe delivery." Once again, Camille found herself in a battle against tradition but knew if change would ever happen, she had to prove herself. "Which brings me to the reason I came to see you. Would you please make a clear broth of either chicken or beef?"

"You want me to make a gravy?"

"No, not something thick like that. A bouillon, boiled broth, and not too highly seasoned. Spicy foods are hard to digest and can give the mother heartburn."

Ida laughed out loud. "Never hurt me!"

Sukey came back into the kitchen and smiled at Ida, and Camille felt as if the two of them were laughing at her.

"I can make it myself if it's a problem for you."

Ida's eyes shot fire. "No, ma'am. Not in my kitchen you don't. I does all the cooking here."

Realizing her offense, Camille offered her sweetest smile. "Oh, I don't mean to interfere with your cooking. I was just offering my help." Perhaps she should suggest something else. "Do you have any soda crackers?"

Ida shook her head.

"Any lemons?"

"We might have some or I can get some. You put lemons in your soup?"

Sukey laughed, and Ida smiled at her.

Camille faked a laugh too. "Oh, of course not. However, sometimes sucking on a lemon can help ease some of the sickness that goes with being pregnant."

Another roll of the eyes. Ida motioned with her head. "Over there in the pantry. If we have any, they'll be in there."

Camille found the pantry door and walked inside. She scanned the assortment of items before finding a lemon. When she returned to the kitchen, she spotted a cutting board. "Do you have a small knife I can use?"

Ida was glued to her spot by the stove, obviously unable to leave her concoction for a moment. "Sukey, show her where the knives are. I burn this roux, the gumbo won't be no good, and Mr. Rousseau gonna be mighty angry."

Sukey stalked over to a drawer and retrieved a knife, then carried it to Camille, who hesitated to grab the point facing her. Sukey dropped it on the cutting board. "Thank you, Sukey."

Camille cut the lemon into thick slices. Unwilling to ask for anything else, she found a glass and a saucer in a cabinet, then saw the icebox. Taking the glass to the box, she used an ice pick to chip some ice into the glass. Next she squeezed a couple of the lemon slices over the ice, and put the others on the saucer.

"This will do for now. I'll bring over some other things the next time I come." She smiled before turning to go. "Thank you, ladies, for all your help." The surprised looks on their faces were worth her effort to stay composed.

She managed to find her way back to Adelaide's room. She tapped on the door, then balanced the glass and saucer so she could turn the doorknob. When she walked in, Adelaide's eyes opened.

"You're still here?" The young woman looked up with surprise.

"For the time being. I brought you something that should help you feel better."

Adelaide pushed herself to a sitting position, focused on what Camille carried. Camille handed her the glass. "Here. Try to sip this. Once the ice melts, you can drink it. It's a little like lemonade."

Adelaide put the glass to her lips and sipped the small amount of liquid already melted. She scrunched her face. "That's sour! Can you bring me some sugar?"

"Sugar can make you feel worse, so if you can tolerate a little sourness, you'll be better off. If you don't want to drink that, just suck on one of these lemon slices." Camille set the saucer down on the bedside table.

Adelaide picked up a slice and tasted a tiny bit. "I hope this works."

"It will." Camille glanced at the leather pouch on the bedpost and pointed to it. "Can you tell me what that's for?"

Adelaide followed her gaze. "It's gris-gris. Madame LaFleur sent it and Sukey hung it there."

"Gris-gris? What is that?"

Her patient shrugged. "It's to keep evil spirits away from me and my baby."

Camille tried not to show surprise. "Is that so? What's in it?"

Adelaide shook her head. "You don't open it. That's bad luck. Madame LaFleur knows what to put in it, so you just trust her."

"I see. So gris-gris is beneficial?"

"Some of it is, like this. But she can make some that gives bad luck."

Camille was tempted to ask why the woman would make such a thing.

Adelaide spoke again. "You don't believe it's true, do you? Well, you better, because there are a lot of people in New Orleans who will tell you that Madame LaFleur's powers are not to be trifled with."

Her powers? What kind of powers did this woman possess? Perhaps a little bag of whatever tied to the bedpost wasn't too dangerous to Adelaide, but what other kind of advice might she offer that could interfere with Camille's treatment? And why did Adelaide's words sound like a warning?

Chapter 3

Julian rounded the corner of Canal Street in front of the drugstore, his mind focused on the next patient he was to see. As he was passing the open doorway, he bumped into a woman stepping outside.

Startled back to the moment, he tipped his hat. "Please excuse me, ma'am. I should look where I'm going."

The woman studied him, then smiled the sweetest smile he'd ever seen. "No harm done, Dr. Charbonnet."

Blood rushed to his face as he recognized the attractive midwife he'd met at the Rousseau home.

"Miss Duval. I am truly sorry to be so clumsy."

"I'm certain you did not intend to bump into anyone." Her soft brown eyes twinkled, and the sunlight glinted off her chestnut hair, which was swept up in the popular Gibson Girl style. The high collar of her white lace blouse framed her face like a portrait and gentleness radiated from her, a quality befitting a nurse. Why would someone so lovely want to be a lowly midwife? Especially a young unmarried woman.

"Will you allow me to buy you a cup of coffee?"

"Actually, I was just on my way to the French Market." She tucked a couple of small bags into the straw basket she carried.

"I was heading that way myself. We can get some café au lait at the Café du Monde."

She lifted her eyebrows. "I thought the French Market was the other direction." She nodded in the direction from which he'd come. She joined him on the crowded sidewalk where they were jostled by passersby.

Julian glanced over his shoulder. "Ah, you are correct. I was so lost in thought, I forgot where I was going." He sounded like a complete fool.

She tilted her head as if she didn't believe him, then smiled a mesmerizing smile. "You must have a lot on your mind, Dr. Charbonnet."

At the moment, he only had her on his mind, since he'd completely forgotten where he was going before he ran into her. "Here comes a streetcar." He motioned for her to go ahead to the trolley stop. The driver halted the mule in front of them, and Julian and Miss Duval stepped up and found a seat on the Canal Street streetcar. The route would take some time as it stopped at each block to allow passengers to board and disembark. When they reached Decatur Street, the streetcar would turn toward the French Market and the coffeehouse. Plenty of time for conversation, Julian hoped.

Snippets of speech from other passengers reached his ears, a combination of French, Spanish, English, and even some Irish brogue, evidence of the city's mixed heritage. French he understood, as his paternal grandparents spoke only French, arriving in New Orleans in the early 1800s. Several of the men on board eyed Miss Duval and tipped their hats, muttering to their friends something no doubt referring to her beauty. Julian sent a glare toward them as if he had a right to defend her. He was certain that had she taken the trip by herself, she wouldn't have been alone for long.

"How long have you been in town, Miss Duval?"

"Only a couple of months. My mother passed away two years ago, and I lost my father just a few months ago. Uncle Claude didn't want me to stay in Charleston alone. He became my guardian, so I moved here to live with him."

"I'm sorry for your losses. Did you say Claude Duval is your uncle?" If he was the same man Julian knew, he was fairly well off and should be able to care for his niece without her needing to go to work, especially as a midwife.

"Yes, he is. I suppose you know him?"

"Is he an attorney?"

"He no longer practices, but yes, he was an attorney."

"He lives in the Garden District also?" It was common knowledge that Vincent Rousseau had married his way into the neighborhood, but how did Mr. Duval, another Frenchman, end up there?

"In the Lower Garden, in one of the smaller houses. My aunt was from Virginia, God rest her soul, and preferred the quiet of the Garden area with its smaller Victorian cottages to the busy downtown neighborhoods of the city."

"I'm sure he's happy to have you around to keep him company."

"I enjoy his company as well. He is my father's twin brother."

"Is that so? And your mother, was she French too?"

Miss Duval frowned and shook her head. "No, she wasn't. She was of English descent and demanded that everyone in our home speak English, not French. So, while I can understand some

French from my father's side, I'm not very fluent in it."

They rode in silence a few minutes while Julian tried not to notice the sweet scent of cologne water wafting from his companion. The streetcar stopped, letting more people on and off.

"Dr. Charbonnet, what about you? Are you a native of the city?"

"Yes, I am." He didn't want to tell her where in the city though, as he lived over a bar in the French Quarter. She might not approve of his lowly background. Instead, he asked her another question. "Have you been down to the French Market by yourself before?"

"No, not alone. But I accompanied our housekeeper once. She gave me directions today, telling me to catch a trolley down Canal to Decatur Street. I assume that's where we're going."

Julian nodded. "That's correct."

"I'm trying to become more familiar with town because I'll have patients all over and need to be able to find them. I'm thankful there are streetcars here."

Miss Duval was certainly not afraid to be alone in the city, a surprising trait, yet one that merited respect. "Yes, they run on the major streets, and most other streets branch off."

She gazed out the window as another streetcar rolled past going the opposite direction. "I've never seen such a broad street."

"They say it's the widest street in the world. There was originally supposed to be a canal down the middle of it, but that plan never materialized."

"It seems that the buildings on one side are newer than the buildings on the other side."

"That's true. For many years, the south side of the street has been the French side, and the opposite side is now considered the American side."

"So the street divides the two?"

He nodded. "For the most part, yes."

"I'm surprised that division still exists."

"Unfortunately, it does. At least in the minds of longtime residents." Like his family and so many others from the French Quarter.

Miss Duval focused on each street they passed, asking the name when it wasn't evident. As they continued on, noises from the waterfront let them know the Mississippi River was just ahead. Ships' masts were visible above the levee where they were anchored in the water on the other side. Sounds of the busy seaport grew louder, with ship horns, men shouting, and cargo being loaded and unloaded. Horse- and mule-drawn wagons lined the levee road beside the waterfront to carry goods away to markets and warehouses.

"Let's walk the rest of the way," Julian suggested. Miss Duval accepted his hand to step onto the cobblestone pavement when the streetcar stopped at Decatur Street. The French Market extended several blocks from the river to Jackson Square in the Vieux Carre, its long roof covering multiple booths displaying their wares with the tent canopies rolled up on each side. Farmers from the countryside exhibited crates, barrels, and bins of locally grown vegetables alongside other vendors selling imported fruit like bananas and coconuts.

"Was there something in particular you were looking for?"

"Yes, I'm looking for lemons and oranges." Miss Duval strolled along the displays, eyeing the produce while vendors hawked their wares.

"I'm sure you'll find them here." Julian pointed to the large clusters of bananas hanging from the rafters. "Would you like some bananas too?"

She looked up and smiled, then shook her head. "Not today, but maybe next time I come."

They strolled past bins of yams, onions, and corn before they came to some fruit displays where she spotted the citrus. She picked up, examined, and sniffed several lemons before purchasing a dozen and placing them in her basket. At the neighboring booth she did the same with oranges.

"There. I've gotten what I came for. Was there something you wanted to buy too?" Miss Duval looked at him, eyebrows raised.

"Actually, I was looking for a particular gentleman who is usually here, but I don't see him today." Julian prayed his fib wasn't too terrible a sin. He didn't want to tell her he had no reason to be there besides being in her company. How else would he find out more about her? "So, shall we have some coffee and beignets?"

"I'd like to try some."

He motioned to the Café du Monde ahead. They found seats at one of the wrought iron bistro tables while an aproned waiter approached. "You haven't been here before?"

"No, I haven't. I'm not too fond of coffee though."

"Then you must try some café au lait. It's made with steamed milk." Julian looked up at the waiter. "Two café au laits, please, and a plate of beignets," he said.

"Yes, sir." The waiter scurried off to fetch the order.

"Miss Duval, I'm curious about why you would choose to practice midwifery."

She tilted her head. "I'm sure you're thinking what most people think, that midwives are only older women who have had children themselves."

"Indeed, that is what I thought. That's one of the things that makes you different. But you're a nurse as well? Why wouldn't you use your nursing skills to aid sick women or children?"

"I am. Are you aware how many women die because of poor health during their pregnancy and how many babies are lost as well?"

The coffee and sugar-coated doughnuts arrived piping hot. Julian took a sip of coffee. "I must admit I don't know much about childbirth. They don't teach us much about such matters in medical college. We doctors leave that business to women."

"Yes, I do know that. Doctors provide no care for expectant mothers before or during their pregnancy. That's why I chose to be a nurse and midwife too. These women need health care all through their pregnancy. Often, doctors are called only when the woman is having a difficult birth, and often they do more harm in those situations than good."

Julian's face warmed, and it wasn't from the coffee.

"How so?" He stiffened under her subtle anger and accusation.

"Doctors only know two ways to help, forceps or hospitalization, neither of which are safe measures."

"Why wouldn't a hospital be safe? We have the most modern equipment."

"I don't know. However, more women die in childbirth or shortly after when they go to a hospital. I personally believe that hospitals are not clean enough."

He drew back. "Not clean enough? You think homes are cleaner?"

"Not all of them, but I certainly try to keep all equipment clean, and myself as well."

"So you adhere to the Pasteur theory?"

"Yes, I do believe in the existence of germs. Our nursing school taught good sanitation methods, such as frequently washing our hands."

He wanted to defend all doctors and hospitals but preferred not to argue. Miss Duval was passionate about her job, and he appreciated that quality. Indeed, he had not concerned himself with childbirth. A twinge of guilt wounded his conscience for not caring about women's health as much as she thought he should. Nevertheless, he hoped he was never called upon in such situations.

She picked up her cup, blew on the coffee, then took a tiny sip.

"I'm sure Vincent Rousseau is happy to have you care for his wife." Perhaps a compliment would soothe her anger.

"I believe his health could improve too. I hope you will be able to help him."

"I'm thankful Dr. Bennett recommended me in his absence. But I don't know how much Mr. Rousseau will listen to me. I made some suggestions, but I don't think he took them seriously. I think he'll only listen to Dr. Bennett."

"Why is that? You're a doctor too."

"Yes, but I'm young, and sometimes patients prefer an older, more experienced doctor."

"So in a way, you and I are in the same boat." She sent a sweet smile, and he relaxed.

"How so?"

"I must prove myself as a midwife despite my assumed lack of experience, and you must prove yourself as well."

He stroked his mustache. "Yes, that's true. But I think you have an easier time being accepted in your line of work."

"Why would you say that?"

"Because you're half American." Even if she did have some difficulty convincing people she was a qualified midwife.

"That's nonsense. You're American too."

"Oh, but here in New Orleans, I'm considered French, and the Americans prefer to deal only with Americans, and the French with French."

"But Mr. Rousseau is French."

"Yes, but his wife is American. That's why he's in the Garden District."

She nodded. "Uncle Claude explained that to me. Surely things are changing now."

Julian shrugged. "Slowly, perhaps. Dr. Bennett is American, so his recommendations have literally opened doors for me to care for patients that I would otherwise have no opportunity to treat. And yet there are still some who consider me a Frenchie."

"I had no idea there was such division here," Miss Duval said. She took a bite of beignet, then another sip of coffee. "But if that is true, I'm sure there are still plenty of French people who need doctors too."

"Yes, of course. After all, this city is predominantly French or Creole." He motioned to the cup in her hands. "So do you like the coffee that way?"

"The milk certainly improves the taste. And the beignets make it taste even better." Her eyes sparkled as she took another bite.

"You figured out the secret." He smiled back and relaxed even more, enjoying her company as they drank their coffee and ate the beignets in silence for a few moments.

"Since you're a native of New Orleans, perhaps you can tell me about Madame LaFleur," Miss Duval said.

He raised his eyebrows. "Why do you want to know about Madame LaFleur? Surely you're not interested in voodoo?"

"Not for myself, but because Adelaide Rousseau wants to follow Madame LaFleur's advice concerning her pregnancy. I need to know what kind of advice she might offer and whether it might interfere with the health of the mother or the baby."

"First of all, you need to know the woman wields a lot of influence around here. She's New Orleans's voodoo queen."

"So is she a witch? Does she deal in magic?"

Julian put his fingers to his lips and looked around. "She wouldn't like to be called a witch. She's a very devout Catholic."

"I don't understand. How can she delve into spells and hexes and call herself a devout Christian?"

Julian shrugged. "I don't know, but she does. But I also know she doesn't like competition."

"Competition? For what? Power?"

Julian nodded. "Yes, power, control. And you could be perceived as her competition."

Miss Duval's face reddened, and her expression hardened. "That's ridiculous. She can think what she will, but Miss Rousseau is my patient, and I intend to care for her professionally, whether Madame LaFleur likes it or not."

"For your sake, I hope she likes it."

Chapter 4

When Camille walked into Adelaide's room the next day, her gaze fell on an open box of bonbons lying on the night-stand. A couple of pieces had been half eaten.

"Where did these come from?" Camille asked.

Adelaide was lying on a fringed, rose-hued brocade chaise beside the window. She glanced at the box. "Vincent. He knows I love them, and I guess he's trying to make me feel better. I really don't feel like eating them right now anyway."

Camille closed the lid. "I'm sure he means well, but candy is not what you need right now." She pulled a bag of soda crackers from her satchel and handed them to Adelaide. "Here. Eat some of these. They'll help settle your stomach."

Adelaide took a cracker and nibbled on it.

Camille reached into the bag again, this time retrieving a glass bottle she'd bought at the drugstore. "This is ginger ale. It should help too. Just sip it, a little at a time." Camille removed the cork from the bottle, then wiped off the top with her handkerchief and handed it to her patient.

Adelaide put the bottle to her lips and took a sip. She glanced at Camille, took another sip, then handed the bottle back. Camille replaced the cork and put it on a small table beside the chaise.

"Have you been out of your room at all?"

Adelaide shook her head. "No. And I'm terribly bored. But what choice do I have in this condition?"

"You can't stay in here your entire pregnancy. You need to move around. It's good for you and for your baby."

"My mother said she lost her babies because she moved too much."

"I doubt that was the reason. There was probably something else wrong. You know, many women work while they're carrying a baby. They cook, do laundry, other jobs."

Adelaide's eyes flashed. "Are you telling me I need to do maid's work? I surely don't believe Vincent would approve of such. Nor would I. Besides, women who do hard work like that are sturdier than ladies."

Camille wanted to roll her eyes but refrained.

"No, I'm not saying you should do those things. I'm trying to explain that just because a woman is with child is no reason for her to do nothing else." Camille glanced out the window and saw a man and woman strolling on the sidewalk. "Perhaps when you feel better, we could go for a short walk. The fresh air and exercise would do you good."

"*If* I feel better."

"You will. Take my advice, and I'm sure your morning sickness will be gone soon." Camille looked around the room to see if there were any more unusual items like the leather pouch she so wanted to remove, if she could just figure out how. What if it had some unsanitary, unclean item in it? To keep such a thing in the room went against everything Camille believed about cleanliness. Yet Adelaide thought it was bad luck to look inside, and Camille didn't want to upset her by doing so. All she could do at the moment was pray about it. *Lord, please protect Adelaide against anything in that bag.*

"What else have you eaten since yesterday?"

"Sukey brought me some bouillon and I had a little."

"And did you keep it down?"

Adelaide nodded. "Yes, but I was afraid to eat too much."

"At least you had something. You don't need to lose weight while you're carrying a child. Next time try the crackers with the soup." Camille's smile was as much for Adelaide eating the soup as for her convincing Ida to make it.

"I need to see your stomach. Will you please lie on your back?"

Adelaide shifted her weight and turned. Camille propped a pillow under her head. She carefully lifted the woman's nightgown and touched her stomach, pressing slightly to see if she could feel the baby, not that she expected to yet. Adelaide watched her as anxiety marked her face. "What can you feel?"

Camille straightened. "Nothing yet, but that doesn't mean the baby's not growing. It won't be long, though, before your stomach begins to enlarge. How do your breasts feel?"

Adelaide grimaced. "They hurt. And I swear, they're bigger."

Camille smiled. "That's to be expected. They have to get ready to feed the baby."

Adelaide's eyes widened. "I don't know how to do that."

"You'll learn. I'll help you get started, and the baby will do the rest."

Tears welled in the young woman's eyes. "I wish my mama was here to help me."

Camille's heart wrenched. "I know you do, but I'll do all I can to help you. And you'll be surprised how much will come naturally."

"I hope so."

"Trust me. It will." Camille picked up her bag. "I'll leave you now, but I'll see you in a few days. Just keep doing what I suggested. You can send for me if you need me, and I'll come if I'm not tied up with a delivery."

"You're going to deliver *other* babies?"

"Yes, that's what a midwife does, you know. But you're a ways off from that yet. I don't usually see patients who are so early in their pregnancy, but you're special, and I'll be with you all the way through your baby's birth."

"I thought you said you came here just for me."

Camille took a deep breath. "I did, but you don't need me all the time, so I must care for others in the meantime." Did Adelaide expect her to be a companion? "Do you have any friends who can come over and spend some time with you?"

"I have a few friends who aren't married yet. But I can't see visitors in this state."

"Then that gives you even more reason to feel better so you can get out of bed."

Adelaide placed her hand on her stomach. "Do you think it's a girl?"

Camille lifted her eyebrows. "I couldn't predict such a thing. Only God knows right now."

"Sukey said if you have the morning sickness a long time, you're having a girl."

Camille had heard that old wives' tale before. She shook her head. "Actually, I've seen women who've been sick up to four months into their pregnancy and had boys, so I don't believe that."

"Well, I really hope it's not a girl anyway."

"Why is that? Does your husband want a boy?"

Adelaide nodded. "Probably. Most men do, don't they? But I don't want a girl, because they make the mama get ugly."

"That is not true. Did Sukey tell you that too?"

"Yes. She said girl babies take away the mother's beauty, but boy babies don't."

Camille hated those inane superstitions. She laid her hand on Adelaide's shoulder. "Adelaide, you are a beautiful woman, and you will be a beautiful mother." Camille noticed a framed photo on top of the dressing table. "Is that your mother?"

Adelaide nodded. "Yes, that's Mama."

"She was a lovely woman. And so are you. So you see, that myth is just nonsense."

"Oh, you're right. Mama was always beautiful, even when she was older."

"So you will be blessed whether the good Lord gives you a girl or a boy. Isn't that true?"

The young mother-to-be smiled and relaxed. "Yes." She yawned. "I'm so tired all the time. I think I'll take a nap."

"You go right ahead, and I'll see you again soon."

⌒

Camille strode down the street past Jackson Square, paying little attention to its namesake, the statue of Andrew Jackson astride his horse. She turned at the corner, looking for the house of her next patient. The buildings seemed to be connected by concrete walls, as there was no obvious separation between them. Many had shuttered doors and windows on the overhanging balconies above, accented by the typical iron scrollwork of the area. She shook her head as she passed doors that had the doorknobs and keyholes reversed with the keyholes above the knobs, another superstition her uncle had told her about. This practice was supposed to confuse evil spirits and keep them from getting inside the houses. Occasional narrow iron gates provided breaks in the walls and a glimpse into open courtyards beyond, surrounded by more balconies. To peer within felt as though she was invading someone's privacy, yet how else was she to find the place?

A man stepped out of a doorway in front of her.

"Excuse me, sir. Can you tell me where the home of Madeline Poydras is?"

The man tipped his hat. "You just passed it. It's right there."

Camille spun around, looking at the wall of shutters she'd just passed. She glanced back at him. "Oh, thank you. But how does one get in? Is there no door to knock on?"

He laughed. "You've never been in the Quarter before? Open that gate there and go down the alley. You'll see the entrance to the place."

"Thank you," she said. She walked back to a wooden gate painted the same dark green as the shutters, pushed it open, and found herself in a narrow alley between two buildings. Children's voices sounded through an open door in the wall, and she stepped through the opening, finding herself in a courtyard. A woman was hanging clothes from a rope stretched from one of the balcony railings across to another as two barefoot boys and a girl ran around her playing hide-and-seek in and out of the clothes. Camille approached the woman whose back was to her.

"Hello? Mrs. Poydras?"

The woman turned around with a clothespin in her mouth and Camille was able to see that she was very pregnant. She removed the clothespin and jammed it onto a pair of children's underwear on the line. "That's me. I'm Madeline Poydras."

Camille smiled and walked closer. "I'm Camille Duval, the midwife."

"You are? My husband said someone recommended you. He doesn't like Madame LaFleur and said he doesn't want that voodoo woman back in his house." She motioned to the children in the courtyard, then patted her abdomen. "As you can see, I'm not new to this."

"Did she deliver your other children?"

"No, I had an older woman, Mama Cree, but when she died, Madame LaFleur said she'd be in charge of my babies from now on. But my husband said no, even though Madame LaFleur threatened that our babies wouldn't survive without her help."

"I believe you and I will do just fine without her help. Do you know how far along you are?"

"Eight or so months, near as I can figure. By the size of me and how heavy I am, I hope he's going to come pretty soon."

"Is there a place I can examine you? I'd also like to see the birthing room."

"The birthing room will be my bedroom." She nodded toward an outside staircase. "Come on, I'll show you." Glancing back at the children, she said, "Y'all stay out of trouble while I talk with this lady."

Mrs. Poydras arched and rubbed the small of her back. "Lawd, my back is killing me." She crossed the courtyard to the stairs, then grasped the railing to pull herself up. Camille followed, hoping the woman could manage the effort. Mrs. Poydras climbed halfway up, then paused and looked down. A puddle of fluid formed at her feet. "Oh my, I think my water's broke."

Camille hurried to Mrs. Poydras's side and put her arm around the woman. "I'm here. Can you make it to the top?"

Mrs. Poydras glanced toward the top of the stairs, then nodded.

"All right, just take it slowly."

They slowly climbed the remaining steps. "That way." Mrs. Poydras nodded toward an open door between four windows, their shutters open against the pale stucco wall. "In there." The woman paused several times to catch her breath when a labor pain hit. Camille helped her into a bedroom then unbuttoned Mrs. Poydras's dress and let it fall to the floor before assisting the panting woman onto her bed.

Camille opened her bag. "Did you have any problems when your other children were born?"

"No, except they came fast when my pains started."

Camille suspected as much. "Do you have anyone to watch your other children while you're giving birth?"

"I have a neighbor, Isabella, who will come over, and my husband can too, when he gets off work."

Camille looked around the plain bedroom, the only wall accessory a crucifix hanging above the headboard. The windows were open, but the hot, tropical atmosphere prevented any breeze from blowing in. The room looked clean enough. "Do you have extra sheets and cloths for the delivery?"

"Yes, they're over there in that drawer." Mrs. Poydras eyed Camille. "How many children have you had?"

"None. Yet. I'm unmarried. Shhh." Camille removed the

Pinard horn from the bag and leaned over Mrs. Poydras, placing the large end on the woman's abdomen, then her ear on the smaller end, and listened. A strong thumping sound denoted the baby's position. She removed the horn and dropped it back into her bag, then gently pressed her fingers in various places on Mrs. Poydras's abdomen, confirming the child had moved down and was ready to be born.

Mrs. Poydras cried out in pain.

"Where can I find your neighbor?"

"Isabella is just next door," she huffed out. "Alphonse, my oldest, can go fetch her."

"Good. I'll go tell him to do so. Where can I find fresh water?"

Mrs. Poydras told her, and Camille went out on the balcony and called out. "Alphonse!"

The tallest boy glanced up.

"Get Isabella for your mother. Hurry!"

When the boy left, she hurried inside, put on her apron, and rolled up her sleeves. Then she went to boil water and fetch the cloths. Soon she heard another woman's voice.

"Madeline? Are you all right, *mon ami*?"

"In here!" Camille answered.

A woman appeared at the door, and Camille advised her of Mrs. Poydras's status. Isabella nodded, then called to the children, telling them she had just baked a cake they could enjoy. Thank goodness someone could come so quickly.

"Oh! Oh!" Mrs. Poydras hollered, sweat beading her brow.

Camille hurried to her bedside with the warm water. She moistened one of the cloths, wrung it out, and placed the warm cloth over the woman's abdomen to relax the muscles.

"I feel like pushing," Mrs. Poydras said.

Camille laid dry cloths under her patient. "Just pant like a dog when the pain comes."

Mrs. Poydras nodded, gritted her teeth, and started panting.

"Bend your knees and get ready to push."

"Oh!" Mrs. Poydras yelled.

The top of the baby's head was visible now. "All right, push!" Mrs. Poydras hollered as she pushed, and the baby's head came out.

"Another good push and it'll be here."

Her patient groaned loudly, pushing again.

The dark-haired baby girl slid out into Camille's hands.

"You have a lovely baby girl." Camille wiped the baby off, then tied the umbilical cord and snipped it before wrapping the infant in a towel. Handing the baby to her mother, Camille smiled. "Here she is."

Mrs. Poydras cradled the baby in her arms. "Another girl. My Marie wanted a sister. She'll be so happy to have one. Hello, little Anna."

"Anna. That's a nice name."

"It was my mother's name. Marie was my husband's mother's name."

"You rest, and I'll clean up here. How are you feeling, besides tired? Any pain?"

Mrs. Poydras shook her head and closed her eyes. Camille felt her forehead and took her pulse. Both normal. "I'll come check on you tomorrow."

Camille blew out a breath. She'd delivered her first baby in

New Orleans. Thank God it was an easy delivery. Wouldn't it be nice if they all were so easy?

She washed up, gathered her things, and slipped out of the house, leaving mother and baby sleeping soundly. Making her way back down the alley, she returned to the sidewalk, noting details of the surrounding area so she could find the house easily the next time. As she proceeded toward the streetcar stop, a woman came out of an adjoining alley and stepped in front of her.

A well-proportioned Creole woman, tall and striking with high cheekbones and hair wrapped in a high red turban, straightened her back and held her head high. She wore large gold hoop earrings and multiple necklaces including a cross, as well as several multicolored bracelets. The color of her skin reminded Camille of the creamy café au lait she'd had at the Café du Monde. The strange woman looked Camille over from head to toe and focused her attention on the medical bag Camille carried. She frowned; then a sly smile spread across her face.

"Good afternoon," Camille said, wondering why the woman didn't move out of her way.

The woman tilted her head and crossed her arms. "Is it now?"

Camille was confused by the strange response. She forced a smile. "I believe so." Her skin began to crawl when the woman continued to stare as if trying to see through her. She attempted to pass. "Excuse me."

The woman didn't step aside though. "So you the midwife I hear about." She gave a low chuckle. "You be careful, *chérie*. You might be trespassin' where you don't belong."

"I don't know what you mean. I haven't gone anywhere I wasn't invited."

The woman chuckled again with a grin. "But I didn't invite you, chérie."

"And who might you be, ma'am?"

At this, the woman laughed out loud. "I might be Madame LaFleur. I'm sure you've heard of me."

Camille froze, but took a deep breath and stood her ground. "Nice to meet you, Madame LaFleur. My name is Camille Duval, and it seems you've heard of me too."

Madame LaFleur chortled. "And so I have." She leaned in close to Camille, and unusual scents of spices and other things accosted Camille's nose. Lowering her voice to a throaty whisper, the woman said, "Remember what I said about trespassin'. You better watch out or you'll find yourself in trouble."

Camille stepped back and straightened. "Thank you for your concern. I'll be careful where I step. Good day, Madame LaFleur." She edged past the woman and strode away, trying to put as much distance between them as she could.

Madame LaFleur's loud cackle followed her down the street.

Chapter 5

Julian trotted down the back steps outside the family's apartment, hoping to avoid contact with any of the early customers at the bar downstairs. He stepped onto the pavement and hurried past the open door when a voice called out.

"Julian! Come here, Son!"

Dread dragged his steps inside the dimly lit room that smelled of stale liquor and cigar smoke where his father was wiping off the bar counter. He motioned Julian over and pointed to a customer seated at the bar, a regular Julian recognized.

"Here's my son, the doctor!" He nodded toward Julian. "Julian, tell Mr. Fontenot where your patients are."

"Papa. . ."

"Go ahead and tell him."

But before Julian could answer, his father continued. "The Garden District, that's where. Who would've thought—a Frenchie doctor in the Garden." Father laughed.

"It helps that my patient is also French."

"But Mr. Rousseau is not your only patient."

"No, but. . ." Julian glanced at his pocket watch. "Speaking of patients, I must hurry. I have calls to make." He nodded to Mr. Fontenot, who raised his glass in salute.

Julian hurried out the door and made it just in time to the streetcar stop.

Climbing onboard, he scanned the car for a place to sit and was delighted to see the pretty midwife. Their gazes met and he smiled, then walked over, motioning to the seat beside her. "May I join you?"

"You may," Miss Duval said, in a rather stilted tone. She didn't act very friendly today.

He sat down beside her, anxious to make conversation, but she stared out the window.

"Is everything all right?" What was bothering her?

"Isn't it a bit early in the day to imbibe?" She continued to look away.

"Imbibe?"

"Yes, imbibe. Didn't you just walk out of a bar?" Would she just look at him?

"Yes, but. . ."

"It's really none of my business what you do. However, I wouldn't want my doctor to drink before he treated me."

So that was it. She thought he'd been drinking. "I wasn't drinking. I have, uh, a patient who works there. So I stopped in to see how he was doing."

She faced him with an apologetic look. "Oh. I'm sorry. I shouldn't have jumped to conclusions."

His conscience pricked, having told her a lie. But what would she think if she knew where he came from?

"No offense taken." He changed the subject. "So what brings

you to the Quarter today? More shopping?"

She frowned. "I had a patient as well. I delivered a baby girl an hour ago."

His face heated with embarrassment. Why couldn't he say the right thing to her? Apparently, she wasn't the only one jumping to conclusions. "You did? Why, how marvelous. Did everything go well with the childbirth? The mother and baby are healthy?"

Miss Duval smiled with pleasure. "Yes, quite well."

"Good to hear. I didn't realize you had patients in the Quarter."

"Why wouldn't I? I expect to have patients all over town. In fact, I'll be getting off in a few blocks to see another patient, a Mrs. Martinez."

"I hope your visit is as successful there. I'm going uptown to see a few patients."

"I met Madame LaFleur today."

Julian flinched, imagining the scene. "You did? What do you think of her?"

"She's a strange person. She warned me not to 'trespass,' apparently, on what she considers her property. However, I don't know what property she referred to."

A sinking feeling hit Julian's stomach. "I think she meant the whole city, especially the French Quarter."

"You mean she owns that much property?"

He shook his head. "No, not the property, the people."

Her eyes widened. "As in slaves?"

"No, no. She just thinks she has that much loyalty from her 'people.'"

"Hmm. Well, she can't be everywhere, and I think this city needs a skilled midwife, not some superstitious beliefs. If she meant to frighten me away, she's wrong. I came to do a job, and she won't stand in my way, even if she tries."

Julian couldn't help but admire her spunk. But a lot of people followed Madame LaFleur. Would the woman give her any trouble?

"I believe this is my stop." She rose from her seat.

Julian stood and let her out, then watched her step from the streetcar onto the cobblestones. Miss Duval looked around, straightened her skirt, glanced back at him, and gave a little wave before walking away. Her gentle appearance hid her courage, a combination that both intrigued and frightened him. Did she really know what she was getting involved in?

As Camille walked down Toulouse Street, she couldn't help but wonder about Dr. Charbonnet. Was he telling the truth about not drinking? He seemed sincere, but she'd noticed a stale odor when he sat beside her. Why did he act like he was hiding something? In a way, she wanted to know him better, yet why? She had to admit he was handsome and polite, but she was not interested in finding a suitor. She had enough work on her hands to keep her busy and didn't need a man to interfere. Every day, she received word of another patient she needed to see.

When she came upon a row of almost identical cottages, she knew her patient lived in one of them. They had no yards or fences to distance them from the sidewalk, but rather opened right onto it. Each house had four dark green shuttered full-length openings, two being doors and two windows. Camille found the address she was looking for and stepped up to a small concrete stoop between the sidewalk and the door.

The aroma of food wafted from the windows, a sure sign some-one was home. Camille knocked on the door. A few minutes passed before the door opened and a pregnant woman with charcoal black hair in a long, thick single braid stood before her.

"Are you Rosa Martinez?"

"*Sí*, I am Rosa."

"I'm Camille Duval, the midwife."

"*Gracias, Dios!* Come in, come in." Camille followed her into the house and observed it was two rooms wide and two rooms deep.

"*Abuelita*, here is the lady who will help me have the baby." Mrs. Martinez spoke to a tiny elderly woman who sat in a chair in the kitchen. A little girl of maybe four or five stood beside her while the woman braided the girl's long dark hair. Peering up at Camille, the woman didn't speak or respond to Camille's smile but returned her gaze to the task at hand. The little girl stared up at Camille with big black eyes. "That is my daughter, Sophia."

"Hello," Camille said to them both.

Mrs. Martinez went to the stove where she stirred a pot, then laid the large wooden spoon down beside it and pointed to the contents. "Sausage jambalaya. Would you like some?"

Camille shook her head. The rice dish smelled wonderful, but she needed to examine her patient. "No, thank you, but I'm sure it's delicious. Where can we go so I can examine you?"

Mrs. Martinez beckoned, and Camille followed her into one of the two bedrooms of the house.

"Would you loosen your clothes, then lie down, please?"

Her patient removed her dress and let it fall to the floor, leav-ing her undergarments on. She lay down on the bed. Her abdomen was huge.

Camille listened for the heartbeat, thinking she heard an echo each time. She moved the Pinard horn around, confused as to where the heartbeat was coming from. "Do you know how far along you are?"

"I think eight months. It must be a big boy because I'm so much bigger than I was with Sophia."

Camille put the horn away, measured the size of the woman's abdomen, then pressed around, feeling for the baby. Were her suspicions correct? She felt the heel of a foot, then she felt another, then another. Yes, there were two babies.

"Mrs. Martinez, is your husband at work?"

She nodded. "Sí, yes, he works hard on the docks. Why?"

"When does he come home?"

"He's always here for supper. Why? Is something wrong?"

"No, I just wanted to make sure you had extra help." Camille wasn't sure how useful the frail old woman in the kitchen would be. "Your grandmother. Will she be able to help you with the babies?"

Mrs. Martinez shrugged. "She helps some. She can hold a baby and rock it." Her eyes widened. "Wait, did you say babies? Is there more than one?"

"Yes, I believe you're going to have twins."

"Dos? Two babies?" She placed her hand over her heart. *"Dios mia."* She looked at Camille, alarm etched on her face. "Are they well?"

Camille smiled. "They appear to be. I think they're fighting over who's going to be first."

"Sí, they move so much. I hope they don't come out fighting."

"I'm sure they'll be glad to get out and have more room," Camille said. "But you still have some time." She glanced at Mrs.

Martinez's feet. "Your feet are swollen. You need to stay off of them and get lots of bed rest."

"Stay in bed? Ha! Who will cook? Who will clean? Abuelita cannot do such things."

"You must find a way to rest part of the day. Sit and prop your feet up. And don't put as much salt in your food."

"Juan would not like it if I don't salt the food."

"You may use it; just don't put in as much as usual." Camille noted Mrs. Martinez's frown. "Do you have any bananas?"

"Bananas? No. Why?"

"Sometimes eating bananas helps reduce swelling."

"I will get some at the market next time. So, the babies, when will they come?"

"I suspect three to four weeks. And get someone else to go to the market for you so you can stay off your feet. I'll come check on you every week to see how close you are to delivering."

"Gracias. Thank you."

The front door opened, and footsteps sounded on the wood floor. "Rosa! *Dónde estás?*" A male voice came from the front room.

Mrs. Martinez strained to push her heavy body up. "*Aquí*, Juan. In here. With the midwife."

A swarthy, muscular man with curly black hair appeared in the doorway. He glanced from his wife to Camille. "*Está bien?* Is everything all right with the baby?"

Rosa grinned and walked to him. "Sí, they are both fine, Juan."

His dark eyes rounded. "Both? There are two?"

His wife nodded, laughing and patting her abdomen. "Sí, we need two names now."

"Hello, Mr. Martinez. I am Camille Duval. I will be taking

care of Rosa and the babies. Will you help me?"

"Help you? I don't know about a woman's business."

"Don't worry about that part. I need you to make sure she rests and gets off her feet. See how swollen her ankles are?"

He looked down at his wife's feet. "Yes. Is that bad?"

"It's not good. But it helps if she doesn't stand on them all day."

"Rosa, you do what the lady says. You rest."

Mrs. Martinez protested. "But what about Sophia? Who will take care of her?"

Camille wondered the same thing. "Have her lie down with you when you take a nap. Is there anyone else who can help after the babies are born?"

"I have a sister, Teresa," Mrs. Martinez said. "She lives in the city, but she's busy with her own children."

"Nonsense. My Rosa does not like to ask for help. I will tell Teresa, and she will come. Besides, she has a girl old enough to help too. Two babies!" Juan Martinez hugged his wife and kissed her. "We must take care of them!"

Camille packed up her bag. "I'll check in again next week. Remember, feet up, not so much salt, and eat some bananas."

Mr. Martinez walked Camille to the door. "Thank you, miss. Rosa lost the last baby, so I'm very happy there are two healthy ones now!"

Camille smiled and stepped outside. She had forgotten to ask if Mrs. Martinez had had any previous problems. She certainly hoped these babies were healthy. At least she had carried them this far. Would she be able to carry them full-term?

Next time she was near the St. Louis Cathedral, she'd go in and pray for her patients—their health and their babies. A vision of

Madame LaFleur's face crossed her mind, and Camille decided to add prayers for protection against whatever obstacles the woman threw her way.

Soon Camille was traveling all over the city, from Royal Street in the French Quarter to upscale townhomes on Esplanade. Her patients were of a mixed variety, from French to Creole, Spanish to American. Women both poor and wealthy needed a midwife, and although Camille wasn't the only one in town, she stayed busy treating mothers and delivering babies. Some of the deliveries were fast like Mrs. Poydras's, yet sometimes Camille had to wait hours for the babies to come.

Little bags of gris-gris were present in many of the homes Camille visited, signs of Madame LaFleur's influence. The woman's sway over the mothers-to-be was also displayed by their resistance to Camille, some refusing her help completely, quoting some foolish superstitions the voodoo queen had told them. On more than one occasion, she was sent away, once by a broom-wielding aged Creole woman who fussed at her in French. New patients were recommended by women she'd helped deliver, helping to open doors for her that previously might have been closed.

She had been stopping by to check on Adelaide each week, glad to see her morning sickness was going away. But one morning when she went into the room, she was accosted by an acrid odor.

"It smells awful in here."

"I know, but Sukey said Madame LaFleur told her it would make the sickness go away."

"What is it?"

Adelaide pointed under the bed. Camille looked and found a

dish of rancid onions. She pulled it out.

"Adelaide, this will not help you. You must believe me. How can such an odor make you feel better?"

"It scares away the spirits that make me sick."

"I beg to disagree. It keeps everyone else away, and the odor alone makes you and anyone who enters this room sick."

Adelaide nodded. "I must admit the smell has been offensive. I've been keeping a bottle of lavender in here to sniff and keep me from breathing the odor."

Camille put the foul dish outside the door. She'd discuss this with Sukey after she finished examining Adelaide. Now at four months pregnant, the young woman's belly was beginning to swell and show signs of the pregnancy.

"You've been doing better, but you must remember to eat."

"These crackers are all I've wanted. I asked Ida to buy them for me when she goes to market so I won't run out."

"You can't live on crackers only. You must eat more to feed the baby. You want a healthy baby, don't you?"

Adelaide nodded.

"Just make sure the food is not too spicy, all right? Rice and vegetables will be good, and some good soup, like chicken gumbo. I'll ask Ida to make it for you." She packed her bag and turned to leave. "No more onions under the bed, understand?"

"Yes, ma'am." Adelaide offered a timid smile to Camille.

"Thank you." Camille offered a smile in return, but wondered what kind of superstitious talisman she'd find on her next visit.

Chapter 6

A s Camille passed by a row of older cottages in the Quarter one day, she heard a woman scream. She paused and looked around, trying to determine the direction the scream had come from. Another scream, and she wondered if the woman was in danger. And if so, what could she do? Where would she find help?

A young Creole man ran out of one of the cottages, looking desperate.

Camille bolstered her courage and called out to him. "Sir, can I help you?"

He glanced at her, then her bag. "My wife is having our baby. She's in terrible pain. She told me to go find Madame LaFleur. Do you know where she is?"

Camille shook her head. "I do not. But I am a midwife. Perhaps I can help."

He stared at her a moment, as if trying to decide whether to believe her or continue to search for Madame LaFleur. Another scream seemed to help him make up his mind. "Come."

She trotted behind him as he ran back to the house and entered. Camille followed him, noticing the mirror hanging on the door, another voodoo superstition thought to keep evil spirits outside. Inside the house, a young Creole woman lay writhing in bed. An older, dark woman sitting beside the bed glared at Camille. "Who's that, Émile?" She cut her eyes toward the man.

"She's a midwife, Maman. She can help."

The pregnant woman's eyes widened and she lurched forward. "No! I want Madame LaFleur!"

Camille took a fresh apron from her bag and put it on, then pushed up her sleeves and glanced around. The house was not sanitary, and she shuddered at the thought of bringing a newborn child into the dwelling. "Where can I find a basin of clean water? And a clean cloth or towel too, if you have one."

Émile ran out of the room and returned soon after with the water. He set it on the washstand and grabbed a cloth hanging next to the basin, tossing it to Camille.

Camille washed her hands, using a piece of soap from her bag. She wet the cloth and washed it too, then wrung it out and approached the woman in the bed whose appearance was like a wild woman with matted long black hair scattered in all directions and perspiration covering her face. "May I examine you?"

"No!" the woman screamed. "I want Madame LaFleur!"

"Angélique, please. Let her help," the man implored.

Camille patted Angélique's face with the damp cloth as she spoke softly. "I understand you want Madame LaFleur, but she isn't here right now. I'm a nurse and a midwife, so I can help until she arrives. Trust me, I have delivered many babies." Camille prayed a silent prayer for the woman to calm down.

Both women glared at Camille with suspicion.

Angélique screamed again, clutching her stomach. "It hurts!

This baby is killing me!"

Camille patted Angélique's face again, and this time the woman relaxed, appearing completely exhausted. Camille looked over at Émile. "I may need your help."

The expression on his face reminded her of a frightened animal ready to run away. "I don't know what to do."

"I will show you." She glanced at the older woman. "Perhaps you can help too."

The woman looked at Émile, who nodded. "We will do what we can."

Camille lifted Angélique's nightgown and found the bed soaked. She placed the towel under the woman, then felt her abdomen. She cringed when she discovered her initial assessment was correct. The baby was breech.

She glanced at the other two and said, "I need you to hold her down, one of you on each side. The baby is facing wrong and I need to turn it."

"It will strangle!" Angélique cried out. "Bring some rope."

Camille had heard the myth that holding a rope could prevent the umbilical cord from strangling the baby. But these myths did no good for the child.

"We don't need that. We need you to calm down so I can turn the baby. Will you help me deliver your baby?"

Angélique stared at her, wild-eyed, but nodded and seemed resigned to whatever Camille said.

"All right." She glanced at the two others, who nodded and held Angélique down.

Camille reached in her bag for her tube of petroleum jelly, rubbed a little on her hands, then reached into Angélique and felt the baby. She too knew the danger of the baby strangling on the umbilical cord and prayed that wouldn't happen. Carefully, she grabbed hold of the baby's shoulder and began to turn it, feeling for the cord. Angélique moaned and tried to move, but the others kept her still.

"Hold on, now. I have to be careful."

Camille continued to turn the child until it faced the correct way. Once she was certain it was in the proper position, she blew out a breath.

"All right now, Angélique. I need you to push."

Angélique pushed, screaming again.

"Breathe like a dog. Pant, Angélique." The crown of the baby's head appeared.

Her patient did as she asked, then Camille asked her to push again.

The next push brought the child halfway out.

"The baby's almost here. Push one more time, hard."

With her last ounce of energy, Angélique pushed, and Camille was able to pull the baby the rest of the way out.

Émile hooted. "The baby came!"

Angélique tried to sit up to see but fell back. Camille tied off the cord and cut it, then wiped off the baby, wrapped him, and handed him to the mother.

"He looks like a fine baby boy," Camille said, a weight lifted from her shoulders.

Angélique checked the baby, counting fingers and toes. She smiled up at her husband. "He is handsome like his father. He is a little Émile."

Émile beamed, and even the old woman smiled.

"Do you have any fresh clothes you can put on, or any clean bed linens? It's important to keep everything as clean as possible for the baby to stay well."

"I have some," the old woman said. "I will go get them and bring them to you."

Camille nodded. "Very good. I'll just wash off my things; then I'll be leaving." When she leaned over to put her items into her bag, she saw the knives under the bed. A chill ran down her back. She wanted to ask but did not want to take away the joy of the moment. Her gaze returned to the happy parents and the baby now suckling at his mother's breast.

When the older woman returned, Camille helped change the bed linens and dress Angélique. Camille smiled at the new mother gazing at her baby. "I'll check back in on you in a few days."

"Thank you, miss," Angélique said.

Camille picked up her bag and headed toward the door. Émile followed her.

He opened his hands. "I do not know how to pay you. We have very little. Will you take a chicken? We have a few in the yard. Good egg-layers."

Camille smiled. "No, thank you. Keep your chickens. You need to feed your family."

"You are a good person, Miss. . .I didn't even ask your name."

"It's Duval. My name is Camille Duval. I'm thankful I was nearby when you needed me and very thankful the baby was born healthy."

Émile crossed himself. "I will light a candle at church for the baby."

"May I ask you a question before I go?" Camille had to know.

"Of course. What?"

"Why were there knives under the bed?"

"They're supposed to cut the pain."

"I see. Well, I suggest you put them back in the kitchen where they can do the most good."

"Yes. You are right. I will do that, Miss Duval."

By the time Camille finished her calls that day, the sun was already beginning to set. Dusk was snuffing out the daylight, and fog creeping in from the river on one side of the city appeared to join fog from the opposite side, cloaking the city in a ghostly haze. Because the streetcar route didn't run from her last call, she was forced to walk farther. As she approached the thick masonry walls of Lafayette Cemetery, the roofs and crosses of its multiple crypts peeking out above the enclosure, she heard a sound coming from the other side. Was someone crying or laughing? She listened, and the sound changed to moaning. Someone must be grieving.

She lifted her eyes toward heaven and prayed the psalm she'd memorized as a child—"What time I am afraid, I will trust in thee"—before quickening her step. She kept her focus straight ahead, resisting the urge to look through the double iron gate to determine the source of the noise when she walked by.

But as she stepped in front of the gate, a small skull rolled in front of her feet. She gasped and froze. Where did it come from? How did it get there? Her heart pounded as she glanced to her left and right yet saw no one. *Lord, protect me.* Shuddering, she lifted her skirt and ran all the way past the walls of the cemetery. A loud cackle followed her, a sound she was pretty certain she'd heard before. Madame LaFleur. Was the woman following

Camille? Was she sending a message? Camille didn't know exactly what the message was, but skulls and cemeteries could mean only one thing—death.

⌒

Julian knocked on the door of the Rousseau home. Would Camille Duval be there today? He hoped so, as it had been weeks since he'd seen her. But he'd heard talk about the new midwife in town—some of the talk had been good and her work had been praised. On the other hand, rumors abounded that Madame LaFleur wasn't happy with the intrusion of this part-American woman into her realm of influence. To be honest, he was worried that the voodoo queen might seek to harm Miss Duval in some way, maybe put a curse on her. But if she didn't believe in such things, would they work?

When Joseph admitted him, Julian glanced upstairs, half expecting, or perhaps hoping, to see the midwife. His last encounter with her had stayed on his mind. Her attitude showed she didn't believe his story about not drinking after seeing him come out of his father's bar. She must think less of him now. If only he could spend more time with her and change her opinion of him. But with her dislike of doctors and their neglect of women plus her assumption that he was a drinker, what could he possibly do to improve himself in her eyes?

Joseph pointed him to the study where he found Vincent Rousseau sitting at his desk, a smoldering cigar resting in a brass ashtray next to a glass of amber liquid. The man glanced up from some papers on his desk as Julian entered the room.

Julian gestured toward the papers. "Some paperwork keeping you busy?"

"Ha-ha." Vincent coughed before leaning back in his chair.

"You might say so." He held them up. "Race forms. Just came back from the Jockey Club. Gotta figure out who tomorrow's winner is going to be." He took a sip from his glass, then drew on his cigar before putting it back down, and coughed again. He motioned to a chair. "Have a seat."

Julian obliged, sitting on the edge of the chair. He really didn't have time to stay long, but sometimes his patients just wanted him to visit with them for a while.

"How's your luck running?" How much money had the man won or lost was what Julian really wanted to know.

"Pretty good this week." Vincent took another sip.

"Glad to hear it."

"I bet you are, so I can pay your bill." Vincent laughed, followed by a cough.

"Yes, of course." Julian smiled. "Do you have a favorite horse?"

Vincent pointed to the form. "Lucky Rose. I like that name, and so far, she's been pretty lucky for me."

Julian was out of small talk. "So how are you feeling?"

Vincent waved his hand. "So-so for a man my age."

Vincent was only in his forties, but his health was poor. Julian saw this type of thing too often among the wealthy. With too much money and too much time on their hands, they ate too much, drank too much, and smoked too much. But Julian's warnings were disregarded as if he were foolish to even suggest putting limitations on their lifestyle. These people felt they were entitled to their standard of living, something that set them apart from the poor and working class. But he would keep trying.

"You are not old, but you could be feeling better if you took my advice."

"What else am I going to do? I have a wife upstairs who won't even see me, much less welcome me into her boudoir. Many men in my position would have a mistress. But I promised to be faithful, and I'll keep my word." His voice was raspy, as if strained from speaking.

"How is your wife doing? Is she feeling any better?"

Vincent shrugged. "Miss Duval says she is. She was here earlier today."

Julian wanted to kick himself. Why hadn't he come by earlier too? But it couldn't be helped. He'd had other patients to see beforehand, others who actually listened to him.

"Apparently, Miss Duval has been pretty busy around town. I've heard her name mentioned."

"Yes, well, why would anyone want some old hag midwife when they could have a *nurse*-midwife, and one that's as lovely as Miss Duval?" Vincent laughed, then coughed.

Julian smiled at the comment, one he had considered himself. "But who is hiring Miss Duval? The husband or the woman with child?"

Vincent coughed out a chuckle. "I believe we know the answer to that."

Julian reached into his bag, pulled out a bottle, and handed it to Vincent. "Here. Take this for your cough, one or two spoonfuls, but not more than three times a day."

"All right, Doc. We'll see if it helps."

Julian doubted it would, as long as Vincent smoked, but he had to do something to validate his profession.

⌒

Every time Camille visited the Rousseau house, she half expected to see Dr. Charbonnet, but every time she discovered they'd missed each other. Why she was disappointed, she couldn't explain, but she brushed the thought away to focus on Adelaide.

On today's visit, Camille was happy to find the mother-to-be seated on her chaise near the window, working on a needlepoint.

"You're looking well today."

Adelaide smiled and pointed to her bulging tummy, now close to six months pregnant. "And fat."

"You're not fat. There's a baby growing inside you, so it's good for you to grow bigger. How are you feeling?"

"Pretty good. I think the sickness is almost gone."

"Then you should be able to get up more often. Are you ready to take a stroll—maybe just through your garden?"

Adelaide shrugged. "Maybe. Sukey told me not to go downstairs though. I could fall."

"I'd suggest you hold on to the bannister, or even have Sukey hold on to you. In fact, if you're up to it, I can take you outside now."

Fear shone in Adelaide's eyes. "I'm not sure."

"Lie down and let me take a look at you."

Her patient did as ordered, and Camille measured her abdomen. She glanced up at Adelaide's face. "I believe you only have about three months left, maybe less."

Adelaide's stomach moved, and she jumped. "It's moving! The baby is moving. Is that all right?"

"Of course it is. It's a good sign."

Adelaide felt her tummy. "I wonder where his head is?"

Camille pushed a little on the stomach and something pushed back. She laughed. "Well, I found the foot. I just got kicked."

Eyes wide, Adelaide said, "Truly? The baby can do that?"

"Yes, indeed. And the bigger it gets, the more it's going to move around to get comfortable."

"But Sukey said. . ."

Camille gritted her teeth. What now?

"What did she say, Adelaide?"

"She said if the baby moves a lot, it's trying to get away from something in my stomach."

"Pure nonsense! The baby's movement is perfectly normal, and don't you believe otherwise!" She was so tired of the ridiculous superstitions the maid was filling Adelaide's head with. "Will you please believe me? I *do* *k*now what I'm talking about."

"Yes, ma'am. I'll believe you."

"Just think of the baby dancing, happy to be alive and eager to meet its mother."

"Dancing?" Adelaide grinned. "What a delightful thought!"

"Yes, it is. So, what about that stroll?"

"Maybe next time." Adelaide glanced away, looking as if she was hiding something.

"Adelaide. Is there something else you should tell me? Did Sukey give you something?"

She nodded, a guilty look on her face as she reached under her pillow and retrieved a small vial. The dark amber glass did not reveal its contents.

"What is it?" Camille suppressed a groan. Another charm, no doubt.

Adelaide handed it to Camille. "Sukey said it's chicken blood. It's supposed to give good health, make the baby's blood strong."

Camille fought the wave of nausea that swept her. She drew in a deep breath and blew it out. "Adelaide, can you see the error in that kind of thinking? Whatever is in this won't help you or your baby. And it certainly didn't help whatever poor creature it came from."

"I guess you're right."

"I know I'm right." Camille dropped the vial into her apron pocket, anxious to rid herself and her patient of its presence.

Camille eyed the gris-gris bag still fixed to the bedpost, worried that it might contain something unhealthy.

Adelaide followed her gaze. "Don't take my gris-gris. I have to keep it."

"Adelaide, I know you're a Christian, so you must believe God will take care of you and trust in Him, not in such superstitious things. Why don't you pray to Him?"

"I do, but Madame LaFleur does too. She took my gris-gris with her to the cathedral and prayed over it."

Camille sighed and decided to let the matter go for a while longer. How could that voodoo queen believe her tricks were blessed by God? The cemetery incident was proof that the woman controlled others by fear. Camille would have to increase her own prayers and pray that Madame LaFleur's power over people would decline and their faith in God would grow.

Chapter 7

Camille was so tired. She'd been going from patient to patient every day, getting up early and going to bed late. Tonight, she hoped to get to bed early. She took her medical bag to her room and washed her hands before having dinner with Uncle Claude. She needed to spend some time with him. He'd been lonely since her aunt died, so Camille gave him an update on her work, but spared him the details. Like most men, he wasn't interested in the specifics of female affairs like childbirth.

She mentioned the signs of voodoo she'd run into but did not share the incident at the cemetery, certain he would become too worried about her safety and perhaps even suggest she limit her deliveries to the nicer areas of the city. Uncle Claude explained what he knew about some of the voodoo superstitions.

"It's all so foolish," Camille said. "Why do people believe those ideas?"

He shrugged. "Some of those beliefs came with the slaves from their ancestors in the islands. It was the religion they practiced, and it carried over here through their descendants."

"But Madame LaFleur calls herself a strong Catholic believer.

Adelaide said she takes her gris-gris to the cathedral and asks the saints to bless it."

"I know the priests, and they don't condone her measures. She usually hides those things in her clothes because if the priests saw them, she wouldn't be allowed to carry them inside. They've warned her about such practices but know she still does it."

"So why don't they keep her out of the cathedral?"

Her uncle shook his head. "Believe it or not, Madame LaFleur gives to the church. She is known to be generous to those less fortunate too, so to keep her out of the church would not set well with the Creole community."

"No wonder. The woman does wield a lot of power, in many ways."

"I suppose you'd say she's not completely evil. Even a voodoo queen has redemptive possibilities."

"What an enigma she is."

"That she is, dear; that she is."

Camille stifled a yawn, then excused herself to the kitchen where she heated a pot of water on the stove. She carried it to her bedroom and poured it into the basin, wishing she had the energy to fill the tub and take a bath. But the basin bath would have to do tonight. She unfastened her skirt and blouse and let them drop to the floor. After washing and patting herself dry, she put on a nightgown and turned off the gas lamp before climbing into bed. She fell asleep quickly, but sometime during the night something woke her.

An obnoxious odor assaulted her nose. What was that smell? She sniffed, trying to identify it, then covered her mouth at the repugnant stench, like something dead. She sat up, turned on the light beside her bed, and looked around. Where was the odor coming from?

She stepped out of bed and slowly made her way around the room, trying to determine where the smell was the strongest. When she drew close to her medical bag, the odor was overpowering.

Gingerly opening the bag, she looked in, not seeing anything unusual right away. But when she felt down into the bottom, her hands touched something slimy but stiff. She jerked her arm out of the bag and carried it over to the lamp so she could see the contents better.

She gasped at the sight of a dead frog lying at the bottom of her medical bag. Where had it come from? How did it get in her bag? Surely she would've noticed a frog in her bag sometime during the day. Had it gotten in there and died? She peered in closer and a tremor ran down her spine. The frog's stomach had been slit from top to bottom, exposing its entrails. Someone had killed the frog and put it in her bag. There was only one place she had left her bag long enough for anyone to put it in. The last place she had visited. The Rousseau home.

Obviously, the frog was meant to send a message. To scare her? Or threaten her? Or was it a curse? There was no doubt in her mind that Madame LaFleur was behind the scheme. And Sukey had to be involved, because she was the last person who had access to Camille's bag.

Why would anyone resort to something so repulsive? Here was proof that the voodoo queen meant the message only for Camille. Was she so obsessed with control? Obviously, she didn't like competition from others. But did she really think this prank would scare Camille away? Camille had assisted in autopsies, so the sight of a dead frog was not such a fright. The act angered her more than anything else. Such a thing in her medical bag was not sanitary and had certainly contaminated her instruments. She'd have to thoroughly clean everything in the bag before she could see any patients again.

Camille closed her eyes and breathed a prayer. *Lord, I will not submit to these evil attempts to scare me. Please give me courage to stand firm.* As if in answer to her prayer, the words came to her, *"Fear not, for the Lord is with you."*

Dead frogs wouldn't keep her from her work. However, they might scare someone else more easily frightened, like Adelaide. Tomorrow, she would confront Sukey and also tell Vincent Rousseau about the woman's involvement with Madame LaFleur's voodoo. It was time to put a stop to this nonsense.

Julian walked past the French Opera House at the corner of Bourbon and Toulouse Streets, glancing up at the marquee announcing *El Cid*, the French opera by Jules Massenet. He remembered reading in the *Picayune* newspaper that the opera was making its premier in the United States here in New Orleans. On impulse, he strode to the ticket window and bought two tickets.

But doubts plagued him as he walked away. Would Miss Duval accept his invitation to the opera? Had he been too hasty in his decision to purchase them? He tucked them inside his coat pocket where they imprinted his heart with the hope that she would accept.

Now to present her with the invitation. He couldn't rely on running into her by accident. Besides, that wouldn't be the proper way to invite her. Had his time in medical school made him socially inept? He blew out a breath. No, he should send a card requesting she accompany him to the event.

Down the street, a stationery store's sign grabbed his attention, so he headed to it. Inside the store, drawers and shelves of paper in every size and color filled the walls and the center aisle. After telling the salesclerk he wanted some simple paper for invitations, he was shown to the billet section where the smaller, six-by-four-inch paper was displayed. He selected some quality, heavier paper, then bought the traditional red envelopes gentlemen used for enclosing invitations.

Julian purchased the items, then penned the invitation there in the store while the surprised salesclerk glanced away. He hoped Miss Duval would be as excited about the invitation as he was to give it to her. After sealing the envelope, he left the store and hopped on the closest streetcar to the Garden District. When the car stopped at the street where Miss Duval lived, he stepped off and turned in the direction of her address, startled to see her coming toward him.

Her straw hat barely concealed the worried expression on her face as she strode along the sidewalk, focused ahead. She didn't even notice him until she drew close.

He tipped his hat. "Hello, Miss Duval. I was just on my way to your house."

She halted her steps and studied him with raised eyebrows. "You were?"

"Yes, ma'am, I was." He offered his best smile, hoping to get one in return.

"May I ask why?"

He withdrew the envelope from his coat and extended it

toward her. "I wanted to leave this for you."

She eyed it with wonder, then took it from him. "Should I open it now?"

"Of course."

His heart fluttered with anticipation as she carefully tore the envelope open and pulled out the invitation. She studied it, then looked up at him, tilting her head.

"You're asking me to go to the opera with you?"

His face heated. "Yes, yes, I am. Can. . .I mean. . .will you?" Perspiration ran down his back as he held his breath waiting for an answer.

"Why, yes. I'd love to go, that is, if I can." A smile eased its way across her face, and his heart melted. "Thank you for inviting me. I love the opera. I've been so busy, an evening out sounds wonderful."

"It's been awhile since I've been to the opera myself." Or enjoyed the company of a beautiful woman. "But what do you mean by 'if' you can?" What if she couldn't?

"As long as my patients don't have babies at that time."

"I pray they won't." He exhaled. "By the way, I've heard about you all over town. You've developed quite a reputation."

"A good one, I hope." A shadow crossed her face.

"Why, yes. Why would you think otherwise?"

"Remember I told you I received a threat from Madame LaFleur?"

"Yes, I remember you telling me you ran into the woman. Have you had any problems?" Rumors of the voodoo queen's tactics concerned him.

She frowned, then lowered her voice. "A couple of strange instances have occurred. Last night I found a dead frog in my medical bag. It had been cut open. What do you think that means?"

His temper flared. "I'm not certain, but I'd guess it was supposed to frighten you."

"I assumed the same. I'm not frightened, but I am annoyed. I keep my supplies very clean, and putting such an unsanitary thing in my bag contaminated them. I had to wash everything thoroughly after I found it."

"How do you think it got in your bag?"

Anger flashed across her face. "I think it was put there during my last stop yesterday, at the Rousseau house."

He drew back. "Do you really think so? But who would do such a thing?"

"I think it was Sukey. She's the one who put the gris-gris bag and other strange things in Adelaide's room, and I believe she consults with Madame LaFleur."

"What will you do?"

"I'm going to tell Mr. Rousseau. In fact, I was on my way there now."

"May I accompany you? I can use the time to check on him as well."

She studied him a moment, then nodded. "That would be nice. Perhaps he'll be more candid with you there."

They began walking the few blocks to the Rousseau house instead of waiting for the next streetcar. The weather was pleasant and not as sticky hot as it could be in New Orleans. Julian wanted to take her arm in his but restrained himself from doing so. She didn't know him well enough for him to be so forward. After all, in her eyes, they were merely business associates. But he hoped someday they'd be more. Perhaps she would see him in a different light when they attended the opera together. For the moment, though, he would try to serve as her protector.

⌒

Camille cut a glance at Dr. Julian Charbonnet as he walked beside her. He was a handsome man, to be sure, his wavy dark hair combed back from his face and, except for the mustache, clean shaven. And he had invited her to attend the opera with him. Her pulse quickened at the prospect. It had been some time since she'd enjoyed an evening out with a gentlemen friend. In fact, the only man she'd gone anywhere with in New Orleans was Uncle Claude. Was it the thrill of attending the opera, or just the fact that she had received an invitation that excited her? Yet the idea of spending an evening with such an attractive and pleasant gentleman as Dr. Charbonnet warmed her heart most of all.

Thankfully, the event was still a month away. She needed to work on her gown, perhaps even purchase a new one. Thoughts raced through her mind as she envisioned the evening, relishing the thought of being entertained in such a manner.

How timely that the charming doctor had arrived when she was on her way to the Rousseau house. She had become so accustomed to going everywhere by herself, much as she had in Charleston, that she hadn't felt a man's escort was necessary. But she was thankful for the doctor's company, especially under the circumstances. Somehow, his presence bolstered her courage. Surely Mr. Rousseau would listen to them both.

⌒

Joseph raised his eyebrows as he admitted the two of them to the Rousseau mansion and ushered them into the parlor. A few minutes later, Mr. Rousseau joined them.

A smile crossed his face. "So the two of you are working together now?"

Camille and Julian exchanged glances. Her face warmed, and Julian squirmed in his chair.

They both spoke at once. "We—"

Rousseau laughed. "And you're talking together. Haha."

Julian's face turned red, but he said, "We happen to be here at the same time because I was planning to see you anyway and ran into Miss Duval on the way."

Rousseau faced Camille. "Weren't you here yesterday? Why did you come back today? Is there a problem with Adelaide?"

Camille shook her head. "Not Adelaide, exactly, but her dependence on voodoo."

He pulled on his beard. "I told you she believed in that nonsense."

"Yes, you did, but I believe someone in this house is adding to the problem."

Lifting an eyebrow, Rousseau said, "I suppose you mean Sukey."

"Yes, exactly. I believe Adelaide would listen to me if Sukey wasn't trying to undermine my efforts."

He lifted his hands. "What harm is there? If you don't believe in that stuff, how does it interfere with your work? Adelaide is young, and Sukey's been taking care of her all her life. My wife believes what her maid tells her. 'Bout forty years ago, Sukey used to go to the voodoo dances in Congo Square when they were allowed, and she was much younger. She's been a follower of voodoo a long time."

Camille gripped the arm of the chair. "What *harm* is there? For one, she brings unsanitary items into Adelaide's room that can make her unhealthy. For another, Adelaide is confused about who to listen to, what to believe."

"Unsanitary, you say? Such as?"

Camille mentioned the gris-gris, the vial of blood, and the onions under the bed. "And I don't know what else, although she did tell me Sukey brought her something to drink that repulsed her, not to mention telling her ridiculous superstitions."

Julian cleared his throat. "If I may speak here, Miss Duval received a direct threat from Madame LaFleur a couple of months ago. And someone put a dead frog in Miss Duval's bag yesterday. She believes Sukey put it there when she was here."

"Is that so? Now that's a different problem. I won't allow anyone, especially my household help, to threaten you, Miss Duval." He rose from his chair and went to the door and called out.

"Joseph! Please find Sukey and bring her here. I need to speak to her."

A few moments later, the maid appeared in the doorway and Rousseau ushered her into the parlor. She kept her head down but glanced up long enough to cast an angry glare at Camille.

"Yes, suh, Mr. Rousseau. What did you need me fo'?"

"Is it true you've been bringing voodoo charms into my wife's room?"

She nodded. "Yes, suh. But it's nothin' bad. Theys s'posed to give Mrs. Adelaide and her babe good luck."

He scratched his beard. "I see. And have you ever put any sort of voodoo charm in Miss Duval's medical bag?"

The maid glanced up with widened eyes. "No, suh! I wouldn't do nothin' like that."

Rousseau peered into her face. "Are you telling me the truth, Sukey?"

"Yes, suh."

"Sukey, I know you mean well, but I don't want you to bring any more charms to my wife. Do you understand?"

"Yes, suh, I do."

"Thank you. You may go back to your duties now."

Camille and Julian glanced at each other as the maid left. Camille wanted to grab the woman and shake her. She was lying. But how could Camille prove it? She could take some solace from Mr. Rousseau's demand that the maid stop bringing voodoo charms into Adelaide's room. Unless Sukey lied when she said she'd stop.

Mr. Rousseau grinned and brushed his hands. "Now, that's settled. You shouldn't have any more trouble with Sukey."

"You believed her when she said she didn't put that frog in my bag."

"Yes. Sukey wouldn't lie to me, so you must've gotten that frog at one of your other patients' homes before you came here yesterday. I'm sure you've run into other voodoo followers elsewhere in the city, especially in the Quarter."

"I have, but I think I would have noticed it when I used the bag here yesterday. Don't you agree?"

"Seems likely. But I must take Sukey's word for it. She's been a loyal employee of the family for a long time, so why should she lie?"

Why indeed, thought Camille. *Why indeed.*

Camille stood to leave, and Julian did as well.

"Did you need to see me, Doctor?"

"Yes, for a moment." Dr. Charbonnet turned to Camille with an apologetic look. "Would you please excuse us?"

"I'm finished here today, so I'll just take my leave," she said, moving to the door. "Please excuse me, gentlemen. Mr. Rousseau, I'll be back next week to see Adelaide."

As she walked back through the grand foyer, her gaze fell on a beautiful piano at the opposite side of the room. Did Adelaide play the piano? Perhaps Camille could convince her to leave her room and start playing. The exercise and activity would be very beneficial to the young woman. Next time she visited, she'd offer the suggestion. As she turned toward the front door, she had the sensation of being watched. Glancing up at the railing at the top of the staircase, she spotted Sukey staring down at her. Their eyes met, and Camille felt as if they were each giving the other a warning.

Chapter 8

Julian was as nervous as a horse in a thunderstorm, never knowing where the next bolt of lightning might hit. Tonight was the long-anticipated event he'd looked forward to, a social evening with Miss Duval.

He'd gotten a haircut and rented a tuxedo and a nice carriage with a driver to convey them. Tugging on the high, tight-fitting collar, he hoped he didn't look like what his father had said when he saw him leave. "You can't make a silk purse out of a sow's ear." Was that what he was doing—trying to look better than he really was? Yes, he had to admit that was true. He wanted to impress Miss Duval, and he could at least look the part of a gentleman, even if he was just the lowly son of a barkeep.

The carriage stopped in front of Claude Duval's house, and Julian climbed out. He sucked in a deep breath, then exhaled before knocking on the door. Mr. Duval opened the door himself and welcomed Julian in. He extended his hand. "Dr. Charbonnet. It's very nice to meet you. I've heard many good things about your work."

"Thank you, sir." Julian shook hands. "It's a pleasure to make your acquaintance as well."

"My niece tells me you're from the city. I'm trying to place your parents. What type of business is your father in?"

Julian's shirt tightened around his neck.

"Good evening, Dr. Charbonnet."

Julian glanced up to see Miss Duval descending the stairs. His breath caught at the vision before him. She was stunning in a pink satin dress with a square neckline and puff sleeves. The dress fit her hourglass shape, calling attention to her impossibly tiny waist. A small feather headpiece adorned her beautiful upswept hair, and a pearl-studded choker necklace graced her elegant neck.

He swallowed before answering. "Good evening, Miss Duval. You look lovely." A catalog of words ran through his head, yet none would adequately convey the depth of emotion that stirred him as he gazed at her, his heart thumping against his chest. He glanced at her uncle, avoiding an answer to his question, then looked back at Miss Duval.

"Are you ready to go?" He reached for the lace shawl she carried draped over her arm and helped place it over her shoulders, his hands warmed by the touch of her cool, creamy skin.

She adjusted her elbow-length ivory lace gloves and nodded. "Yes, quite ready. I've been looking forward to this evening." She faced her uncle and kissed him on the cheek. "Good night, Uncle Claude."

"You two have a wonderful time!" Mr. Duval beamed approvingly as he ushered them out the door.

The ride to the opera house seemed too short as Julian sat next to Camille in the open carriage, trying hard not to stare at her and enjoying the nearness of her body to his. The streets around the opera house were lined with carriages waiting to be unloaded.

"My, I believe everyone in New Orleans is here tonight," she said.

"I heard the performance is sold out. Thank goodness I bought our tickets early." He certainly was thankful he'd responded to the impulse to get the tickets when he did.

"Miss Duval, would you prefer to wait our turn in the carriage or get out now and walk the rest of the way?"

She gave him an endearing smile. "Let's get out. It's a lovely evening for a walk. But could you please call me Camille? I believe we can dispense with the formal address tonight."

His face warmed. "I would love to call you Camille. And will you please return the favor by calling me Julian?"

"Yes, I'd like that."

Camille took Julian's arm as they strolled to the grand entrance of the French Opera House. The assortment of attendees was fascinating, and representative of the diverse city. Ball gowns of all colors, fabrics, and designs added as much variety to the attendees as the people themselves. From luxurious beaded silk and satin to plain black or beige linen to the overly embellished and jeweled gowns of the wealthy Creoles, the display was dazzling. She recognized a few people, having seen them in church or in the Garden District, but none of them had been her patients. In fact, only one of the women appeared to be with child, if indeed that was the reason for her extended abdomen.

Camille inhaled, and the mixed scents of perfume, cigar smoke, and smoke from the gaslights on the street filled her nostrils. The air was full of excited female chatter, boisterous male laughter, and the snorting of horses as they stomped their hooves on the street.

"What a festive atmosphere!" Camille said to Julian.

"You should see it during the Mardi Gras celebration. You haven't experienced the carnival yet, have you?"

"No, I arrived after Easter, when it was over. But I look forward to seeing it next year. I hear it's quite the soiree."

"There are actually quite a few soirees held during the Lenten season. Perhaps we can attend one of them." He smiled at her with a sparkle in his eye that made her heart flutter.

She smiled in return, momentarily at a loss for words. Had he just invited her to next year's Mardi Gras balls?

"Dr. Charbonnet." A gentleman nodded to Julian on their way into the opera. Julian nodded back. The scene was repeated several times, prompting Camille to comment.

"You're rather well-known, it seems."

Julian lifted his chin. "At least a few of my patients remember me."

Camille gave him a little squeeze on his arm. "I'm honored to be on the arm of such a distinguished doctor."

A tinge of red traveled up his neck, and he smiled, then gave his collar a tug as if it were too tight. "You flatter me, Miss Duval."

They found their seats inside the theater, and the performance began. Camille sighed as she relaxed to watch. What a welcome respite from her daily life. She'd almost forgotten what it was like to slow down and enjoy herself. Much as she loved her work, the demands of others' needs could be taxing. Only the pleasure of holding a newborn baby she'd delivered and presenting it to its mother kept her from getting overly tired.

The faces of mothers and babies she'd delivered ran through her mind. The Martinez twins had arrived a few weeks ago, much to the delight of their parents and big sister. She'd checked in on them afterward to make sure there were no problems. The same was true of her other patients, who welcomed her back, even though some still held to the old charms from their voodoo queen. She'd delivered French, Creole, Spanish, Irish, and German babies, not to mention the American ones. In fact, it seemed to her that childbirth was one of the few things the different cultures had in common, all of them treasuring that sacred occurrence. Camille thanked God every day for the opportunity to be a part of the process.

She scanned the crowd, wondering if any of the younger ones would be her future patients. Perhaps she'd deliver the grandchildren of the older patrons present.

Camille caught Julian looking at her a couple of times and smiled in return. His admiring gaze made her stomach flutter, and she glanced away as her face warmed. Perhaps she'd spoken too harshly about doctors when they'd shared coffee that day at the Café du Monde. All doctors weren't bad, and she knew he wanted to be a good doctor as much as she wanted to be a good nurse and midwife. They shared their desire to help others, a realization that filled her heart and drew her toward him.

During the opera, Camille noted several people glance at them. Were they looking at her or at her handsome escort? No doubt the women found him attractive. Camille had the urge to take his arm again, as if to assure her status as his companion for the evening, but that would have been too forward. Soon she was lost in the performance and would have forgotten where she was, except for the scent of sandalwood wafting from her escort, reminding her of his proximity.

When the opera ended, they stood and made their way toward the exit with the throng of others.

"Did you enjoy the performance?" Julian took her hand as they descended the stairs.

"Immensely. I was thoroughly caught up in the story."

He beamed. "I'm very happy to hear that."

They were in the grand foyer discussing one of the scenes from the show when a woman nearby collapsed onto the floor. Several other women screamed, and a group of people gathered around the woman. Camille and Julian ran to her, shooing away curious onlookers as they knelt beside her. Camille recognized her as the pregnant woman she'd seen earlier. Julian felt for a pulse while Camille opened her evening bag, retrieved a small bottle of smelling salts, and passed it under the woman's nose. Soon her eyes fluttered open.

"Is she all right?" The man Camille assumed to be the husband knelt near the woman and kissed her forehead. "Danielle, love, can you hear me?"

The woman's eyes came into focus as she sought her husband's face. Then she looked at Julian and Camille. "What happened?"

"You fainted, I believe," Julian said. "I'm Dr. Julian Charbonnet."

"How far along are you?" Camille asked. "I'm a midwife and a nurse."

"Between eight and nine months, I think. I didn't want to miss the opera, although Louis begged me to stay home." She smiled apologetically at her husband, then looked back and forth at Julian and Camille. "Are you two married?"

Julian's face turned red and Camille felt her own doing the same. "No, we're not," she said. "We just happened to be here together. May I?" Camille reached out to Danielle's stomach, and she nodded. Camille felt the baby through the loose ball gown the woman wore. "Have you had any labor pains?"

"I don't think so."

"Do you have a midwife? If you need one, I can come by your house tomorrow and do a full examination. I don't think you're in labor yet, but you aren't far off."

Danielle glanced at her husband, who said, "A nurse too, you say? Yes, that will be fine. It wouldn't hurt to have a more learned person check on you than the old woman who's our midwife."

"Good. Tell me where you live, and I'll see you tomorrow." She faced the young woman. "Can you stand?"

Danielle nodded, and they helped her to her feet. Danielle's husband gave Camille their address; then the men helped the woman to the waiting carriage and lifted her in.

Camille and Julian watched it ride away, then looked at each other and smiled. A bubble of laughter escaped Camille, and soon they were both laughing.

"I don't think we can ever get away from our work, can we?" Julian said.

"No, I think not. Such is the life of a doctor and nurse," Camille said.

"We make a pretty good team, don't you think?" Julian's eyes twinkled as he winked at her.

"Yes, I believe you're right. We do make an excellent medical team," Camille said.

The twinkle left Julian's eyes, and Camille knew he hadn't only been referring to their medical association. Perhaps they did share a bond beyond their professions. And the prospect of such a bond was rather appealing.

As the carriage carried them back to Camille's house, the conversation returned to the opera, avoiding talk about anything related to their work. Julian was afraid he'd overstepped his boundaries, as Camille had made it clear their association was mostly due to their professions. True, they had met because of their work in the same field, but Julian yearned for their relationship to develop into something more. And even though she didn't acknowledge it, he sensed her interest in him was more personal as well. The way her eyes sparkled when she looked at him tonight gave him reason to hope.

When they arrived at the Duval house, she turned to him.

"Thank you for a wonderful evening. I truly have enjoyed myself. It was such a welcome respite."

"I'm very pleased that you did. Perhaps we can have another outing in the near future."

"What do you mean?"

"Have you been down to the beach yet?"

"The beach? I'm confused. I didn't know there was an ocean near here."

"There isn't, but there's a very large lake that looks as large as an ocean. Lake Pontchartrain. There's a beach there, right next to the lighthouse."

"It sounds wonderful. How far away is it?"

"About ten miles north of here. We could take a picnic."

"I'd love to do that."

"How about next Saturday?"

"Perhaps. It depends on my patients, of course. But we can try to plan on it."

"Excellent." He lifted her gloved hand and kissed the back of it. "I look forward to showing you our beach."

He helped her out of the carriage, then walked her toward the house. She stopped.

"What is that?" She pointed to something in the yard.

He followed her gaze and saw it too. A chill raced through him when he realized what it was. Julian walked over to the round object. "It's a conjure ball."

She joined his side to see the tar-blackened sphere with feathers sticking out of it. Julian kicked it, and it rolled enough to show a cross marked on the side.

"What does it mean?"

"It's a voodoo curse. Whoever brought the thing rolled it across the yard to bring bad luck to the people who live in the house."

Camille set her hands on her hips. "Julian, this has gone too far. This witch is coming onto my uncle's property for the purpose of doing harm. I won't stand for this anymore. Tomorrow, I'm going to find that Madame LaFleur and give her a piece of my mind."

"I'll go with you."

She shook her head. "No. This is between her and me. It doesn't involve you." Her voice softened and she searched his face. "I don't mean to offend you, and I appreciate your offer, but I need to do this by myself."

The determination in her voice suppressed any objections he had. "Please be careful, Camille."

They stopped at her front door and she faced him. "Julian, you believe in God, don't you?"

"Of course. Why?"

"Then you must believe what the Bible says. 'Greater is he that is in you, than he that is in the world.' *I* believe it, so I'm not afraid. If you want to help me, you can pray for me."

"That I will do. I promise I will pray for you."

He kissed the back of her hand, wishing he could kiss her lovely lips instead, before she turned to go inside. After the door closed, he went back to the ball in the yard and kicked it out into the street where a horse and carriage passing by rolled over it, smashing it to pieces.

Chapter 9

Camille asked several people in the French Quarter where Madame LaFleur's house was. Some refused to answer. Others shrugged as if they didn't know. But Camille was certain that everyone in the Quarter knew where she lived. They just didn't want Camille to know. She stopped in on a few patients to check on them while she was in the area.

One of the women whose baby she'd delivered was crying when Camille stopped by.

"Lizette, is everything all right? Are you feeling badly? How is the baby?" What had happened since Camille's last visit?

Lizette backed away and let Camille in. Camille hurried to the cradle to check on the baby, but he wasn't there. "Where's the baby, Lizette?"

The woman didn't answer, and Camille realized Lizette was suffering from melancholy. Camille had seen this before, when mothers became sad after a baby was born and paid no attention to the child, sometimes neglecting to feed it and, in rare cases, even harming the baby or themselves.

Alarm gripped Camille. She grabbed Lizette's arms, trying to make the woman look at her. Camille leveled her gaze on Lizette's face and raised her voice. "Where is your baby?"

Lizette's vacant stare drifted to the back of the house, and Camille let go of her arms and rushed to the back door of the cottage. She opened it and found an older girl of around thirteen holding the baby and rocking it in her arms. The girl looked up at Camille. "Lizette cries all the time. She barely feeds the baby. I'm Lizette's sister, Elise. I've been staying here to take care of the baby until Lizette feels better."

Camille breathed a sigh of relief that the baby was being taken care of. But Lizette still needed help. "Does Lizette ever leave the house?"

"No. She stays inside all the time with the shutters closed. It's too dark in there, so I come out here."

"Lizette needs to get outside too."

Camille went around the house, going from window to window, opening the shutters. She grabbed Lizette's hand and pulled her outside where her sister and the baby were. "Lizette, you stay out here for a while." She pointed to a chair and Lizette sat down. "You need some fresh air and sunlight."

"Elise, is there a baby carriage here?"

"No, ma'am, but the neighbor has one."

"Then see if she'll let you borrow it. You and Lizette need to take the baby out for strolls. Lizette needs to get out of the house and exercise."

Camille leaned over in Lizette's face. "Lizette, I want you to take your baby for a stroll. Elise will come with you. I want you to do that every day. You will feel much better if you do what I say. And the baby will be happier too. Understand?"

Lizette nodded.

"Elise, you see to it that she does, all right?"

"Yes, ma'am."

Camille walked closer to Elise and lowered her voice. "Elise, do you know where Madame LaFleur lives?"

Elise cut her gaze back and forth as if the walls around the yard had eyes. She nodded.

"Would you please tell me where it is?"

"Yes. She doesn't live by herself. Her daughter lives with her because her daughter's husband went out on the ships."

Camille was surprised. Madame LaFleur was a mother?

After Elise gave her the directions, Camille left the house and set out to find the voodoo queen's home.

Julian watched Camille exit the cottage on Orleans Street. He'd been following her since she left home that morning. He knew she'd be angry if she discovered him, so he'd stayed a safe distance behind, darting behind something or into a store when she stopped. He didn't know what Madame LaFleur would do to her. In fact, he'd never heard of the woman personally doing harm to anyone, other than putting curses on them, but he wondered what she'd do if confronted as Camille intended. Or what her loyal followers would do. Rumors abounded of people who'd crossed the voodoo queen and disappeared. Julian couldn't allow anything to happen to Camille.

Since their evening together, his affections for her had deepened, and he was determined to grow even closer to her. He admired her courage as well as her faith. Perhaps his own faith needed to be stronger. But he had done as she requested and prayed for her. In fact, he hadn't stopped praying for her as he trailed her all over the Quarter.

Her face set with determination, she was surely going to Madame LaFleur's house now. Although he wasn't certain of its location, he had a general idea, and Camille was headed in that direction. He kept her in sight as she walked several blocks, crossed streets, and turned corners. When she stopped in front of a brightly painted Creole cottage, he assumed she had found the house. She knocked on the door and waited.

No one came to the door, so she knocked again and appeared to be listening for sounds coming from the house. She stood a while longer. Then he heard a scream that seemed to come from inside the house. Camille appeared undecided about whether to leave or stay. He hoped she would leave.

But while she stood there, Madame LaFleur came around the corner and approached her.

⁓

"What are you doing at my house?"

Camille jumped and spun around. Madame LaFleur walked toward her. If the woman was outside, who screamed inside?

"I wanted to talk to you." Camille squared her shoulders.

Madame LaFleur cocked her head, her eyes dark as she studied Camille.

"You want to buy some of my charms, yes? I have many charms for women having babies."

"Yes, I've seen some of them, and I don't want any of them. They're disgusting, not to mention unsanitary."

"You think so? You do not know the power."

"Oh yes, I do. I know the true power, and it's not you or your charms or curses."

The woman crossed her arms. "The true power? Your power?"

"No, not mine. God's. I believe in God's power."

The voodoo queen threw her head back and laughed. "God's power is my power too. I pray to the saints to bless my charms, and they do."

"You might think so, but you're wrong. And speaking of wrong, I want you to stay away from my patient, Adelaide Rousseau. You are interfering with my treatment."

"Ha! Your treatment? I was treating her before you came to town. How you think she got pregnant anyway?"

"I know how she got pregnant, and you didn't have anything to do with it. You are not God. Her husband hired me to take care of her through her pregnancy, not you, so stay away from her."

"I've never been there."

"Perhaps not, but you give things to Sukey and put silly superstitions in her head. You need to stop."

"You think you can make me stop, chérie? Nobody can stop Madame LaFleur."

"You don't scare me. Your dirty little tricks like putting a dead frog in my bag or putting that ridiculous ball in the yard will not stop me from doing my job. And stay away from my uncle's house too."

"I've never been there either." She laughed. "You see, I don't have to go anywhere to do my work. People come to me, and I help them, so they do favors for me."

Camille pointed at the woman's chest. "You are evil. Leave me and my patients alone!"

Another scream came from inside the house. Madame LaFleur glanced at Camille, then at the house. "My daughter. Her baby comes! Get out of my way!"

She swung her arm to move Camille, then gasped and grabbed her chest, crumpling to the ground. Camille knelt beside her. "What is it? What's wrong?"

"My heart." Gasping, she said, "You did this when you pointed at me."

"I did not. I don't have that kind of power. But I want to help you."

Another scream, and the woman gazed toward the house. "My daughter. Please. Help my daughter."

Out of nowhere, Julian appeared beside the woman. He glanced at Camille. "You go help her daughter." He looked back at Madame LaFleur. "I'll help her."

How did he happen to be so close? She pushed aside her questions and nodded, then shoved the door of the house open and went inside. The house was dark, except for low candlelight on the fireplace mantel, the scent of melted wax among the many odors permeating the room. As her eyes grew accustomed to the dim light, she saw something sprinkled around the edges of the room. What appeared to be some kind of crude altar was set up on the mantel with a variety of odd objects, including a human skull and several animal skulls. Candles of various colors and sizes burned and dripped down the sides and onto the wood. Camille shuddered and looked away.

A moan came from an adjoining room, then a scream. Camille hurried into the room and found a young Creole woman writhing in the bed. When she saw Camille, she said, "Where is my mama? I need her!"

"She asked me to help you until she can get here."

"No, I don't believe you." She groaned. "What did you do with her?"

"I did nothing to her, I promise. Please. I want to help you. What is your name?"

"Josephine."

"Josephine, I need to examine you. Please try to be still."

Camille felt around Josephine's stomach and could tell the baby had moved down to the birth canal, but Josephine was still not dilated enough. "Josephine, I think the baby wants to come out pretty soon. Let me find some water so we can wash off and get things clean for the baby."

Camille rushed out the back of the house to find a separate small kitchen building. Strange odors were in the kitchen and jars of unknown things sat on the windowsill. She held her breath as she pumped some water to wash her hands, then put some into a pot and brought it back inside. Rusty crossed knives lay under the bed, ineffective against Josephine's pain.

She felt in her bag for a clean cloth, dampened it, and placed it on Josephine's forehead while the woman moaned. Camille had another cloth in her bag that she placed underneath Josephine. From the position of the baby, Camille knew Josephine needed to lie on her side.

"Josephine, I need you to roll over to your right side."

Josephine moaned. "I can't."

"You can, and I'll help you. Ready? One, two, three!" Camille pushed as the woman turned.

"Is the baby gonna come now?"

"Not quite yet. We have to wait a bit longer."

"I can't! It hurts too bad!"

"Just breathe and push the air out like this—puff, puff, puff— each time you feel a pain."

"I want my mama!"

"I know, but I'll stay with you until your baby's born. All right?"

She moaned again, and Camille rubbed the young woman's back, hoping to bring some comfort and reassurance to her. She couldn't possibly tell Josephine that her mother was ill. Meanwhile, Camille prayed for God's presence to be near and protect her against the evil that was in the house. She also prayed for Josephine, for her baby, and for Madame LaFleur. Camille's own back was beginning to ache as time dragged on into the evening.

As the hours passed, Josephine's pains increased and grew closer together until the baby had moved far enough down into the birth canal.

"Okay, Josephine. I think this baby is ready to meet his mama. Now let's get you on your back. Sit up a little. I'll prop you up with the pillows." Camille helped her get into position. "Okay, now. . .push!"

Josephine hollered but pushed, and the baby's head crowned.

"All right. Take a deep breath and push again. Now!"

Josephine pushed again, and more of the baby's head came out, but Josephine went limp.

"Come on, Josephine. You can do it. One more time. Push!"

Josephine pushed with one final scream, and the baby came all the way out. Camille quickly wiped off the baby, but it didn't cry.

Josephine rolled back over. "My baby. Is it. . . ?"

Camille rubbed the baby's skin vigorously until finally the little boy coughed, then cried.

She wrapped him up and handed him to his mother. "Here's your baby boy. What are you going to name him?"

"Jacques, after his father."

"Your husband will be very proud."

"Where is my mama? I want to show her my baby."

Camille wondered the same. How was Madame LaFleur?

"I'll go find her and tell her. You rest now." Camille straightened and stretched her back. It had been a long delivery, but thank God, she had been there at the right time.

When Camille went outside, the neighbors told her Madame LaFleur had been loaded onto the hospital carriage and that the doctor had gone with her.

"The doctor said he thought she had a heart seizure. He said she had to go to the hospital to get some rest," one of the neighbors said. "How is Josephine?"

"Mother and baby are doing fine. Madame LaFleur is a grandmother. Her daughter wants to see her, of course, and show her the baby. I hate to upset her right now and tell her about her mother's condition."

Another woman approached. "I'm Madame LaFleur's friend. Did I hear you say Josephine had her baby?"

"Yes, that's true. She had a baby boy."

The Creole woman grinned and clapped her hands. "Oh, that's so good!" She turned to the people behind her and said something in French.

A cheer rose from the crowd.

"Perhaps you can help. Someone needs to look in on Josephine and the baby. Would you mind? Josephine will be missing her mother."

"Oh chile. We'll all take care of Josephine and the baby. We love Madame, and we'll do all we can. She don't need to worry about nothing."

"Thank you. I'm sure she'll be very grateful to you."

"She's helped us out a lot, so now it's our turn to help her. How long will she be gone?"

"I don't know. As soon as I find out, though, I'll send word."

"Can we come visit her at the hospital?"

"Let's give her time to rest first."

The woman nodded and turned to her friends, telling them in French what Camille said.

"Can we see the baby now?"

"I think the baby and mother are sleeping now, but you can look in on them, maybe one at a time, because Josephine is very tired too. She'll probably be hungry when she wakes up. Can you bring her something to eat?"

"Yes, ma'am. We sure can. We'll make sure she gets plenty."

The gaslights had been lit when Camille trudged down the street to the next trolley stop, a long three blocks away. As she approached the stop, she realized it was in front of the bar that Julian had come out of that day awhile back. While she waited for the streetcar, she couldn't help but hear the loud voices coming out the open door of the establishment.

"Yes, sir, my boy Julian, he's an important doctor now!"

"You have good reason to be proud of him, André."

"That I do. Graduated from Tulane University with the highest grades!"

"Where'd he get those brains from, André? Not you, that's for sure!"

"Ha, you're right about that. His mother, God bless her soul. She was the smart one. The boy takes after her."

"Julian is gonna do well, André. You done good."

"Naw, Julian's done it all by hisself. He's a good boy."

Camille looked over her shoulder, hoping to get a glimpse of the man talking. She turned slightly and saw him behind the bar, seeing a resemblance to Julian right away. So that man was Julian's father? She glanced up at the balcony overhead. Was this where Julian lived? Why hadn't he told her that when she saw him come out of the bar? A sinking sensation in the pit of her stomach told her he was embarrassed to tell her. Did he think she'd think less of him? The image of Julian tending to Madame LaFleur came to her mind, and she saw how tender and gentle he'd been with the woman. Yes, he was a good man, and he'd captured her heart.

Chapter 10

Camille entered the ward at Charity Hospital and walked to the bed of Madame LaFleur. The woman looked so different and peaceful as she lay still with her eyes closed, her long braids lying across her shoulders instead of piled high in a turban. Camille tiptoed over to the bedside table and set down the vase of flowers she carried.

The woman's eyes fluttered open. "You sneakin' up on me?"

Camille froze. "No. I just didn't want to disturb you."

Madame LaFleur glanced at the flowers. "So pretty. You bring them to me?"

"Yes, I thought you might like something colorful in here."

"You right about that. This place is so dull. I think grits got more color."

Camille chuckled. "How are you feeling?"

"Like I want to go home and see my grandbaby."

"When did Dr. Charbonnet say you could leave?"

"Don't remember. Don't know how long I been here. But I need to get up and do something. My people need me."

Camille's heart leaped as Julian walked toward them and stood at the end of the bed, looking very professional with his doctor's coat on and stethoscope hanging around his neck. "Did I hear my name?" He smiled at Camille and winked, radiating warmth through her body.

"Yes, sir, Doctor. When you gonna let me go home?"

He went to her side and placed the stethoscope on her chest, listened a moment, then straightened. "Your heart sounds good. You've been here three weeks now. Do you feel well enough to go home?"

"Yes, sir, I sure do. Lying here all day makes me weak."

"Sit up on the side of the bed for me."

She complied and he put his stethoscope on her back. "Can you stand?"

"Of course I can stand." She stood up and took a few small steps. "See?"

He crossed his arms over his chest. "Well, it looks like you can get around. So I'm going to let you go home. But you must take it easy and not overtax yourself."

"I will. By the saints, I promise." She made the sign of the cross, then pointed skyward.

Julian excused himself, leaving Camille and the voodoo queen alone.

"I need to set things straight between us," Madame LaFleur said, plopping back down on the bed.

Camille nodded. "I'm listening."

"I hear you're a good midwife and not too bad a nurse. My people say you're nice and they trust you. And you brought my grandson into this world. I have to thank you for that."

"I was just doing my job, which I love very much, especially when I can assist in the birth of a fine young boy like your grandson."

Madame LaFleur beamed with pride. "So you go on doing your job, and I'll do mine. I think this city is big enough for the both of us."

"And will you promise not to leave nasty things in my bag or at my house?"

The woman chuckled. "You don't worry. I won't be sending any bad gris-gris to you."

"Or my patients?"

Madame LaFleur arched an eyebrow. "We might have to decide whose patient is whose."

"All right. Why don't we let them choose?"

Madame LaFleur nodded. "I can go with that."

"Then we have an agreement?"

"We do. But one more thing, Miss Duval."

"Yes?"

"Thank you. You and your man, for taking care of me and mine. If you was my enemy, you wouldn't have done that."

"I never wanted to be your enemy."

"Or steal my power?"

Camille smiled. "I don't want any of your power. I have all the power I need, and it comes from God, no one else."

⌒

When Camille raised her hand to knock on the Rousseaus's door, it opened.

"Yous better get up there quick, Miss Duval," Joseph said, glancing up the stairs. "Mr. Vincent done worn out the floor pacin' till you got here."

Camille lifted her skirt and ran up the steps and into Adelaide's room. Sukey stood by the young woman's bedside, holding her hand.

Adelaide glanced at Camille. "Thank God you're here. Oh!" She jumped as a pain hit her.

"How long have the pains been going on?"

"All mornin'," Sukey said. "They's gettin' closer together."

"Will you please get me a basin of warm water and a few towels?"

"Yes, ma'am." Sukey hurried out the door. She'd become much more cooperative since Camille and Madame LaFleur had reached a truce. The voodoo queen had kept her word, so no more charms or other voodoo objects appeared at the Rousseau house.

Camille tied on her apron and examined Adelaide, checking her pulse and temperature, noting the baby's downward movement. She listened to the baby's heartbeat and found it strong. When Sukey returned, she wet a towel and wrung it, then placed it on Adelaide's forehead, now beaded with perspiration.

"Oh! Oh! I can't do this!"

"Yes, you can. We've been waiting a long time for this baby to come into the world. Do you remember what I told you? Short breaths when the pain hits. Like this." Camille demonstrated with little puffs of air.

She stood beside Adelaide and held her hand while Sukey stood a few steps away, watching with a worried look on her face. Camille spoke softly, patting Adelaide's face with the towel. "Everything will be all right and your baby will be here soon."

Adelaide tensed and yelled. "God, help me. I'm dying!"

"Puff, puff, puff," Camille demonstrated.

Adelaide copied Camille, and Camille checked the time on the watch pinned to her shoulder. The pains were much closer now, about two to three minutes apart, and lasting longer. Adelaide screamed and panted through each one. Camille glanced over at Sukey. "Sukey, I need your help."

The woman nodded and came close to the bed. "Hold her other hand, please. Adelaide, when the pain hits, squeeze Sukey's hand."

Camille checked the birth canal and saw that it was fully dilated. "Okay, Adelaide. It's time to push. Take a deep breath, squeeze Sukey's hand, and push. Ready?"

Adelaide shook her head. "No, I can't."

"You have to if you want to hold this baby. It's waiting to meet its mother."

Another pain hit Adelaide, and Camille said, "Push! Now!"

Adelaide gritted her teeth and pushed.

"There you go. I can see the head. Now do it again."

Adelaide pushed again and again until the baby girl finally slid out into Camille's hands. Adelaide fell back against the pillow, exhausted. Then she raised her head and looked at Camille. "What is it? Is it well?"

As Camille rubbed the baby with a towel, the little one cried out. Camille smiled and wrapped the baby in a clean cloth, then handed her to her mother.

"Here is your new baby girl."

Adelaide reached for the baby, her eyes filled with awe and love. She peeked inside the towel and looked at the baby's fingers and toes. Then she looked at the baby's eyes that were fixed on her mother. "She's so beautiful."

"She look just like you, Miss Adelaide. She got that thick black hair and big pretty eyes, just like you did when you was born."

Sukey brushed tears away from her face.

Adelaide looked up at Camille. "Thank you."

"Thank God. He's blessed us all with this beautiful, healthy baby. What will you name her?"

"Angeline. My little angel."

Chapter 11

Camille and Julian sat under the sunshade on the beach watching the bathers in the lake. A gentle breeze blew off the water, fluttering the lace edges of the umbrella and ruffling tendrils loose from Camille's hair. Behind them, the Port Pontchartrain Lighthouse stood sentry.

"I saw Madame LaFleur yesterday. She and Josephine were strolling baby Jacques in the carriage. She's quite proud of that grandson," Julian said.

Camille sighed. "I'm so thankful we were able to settle our differences."

Julian leaned toward her. "I'm thankful she didn't scare you away."

Camille laughed. "I'm not that easy to get rid of."

"Did you know Vincent Rousseau has given up his cigars?"

Camille's eyes widened. "Is that so? You convinced him it was an unhealthy habit?"

Julian chuckled. "Afraid I can't take credit for it. Adelaide told him he couldn't come near the baby as long as he smelled like cigars and coughed all over the place."

"Babies can change lives," Camille said, smiling.

Julian stroked the back of her hand, then lifted it to his lips and kissed it.

"Julian, why were you afraid to tell me your father was a bar-keeper? Do you think that matters to me?"

"I wasn't sure, but I didn't want you to think less of me. I've tried to make a good name for myself, but some people care about family background."

"I don't. Your father's very proud of you, and you should be proud of him too. He worked hard to help you through medical school."

"You're right. He's a good man."

"So are you."

He smiled at her and winked. "I told you we made a good team."

She leaned toward him as their lips met. "I completely agree."

Award-winning author **Marilyn Turk** writes historical fiction usually set on the shoreline of the United States. Marilyn is a lighthouse enthusiast. She and her husband have traveled to over one hundred lighthouses and climbed most of them. In addition, they served as volunteer lighthouse caretakers at Little River Light on an island off the coast of Maine.

Lighthouses always show up in her books, either as part of the setting or in cameo appearances, and on her lighthouse blog at pathwayheart.com. Her book, *Lighthouse Devotions*, features inspiring true stories about lighthouses. When not climbing or writing about lighthouses, Marilyn enjoys gardening, boating, fishing, and tennis.